PREHISTORIC

Daniel C Tuck

Published by Bat From Beyond

Copyright © 2023 Daniel C Tuck

All rights reserved.

ISBN: 9798858633006

For Cath and Robert.

PROLOGUE

Lyme Regis, England.
October, 1811.

The beach glowed orange in the early morning, the water pooling on the surface of the sand from the storm that had just passed, blazing like fire as the sunlight hit it. The sea still frothed angrily, grasping at the shoreline for anything to snatch away and pull under. But the danger was slowly receding away from the land as the tide started to retreat.

The clay and limestone cliffs loomed over the beach, casting long shadows at their bases, shrouding areas of the beach in darkness despite the rising sun. It was so dark it was easy to imagine cave mouths must exist in the blackness, though that was not the case there. As the tide was only just pulling back, the large rocks at the base of the cliffs were slick with water, slippery and dangerous to anyone who might try climbing them without taking due care.

It was the perfect morning, as far as eleven-year-old Mary Anning was concerned:

The beach was empty, and the current weather was finally dry, albeit cold at that hour of the day. Having just had a relatively large storm pass through, the beach was sure to have some secrets it was waiting to reveal that morning. And she was going to be the one to find them.

Dressed in several layers of ill-fitting clothing, making her look far more plump than she was (the only way that she could persuade her mother to allow her out of the house at the temperature it was in the early hours of the morning), Mary was armed with a bucket, trowel and her father's trusty rock hammer. She was confident that she would find a good collection of snake stones, if nothing else, this morning.

They were remarkably easy to find along the beach in Lyme Regis if you kept your eyes open and knew where to look. But you had to be up early to get in with a chance to collect the best specimens.

Mary's parents ran a small shop in the town, selling all manner of natural curiosities, like the snake stones. Her father, Richard, had collected them for years and taught Mary and her older brother, Joseph, where to find them and how to prepare them so they were cleaned and polished beautifully for tourists to buy and take home as souvenirs. Joseph, like Mary, was a natural at finding remarkable objects, but his heart was not in it quite the same way as Mary. At fourteen years of age, he was already keen to leave Lyme Regis and make a name for himself elsewhere in the country where industry was thriving. There were few opportunities in a small seaside town for someone with ambition like himself.

The sale of natural curiosities was one of the very few growing businesses in their small town, and each year more and more people headed to the coast - more often than not, *wealthy* people who could afford to travel so far for a stroll beside the sea - and all were amazed by these beautiful, spiral wonders that had been spewed up on the shore by the waves. There was a lot of business competition, with many people finding collecting them a relatively easy way of making money. But fortunately, most of their competition lacked the resolve to awaken early enough in the morning to beat Mary Anning out of the house and onto the shore. Even her father had been frequently amazed at the specimens she brought home.

To Mary, being out on the beach by herself first thing in the morning was magical. She didn't want to be cooped up inside their small, dark house, helping her mother do chores, or having it explained to her repeatedly how such-and-such is not something a *lady* should be doing. Since her father passed away the year before, Mary had felt that her mother had started trying to strip everything that Mary and her father had done together away from her very being. She couldn't blame her mother: Mary "Molly" Anning was expected to bring her daughter up a certain way, and she was finding things hard enough without Mary's father being there to support them financially and emotionally. Looking after Mary and Joseph and keeping the shop going was a huge burden for one woman to take on, and even now, her health was starting to fail her. Mary was finding that more and more of her time was being taken up with helping her mother in their shop, doing all of the heavy lifting (which, as Mary pointed out to her mother, was indeed *also* something that a lady should not be doing), re-arranging, wrapping and displaying. Molly wanted to ensure that Mary was set up in the best possible way for the life she would be living, ready in case Molly herself was taken to her eternal Home sooner rather than later.

Mary had always been something of a tomboy, clambering over rocks, digging in the sand until she was filthy from head to toe, fearlessly flinging herself into the waves at the merest glimpse of something that might be worth saving from the sea. If a tourist arrived at their shop proclaiming himself to be a man of science, heaven help him if Mary caught wind of that fact: she had been known to grill visitors, asking about anything and everything that filled the young girl's head, until they were itching to leave, usually distracted from actually buying anything.

She was keenly interested in science, particularly the natural sciences, and always asked questions about the world around her.

Not things a *lady* should be doing.

So Mary was always grateful for the few hours she could spend alone on the beach. She became lost in her thoughts of what the world might have looked like long before she had come along. Wondering precisely what these magical, incredible, spiral snake stones and long, pointed devil's toes were that were so abundant along the coast and dreaming of finding that one remarkable specimen that would allow her to truly call herself a woman of science.

Mary walked the road alongside the sea, watching the waves churning against the pebbles, crackling like lightning as they bashed together. Although it was early, a few people were already around: tradespeople and fishermen, mostly, preparing for the upcoming day's work. A familiar sight to the whole town, they were not surprised to see Mary up and about at that hour, armed with her hammer. They knew she was a bit strange, with all those fancy notions running through her head and talk of science when she should instead be doing her Bible studies. Her parents were not exactly the most welcome within the small town. Classed as dissenters from the church for attending a congregationalist chapel rather than the more strict, fundamental Church of England, it was assumed by those who did not know any better that the whole family were essentially being taught a completely different religion. That was not the case, of course: there was only one God that both churches worshipped, but it was true that the congregationalist church had encouraged the congregation to look outside of the Bible itself for answers to questions, to think about the wonder of nature and to study and learn about it outside of the realms of the fundamentalist belief that God created everything as it is, as it was, perfect from the beginning and without change. Mary had read enough scientific journals whenever she could get her young hands on them to know that there was mounting evidence that other life had once roamed the planet, life that was no longer known to them. If God had created everything so perfectly from the very beginning, and everything was then as it is now, where had that life gone?

But she was only young; she would grow out of these peculiar, un-Godly notions, given time.

A few familiar faces tipped their hats to Mary as she passed them by, giving her a friendly 'Morning, Miss Anning,' to which she always replied in an equally friendly manner.

She followed the sea wall across to the Cobb - the town's harbour, built in a horseshoe shape. Steep steps led up to the top of the wall of the Cobb, slippery and uneven, but Mary had climbed those steps so many times in her short life that she skipped up them with ease, barely even noticing their presence.

She walked along the wall, right to the end and looked back towards the land.

This particular spot had always been her favourite view. From there, looking to her left, she could see Lyme Regis' cliffs, the very place towards which she was heading, and her personal preference for looking for any secrets the sea may have decided to reveal on a particular day. To the right, the town stretched out, small but slowly growing, with the recent increase in tourists helping shape the town's future. Beyond Lyme Regis were the mud and clay cliffs of Charmouth, another good place for collecting, Mary had found, but it was a few mile's walk along the beach from Lyme, so it was rare that Mary found herself able to make the time to head out that far.

The view wasn't especially great that morning, with the remnants of the night's rain still hovering. Clouds in the sky here and there, parting occasionally to illuminate the landscape, and a misty haze across most of the view. Nevertheless, it was a view firmly imprinted in Mary's memory, so there was no real need for her to see it perfectly with her eyes; she could easily match up her thoughts to what she could see, and the picture would be complete.

Mary skipped across the top of the Cobb, jumped down the steep steps again, and headed towards the cliffs to begin her morning's work.

A section of the cliff face had fallen overnight, crumbling from high above the beach and tumbling to the ground, pulling down clay and rocks and landing in a crumpled heap on the floor. It was a common sight for Mary, which happened at least once every few weeks, usually after terrible storms. The large chunks of rock that littered the beach were a firm reminder of just how dangerous the environment could be if you weren't careful; stand in the wrong place at the wrong time or act without caution beside those cliffs, and you could easily find yourself badly hurt, or even killed. Mary had known a few people from the town who had lost their lives that way: carelessly. Having grown up there and with a father imbued with common sense, Mary knew to respect and fear the landscape. Despite its beauty, it could turn on you in a second.

Nevertheless, despite the danger inherent in rock slides like that, Mary was always excited to see them. As the debris from the cliff tumbled down, it more often than not exposed some of the cliff's long buried treasures, exposing larger snake stones, unidentifiable bones and other such mysterious artefacts.

She couldn't help but run towards the site when she saw it, the thrill of anticipation driving her faster forward.

Mary trod over the rocks that covered the floor, scouring over them, inspecting each one, lifting the ones she could, and heaving aside others. One large, round rock caught her eye. Smooth and grey, except for an inch-long indent in the side, a slight browny-cream extrusion sticking out from the gap. She smiled, knowing exactly what she had found. Carefully setting the stone down on top of a larger, flatter rock, Mary took out her rock hammer. She lined up her blow and gave a swift, firm tap against the stone. It immediately broke into two pieces. She picked both pieces up, holding them together, savouring the moment she knew was coming.

Carefully, she pulled the stone pieces apart from each other.

Sandwiched between the two pieces was a beautiful, creamy-coloured snake stone. It was revealed outside of that stone encasement for the first time: about an inch in diameter, with clear, detailed ridges all along its spiral shape — a perfect specimen. Mary had found many similar stones over her years, but it never failed to please her when she saw another, especially one as perfectly formed as this. She placed the two pieces back together, wrapping the snake stone back in its protective shell, and put it carefully in her bucket.

More people were starting to venture onto the beach as Mary began to think it was time for her to leave. There were the usual faces, others keen to find something of worth on the beach and willing (though not quite as willing as Mary) to get up early to make it worthwhile. A familiar few who knew Mary's talent for finding things of interest hovered nearby and watched her out of the corner of their eyes lest she stumble upon something, that they may able to be a part of her discovery. A couple of tourists were out for an early morning stroll, enjoying the chilled embrace of the cool sea wind on their skin, brushing off the dust from a night's sleep.

Mary had a reasonable collection for a couple of hours of work: some lovely snake stones, several decent-sized devil's toenails and various exciting and unusual stones and pebbles.

She glanced around for one last look, making sure there wasn't anything obvious she had missed before she ventured home. Her eye fell upon something partway up the recently exposed cliff face: an unusual shape jutting from the clay. She scrambled up the fallen rocks to where the object protruded and started to pull away the surrounding debris.

It looked like the face of a creature.

A long-snouted creature with two rows of sharp teeth.

Eyes wide with excitement, Mary continued to work away at the rock and clay, uncovering more of the skull from the cliff. A large, round eye socket stared out at her, browny-grey from the clay it had been buried in, fractured in multiple places but still remarkably intact. It was like nothing she had ever seen before. Mary took a step back to admire the discovery. Her foot slipped. In a well-practised movement, she changed her footing and stopped herself from tumbling backwards from her viewpoint on the fallen rocks.

If a head was in there, the rest of the creature could surely be.

This find on its own was so unique, so remarkable, that Mary could hardly bear even to dream that there could be more of the beast waiting to be unveiled. But her head was practically exploding with thoughts, dreams, and ideas, taking her off on all kinds of adventures in presenting her discovery to the world's greatest scientific minds, all genuinely astonished by what she had found.

The rest of the mysterious beast was there, buried in the cliff. She was sure of it.

Even the head on its own - a two-foot long beak-like profile with a large bowl-shaped eye - would be too heavy for her to carry home alone. If she found the rest of it, there was no hope.

She would need help.

Mary turned around to look to see if there was anyone else nearby who might be able to assist her.

In her excitement at uncovering such a discovery, Mary had failed to realise that everyone on the beach had stopped what they were doing to watch this young girl revealing her mysterious prize. A crowd had gathered at the base of the cliff, watching her every move, each as astounded as she was by such a sight.

'Might somebody be able to help me, please?' she asked the assembled congregation, her voice sounding young and foolish against the thought of the immense task that awaited her.

Extracting the sea lizard from the stone took several days of hard work. Back and forth to the beach Mary went, every single day, whenever the rocks were reachable without risking getting washed away by the tide (and even at times when she knew that, strictly speaking, she shouldn't be there and was putting herself in danger by doing so). There was no fear of her find being stolen by others: everyone in town knew that this was Mary's prize, her reward for the years of her life spent searching the beaches for anything and everything of the slightest interest. There was little to no chance of a similar discovery being made shortly after Mary had found hers, so anything that appeared to resemble her creature would be treated with utmost suspicion by the residents of Lyme Regis.

Even once the creature had been extracted from the rock face, Mary knew there was still plenty of work to do back at the shop. She would need to carefully chip away at the rock surrounding the lizard, removing anything where it was safe to do so, cleaning around the creature's shape, revealing its full nature. There were hours of work ahead of her. *Hours.* She smiled to herself as she thought about it. She could think of nothing she would rather be doing.

With the assistance of some local men, Mary wheeled the lizard back to the Anning shop on a makeshift transportation device. Mary herself pulled from the front. The men bent over around the vehicle, ensuring that the lizard, covered as it was with a canvas to protect it, would not fall off as Mary drove it across the cobbled streets. Every bounce drove a shiver of fear through Mary that her find might be damaged.

By the time they reached the shop, a line of people was waiting outside, practically a welcoming committee. Everyone in town had heard about Mary's find and wanted to see what she had discovered. She had found some remarkable things in her short life to date, but from what they had all heard, this was the most astonishing yet: the shape of a giant crocodilian creature, preserved almost perfectly in the rocks along the shore of their town. As she passed along the line of spectators, Mary looked up at the faces peering down at her and her discovery, all wanting to see the incredible sight she was wheeling behind her. So many adults staring down at such a young girl, watching, inspecting, asking themselves how someone so young could have found anything significant. Whispers that it was nothing more than imaginative child's play. Mutterings amongst several sneering individuals that the creature was a hoax, designed purely to con some money from the purses of visitors from out of town. Mary had heard it all before, though: whenever she came back with anything slightly different from the usual, the expected torrent of disbelief poured down upon her and her family.

'Don't listen to them,' Mary's father used to say to her. 'They're just jealous they haven't got half the brain you were born with. They wouldn't recognise something special even if it hit them square in the face.'

The remembrance of her father brought tears to Mary's eyes and a smile to her mouth simultaneously. If only he could see her now...

Reaching the steps to the shop, Mary turned and helped the men lift the creature up and through the front door. They heaved it onto the table where Mary (and previously her father and brother) prepared the items for sale and display, and the men stood around awaiting further instructions.

'That will be all,' Mary's mother told the men, stepping forward and ushering them back out the door. 'Thank you for your assistance.'

The men tipped their hats and, although vaguely confused by the sudden request for them to leave without so much as a glass of water for their efforts, they nonetheless complied with Mrs Anning's wishes and filed out of the front door.

Only as her mother closed the door to the shop, Mary noticed a solitary man standing in the corner of the store, watching her intently.

'Mother?' Mary enquired quietly.

Mrs Anning beamed at the man and her daughter.

'Mary, this gentleman has come all the way from London to examine your find.'

'From London?' Mary repeated, the great city's name rolling from her mouth as though she was speaking of some mystical utopian landscape.

'Indeed, young lady,' the man said, stepping forward.

He held out his hand to Mary, who dutifully shook it.

'I heard of your remarkable discovery,' he continued, 'and felt much obliged to pay a visit to take a look for myself.'

His eyes moved greedily towards the covered shape on the tabletop.

'May I?' he asked Mary as he approached.

'Of course you may,' Mrs Anning replied on Mary's behalf.

Mary watched closely as the man from London carefully, slowly lifted back the canvas from her once-in-a-lifetime discovery. As he revealed the long, thick snout with rows of sharp teeth, uncovered more of the bowl-shaped eye socket, and saw the great beast for the first time, his eyes widened, shining with excitement and joy at what he saw. He placed a hand gently against the creature, touching it lightly with his fingertips.

He turned his head slightly towards Mary and, seeing her watching him, quickly threw the cover back over, and his face turned hard and serious.

'It is but nothing,' he suddenly declared.

'What do you mean?' Mrs Anning demanded.

'It is nothing more than a crocodile.'

'That's not true!' Mary cried.

'Are you sure?'

'Quite sure,' the man declared as he pulled his purse from a pocket.

'It is no crocodile,' Mary told him firmly. 'I have seen crocodiles, and that is nothing of the sort. And you know it.'

'Madam,' the man turned to Mrs Anning, ignoring her daughter. 'I can offer you twenty pounds for the item and not a penny more.'

'Twenty pounds?' Even at Mary's age, she knew the value of her discoveries and that twenty pounds was an insult.

'It is worth no more than that,' the man told her. 'I already have several crocodiles in my collection, so I do not wish to pay more than it is worth.'

His eyes slid over to the lizard on the table, and he licked his lips, his mouth drying at the thought of losing his prize, thanks to a young girl.

'Take it or leave it, madam,' he told Mrs Anning, 'but I am sure you will not get a better offer than that.'

'It is rather less than I had hoped,' Mrs Anning told him, chewing on her bottom lip as she thought through the situation.

'I am sorry about that. But you will not find a collector who would pay over the odds for something as common as this.'

Mary stood beside them, listening to the conversation, seething with rage at what was happening right under her nose. Her most significant discovery was being sold for a pittance to someone trying to take advantage of her mother.

'It is not common,' Mary told the man, trying to keep her anger in check, trembling at the exertion of doing so. 'I have read up on these things. I know a crocodile when I see one, and this is not a crocodile. You know it is not a crocodile, too.'

The man smiled and laughed. He turned to Mrs Anning.

'It seems your daughter would like to be a scientist when she grows up.'

'Well, I don't know about that, sir.'

'I would, and I will be,' Mary told him.

'Science is no place for a lady,' he told Mary. 'Now: twenty pounds. Yes?'

'Very well, sir.'

He pulled the money from his purse and placed it on the side next to Mrs Anning.

'Splendid. I shall have someone call by to collect it later today. Pleasure doing business with you.'

He gently placed a hand on the covered lizard once more, then lifted it with a sigh of relief.

He smiled at Mrs Anning.

'Good day to you.'

Passing by Mary on his way out of the shop, the man ruffled Mary's hair.

'A scientist,' he laughed and left.

I

"It is demonstrable from Geology that there was a period when no organic beings had existence: these organic beings must therefore have had a beginning subsequently to this period; and where is that beginning to be found, but in the will and fiat of an intelligent and all-wise Creator?"

Vindiciae Geologicae, William Buckland

ONE

London, England.
December, 1823.

With his quality suit, thick, long black coat and tall, dark hat perched on top of his head, Dr Gideon Mantell was every inch the respected physician. However, it was generally unusual to see such men of high standing scrambling around on their hands and knees on the clay ground of a quarry as darkness descended in the early hours of a late December evening. Guided only by a small lantern, Mantell rummaged through a pile of debris, searching, picking apart small blocks with his bare hands and rubbing the clay to find anything hidden inside.

For the quarry foreman and his crew, this had been a source of amusement the first couple of times that Dr Mantell had arrived at their workplace. But after multiple visits, they had grown accustomed to the peculiar sight and found him to be more of a hindrance to their work than anything else.

Today was no exception.

It had already been a long day, and the foreman and his crew were eager to get home before the expected bad weather set in. Their work had already been disrupted on a few occasions throughout the day by sudden downpours, so they were already at the site later than they should have been to try to remain on schedule. The good doctor made it worth their while to hang around and allow him to do whatever he was doing, slipping them a couple of coins each for the inconvenience, but there were some days when they just wanted to get out of there. They were set up to complete one final task for the day before they could be on their way; preparation had begun, but for now, the men could do nothing but stand around, resting against their tools as they waited for Mantell.

The doctor skittered across the ground excitedly, prancing from one pile of debris to another, ripping it apart, finding something of interest and pulling it open carefully with his fingertips to look at whatever it might be that he had found.

Raindrops started to dot the ground, but Mantell seemed oblivious.

The crew looked towards their foreman, their eyes urging him to move things along.

Reluctantly, the foreman approached the doctor.

'Dr Mantell, we need to clear this area,' he said.

Mantell, lost in his work, ignored him. He sat down in the dampening clay, a small chunk of rock in his hands. He held the lantern up to the rock and examined it closely. A small smile crept across his face. He carefully set it on the ground and placed his lantern beside it. It was hard to see anything in those conditions, though, with nothing but the glow of a small lantern to illuminate his find, the shadows constantly flickering, giving the illusion of detail where there was none.

He looked up at the constantly darkening sky, the black rain clouds doing nothing to help the situation. Only then did he notice the foreman close by.

'Fetch me another lantern, would you,' Mantell requested.

The foreman glared at Mantell. He wasn't there to serve the man; he allowed him on to their site as a favour, but sometimes the doctor seemed to forget his place. This was *their* world, not his. Nevertheless, he knew how tenacious Mantell could be: if he had found something that had piqued his interest, there would be no getting rid of him unless they helped him along the way.

The foreman waved a hand at a crew member lurking nearby, silently passing along Mantell's request.

'My men want to leave,' he tried telling the doctor as he wiped rain from his eyes.

But Mantell was working on the rock that he had found. He carefully chipped away at it using a small metal hammer, working to extract something embedded within the stone. With every couple of glances of the hammer, he used a brush to move away the dust that had formed, ensuring that he could see exactly what he was doing.

Slowly, structures emerged from within, the rock giving away its secrets. Secrets that Mantell, after years of study and first-hand discovery, knew precisely where to find. Some of these treasure hunts ended in disappointment, of course, but other days… other days were like this.

Mantell smiled again as he continued to reveal the hidden treasure in the stone.

Shapes within became more recognisable.

Unmistakable now, and precisely what he had been hoping to discover.

He looked up from his find, eyes wide and excited.

The foreman appeared to be arguing with a couple of crew members, voices raised and excitable, but Mantell paid them no heed: the crew member sent to fetch another lantern was on his way back. Mantell rushed him over, waving frantically with his hands.

'Hurry, hurry,' he told the worker.

The foreman hurried over to Mantell.

'Dr Mantell, I must insist that we leave this area,' he told the doctor. 'It's no longer safe, and we must move.'

Mantell still paid him no attention. He held the newly acquired lamp in one hand, his find in the other.

A row of dark, triangular teeth was stuck in the rock, still attached to a piece of jawbone — the remnants of an ancient fossilised creature.

'Beautiful,' he whispered.

'Dr Mantell!' the foreman shouted as a final warning before the whole ground shook from an explosion nearby.

Servants hurried to fetch warm towels and water as the house filled with pained cries of exertion. Screams echoed throughout the dark hallways, the sound of a woman in great pain.

Jane, a young maid, hurried to her mistress' room, arms loaded with towels. The master of the house, Geoffrey Worthington, strode impatiently back and forth in front of the door to the room, anxiously treading the carpet. Seeing the maid heading in his direction, he stopped her.

'Any sign?' he enquired.

'Not yet, sir.'

'I asked you to call him hours ago,' he snapped.

'I did, sir. Spoke to him directly.'

'And what did he say?'

'He said that he had another matter to attend to first, but he would get here as a matter of urgency.'

A scream of pain came from behind the closed door to the room.

'If I may, sir?' Jane indicated towards the door Geoffrey was blocking.

'Oh, of course.'

He stepped aside to let her by. She pushed the door open a fraction and was about to step through the crack when Geoffrey stopped her.

'Look after her, won't you, Jane?' he asked, allowing worry and fear to show in his face for the first time.

'Of course,' Jane smiled a slight smile.

Turning to head through the doorway, she changed her mind at the last minute.

'I almost forgot, sir,' she said and slid a concealed bottle of brandy from between the towels she was holding after making sure that no one could see what she was doing.

Geoffrey took it from her and smiled.

'Thank you for looking after me too.'

'Of course.'

Jane finally entered the bedroom and closed the door behind her, maintaining her mistress' privacy and dignity.

Geoffrey pulled the top from the brandy bottle and drank from it directly. The liquid warmed his throat and stomach, but it did little by way of alleviating his anxiety.

'Where in the blazes is that doctor?' he enquired of the empty hallway before him.

Chunks of rock flew into the air. Boulders rolled down the quarry face. A dust cloud lifted and started to fall back to the ground like black, filthy snow. His most recent discovery so enamoured Mantell that he barely noticed anything happening. Tunnel vision had set in, and all that he could see was the fossilised jaw he had discovered within the dirt, and all that he could hear was the round of applause from the members of the Geological Society whenever he might have the opportunity to present it to them.

He failed even to hear the foreman yelling at him: 'Move! Now!'

Realising his cries were being unheard, the foreman had no choice.

He rushed towards Mantell and threw him aside with all of his strength.

The fossil flew from Mantell's grasp, yanking him out of his reverie as he was forcibly jolted from where he had been standing. He felt like a horse had just run into him as he fell to the ground, the foreman landing on top of him.

'Where is it?' he cried out once he had a chance to get a breath.

He looked around the ground and spotted the fossil on the floor where he had previously been standing.

Breaking free of the foreman, he rushed to retrieve his precious object.

He grabbed it just as a large rock fall landed precisely where he had been standing. If the foreman hadn't acted the way he had, Mantell himself would have had to have been excavated. Even as a cloud of dust billowed up from the ground and into his face, Mantell focused on his find rather than giving his mortality a second thought.

He wandered across the quarry floor, passing by the foreman.

'You're welcome,' the foreman told him, his voice ripe with sarcasm, as the doctor walked away without a word.

As a knocking sounded against the front door to the house, Geoffrey Worthington rushed to answer it, ready to greet the late arrival with a fierce scowl etched onto his face.

Opening the door, however, the scowl evaporated and was replaced by a gasp of surprise. He had been expecting to see Dr Gideon Mantell on his doorstep, certainly, but not precisely in the condition in which he had arrived.

His clothes were filthy, covered in mud and dust, and wet from rain. His face was black, smudged in places from where he must have tried to clean himself with a rag of some sort.

'What in the blazes happened to you?' Geoffrey asked.

'My apologies for the delay,' Mantell said and stepped into the house, pulling his rain-covered hat from his head. 'How are things proceeding?'

He looked past Geoffrey and into the house.

Jane walked down the stairs towards the pair of men.

A newborn baby wrapped in her arms.

Two

Lyme Regis.

The festive spirit had captured Charlie and his fishing crew early. Over the previous week, they had landed a more significant haul than anyone could have expected or even hoped for at that time of year. So much so, that they had to return home a day early for lack of room on the boat to store anything else. Having returned to land, they all greeted their wives and families and swiftly made their way to the local public house to celebrate what was looking to be a good Christmas all around.

A few hours later, they emerged from the tiny, cramped building and staggered into the bitter but fresh air of the winter's night. The cold had an almost sobering effect on a few of them, and they wrapped their coat collars around their necks to ward off the worst of the chills.

Nathaniel, the youngest of the crew at seventeen years of age and less experienced at drinking than the rest, staggered and lurched along the cobblestone path, heading away from the group towards home. At least, he hoped he was heading home; it was hard to tell.

The rest of the crew watched him trip and stumble across the stones, laughing and joking about his lack of balance on land and off. It was his first time out drinking with them, and they didn't hold back.

'Sure you'll find your way home, Nathaniel?' the Skipper called out.

'I'm fine,' came a slurred response.

'Bright and early on the morrow, lad.'

Nathaniel lifted a hand, waved acknowledgement in Charlie's general direction, and continued drifting down the dark street until he was almost out of sight.

'His mother'll kill us when she sees the state of him,' Charlie muttered, mostly to himself.

The door to the public house swung open and clattered shut again. Charlie looked to see who was joining them outside and was greeted by a massive boulder of a man, towering over them all and almost as wide as his boat.

'Busy tomorrow, Jessie?' the Skipper asked the large man.

'How much?' Jessie fired back gruffly.

'I haven't told you what I need yet.'

'Doesn't matter what it is, does it?'

'Anything for a price, aye, Jessie?' a young fisherman named Jack piped up from the relative safety of the group.

Jessie glared at him in silence, a glare that Jack could practically feel crushing his bones without even touching him. He involuntarily sank back into his crew mates, engulfing himself within the group and tucked away from sight.

'Might be a guinea or two in it for you,' Charlie told Jessie.

The large man grunted in disdain.

'Not worth it,' he growled and strolled away.

Nathaniel vaguely heard Jessie's booming voice coming from behind him as he spoke with the Skipper, and he vaguely recognised the street he was heading down, trying to find his way home. He had walked those streets many times throughout his relatively short life, but it had never been this dark and... wobbly. It was the first time he had been invited out for drinks with the crew, and when the Skipper asks you to do something, you do it. Not that he had put up much of a fight; he had heard so many tales of what had gone on in the public houses after the boys had a few too many, and he had always found them hysterical, so he had waited patiently for the opportunity to witness them.

Tonight had been that night, and he had not been disappointed.

But after the almost violent noise of laughter, out-of-tune singing and arguments, the blurry, empty street that emerged before him and the silence it contained felt oppressive and frightening. He considered turning back and going a different way, but that would mean passing by the crew again, who would wonder what he was up to and no doubt laugh at his drunken inability even to make it home. Plus, he had an innate dislike for Jessie. The man was loud, brash and quick with his fists. Not that the crew members he worked with daily were exactly gentle creatures, but there was something about Jessie that put him on edge. Probably the fact that he was the size of a bear; that was enough to intimidate the best of men.

If he didn't want to be mocked mercilessly for the rest of his life, he had no choice but to continue straight on.

He felt a splash of water on his face. Nathaniel looked up just as the heavens opened. Sharp, stinging, cold drops of rain streaked from the sky, lashing against his bare skin like an onslaught of needles. He wrapped his coat tighter around himself, pulled his collar up and ducked his head down to protect himself as best as possible. He picked up the pace, eager to get home before the weather worsened. The last thing he needed was to become too unwell to be able to work in the morning, particularly with the way things were at home.

But the rain made the cobblestones slippery and treacherous underfoot, especially with his balance and vision already somewhat impaired by the alcohol consumption.

Nathaniel slipped, stumbled, and fell to the ground, putting his hands out in front of him just in time for them to take the full impact of the fall rather than it being his face doing so.

He lay there for a second, relieved at landing unhurt but wondering how he would ever make it home in one piece.

The lashing rain paused momentarily, the briefest respite from the constant sting. At the same time, a shadow seemed to pass by overhead. The moment the shadow had passed, the rain continued to fire at Nathaniel. It was as though something was in the sky directly above him, blocking the rain.

He climbed to his feet from where he had fallen and looked up, trying to see what it could have been. But the rain hurt his eyes with its fierce, cold drops, and did nothing to help his already blurred vision. Then he heard it: through the sound of the falling rain hissing and smattering against the cobblestones, the sound of something flapping in the darkness. Something large. He knew the sound of seagulls flying around, and this wasn't that.

This was something far larger.

And the sound of the wings was different, too.

It didn't sound the way gull wings did - not like feathers, but more of a leathery sound, perhaps. The sound got louder, as though whatever it might be was getting closer. There was a *whoosh*, and something huge glided through the rain, heading directly towards him. Nathaniel dove to the ground. The thing swooped straight over his head, and he could feel the air moving with it, the rain being pushed away from him as the great creature headed on by.

Then, a soft, wet *thwack*. Feet slapping against a damp surface.

Nathaniel wiped the rain from his eyes as best as he could, though it was a fruitless endeavour, as it didn't seem to be stopping any time soon.

He peered into the darkness of the street, trying to make out the form of whatever it was that was down there.

Thwack, thwack, thwack.

The feet were heading closer.

It had to be a joke, Nathaniel decided. The rest of the crew had seen how drunk their youngest member had been in the pub and had decided to play a trick on him. That's all it was. He felt surprisingly sober and wasn't in the mood to play games.

'Who's there?' he called out into the darkness, attempting to sound forceful, but the rain further weakened his trembling voice.

Thwack, thwack.

'Jack?' he called again. 'Skipper? This isn't funny.'

He took a couple of cautious steps forward.

'Is anyone there?'

The soft sound of leathery wings flapping came from down the street. The same large shadow passed over Nathaniel's head. Whatever it had been seemed to have gone. He stood silently for a moment, listening for any indication that the giant bird was returning. Hearing nothing, he turned back the way he was initially heading, pushing on, eager now to return to the safety and comfort of his home.

But a shape emerged in front of him.

Gliding through the rain, straight towards him.

A huge creature - like a bird, but of unimaginable size, long thick wings stretched out as it silently darted towards him. Its beak, long and ending with a sharp point, opened wide as it approached Nathaniel, exposing many razor-sharp-looking teeth.

Nathaniel barely had time to react.

He twisted around, trying to run, but the slick stones again fought against him. He lost his footing, slipped and tumbled. Frantically trying to regain some grip on the ground, he continued to stumble forward.

A sharp pain ran through him, starting in his back and spreading throughout his whole body.

Then, the ground was moving away from him.

He was going higher, higher into the air.

The creature had grabbed him with its massive feet, sharp claws gripping his flesh and lifting him from the ground, flapping through the rain-filled air.

Nathaniel was unsure what to do because he had no previous experience with a giant winged creature attacking and kidnapping him. Every instinct told him that he had to fight the beast to escape its sharp grip and its monstrous claws. But, on the other hand, the drop to the ground was becoming greater by the second. He was unsure whether it was the creature or the fall that was most likely to kill him. He finally decided that, as he had no way of knowing where this beast was taking him or what it would do with him when it got him there, at least a fall from a great height was something of a known quantity. He would rather take the chance against gravity than whatever diabolical plans the creature might have for him.

Every movement he made seemed to twist the sharp claws further into his flesh, coursing waves of agony throughout his whole body. But he twisted, turned, writhed around in the firm grip, frantically trying to hit out against the creature, striking at the claws with as much force as he could muster.

His fist made contact with a particularly fleshy part of a claw. It must have been a weak spot for the beast as that claw's grip on Nathaniel weakened. Nathaniel took the opportunity to strike the same way against the other claw.

That grip, too, loosened.

Nathaniel wriggled, fighting against the hooks embedded in his flesh.

The ground suddenly rushed back towards him at an alarming speed as the winged creature released its grip.

He would have screamed, but the impact of the landing came much quicker than allowed him the opportunity. As he bounced against the ground, he rolled up into a ball, trying to minimise the damage it might do to him. He skimmed like a stone across water, scraping and grazing himself on the harsh rocks he'd arrived on.

Battered, bruised and bleeding, but - surprisingly - alive.

Nathaniel staggered to his feet. He winced as he tried to put weight on his left foot. His leg bucked immediately from the pain and strain of that small action. It felt like something was broken. He looked around and tried to get his bearings. The creature must have concentrated more on gaining height than making distance, as he found that he had landed not too far away from where he had initially been taken.

The rain mercifully began to slow, the force of the drops softening to the point where they were no longer stinging bites and, finally, eased off completely. The night was eerily silent without the rain falling on the stones. It could have been quite easy to believe that everything that had gone before had been a product of his imagination if not for the injuries he had sustained. But anyone could have put that down to an unfortunate tumble after the excess of alcohol he had consumed earlier in the evening.

The darkness of the street slowly dissipated, the path glowing a yellowish-white from the wet as the large winter moon emerged through a gap in the clouds. Relief flooded over Nathaniel; the weather had improved, and the moon had come out of hiding to guide him home. These were both clear signs to him that everything would be alright.

A shadow fluttered across the moon, casting the path back into pitch blackness and throwing an unholy silhouette on the ground.

'No, no, no, no, no,' Nathaniel muttered to himself.

He looked up into the sky.

The creature was bearing down on him.

Fast.

Its immense wings were tucked in against its body, the sharp beak rocketing in his direction, a vast arrow aiming for a target.

Nathaniel could do nothing but run.

But even that, he couldn't do properly. Every step was agony as he hobbled along the street, trying to escape the advancing missile. A fearsome *screech* filled the air. Nathaniel risked a glance over his shoulder and saw the creature was close - *too* close - behind him, its beak open, sharp teeth exposed. It emitted the horrendous sound again as it got closer.

Nathaniel ducked, deliberately falling to the ground.

The creature glided overhead. It flapped its wings, forced itself into the air and looped back around, ready to take another shot at its prey.

Nathaniel frantically searched the ground, pulling at the stones, looking for anything he could use to fight back.

One of the cobbles came loose. A large, rounded stone, heavy in his hand. He waited until the creature was close enough to see its tiny little eyes on either side of its head and then threw the rock with all his might towards the beast's face.

It hit. The creature screeched again, a sound filled with anger and pain. It slowed, flapped its wings and backed away slightly. Nathaniel grabbed another rock and threw it, hoping for another hit. But already, the creature was wise to his plan: it skittered to the side in the air, the rock tapping harmlessly against the side of its wing. It hovered above the street, watching Nathaniel and practically daring him to try again.

Nathaniel realised he had no option but to get out of there. He could be engaged in this battle with the creature all night, but it had the entirety of the sky to duck and weave away from anything Nathaniel might throw at it. He had no choice but to run and hide.

He stared at the creature in the sky for a long moment, then, without any warning of what he was about to do, he turned and hobbled away from it.

The creature screeched and immediately pulled into a dive.

Favouring his left leg as much as he could, Nathaniel hopped towards the church by the cliff. There was no logic or reasoning behind it. Perhaps it was merely the fact that it was a church and, therefore, a place of refuge and sanctity; the Lord would not allow such a hellish creature to enter those hallowed grounds, surely. He swung open the iron gate in front of the path towards the building and closed it behind himself. A small gate would offer no protection against a flying monstrosity, but habit made him shut it automatically without a second thought. He fled through the grassy graveyard and ducked behind the largest headstone he could find. He was still exposed, of course; anything above him could easily see where he was. He was merely trying to buy time before the inevitable conclusion.

He closed his eyes and prayed. As he prayed, he realised that it had been too long since he had done so. He wondered for the first time if anyone was listening to those prayers, and if there was any possibility of them being answered, or if this was God's plan for him all along; maybe this was how it was meant to be, and no amount of prayers could change the course of his destiny.

A soft *thump* sounded close by.

The creature had landed heavily in the grass and was stepping towards him.

Nathaniel realised then that he didn't want to die, hidden like a coward crouched behind a gravestone, but would instead go on putting up a fight.

He took a deep breath, preparing himself to step out of hiding.

He opened his eyes.

The creature was right in front of him, staring into his face.

It opened its beak and vomited a cloud of foul-smelling breath as it screeched into Nathaniel's face.

Nathaniel began to think that the creature looked like it was grinning.

But then everything went black.

THREE

London.

After the day's adventures, the large house felt quieter and even more dark and empty than usual to Gideon Mantell. Every time he opened the front door, he still expected to be greeted with exuberance by his son, Walter, running the length of the hallway to meet him or a welcoming kiss from his wife, Mary-Ann.

It had been some time since those things had been a part of his daily routine, and he did miss it.

It was his fault, of course.

Mary-Ann had warned him that this was how it would turn out if he couldn't find time and space for them within his life. When he had reminded his wife that he was a busy general practitioner and he could not simply tell patients not to call, Mary-Ann had swept an arm around the house, showing him the evidence that he had always been able to find space and time for his fossil collection, and his various expeditions that had resulted in all of this… *stuff*.

Every available space was covered in fossils, bones and rocks. Some were displayed carefully in glass cases, on show, like pieces in a museum. Others were more liberally scattered around, waiting to be examined, identified, catalogued and indexed.

It was the thrill of the hunt for Mantell rather than the exhibition. He liked nothing more than being out in the wild, trying to find his next great specimen. It was like an addiction. The more he found, the more he wanted. The larger the discovery, the bigger the next one had to be for him to satisfy that hunger.

He stood in the open doorway of his house looking inside, his medical bag clutched in one hand and a larger, fuller bag of rocks and more exciting discoveries slung over his shoulder.

That particular night, there was nothing but darkness to greet him and the cold, empty shell of a house far too large for just him.

Of course, even if Walter and Mary-Ann had still resided with him, it would have been too late for Walter to be up still in the evening. But in those instances, Mantell would head up the stairs and look in on his boy, ensuring he was safe and comfortable in his bed for the night. He would say a short prayer over the boy at his bedside and bid him a whispered goodnight.

Occasionally, he would still find himself automatically looking through the boy's bedroom door to check on him and feel the briefest moment of shock as he realised Walter wasn't there before remembering the actual state of the situation.

Mantell closed the front door and headed into the house.

Inside his large study, he lit a couple of lanterns and threw his medical bag in the corner of the room. He swept the papers that covered his large wooden desk to the floor with one arm, overlooking the gift left for him, wrapped in paper and labelled, with a child's hand: 'Father'. The gift landed on the floor amongst the miscellaneous items he had thrown aside.

Mantell carefully placed his specimen bag on the cleared space on the desk. He pulled up his chair and slowly opened the bag as though something might escape should he not be careful about it.

Using both hands to hold even the smallest pieces, Mantell carefully extracted each find from the day, laying them out on his desk for inspection. There were dozens of items. It had been a worthwhile visit. Yet it was still the piece with the teeth he had discovered in the quarry that continued to draw his attention. He picked it up and turned it over in his hands. He pulled a magnifying device closer to himself and placed the specimen underneath it. He took a small brush and chisel from a compartment in his bag. Looking through the magnifier, he gently chipped away at the matrix surrounding the fossil, brushing aside the debris as it blocked his view. Through this slow, painful process, he revealed more of the find. Several additional teeth were hidden within the stone, and the jawbone they were attached to was in surprisingly excellent condition.

Mantle smiled. Christmas had come early.

He jumped from his seat and rushed out to the entrance hallway of the house, his voice echoing within the empty building as he yelled:

'Justine! Justine!'

Impatient for a response, he swept across the hallway to the bottom of the large staircase and yelled up the stairs in case she was up there for whatever reason.

'Justine!'

'Yes, sir?'

The voice made Mantell jump. He turned to find his young maid standing directly behind him, holding a candle to light the way to her master. Her hair was messy, and her nightgown rumpled; the shouting had just awakened her. Mantell took in her appearance and looked disappointed.

'You went to bed early,' he reprimanded her.

'No, sir. It's late.'

'What time is it?'

'Around two o'clock in the morning, sir.'

Mantell was surprised. Little wonder the household with the pregnant woman was not best pleased upon his arrival. By the time he had reached them, it must have already been past midnight.

'Is that so?' Mantell replied calmly, trying to mask his shock. 'Nevertheless, you should be available whenever you are required.'

'Of course, sir.'

Justine had worked for the Mantell family for several years and was used to her master's whims and mood swings. She knew he wasn't angry with her, and he certainly did not expect her to stay up all night just in case he felt a specific urge to use her services. It was just one of those things he would say when he was distracted by something else or to cover his tracks if he had been caught in a moment of saying something ridiculous.

'How did it go, sir?' she asked.

'Fine,' he replied distractedly. 'Just fine.'

'What was it?'

Mantell looked puzzled. The girl was tired; she was asking nonsensical questions that had nothing to do with the conversation in which they were currently engaged.

'What was *what*?'

'The child, sir. Was it a boy or a girl?'

'Oh. Yes. One of those.'

Mantell realised that he honestly could not remember.

It made little difference to him since he hadn't been there for the actual birth. He had given the child a cursory examination upon his arrival. It seemed in good health, but for all the time that he was there - and indeed the entire journey back, and all the time he had been back in his own home - he had been thinking of nothing but the discoveries he had come across earlier in the day at the quarry. He had attended enough births that, to him, another one was inconsequential.

'Filthy house, was it, sir?' Justine smiled as she brushed dust and dirt from Mantell's coat, which he had not yet taken off.

Mantell shrugged away from her and stepped towards his study. He continued talking as he went, forcing Justine to skip behind him to keep up with the pace of both his words and his stride.

'I shall be going to visit the Reverend Buckland for a couple of days to show him a new specimen,' he told her. 'I shall return on time for Mrs Mantell and Master Walter's Christmas visit.'

'Very good, sir.'

'If Mrs Mantell should enquire as to my whereabouts, you are *not* to tell her, under any circumstances, that I am visiting Buckland again.'

'Yes, sir.'

He stopped suddenly and spun around to look Justine square in the face, causing her to almost collide with him. His expression was one of utmost seriousness.

'Do you understand what I am telling you?' he asked gravely. 'You know how Mrs Mantell feels about the Reverend, and indeed how she feels about me visiting him.'

'I shan't volunteer up that information, sir. You have my word.'

'Very good. Then fetch my case; I leave immediately.'

'What of your patients, sir?'

Mantell thought for a moment.

This was part of the reason Mary-Ann had taken Walter and left him. He was a well-respected, highly-paid physician, but his mind was no longer on it. When he was with his patients, he - on the whole - gave them his full attention and performed his duties to the best of his ability. But medicine was no longer his first, or indeed second, love. He longed for the thrill of the hunt for discoveries, discussing the latest finds with like-minded individuals, such as the Reverend William Buckland, or even poring over the latest scientific papers. It was true that he was neglecting his practice, but when performing his Hippocratic duties, he felt he was neglecting the scientific world that had embraced him and taken him in as one of their own. He was living two separate lives, and it was exhausting him. He needed to commit to one or the other, but it was a struggle: the physician role paid handsomely yet yielded no personal satisfaction; the scientific role, on the other hand, had presented him with little by way of a financial prize, but the emotional reward was immense.

He looked at the latest finds in the middle of his desk. The sharp teeth. The attached bone. The dust from the surrounding matrix he had scraped away himself until the treasures of that rock were revealed in their full splendour.

'Sir?' Justine prompted after a long silence from her master. 'Your patients?'

Mantell looked at her, his mind made up.

'Tell them I'm sick.'

FOUR

Lyme Regis.

Very little had changed in the intervening years since Mary Anning had made the shocking discovery on the beaches of Lyme Regis. She had grown older, of course. Now in her early twenties, the years of working the rocks along the shore had made her sturdy and tough. She was a woman who would not suffer fools gladly but also a woman of great compassion and a continued respect for the natural world that surrounded her.

The find had not made her and her family wealthy, nor had it made her name known within those scientific circles where she still longed to be a part.

When she wasn't running the shop - which by now she was doing almost single-handedly, her mother confined to her bed with illness for most of each day - Mary still loved nothing more than to read and re-read, examine, annotate, illustrate and otherwise devour any scientific papers of which she was able to get hold.

Mary had succeeded in making a few connections in that world, and the more amenable of them often sent her articles and books that they believed would be of interest to her. Sometimes Mary wondered if they did it simply because they found her amusing - imagine a *woman* who wanted to be a scientist! - but whatever the reasoning, she was grateful to have those people in her life who were willing and able to accommodate her, even if they could not fully accept her into their vocation.

The early morning hours were still Mary's favourite time of day. Getting up from bed just before the sun rose and leaving the house /

shop before most people, including her mother, were about their business. It was when she could fully concentrate on the things she enjoyed rather than the day-to-day business of keeping the little shop going.

This morning, Mary trod carefully down the rickety staircase from the living areas above the shop, trying as best as she could to avoid those steps she knew to squeak a protest should they be trod upon. Having lived in the same property for all of her young life, she had learned the hard way how to avoid detection when sneaking around. Although she could have easily found her way in the dark, she used a small lantern to guide her.

As the light from the lamp descended the staircase, something moved on the shop floor.

A small shape emerged from underneath one of the many tables set up to hold the various specimens on offer for purchase.

'Good morning, Tray,' Mary called out to the shape as it bounded towards her.

The young spaniel had become Mary's companion for her morning walks. She had acquired him as a puppy, and he was now almost a year old - still a puppy in some respects, but obedient, faithful and surprisingly good at locating fossils along the foreshore that Mary may have otherwise missed.

Mary crouched down on the floor and stroked the dog as he excitedly circled around and around in front of her, clearly pleased to have her back in his life after the few hours during the night for which they had been apart.

Mary stood upright again and headed to a corner of the shop where her fossil hunting clothes and equipment awaited her. She checked that everything she needed was in her basket - a hammer for chipping away at the rocks, a brush for performing a basic cleanup on the discovery site, and a blanket, just in case. She pulled out a thick canvas bag and slid it underneath the blanket in the basket, out of sight. There was plenty more room in the basket for the morning's discoveries; it was rare to make a find that would be unable to fit in the basket, and on those few and far between occasions, she would usually require assistance to lift such a thing back to the shop anyway. She was strong, but even for her, a solid chunk of rock was unmanageable.

Satisfied that she had what was needed, Mary pulled on several outer garments. So many layers made her look far broader than she was, and she was more than aware that, at times, she might look a little ridiculous, but it was another lesson she had learned over the years doing this: December mornings were *cold* beside the sea.

She placed the final piece of her ensemble on top of her head: a tall, black hat. This was the part of the outfit that Mary liked wearing the least. She did not mind that it looked more like something that a gentleman might wear - it's not as though she made a great effort to conform to the gender stereotypes expected of her, but rather that the thing was huge and heavy. If she tipped her head to either side, the hat's weight felt like it would pull her head down further. But, once again, it was an addition to the outfit she had made over time following some near misses of rocks falling from the cliffs. She had been struck by plenty of them over time, but one particularly close call with a large boulder that could have done some real damage persuaded her that some additional safety measures were required.

Ready to leave, Mary glanced around the shop, looking for Tray.

It never failed to amaze her, as she looked at their little business, how much she had found on the beach just outside their front door. There were shelves stacked high with her discoveries, tables piled up, and boxes overflowing on the floor. It was a shame, then, that their sales were nowhere near a match to how many items they had to offer for sale. During those winter months, in particular, customers were lacking. It was hoped that trade would pick up again over Christmas; over the past few years, an influx of people, mainly from London, decided to spend their festive period beside the sea. Those who could afford to take a holiday tended to be the same people who would make multiple purchases from their shop. They liked to buy the 'unusual trinkets' as gifts for those back in the city who would be amused by such things.

For now, though, the shop only opened a few hours each day, and locals generally wandered in, not to buy anything, but to look at Mary's latest finds and have a general chat about this and that. They would leave without purchasing anything most of the time, but at least it passed some of the time.

Mary spotted Tray at the side of the shop.

He was sniffing, again, at the bottom of the door down to the cellar.

That room was private and kept permanently locked. Mary didn't want Tray venturing down there, and he knew it.

'Come on,' she called to the dog and opened the shop door.

The sound of the door opening drew Tray's attention. Excited to go outside, he leapt over to Mary, tail wagging and tongue lolling from his mouth.

About to leave, Mary noticed a light heading down the staircase towards her.

'Go back to bed, Mother,' Mary called out. 'It's still early.'

Molly Anning appeared at the bottom of the stairs. Her thin white nightgown and delicate, aged skin gave her a spectral appearance in the light of her lantern. Illness had ravaged her body, leaving the sixty-four-year-old practically an invalid. Her body was deteriorating fast, but her mind was as sharp as ever.

'Where are you going?' Molly asked her daughter.

'I won't be long,' Mary replied, trying to edge out the shop door so as not to let in any more cold morning air than she already had.

'It's not safe.'

'I'll be careful, Mother. You know I will. Go back to bed before you catch a chill. I'll see you on my return.'

Mary stepped onto the steps leading up to the shop, Tray skipping beside her, and closed the door behind them.

FIVE

As expected and indeed hoped for, the streets of Lyme Regis were almost empty at that time in the morning. A few local folks were out and about, ready to start their day's business, but the majority had no reason to be awake at such an ungodly hour. Not that Mary had ever thought there was anything "ungodly" about this time in the morning. It was perhaps the best time of the day to encounter God - just her, Tray and the wildness of nature. She felt little need for anything much else.

Of course, one of the few professions that did tend to be active at that time in the morning was that of the fishermen; being a town built on the seafront, there were plenty of those around. So Mary was not surprised to see Skipper Charlie and one of his older crew mates, Bill, heading towards the harbour. She tried looking for an alleyway to duck into, not feeling particularly in the mood for a social encounter even at the best of times, but it was too late as she had already been spotted.

'Cold one this morning, Mary,' Charlie called out to her by way of a greeting.

'It is that,' she agreed.

Charlie and Bill headed over to join her, Bill looking her over with an amused smirk stretched across his face. Mary tried to ignore him as Charlie crouched down and stroked Tray. The dog wagged his tail appreciatively.

'How are you doing, boy?' the skipper asked Tray. 'How are you doing?'

'Don't be rude, Tray. Speak,' Mary commanded.

Tray sat down and let out a single bark as if replying to the skipper.

Charlie smiled and heaved himself back up to his feet. He eyed

Mary's outfit and basket, the tools she was carrying.

'Still chasing your fortune and glory?' he asked.

'No chance of glory for the likes of me,' Mary admitted. 'But I'll settle for the fortune.'

Charlie laughed lightly at Mary's joke as Bill silently smirked beside him.

'There's word of a slide,' Charlie told her, 'after all the rain last night.'

'Is that so?'

Mary's eyes lit up at the news. The times when parts of the cliff face slid away were always the best opportunity that Mary had to find something of worth. The larger the slide, the larger the pieces that would have landed on the beach, and potentially the larger the discovery waiting to be made. It was after one such slide that she had made a recent discovery, one she had tried to keep quiet from others in the town lest they try to buy it from her. She was waiting for the opportunity for it to be given a complete independent analysis before others could try to make any claim on it or attempt to persuade her that it was of little worth. Mary had discovered over the years that the greater the value of the find, the more people tried to put it down and devalue it to her face whilst trying to take it away from her at the lowest possible price, knowing full well that they were getting themselves a bargain. She had taken the deal on more than one occasion despite knowing she was being played for a fool. Times were hard, and she had to make the occasional sacrifice to keep the shop open and a roof over her and her mother's heads.

Charlie could see that Mary was itching to get away and investigate the site. He'd known her since she was first born, and, despite finding her something of a peculiar woman, he both liked and respected her. She appreciated and feared the sea; they were similar people in that regard. Charlie was sure she would have made a fine fisherwoman in another life.

'Take care of yourself, won't you,' he told her.

'And you,' Mary replied.

She and Tray hurried, trying to move quickly without looking like she was eager to escape Charlie and Bill. She had always found Charlie to be pleasant enough, but Bill - despite having never had an entire conversation with her - had always come across much like many of the older folks in the town: a traditionalist who wanted nothing better for the womenfolk than to sit at home and wait upon their husband's every whim. His constant sneer whenever he was looking at her gave Mary the creeps. She tried to push him from her mind but couldn't escape the feeling that she was being watched, even as she and Tray hurried towards the beach.

Mary turned slightly to look behind her at where they had just been. Charlie and Bill were still standing there, watching them go. Even from that distance, Mary could see Bill say something to Charlie. The skipper laughed slightly but looked uncomfortable when he realised Mary was looking at him. He raised a hand in a brief wave, looked away sheepishly and turned to leave. Bill grinned and continued laughing; he didn't care if she knew what he thought of her.

Mary quickly shook off the wave of sadness that briefly engulfed her.

She looked down at Tray and smiled at the thought of what their visit to the beach might bring.

'Let's see what's to be found this morning,' she told the dog.

Sure enough, Charlie was right about a cliff fall during the night. A large section of the rock face had tumbled to the ground, spreading like a fallen log across the beach. Even now more, smaller, rubble fell from the recently exposed surface, landing atop the fallen rocks and soil.

Mary pressed her hat firmly against her head and hurried to the slide, Tray racing before her.

It looked as though she was the first one there that morning. That was usually the case, but occasionally, if word got around that there had been a fall, others would be out there, trying their luck. They seemed to assume that a magnificent specimen would magically present itself to them without them having to do any hard work. Generally, they gave up after a short time looking, having realised that it wouldn't be as easy as they had expected. There had been times, though, when a lucky few *had* been gifted an easy find, much to Mary's annoyance; they were usually the types of people who cared nothing for the actual discovery but only for the value of the discovery should they get it in front of the right person.

Mary was there for the science, others more so for the money.

Mary carefully stepped onto the freshly fallen debris. It was slippery from the rain and treacherous underfoot. Not as stable as other parts of the beach, this was still little more than a loose collection of rocks;

certainly not an easy climb. Nevertheless, Mary had plenty of experience, and, with care, she found it reasonably straightforward to traverse.

The sun had not yet risen, so Mary had to be guided by the natural light that reflected onto the beach from the sky and the sea.

Tray, of course, thought nothing of the potentially dangerous conditions. The dog clambered up the rocks, scrambling across the higher or more slippery parts, enjoying sniffing at the fresh new scents the cliff had revealed.

He stuck his nose in a looser area of mud and yapped at Mary, his wet nose covered in dirt.

'Have you found something?' Mary asked, treading cautiously to where Tray stood waiting for her.

The dog took a step back to give Mary space to work. She knelt on the wet ground and examined the area Tray had been sniffing. A large, round rock was peeking through. A slight seam ran along the exposed face, an indent with something inside poking through. Mary smiled and stroked the dog.

'Good boy,' she told him.

Tray wagged his tail happily and scampered away as Mary pried the rock from the ground. It was a good size - around a foot across - and heavy. Mary heaved herself to her feet, clutching the rock against her chest, and stepped back down from the fallen ground.

She set the rock on top of a large, more stable slab on the beach and pulled her hammer from her basket. Taking careful aim, she gave the rock a swift, sharp tap. The sound echoed in her ear like a crack of thunder, but the sound of the wind and waves wouldn't have allowed it to carry very far that morning. She struck down at the rock again, twice, three times more. It soon parted along the seam, splitting in half beautifully. Mary set down her hammer and took a breath. It was always such an exciting moment, awaiting the reveal of what was hidden within the rock - especially one this size - that Mary liked to savour the moment.

She slowly pried the two sections apart and looked inside the rock.

A perfect, browny-white snake stone. It was in remarkable condition, too - almost complete and without too many imperfections. The ridges were all intact; the intricate pattern of the spiral ran beautifully from the outside right into the middle. Mary wrapped it carefully in the blanket she had brought and placed it gently in the basket.

An excellent first find for the day. It bode well for the rest of the morning.

Six

Oxford.

It was standing room only in the lecture hall. Should you ever have wished to see the Reverend William Buckland present one of his lectures first-hand, you had to be up early to be able to find a space in that room. Throughout the University of Oxford, and indeed within academic circles throughout the land, Buckland was known as what could only be described as "a character".

Permanently dressed in his long, flowing, clerical gown, the thirty-nine-year-old professor looked older than his years, with his hair escaping from the top of his head and only continuing to exist in its full, black form around the back and sides. His infectious passion and joy for the subjects he spoke about made up for the physical ageing as he presented with the boundless energy of youth.

Generally, two types of people attended Buckland's lectures: those who appreciated and enjoyed his enthusiasm and unconventional presentation style, and those who wanted nothing more than to catch him out and have the opportunity to make an example of him for his often controversial opinions.

The table at the front of the lecture hall was weighed down with numerous specimens, models and illustrations, all of which had a purpose within the lecture to aid his presentation of the topic. Buckland rushed back and forth in front of the table as he spoke, as if the physical act of movement helped to make the words come forth. He held the large fossilised skull of a hyena in his hands. Its curved, glossy shape and sharp, jagged teeth had yet to make their purpose known within the lecture, but there were persistent rumours that the professor kept a very much alive hyena of his own as a pet within his quarters. Indeed, many students (and professors) had passed by his residence and heard the most peculiar sounds coming from within. Knowing Buckland as they believed they did, the sounds could have been coming from anything within there, not necessarily a hyena. Few doubted the validity of this particular rumour; keeping a wild creature such as that as a pet sounded like it was something William Buckland would do.

Buckland looked out across the assembled faces in the lecture hall.

He had their full attention. They were enraptured by every word that came from his mouth; exactly how he liked it. A twinkle shone in his eye. A mischievous grin edged its way onto his face. They had come to hear him speak of his discoveries within the Kirkdale Cave in Yorkshire, which was all well and good, but he knew that they would be leaving with something to talk about. Some would be impressed, others... well... Buckland looked across at the other professors in the hall, those who had done nothing but lecture for years, without getting their hands dirty or helping to advance the sciences, stuck in their decades-old ways of thinking. He knew that he would have a challenging time following this lecture and the presentation of his findings.

The cave in Kirkdale had been a fascinating investigation. Buckland had been brought a sample of specimens discovered there by one of his younger, more open-minded colleagues at the university, who had known they would interest him. Buckland had thought little of it at first - many a time, he had been brought "discoveries" for analysis and identification for them to be of little consequence, most likely something that he already had dozens of within his collection. A few weeks later, he remembered he had been given the samples and decided to take a look. After close inspection, he packed a bag and left immediately for Yorkshire, much to the chagrin of other professors who had to fill in for him at the university without the slightest notice.

Now, here he was, ready to present what he had discovered to a roomful of students and peers.

He paused in front of the table, taking a moment to look each audience member in the eye. Buckland could feel every one of them lean forward slightly in their seats - those who arrived early enough to be able to get a seat, that was - waiting for whatever it was that he was about to say.

He took a breath.

'The Kirkdale Cave presented me with a great mystery,' he began, his voice filling that vast space, every syllable clear and crisp as it bounced across the walls and ceiling. 'The floor to the cave was covered - *carpeted* - with bones. Hundreds, perhaps thousands of them.'

Buckland placed the large hyena skull on top of the table and instead picked up a handful of small bones. He sprinkled them across the floor in front of the table, illustrating his point. He stepped on them as he continued to pace, the bones crunching and cracking with each step.

'It was initially thought that these bones belonged to creatures such as cattle. Poor, unfortunate souls that had wandered away from their grazing ground and become stuck within the cave; the entrance at Kirkdale is, after all, a narrow passageway, so a creature such as a cow could get stuck very easily. I had no problems in this regard; as you can see, I am a fine figure of a man.'

He paused momentarily, his eyes twinkling as he waited for a titter of laughter to complete its round of the room.

'*But!*' Buckland suddenly exclaimed with such vigour that several audience members jumped in their seats. 'After careful analysis of the samples I was provided by so gracious a colleague, I deduced that this was, in fact, not the case. The bones in the cave belonged to no creature as common as the humble cow. Nor, indeed, much of anything that one would find venturing across the wild lands of Yorkshire.'

The words had their desired effect, and Buckland could see that he continued to hold his audience's rapt attention.

'There was a mixture of different creatures. Some are identical - or at least very similar - to those we know of in our current times, others of which are yet to be identified by science. Some of the beasts these bones belonged to would have been of great size - horses, deer, even elephants and rhinos. How could these bones have arrived within this cave when the entrance to the system is barely wide enough to allow a trim man such as myself through?'

He looked out at his audience, looking for anyone willing to answer his question. Most had learned from experience that even a simple question within one of Buckland's theatres was likely to be a trick; the expected answer was never the one they would have expected it to be. Everyone remained silent, absolutely still, in case their professor took their slightest movements to mean they had something to add to his discussion.

'The Great Flood, one might say,' Buckland eventually answered his own question. 'A giant sweep of water across the whole world would be enough to transport these bones from elsewhere and leave them behind within the cave after our Lord wiped out the savages and heathens. Other than those who appear to have survived and made their way into my lecture, he joked, pointing out a pair of students.

'The waves could carry small items like bones a vast distance, I am sure.'

Buckland demonstrated this by sweeping a wave-like arm across the top of the table, flinging many tiny bones to the ground, some halfway across the room. He scurried across to those that had made the longest journey.

'You see that they have landed far afield,' he explained, 'somewhere they would not be expected to belong. *That* is the explanation, is it not?'

Once again, he waited for some confirmation from his audience. There were a few hesitant nods of the head from those unable or unwilling to be able to imagine any alternative scenario.

'Well,' he said, rubbing his hands together and smiling at the assembled faces. 'As enlightening as I am sure you found that, it is, in fact, the least interesting aspect of my study.'

He retrieved the hyena skull from the table and held it carefully in front of him.

'Many of the bones retrieved from the cave had teeth marks, which I believe belonged to a creature that was most likely a relative of this fellow, the hyena. Likewise, on my visit to the site, I procured numerous samples such as this one.'

Buckland picked up a small, lumpy rock from the table. Irregular in shape and nothing special to look at, he nevertheless held it carefully.

'Excrement, gentlemen,' he explained. 'The excrement of a hyena, fossilised to stone as though Medusa herself had stared upon it. Unless one knew of what one was seeking, it is unlikely that this would be recognisable from a regular stone. It is without scent, and - '

He demonstrated this last remark by placing the coprolite between his teeth and attempting to bite into it, much to the disgust of the crowd before him.

' - perfectly solid,' he continued. 'It would appear that the cave was used as a shelter for a family of hyenas. Somewhere they could bring their prey, most likely already killed elsewhere, and store it to eat in safety when they were ready to do so.'

Buckland carefully placed the skull on top of the table.

'Now, as if that were not fascinating enough, I am sure you will all agree there is yet more to this tale. Upon examination of the bones, one would believe that the creatures they once belonged to were pre-diluvian; that is, they must have been wiped from this Earth by our Creator during His magnificent Flood. They are not currently known species, or, at best, similar in many respects, but perhaps a distant relative of our currently existing wildlife. That is all well and good, but a geological survey of the cave and the rock layers within have proven beyond a shadow of a doubt that the cave itself is *post*-diluvian. The bones of the creatures must have been deposited there *after* the Flood.'

Confused faces look back at the professor, not quite grasping the point he was trying to make.

'Such creatures no longer exist,' he explained. 'This means that if they had been wiped from the face of this, our wonderful Earth, it must have been *after* the Great Flood.'

Buckland jumped up onto the table and perched on the edge. He looked again across the faces, staring back at him, ready to deliver the killer blow.

'Gentlemen, if this is indeed the case - and all scientific investigation appears to point to it being so - then it would appear that our Lord and Creator broke His promise. He, the Almighty, the Beginning and the End, wiped out numerous species *after* the Great Flood.'

There was uproar in the lecture theatre. Students and professors alike jumped to their feet, yelling, waving their arms, demanding apologies from Buckland for saying such things, especially there in so public a forum. An older professor rose to his feet. He had been with the university for many years and commanded great respect and loyalty from the students and faculty. But he was also one of those for whom scientific progress and discoveries had to be tallied precisely against the Bible in its purest form. If the Bible did not confirm that the findings were possible, then there had to be something wrong with the science.

The Word was the Word, and the Word was final.

As people realised that this particular professor was preparing to speak, a hush fell upon the room, allowing his words to fill the space more easily.

'What you say, Professor Buckland, is nothing short of blasphemy,' the professor declared.

Buckland pulled himself from the table and tried to look as humble as possible in front of his colleague.

'It does not rest easily with me either, sir,' Buckland admitted, 'and further scientific research is required before reaching a definitive conclusion.'

'Then you admit you believe it possible that you are wrong?'

'No, sir, with all due respect, I do not. As both a man of God and a man of science, it almost pains me to say that I stand by my conclusions. However much it may discomfort the establishment.'

The noise level in the lecture theatre increased once more as Buckland and the older professor stared at one another across the room, neither willing to make the next move.

SEVEN

Lyme Regis.

It was almost noon by the time Mary returned to the shop. Time always got away with her when she was lost in her expeditions to the beach; before she knew it, she needed to be heading back home. Today, she was particularly late, having ventured further afield than just the beach. Her mother would not be pleased. She had found several reasonable snake stones on the beach, though nothing else had matched the first one that Tray had come across. Other than that, it was similar to most mornings.

However, she needed to get inside the shop quickly before she was seen.

She couldn't have anyone else noticing the now-full canvas bag she held carefully in front of her, the weight requiring her to hold it with both hands, her basket heavy and loaded down with more than just fossils, painfully hoisted on her shoulder.

As was always the case, Tray was excited by the bag. He circled underneath it, yapping at it occasionally as the bag squirmed and rustled, the contents moving. Water seeped through the canvas, dripping to the ground. Fortunately, the streets were still wet from the rain. Otherwise, she would have been leaving a trail showing the exact direction from where she had come.

No one outside of her home could know about it.

So far, Mary had avoided detection, but it was only a matter of time. She knew that and had no idea what would happen when she was discovered.

For now, though, the secret remained thanks to carefully monitoring her path home over time, watching and studying those who were regularly out and about, and devising a route home through trial and error that, with care, would get her back unnoticed.

Mary heaved the basket and wriggling bag up the steps to the shop and pushed open the front door. She ushered Tray inside, checked that she wasn't being watched, and went in, closing the door behind her. She placed the full basket on top of a table and moved her shoulder in a circle, trying to get some feeling back into it, having been numbed by the weight it had carried for some distance.

'Is that you, Mary?' a call came from up the stairs.

'Yes, Mother,' Mary replied. 'Stay upstairs. It's cold down here today.'

Mary pulled out a key hidden behind one of the cabinets in the shop that housed her discoveries. As far as hiding places go, it wasn't the most secure, but there was no reason for anyone but her to venture into that part of the shop, so Mary was reasonably confident that it would not be discovered. She lit a lantern and rested it on the floor momentarily as she placed the key in the lock for the door down to the cellar and turned it. The door unlocked. Mary pushed the door open and picked up the lantern again, taking the weight of the heavy bag in one hand.

'You went back,' Molly said.

Mary turned. Her mother stood at the bottom of the stairs, looking at the canvas bag.

'I told you to stay upstairs.'

'This isn't going to end well,' Molly told her. 'You know that, don't you?'

She did, of course, but there was no way she would admit that out loud. Admitting it to someone else meant that those words took meaning and would be harder to ignore than when they played around only in her head.

Mary ignored Molly's warning and stepped through the cellar door. She pushed Tray gently back with her foot so that he stayed within the shop itself and closed the door behind her.

It was hard work descending the steep steps to the cellar with such a heavy bag in one hand and a lit lantern in the other, but it was a move that Mary had already practised on several occasions. This wasn't the first time she had had to do it, and she was sure it wouldn't be the last, regardless of what her mother said.

The cellar was dark, of course, and it was cold down there. It was surprisingly large, going beneath the ground a fair distance, leaving the space with high ceilings and an eerie cave-like atmosphere. That ambience was added to by the sounds coming from the cellar:

Something moved down there. Or, rather, some *things* moved. Scuffling, squirming and splashing noises emanated across the space. Sounds of life of some description.

Mary headed across to the far end of the cellar and smiled.

She emptied her bag onto the floor, the contents wriggling and writhing as they were set loose.

'Mary!' she heard her mother yelling outside the cellar door.

A scowl quickly replaced the smile, but she knew she couldn't ignore her mother - suspicions would be raised if anyone entered the shop while she was yelling into the cellar. Mary moved the bag's content forward with her feet, making reaching it easier, then turned back towards the steps.

As she climbed back up towards the shop, new sounds came from the cellar:

The sounds of crunching, chewing and swallowing.

EIGHT

Oxford.

The commotion in the lecture hall gradually died down. Buckland had perched himself on the table's edge again, waiting for calm to be restored. He viewed it with no small amount of amusement; it wasn't the first time that one of his lectures had ended this way, and he was sure - and indeed hoped - that it wouldn't be the last. There was little point in science, in research and discovery, if one did not occasionally present some research that went against some pre-conceived notion of how the world worked. Buckland knew this one would be contentious, especially amongst the fundamentalists within the congregation there.

Gideon Mantell slid into the back of the room. Having made his journey from London to Oxford in good time, he wanted to surprise the Reverend. He wondered what could be going on in the hall to cause such commotion; lectures were generally solemn, dry affairs. Not Buckland's, usually, admittedly, but he had never attended one with such a boisterous atmosphere as he encountered upon first entering the room. But then he saw Buckland at the front, looking out at his audience with a faint smile of pleasure. Mantell, too, smiled. His friend was up to his old games of doing his utmost to rile up the crowd and drawing much amusement from the reaction he provoked.

Mantle placed his bag on the floor at his feet and leaned against the wall as Buckland raised his hands, urging for quiet within the room. Gradually, the attendees noticed his plea and fell silent one by one.

'Science and religion have for too long been mortal enemies,' he proclaimed. 'Just look at what happened here in the past few minutes. There is no reason why this should be the case. I want to ask you this:

50

how can science help prove and validate the One Truth in the Good Book?

Buckland twisted around and picked up a copy of the Bible from the table. He jumped down and began his usual energetic pacing back and forth across the front of the room.

'Perhaps our scientific techniques are incorrect, drawing false conclusions,' he continued.

Murmured agreements came from several in the audience, most notably the older professors, many of whom still likened scientific processes to magic and witchcraft.

'Perhaps it is science that is wrong. Or, perhaps...' his voice trailed away as he frowned at the Bible he held.

He took a deep breath and smiled, his usual, more buoyant demeanour returning quickly. He looked towards the clock on the wall of the lecture hall. He threw the Bible back on top of the table, this small action in itself drawing gasps from some, those who were watching carefully for anything that could be used to have Buckland banished from the university. He picked up his hyena skull and tossed it up like a ball, catching it easily each time.

'Anyway. *Tempus fugit*, and I must draw this lecture to a close. After all - '

Buckland rushed forward and aimed the hyena skull at an unsuspecting student in the first row of seats in the hall.

' - what rules the world?'

The student could only gawp at the professor, the fanged skull inches away from his face. He looked at those who sat beside him for a clue, but they were likewise confused and dumbfounded. The student shook his head, open-mouthed, lost for words. Buckland moved on and pointed the skull at another student a few seats away. He repeated the question:

'What rules the world?'

This student was equally unsure of the answer but hadn't been taken by surprise quite so forcefully as the first, so they at least managed to speak a response:

'Haven't an idea,' he replied.

'The stomach, sir, rules the world,' Buckland told him as though there was no other possible answer to that question. 'The great ones eat the less, the less, the lesser still.'

Buckland moved back to stand in front of the table. He put the skull down and looked out across his audience. They looked none the wiser.

'By which I mean: we must stop to partake of luncheon,' he explained. 'Be gone. All of you.'

The assembled students and professors rose from their seats and applauded the professor for his lecture. Some, Buckland could see, did so with enthusiasm, others more because they knew they were expected to do so, and a persistent few stood with their arms either folded across their chests or still against their sides.

As they filed from the room, Mantell took the opportunity to squeeze past them to reach Buckland, who was retrieving the collection of items he had dropped on the floor throughout the past couple of hours.

'Fascinating lecture,' Mantell said to Buckland's back.

Buckland turned and looked up at Mantell. A smile spread across his face at the sight of the doctor.

'Gideon! It's so good to see you.'

The two men shook hands.

'Do you truly believe your research about Kirkdale incorrect?' Mantell asked.

'I believe, sir, in the Good Book and the messages within,' Buckland told him. 'Science is new. Our Lord is wiser than even the eldest in this room today.' He glanced at the remaining professors as they slowly sidled out of the room. 'Which is saying something. But I also believe the evidence I see with my own eyes. Somehow, I have to learn to reconcile the two when there appear to be indisputable differences between them. I am conflicted, Gideon, I must admit.'

Buckland continued to scoop up his illustrative artefacts from the ground. Mantell crouched down to help him, and together they collected the last of the bone fragments they could see, stacking them into a large pile on top of the table.

'Thank you,' Buckland said, then, after a moment: 'Was I expecting you? Did you send word that you were coming?'

'I did not,' Mantell admitted. 'I apologise for the intrusion.'

'It is never an intrusion to see you, my friend,' Buckland smiled.

Mantell smiled back at him. A secretive kind of smile, like he had something he wanted to tell the professor but was keeping it to himself. Buckland frowned at him. With a grin, Mantell pulled his bag onto the table and slid it across to be in front of Buckland, who looked at him quizzically.

'What is it?' the professor asked.

'I have something to show you.'

Mantell nodded towards the bag.

Buckland's eyes suddenly lit up, and his arm shot into the air.

'That reminds me! I have something to show you, too!'

'Very well, but - '

'I'm holding a luncheon this very afternoon for a select few students and members of the faculty. You must join us, and all shall be revealed.'

'But I - '

'You're not leaving for London again immediately, are you?'

'No, of course not.'

'Good,' Buckland smiled. 'Then I shall see you shortly!'

The professor turned his attention back to clearing the table.

Mantell collected his bag. He would have to wait a little longer before showing Reverend Buckland his latest discovery.

NINE

Lyme Regis.

The morning's haul had not been great for Charlie's crew. It had been a slow start first thing, and the situation had failed to improve much since then. The sea was a fickle thing; one day - just the previous day, in fact - she would give away a generous bounty. On other days, barely a scrap. Now, the sky was darkening. Thick clouds were rolling in over the horizon, and the wind was beginning to build up. Charlie's boat was sturdy enough, but, just like himself, it was getting on in years, and he wasn't sure how much battering it could take these days. As the darkness crept in, Charlie got one of his men to light the lanterns that hung from the sides of the boat so they at least had a chance of seeing the water below.

'Pull her up,' Charlie instructed.

The men heaved the vast net out of the sea and back onboard the vessel, spilling the contents into a container. It was another pitiful load. They had still only caught about one-third of their available capacity. There was room to spare, but how much time they had left was open to debate.

The boat began to roll from side to side, the waves increasing in size as the clouds edged closer towards them.

A bright flash illuminated the sea, causing it to momentarily look as though they were stranded in a snow bank rather than floating on the water. The men stopped what they were doing and looked towards their skipper. Charlie watched the sky and counted to himself. A rumble of thunder came from the distance, where the clouds were forming in greater numbers. There were ten seconds between the lightning and the thunder.

Charlie knew his men were waiting for him to make a call, and he was wasting precious time deciding what to do.

'Throw them back over,' he instructed at last.

The crew looked at each other, silently questioning the order they had been given.

'Skipper?' Bill queried.

'We've time,' Charlie told him, perhaps more to appease himself than them. 'The more we get now, the less likely we'll be out here on Christmas Day.'

The men looked at each other once again, otherwise unmoving.

'What are you waiting for?' Charlie growled. 'A choir of angels announcing the Virgin's birth?' Get to it, lads!'

Seeing that their skipper meant business, the men set about their work. They threw the nets back over the side of the boat and busied themselves with the other duties they had to perform.

Charlie looked at the sky. The storm was no longer a distant threat on the horizon. It was edging closer and closer with every second. He had worked on the sea all of his life and had come to rely on his instincts over anything else. He took pride in the fact that he could read the seas and skies, able more often than not to predict how they would behave. Today, though, the waves lapped hard against the side of the boat. The sky grew blacker with each passing second, and the wind tossed them a little bit more. Charlie knew that he had gone against his every instinct. None of them had had the best year, and he wanted to land one more large catch to make sure his men had the Christmas they deserved. They were a hard-working crew, and Charlie felt that he owed it to them to make sure they were financially rewarded for the job they did. Except for young Nathaniel, who, for whatever reason, had failed to show up that morning, most likely ridiculously hung over still…

They still had time against the storm; Charlie was sure of that. But something else about the day didn't feel quite right. He felt unsettled, which was how he usually felt when a storm was coming, but the feeling generally diminished when he saw a storm. Today's feeling came before the black clouds and thunder had revealed themselves. Something told him they had to get out of there, but they would carry out their duties until he could justify that feeling to himself.

'Come on, lads. Get moving,' he ordered and set about helping them with their assigned tasks.

Another flash of lightning lit up the sky, the following thunder coming sooner after than the previous rumble had done.

TEN

Oxford.

When William Buckland had told Mantell that the luncheon was for a "select few" students and faculty members, he did not make it clear exactly what the selection criteria were. As Mantell entered his friend's home, it was clear that Buckland had trouble narrowing down his choices.

The place was crowded.

Being university living quarters, there was not much room to begin with, but there must have been two dozen students, plus half as many professors crammed into that small space. Mantell did not recognise any of the students, but a few professors were familiar to him, having crossed paths with others with similar interests over the past few years.

The state of Buckland's home even put Mantell's house to shame: no surface was not covered with artefacts, journals, research notes, maps or tools of the trade. Mantell, starting to realise how hungry he was, having not eaten since leaving London to speak with Buckland, wondered where they were expected to eat. Any sense of a formal dining situation was thrown out of the window because even the dining table was loaded with miscellaneous items.

With that number of bodies in such a small space, Mantell got relatively warm rather quickly. He took off his coat and looked for somewhere that he might be able to put it to keep it safe. He noticed a closed door to the side, perhaps a closet. He went to open it, but an arm reached out and blocked him from entering. Mantell followed the arm to its owner and saw it belonged to Buckland himself.

'Ah, there you are, William,' Mantell said. 'I hope you don't mind; I'm just looking for somewhere to lay my coat.'

'Perhaps best not to put it in this particular room,' Buckland told him. 'Billy is in there.'

'Billy?'

Buckland beamed, his eyes lighting up with child-like joy.

'Of course! You have yet to meet Billy, haven't you?' he asked with glee.

'Is he a student, or...?'

Buckland smiled again and laughed a little.

'Oh, no, not a student. More... my research partner.'

This was news to Mantell. Buckland had always been one to work alone - not always through choice, admittedly, as many were scared off by some of his more eccentric, peculiar ways and mannerisms. So for him to have someone in his home, whom he described as an actual partner, was a great surprise.

'Would you like to meet him?' Buckland asked.

'Well, yes. Certainly!'

Mantell couldn't help but be intrigued by what sort of a person Buckland had enlisted. He was perhaps also, secretly, a little jealous of this Billy. There had been more than one occasion upon which he had hoped to partner with Buckland for a particular piece of research, only to be denied the opportunity. What kind of a person was allowed the enormous privilege of being a research partner to the extraordinary Reverend William Buckland over him?

'Very well,' Buckland said with a hand on the door. 'Don't make any sudden movements or loud noises, lest you should scare him.'

'Of course,' Mantell agreed, with no small degree of confusion and, indeed, apprehension.

Buckland pushed the door open and ushered Mantell forward, closing it behind them when they were both inside.

'He must have left,' Mantell said, looking around the small room where he found himself but not seeing anyone.

It was a strange little room, not what Mantell had expected. There was hardly anything in there, completely contrasting to the rest of the house. What looked to be a large crate, covered in a blanket, stood in one corner, with various other objects scattered around, including a bowl that was full of water, something that appeared to be the remains of someone's dinner and a huge piece of wood with chunks taken out of it.

'He's probably just being shy,' Buckland told him. 'Billy! Come on out.'

Nothing.

Buckland made a clicking noise with his tongue.

'Billy!' he repeated.

The crate shifted slightly, and the blanket upon it moved.

'Come on, Billy.'

A shape formed within the blanket, something emerging from inside the crate.

And then Mantell saw a hyena's long, brown face staring at him from under the blanket. He couldn't help but take a step back.

'Keep still,' Buckland advised him. 'You'll scare Billy.'

Billy looked at Mantell, silently judging him, perhaps working out if he could be trusted or even if he could easily be run down and devoured. The animal looked from Mantell to Buckland and back again. Buckland made the noise with his tongue again, and Billy fully emerged from the crate.

He was a large creature. Brown with black spots and a line of raised fur running down his long neck to the start of his back. The hyena grinned at Mantell, the most terrifying thing he had ever seen.

'William...?' Mantell whispered.

Buckland crouched down and patted the floor in front of him. Not taking his eyes off Mantell, Billy stalked towards his "partner". Once he was close enough to touch, Buckland stroked the creature's head and neck. He had somehow tamed this wild dog, keeping him like a pet.

'Gideon, this is Billy. My research partner.'

Somehow, even the ridiculous nature of this situation made more sense than Buckland partnering up with an actual person. He should have expected nothing less from his friend.

'Wherever did you get him?'

'From a circus.'

'Why?'

'Because they sold him to me, and it was easier and cheaper to do that than to make enquiries elsewhere. Have you any idea how expensive exotic creatures such as this are these days?'

'No, I mean: why do you have a hyena at all?' Mantell clarified.

'He helped me with the research for the Kirkdale Cave mystery,' Buckland told him. 'I found faeces belonging to a creature there, and I believed it to be from a hyena. I needed an actual hyena to be able to verify my findings.'

'Naturally.'

Buckland rose to his feet and brushed the hyena fur from his hands.

'You may stroke him if you would like,' he told Mantell.

'I am quite content not to do so, thank you.'

'Very well.'

'You said you had something to show me,' Mantell said, eager to leave the room and move on to less potentially dangerous things.

'Ah, indeed I do!' Buckland agreed. 'But first, we must eat.'

Buckland brought silence to the proceedings and asked that they thank the Lord God for the food that He had provided them that day, the bounteous treasures of his works of nature, and the delicious treats contained therein. Having concluded the prayer, numerous servants appeared with trays laden with food. They carried them around to the assembled guests to eat where they stood, seeing as there was nowhere for them to sit. Lunch consisted of more of a selection of canapés rather than a formal luncheon. That was not to say that the guests didn't have their fill: plenty of different foods were being handed around, and Buckland looked on with delight as everyone appeared to be enjoying what they were eating.

There was a light treat of meat pie with delicate lattice work on the top; deep-fried, battered pieces of another kind of meat; some lightly set jelly in a glass... All manner of peculiar varieties of food that tasted delicious but were quite unrecognisable by those consuming them. It was surely to be expected that such a character as William Buckland would provide a lunch that matched the eccentricities of his character.

Mantell took a piece of toast with a mound of lightly coloured meat on top from a tray offered to him. He sniffed at it. It smelled good. He glanced around the room and spotted Buckland speaking with a young man, probably not yet reached twenty years of age, his face pointed and sharp, which was further exaggerated by a tall forehead and long dark hair sweeping from the middle of his head down to his neck. His eyes were intense as he listened to Buckland talking. Mantell worked his way through the other guests to reach the pair until he stood just behind the young man.

'Ah, Gideon,' Buckland greeted him when he saw him there. 'I would like to introduce you to someone.'

The young man turned and faced Mantell, boring those intense eyes into his face as he looked him over.

'This is Richard Owen,' Buckland announced.

Mantell held out a hand towards Owen.

'Dr Gideon Mantell,' Mantell introduced himself.

They shook hands.

'I have heard much of you,' Owen told him, his voice as cold as his eyes.

'Indeed?'

'Indeed.'

The young man turned his back on Mantell to resume his conversation with Buckland.

Mantell sidled around so that he could be a part of it, not yet done with speaking to Owen himself.

'From where, might I ask?' Mantell enquired, trying to remain part of the conversation.

'I have read some of your papers.'

'I have not yet been published,' Mantell cast a look at Buckland.

'I took the liberty of sharing your work with Mr Owen,' Buckland told him. 'I thought he might find them of interest.'

Mantell was not happy about that in the slightest. Until papers were published, there was little proof that the author had written the piece. There was no way to credit findings to the correct person should another plagiarise unpublished works.

'Indeed, you have not been published,' Owen said with a smirk. 'And I can understand why.'

'Is that so.'

There was something about Richard Owen that had rubbed Mantell the wrong way even when he first laid eyes on the man. And now, speaking with him, he realised his initial reaction was correct. For a man over ten years his junior, he showed little respect for his elders and a particularly dismissive attitude towards someone he had just met.

'And might I ask why?' Mantell knew he should have dropped the subject and moved on, but he couldn't help himself.

'A number of your findings are incorrect,' Owen brushed away the question.

Mantell could feel himself becoming angry at the boy.

'I have checked and double-checked those findings and even had them peer-reviewed. There is nothing incorrect about them.'

'You have your opinion, and I have mine.'

'They are not opinions, sir: they are facts.'

'Then they are wrong.'

Buckland stepped in, sensing the atmosphere becoming heated between the two and attention being drawn towards them by the raised voices.

'Gentlemen, please. Perhaps we could discuss this in a more civilised way, at another time, and in a more appropriate setting,' he suggested.

'Very well,' Mantell agreed, staring hard at Owen.

'I fail to see what purpose it would serve, but I would happily show Dr Mantell where his faults lie.'

Buckland smiled as if that was an exceptionally positive resolution. He clapped both men on the arms.

'Good, good. Enjoy yourselves, please!'

Mantell continued to stare at Richard Owen. He realised that he was still standing with a piece of meat-laden toast in his hand. He quickly put it in his mouth and chewed.

Owen grinned.

'You do know that is mouse you are eating?' he asked.

Eyes wide, Mantell looked at Buckland.

The professor shrugged his shoulders in agreement.

'Delicious, though, isn't it?'

ELEVEN

Lyme Regis.

Rain lashed at the boat as the cold, completely soaked crew pulled another half-empty net from the port side and dumped it onboard. Conditions continued to deteriorate, and it was almost as dark as night. The clouds were dark and heavy, with no gap between them and no break in the sky for as far as they could see. Lightning and thunder continued flashing and rumbling as the boat banked and rolled across the increasingly large waves.

Yet they still hadn't pulled in enough for it to have been a worthwhile trip. Certainly not enough to be able to take the day off for Christmas. Charlie had promised his men that he would do everything he could to ensure they could spend the whole day with their families. But he had to balance that promise against the possibility that they might not even make it home for Christmas if things worsened.

He made a call:

'One more haul and you can get back to your wives,' he told them.

'Can we make it two, Skip?' Jack asked him with a grin. 'Bill says it's warmer out here than in bed with his missus.'

Standing right behind Jack as the young man spoke, Bill clipped him around the ear.

'Understandable,' Charlie agreed, 'but let's just do the one.'

The crew laughed, but that quickly ended as the largest streak of lightning they had ever seen flashed down from the sky, shooting straight down to the water. Immediately, the thunder roared across the sea, so loud they could feel it. The rain pelted down even harder, which they had hardly thought possible, considering how bad it already was. The boat deck pooled with water, the men having to tread through an inch or two in places.

They looked at their skipper.

He sighed, resigning himself to the fact that the weather had beaten them this time.

'Sorry, Bill; we'd best head home now. Pull up the last net,' he instructed.

The men heaved the starboard net up on deck, splashing it down into the standing water on the floor.

Jack continued to look overboard, staring into the waves. The lanterns on the side of the boat illuminated small circles of water as the black waves roiled and crashed and pounded against the boat.

'Skip!' Jack called out.

'What now?' Charlie grumbled as he sloshed across the deck to join his now youngest crewman, following the disappearance of young Nathaniel.

Jack grabbed another lantern from onboard and held it over the side, trying to light up the water further to get a better view of whatever he was looking at.

'What is it, lad?' the skipper asked.

'Something was down there.'

Charlie looked over the side but could see nothing but the waves. The motion, the rain and the flashing lightning played tricks on the eyes, and many a seaman had claimed to have seen things in the waters that were nothing but illusions caused by the light. There wouldn't be anything out there, least of all in that weather.

'Get back to work,' he told Jack.

He turned away from the lad and headed back to help the other men prepare for returning to land.

A scream from behind him pierced through the rain.

Charlie spun around.

Jack was gone. The only sign of him ever being there was the lantern he had been holding, lying on its side on the floor, the light extinguished in the water.

'Man overboard!' he yelled.

Immediately, the crew sprang to action. They lined the sides of the boat, armed with lanterns, trying to see where Jack could be in that ink-black, forever-changing landscape outside the boat.

Charlie leaned further over the side, holding the lantern as close to the water as he could safely manage.

A shape drifted through the waves, little more than a silhouette, but it was something long.

'What in all that is good and holy is that?' he whispered.

What looked like a tail flicked briefly against the water's surface, and Charlie could swear that he saw scales upon the body. As quickly as it appeared in his sight, it disappeared again.

'There's something in the water,' he yelled.

He looked behind him to where the rest of the crew were assembled, keeping his arm holding the lantern dangling over the side.

'Anything over your side?'

'Nothing yet, skip,' came the response.

Charlie turned back just in time to see something massive leap out of the waves. A long, crocodilian creature with a pointed mouth, currently wide open and exposing rows of sharp teeth. An *ichthyosaur*. Before Charlie even had time to react, the creature grabbed his arm. Charlie screamed as the ichthyosaur's teeth dug into his flesh. He let go of the lantern. It splashed into the sea, disappearing forever. Completing its leap out of the waves with Charlie's arm in its mouth, the inevitable dive back into the sea began. The grip on Charlie's arm was too tight; he couldn't get free. The creature was strong. As it pulled, Charlie had no choice but to go where his arm went. He fell overboard and followed the creature into the dark waves, the cold waters hitting him violently as he submerged.

Cries rang out along the boat.

'There's another one here!' called Bill from the stern.

'And here,' another yelled from the starboard side. 'Two of them, even.'

The men watched in rising terror as more ichthyosaurs appeared.

They circled the boat.

Twelve

Oxford.

Gideon Mantell had quickly excused himself and found somewhere private to extract the mouthful of food from his mouth and discreetly get rid of it. He had been brought up with manners and common courtesy and tried his best to maintain those standards regardless of the situation. A large flower pot became the receptacle for the partially chewed food. It wasn't that it tasted foul - Buckland was quite correct, and it was delicious - it was merely the thought of eating such a creature as a mouse that disgusted him and made him feel nauseous. He tried not to think about what other things he had eaten before the mouse on toast canapé and decided not to consider asking Buckland about it, for his own sanity.

The guests were starting to leave as Mantell found his way back towards Buckland; perhaps they, too, had discovered the secret ingredients within the food they had consumed.

'Come with me,' Buckland told him as he approached.

The two of them headed to Buckland's private study.

It was in much the same state as the rest of the residence, with artefacts, rocks, illustrations, and papers strewn across surfaces, furniture and even the floor, with no evidence of any logical filing system. Further shelves lined the walls, each stacked high and low with books, journals and more papers. Mantell browsed the shelves, admiring the collection. He picked up a peculiar-looking contraption, a small metallic device slightly smaller than the palm of his hand. It was perhaps the only manufactured object on the shelf.

'Whatever is this, William?' Mantell asked.

Buckland smiled and took the object from Mantell.

'This, my friend, is beneficial when exploring caves.'

He flicked a small lever on the side of the device, and a flame sprang from the top.

'Goodness!' Mantell laughed.

He took the object from Buckland and flicked the switch multiple times, repeatedly igniting and quenching the flame.

Buckland shrugged slightly.

'A simple mechanism that rubs two flints together, with some combustible liquid within.'

Mantell moved to place the lighter back where he had found it.

'Keep it,' Buckland told him.

'You are sure?'

Buckland pulled open a desk drawer.

'I have plenty,' he said.

Inside the drawer were at least a dozen similar objects.

Mantell smiled in gratitude as he slid the item into his jacket pocket.

'Anyway,' Buckland said. 'Onto our more important business.'

He looked towards the study door, checking that no one was watching. He lifted the cranium from a human skull on the top of his desk and fished inside, retrieving a small metal key. He then used that key to unlock a drawer in his desk.

He pulled out an object wrapped in cloth from the desk drawer.

He placed the object carefully on top of the desk and smiled at Mantell.

'What is it?' Mantell asked.

'Take a look,' Buckland nodded towards the wrapped object, still smiling.

Mantell moved forward and carefully unwrapped the package, slowly pulling back one corner of the fabric at a time until the entire object was revealed.

'My God,' he exclaimed breathlessly.

'Incredible, isn't it?'

Mantell could scarcely believe what he was looking at. It was a section of jawbone close to a foot long. Several incredibly well-preserved, pointed teeth were still attached within the fossilised bone, with one colossal tooth all of three inches tall sticking up in the middle. Although the specimen he had brought to show Buckland was also a jawbone, it paled in comparison to this monstrous find. After seeing this discovery, he would be embarrassed to mention his own.

'May I?' Mantell asked, reaching towards the fossil.

'By all means.'

Mantell picked it up and turned it over gently, examining every little detail. It was indeed the most astonishing thing he had seen in his life, and to hold it in his own hands was incredible.

'Megalosaurus,' Buckland announced.

'I beg your pardon?'

'That is my proposed name for the beast,' he explained. 'Megalosaurus - *big lizard*. My albeit conservative estimates place the creature at approximately sixty feet long.'

'Astonishing.'

Mantell handed the fossil to Buckland, who carefully placed it back within the fabric and wrapped it securely, taking all the care one would take when swaddling a baby. He gently lifted it and tucked it away in his desk drawer again.

'You have not yet published about it?' Mantell asked.

Buckland smiled again, more sadly this time.

'I do not believe that certain fossils, such as those which attended my lecture this morning, are yet ready to hear of a sixty-foot monster once prowling the countryside.'

'That may be so, but - '

'Once I have the time to put aside to write up my findings, I shall do so,' Buckland told him. 'However, it shall not be as yet, as I am heading to the south coast this very evening.'

Mantell couldn't help but notice the mischievous twinkle in Buckland's eye as his friend turned to look at him.

'In fact,' he continued, 'why don't you come with me? I could make use of an assistant.'

'Is Billy not up to the journey?' Mantell replied with sarcasm.

'Sadly not. And, alas, he is quite unable to record our findings.'

Buckland reached down to a case at his feet, already packed and ready to go. He opened it up and pulled out a large rolled-up sheet of paper. He swept everything from the top of his desk, allowing it to clatter to the floor, some of the items smashing as they landed, but Buckland paid them no heed. He placed the paper in the middle of the desk and unrolled it.

'I am afraid I cannot come with you,' Mantell told him. 'I must be back to my family for Christmas, and I - '

He interrupted himself as his gaze turned to the paper Buckland had laid before him on the desk. He looked from the paper to

Buckland, back to the paper, then again to Buckland. Buckland grinned as Mantell pored over the details in the document.

It was an illustration of a fossil of some sort of crocodilian species. A long neck and head, ending in a pointed jaw, lined with sharp teeth. It had four flippers, two at the front near its head and two at the back close to where a long tail began. The detail in the illustration was exquisite. The fossil was so well preserved, looking at the image, that it could have been a complete, fresh skeleton they were looking at rather than something that had become stone over many, many years.

It was a *plesiosaur*.

It was not the first fossil of a plesiosaur that either man had seen before, but it was undoubtedly the most complete, the most intact, and the largest. Based on a scale etched beside the illustration, the whole thing could not have been less than sixteen feet long from the snout's tip to the tail's end.

Mantell traced the length of the drawing with his fingertip, unable to comprehend just how incredible this thing was.

'Isn't she beautiful?' Buckland said.

'You will be the first to examine this?'

'I shall be. Or: *we* shall be.'

'I cannot,' Mantell said, but the words sounded hollow and meaningless, even as he spoke them, his eyes greedily taking in every little detail from the picture before him.

'This could be what you've been waiting for, Gideon,' Buckland tried convincing him. 'The discovery to make your name.'

'It is not mine, though.'

'The person who made the discovery is not… part of our scientific community,' his friend explained. 'You would almost certainly be granted permission to publish.'

'Why not you? Why would you let me publish such a thing when it was brought to you in the first instance?'

'I have enough on my hands,' Buckland told him. 'I have yet to write up megalosaur, as I told you, and I have many other duties here at the university that I am afraid I have been ignoring because they simply interest me little.'

Buckland carefully rolled the picture again, clearing his desk. He placed it back in his case and turned to Mantell earnestly.

'I need someone I can trust to write this up accurately,' he told Mantell.

'How long would we be gone?'

Buckland tried to suppress a grin. He was sure now that he had persuaded his friend. There was no way that Gideon Mantell would turn down this, the opportunity of a lifetime.

'A day. Two at the most.'

Unnoticed by the two men, Richard Owen moved away from where he had been listening, out of sight, by the study door, intrigued by what he had heard.

THIRTEEN

Lyme Regis.

The sun was setting, but the rain was still falling as Mary took Tray for another walk. The little dog needed at least two or three walks daily; he became agitated and hyperactive if he was shut inside the shop for too long when there was so much space and open air to explore just outside the door. Not that Mary minded: it was a good excuse for her to get out as well, away from the dusty old shop and the responsibility of running it that she had somehow inherited as her brother moved away and her mother became too unwell to be able to be of much help. Of course, the simple fact was that Mary enjoyed being outdoors, especially on the beach, so she was always more than happy to accommodate Tray's every demand to be taken out, despite her mother's accusations that she was spoiling the creature.

They had already been to Mary's secret place and were heading back to the shop with another load squirming within the bag, assuming there would be no casual walkers out and about due to the inclement weather.

So it surprised Mary when she noticed a crowd gathered around something on the foreshore. The tide had only recently started to go back out, so they were congregated close to the cliff edge. The people were not dressed for walking and certainly not for the current weather; it was unusual to see a group like that on the beach at the best of times, but it was almost unheard of in heavy rain like this. Mary was torn between needing to return to the shop with her full bag and finding out what was happening.

Inquisitiveness got the better of her.

Mary moved towards the group, carefully keeping her distance, hoping to avoid being noticed.

A woman turned away from the group and fled in Mary's direction, a handkerchief over her mouth, her eyes wide, scared, upset. Mary held her bag behind her back as the woman passed by. She was starting to get a bad feeling about whatever the group were looking at.

She edged closer. Wanting to move nearby but keep herself out of sight of the other people, she clambered up some fallen rock. Mary hid behind a permanent protrusion in the cliff face caused by a fall some years previously.

The group parted a little, making enough space for Mary to finally see between them.

On the beach was a fishing boat.

Or, at least, what once had been a fishing boat.

It must have run aground in the high tide, crashing violently against the cliffs. The sides were practically destroyed, with massive holes throughout the whole of the body. It was a wonder it even made its way back to land without sinking without a trace to the bottom of the sea.

Wrecks were relatively common, but what was not so typical was the amount of blood that covered those parts of the deck that remained intact. For all of the rain, a considerable amount of blood must have been lost on deck to still be immediately recognisable for what it was. Mary carefully climbed the fallen rocks to get a clearer view of the boat.

She immediately wished that she hadn't.

Torn clothes were strewn like rags, violently ripped to shreds. An arm, severed from its body at the shoulder, here; a single foot, ragged flesh and bone sticking out of the top where it had been removed over there. It was absolute carnage. If anyone had managed to escape by jumping into the sea, drowning in those freezing waters would likely have been a preferable death than whatever it was that had caused the violence still very much apparent on that boat.

Mary turned around and carefully climbed back down the rocks, suddenly feeling unsteady on her feet for the first time, and headed home.

Mary stumbled into the shop. Relieved to see it empty, she put the writhing bag on the floor and locked the door behind her. She slid to the ground, sobbing quietly as she leaned against the wall for support. Tray sniffed at her, not used to the sight of his owner and friend crying. Whining in concern, he licked at her face, washing off the salty tears that slid down her cheeks.

'Is that you back, Mary?' Molly called from up the stairs.

Receiving no response from her daughter, she crept halfway down the staircase and looked across the shop floor. Seeing Mary sitting there in tears, she rushed down the remaining steps, using a stick for support, as fast as she was able.

'What's happened?' Molly asked.

She noticed the bag wriggling on the floor, and her face became rigid, her voice stern.

'I warned you,' Molly said in her "I told you so" voice.

Mary continued crying, unable to stop the tears from coming now that they had begun.

Molly hobbled across to the wall and, leaning against her stick, slowly lowered herself until she was sitting on the floor beside her daughter.

'You can't do this alone,' she said, her voice softening somewhat.

Mary placed her head on her mother's shoulder.

'I'm not on my own,' Mary told her. 'I have you.'

'You know that's not what I mean.'

Mary closed her eyes and wept.

FOURTEEN

Somewhere between Oxford and Lyme Regis.

The carriage thundered along the road, pulled by a solitary horse who carried Buckland and Mantell as fast as she could. The two men rose and fell within their seats as the wheels hit and reacted to every bump, hole and rock along the way. Buckland had hold of the reigns, unwilling to allow even his own driver along for the journey, lest secrets be revealed. Plus, being in charge of the carriage himself, he was able to set the pace for their journey.

Sitting beside him, Mantell felt particularly unwell. It was cold out front beside the professor, but it had felt rude to sit in the relative warmth and comfort of the back of the carriage whilst his friend sat exposed out front. Fortunately, the rain had stopped; otherwise, the journey would have been especially freezing. The speed at which Buckland was forcing them to go made Mantell uneasy.

"Uneasy" was perhaps something of an understatement; Mantell was, in fact, terrified. He clung to the edge of his seat so hard that both hands had lost all colour, and he wasn't even sure if he would be able to unclasp them once they reached their destination.

'Do we have to go so fast?' he asked, trying to keep the fear from his voice.

'If we are to reach Lyme by morning, yes.'

'What of your horse?' Mantell tried diverting attention away from himself, hoping that if his friend did not care for his well-being, perhaps he would care for that of his animal.

'She's used to it,' Buckland dismissed him with a wave. 'We frequently travel such distances, and I am not one to wish to spend too long on the road.'

The horse made a sudden stop.

Mantell's hands automatically released their grip on the seat and put themselves out in front of him, narrowly preventing his face from smashing into the front of the carriage. Seemingly unnerved, Buckland dismounted, walked around to be alongside his horse and inspected the roadside.

'What are you doing?' Mantell asked.

Buckland held up a finger, indicating for him to wait for a moment.

He picked up a rock and examined it in plain view of the horse. The creature whinnied slightly, and Buckland climbed back onboard. He tossed the rock back to the ground, picked up the reigns and the horse set in motion again.

Mantell looked at his friend, expecting some explanation. Buckland finally looked his way and noticed his expression.

'My dear horse has become so accustomed to me stopping at quarries,' Buckland explained, 'that she will now stop of her own accord should she believe that we are in a location I would normally wish to investigate.'

'I see,' Mantell said, though he did not.

'I have to feign interest in the surroundings at least if I wish to persuade her to continue the journey. Hence allowing her to see me examine the rock.'

'Just as I thought things could not get any more peculiar.'

Buckland smiled at Mantell, but the smile changed to a frown.

'You look a little off-colour, Gideon,' Buckland told him. 'Perhaps a little food will be in order. A box under your seat contains something to eat, should you require it.'

'It is not mice, is it?' Mantell enquired, fearing a repeat of earlier in the day.

'Of course not. They go chewy if left out for too long a period. They are certainly not something to take on a long journey.'

'Indeed.'

Mantell reached under his seat and pulled out a box. Inside were various delicious-looking baked goods. He pulled out a small pie, round and covered with golden, crusty pastry. He lifted it to his nose and breathed in the aroma. It certainly smelled good enough to eat. The scent alone made Mantell realise just how hungry he was. He took a large bite and chewed it carefully. It was superb, full of incredible flavour, stuffed to the crust with meat and vegetables. He closed his eyes and made satisfied noises as he chewed. Buckland laughed at his friend's enjoyment.

'You approve?' he asked.

'Most definitely,' Mantell replied with a mouthful.

'You wouldn't have thought hedgehog would be so delicious, would you?'

Fifteen

Lyme Regis.

The rain had started again, taking the two young lovers by surprise. It shouldn't have done, as that was how the weather had been all day, but they were so wrapped up in each other that anything external to them failed to register properly. Matthew grabbed Rebecca's hand and led her to an enclosed doorway, both laughing at how thoroughly soaked they had become within such a short time.

Matthew pulled Rebecca towards him, wrapping his arms around her, warming her from the chill of the rain. He lifted his head back slightly to look at her face. Beautiful in the lantern light, her hair flat and shining against her head, dripping with water. She smiled, and he could no longer help himself. He gently lifted her chin, raising her face to his and kissed her.

A pattering sound came from somewhere close by.

Not the soft, hissing *pitter-patter* of falling rain, but a more solid, almost squelchy patter of feet splashing in puddles. Distracted by the noise, Matthew reluctantly pulled away from Rebecca's embrace and looked into the street where they were taking refuge.

'Hello?' he called out.

Nothing but the rain called back.

They both listened to the sounds of the street, trying to hear the noise again. But nothing came.

'It must be just the rain,' Rebecca offered.

Unconvinced but wanting to resume their previous activities, Matthew agreed and again took hold of Rebecca.

The sound returned. There was someone - or *something* - out there.

'Who's there?' he tried again, annoyed at the interruptions.

He stepped out of their shelter and into the street for a better view.

'Can we just go?' Rebecca asked.

'Just one minute.'

There was something in the street.

Matthew wiped the rain from his eyes and brushed his hair back to try to stop it from continuing to drip down his face. He squinted into the darkness, trying to figure out what it was, but he could see little more than a dark, motionless shape, probably about waist-high to him if he was close enough.

'What *is* that?' he whispered to himself.

The shape suddenly moved.

Matthew briefly saw its silhouette as it darted across the street and around a corner. It had two long, thin legs, supporting a slender body. Attached to that body were two scrawny arms, ending in what looked like they could only be sharp claws. As the creature fled, a long, thin tail waved behind it.

Matthew stared wide-eyed. He had never seen such a thing in his life. He considered chasing after it, trying to find out exactly what it was, but he wondered if it was dangerous. He had no wish to be hurt, of course. And then there was Rebecca, he suddenly remembered. He turned around to go back to her.

She stood right behind him.

Matthew couldn't help but let out a small, scared squeak.

She looked somewhat unimpressed.

'Can we go?' she asked. 'Now, please.'

Matthew looked down the street towards where the creature had disappeared. He reluctantly nodded in agreement and allowed himself to be led away.

Watching his wife's reaction as he handed his son a Christmas present, Mantell hoped for her approval over his gift choice. Walter opened the large package with excitement, his face alight with the joy of such a large box being presented to him. Mary-Ann stared at her husband, solemn-faced, eyes giving away nothing.

Walter removed the wrapping and opened the box inside.

He burst into tears, screaming, in absolute hysterics.

'What did you do?' Mary-Ann screamed, her voice like nothing Mantell had ever heard before in his life.

'I thought he would like it,' Mantell insisted.

'What did you do?' Mary-Ann screeched again.

Walter removed a hyena skull from inside the box and showed it to his mother, still crying. The teeth bared in a permanent grin. The empty, black voids where the eyes had once been.

'Why would you give that to a child?' she yelled.

She snatched the skull from Walter and launched herself at Mantell, the skull raised high above her head.

With a shriek, she brought it down and struck him hard on the forehead —

Mantell awoke with a start.

He found himself on his knees, his forehead pressed against the inside of the front of the carriage, pain searing through him.

It had been a dream.

Mary-Ann had not attacked him. Of course not. He must have fallen asleep, and the carriage had jerked to a halt, launching him to the ground. He pulled himself upright and pressed a hand to his forehead, wincing as he touched it. His fingertips came away covered in blood. He looked around. Buckland was gone.

'William?' he called out into the darkness of the road on which they had stopped.

As far as he could make it, they were surrounded by trees and very little else.

Mantell unsteadily climbed down from the carriage, his legs not entirely responding as they should have, having sat on the hard bench for several hours. He stretched as he regained his balance and walked around to the front of the carriage. Petting the horse's face as he passed by, he spotted Buckland crouched down by the side of the road.

'William?'

Buckland turned around and smiled as he saw Mantell.

'Ah, you're awake.' He frowned as he noticed the cut on Mantell's forehead. 'What happened to you?'

'I believe I must have slipped from my seat.'

'How careless.'

'Why have we stopped?'

Buckland nodded his head through the trees in front of him.

'We have reached a quarry,' he sighed. 'The choice to stop was not mine.'

'Where are we?'

Buckland reached down and scooped up a handful of gravel from beside the road. He put it up to his nose and breathed in deeply. He thought for a moment.

'Yeovil,' he declared. 'We haven't far to go.'

Mantell was astonished.

'You know where we are from smelling the ground?'

'The one thing I know best, my friend, is stone,' Buckland told him. Then he grinned: 'But, no. I have been here many times and recognised the place instantly. I know exactly where we are.'

He dropped the gravel to the ground, rubbed the dust from his hands and marched back to the carriage.

'Let us continue,' he suggested.

There it was again. The sound of something breaking. Perhaps glass. Mary sat up in bed, listening into the darkness for any other sounds, for some confirmation that she had indeed heard what she thought she had. Definite noises were coming from somewhere within the property. It was rare that they had trouble with theft, so it was unusual to hear such sounds in the middle of the night.

A peculiar noise ventured up the stairs.

Like an animal of some description.

Even Tray lifted his head from where he lay at the bottom of the bed. Mary didn't usually allow him upstairs, but after the previous day, she felt particularly in need of some company, so she allowed him to lie on the floor. She had woken up to find him on the bed with her. The dog tilted his head, also listening. A slight growl began in his throat, so faint and underwhelming that it would not put off even the most cowardly intruders.

Mary climbed out of bed, stepping onto the cold wooden floor.

Tray stood up, wanting to join her, but Mary pointed a finger towards him.

'Stay,' she commanded.

The dog laid back down, but he looked ready to jump back up again at a second's notice.

Mary lit a lantern that stood beside her bed, opened her door and stepped out to the top of the stairs. Her mother's door creaked open a fraction as Mary stood there. Molly peered around the crack.

'I heard a noise,' Molly said.

'I know, Mother. You wait here.'

'You're not going down there by yourself.'

Molly opened the door fully and stepped out to join her daughter. Mary rolled her eyes, knowing that if anything, Molly would be a hindrance more than a help, but she knew better than to argue.

She trod carefully down the stairs, lantern held high, watching for any movement. Her mother shadowed her close behind.

At the bottom of the stairs, they could see that the shop was empty. Mary frowned. She cast the light from her lantern across to the cellar door. It was still locked. But it seemed as if that's where the noises were coming from. The sound of things breaking and the strange animal noises continued, seemingly from somewhere behind that door.

Mary passed the lantern to her mother, retrieved the key to the cellar and unlocked the door. She opened it and took the lantern back.

A growl came from down below.

'Stay here,' Mary told her mother.

She turned the lantern down a little, not wanting to make her initial arrival within the cellar quite so immediately apparent, and headed down the steps.

Water and glass covered the cellar floor. Mary trod carefully, not wanting to step on the fractured shards with her bare feet. Something smashed in the darkness. Mary jumped and lifted her lantern higher. The light from the flame wasn't bright enough to dispel all of the darkness in there; a large portion of the cellar remained hidden. More water splashed against Mary's feet. It must have come from the glass item that had just been smashed. On top of the water flowed some creatures:

Ammonites. Their smooth, spiral shells made them skid across the floor on the water, unable to stop themselves from moving with their tentacles and beak-like mouths. They were water-dwelling creatures and wouldn't survive outside of the tanks that were being smashed on the floor. These were creatures that should no longer exist, now only really known as the snake stones Mary found and retrieved from the beach. Creatures that were wiped from the face of the earth many, many years ago.

Creatures that Mary's mother had warned her against bringing back to their shop because *bad things would happen* if she did.

Creatures that had now been discovered by someone else who was in their cellar.

Mantell stretched his whole body from head to toe as Buckland unharnessed his horse in the stable at which they had finally arrived. He stepped out and looked around. It was quiet, absolutely deserted. A short way off in the distance, the sea glittered under the night sky, shimmering lightly and adding to the peaceful setting.

'I can understand why you like it here,' he called out to Buckland. 'It is so much more peaceful than the city.'

Buckland headed over to join him in inspecting the scenery before them.

'Indeed it is,' Buckland said, placing a hand on his friend's shoulder. 'Indeed it is.'

Crunching noises came from somewhere in the part of the cellar that was still enveloped in darkness. Crunching and munching. Mary took another hesitant step forward, wanting to illuminate whatever was making the sound, but at the same time, not entirely sure that she wanted to know. The light from the lantern caught something.

Mary backed up against the nearest wall and put her spare hand over her mouth to stop herself from gasping.

A creature on the floor of her cellar was chewing on the spilt ammonites, cracking into their shells with its sharp teeth and guzzling them down like tentacled oysters. It was a relatively small creature, around waist-height, but its sharp claws and fast-looking legs gave Mary pause for concern.

Not that she hadn't seen a *proceratosaurus* such as this one before; she recognised it immediately from the peculiar bright red crest on the top of its snout.

She had just never seen one in her cellar.

An ammonite wriggled inside the creature's mouth, thrashing away and trying to escape. The proceratosaurus flung it in the air with its mouth, opened its jaw wide and allowed it to slide straight down its throat as gravity made the inevitable descent happen. Out of food lying on the floor, Mary could only watch as the creature lightly jumped upon a surface in the cellar and pushed against one of the many glass containers filled with water, ammonites swimming inside, blissfully unaware of their impending fate. Though the container was heavy, the small creature was strong and soon toppled the makeshift aquarium over the edge. It smashed loudly on the floor, the water splashing across the ground and ammonites spilling out. The proceratosaurus immediately set to work devouring what it could.

Mary backed away quietly, unsure what to do. She had kept the contents of this room hidden for so long, she did not wish for this to be the way it was discovered; not until she was ready to reveal it herself, in her own time and in her own way. But she could not just let the creature remain loose; once it had finished with the ammonites, it was sure to move on to other, larger things…

The cellar suddenly glowed brighter, and Mary's shadow cast long across the floor.

She turned and saw her mother standing at the bottom of the steps, holding a brightly flickering lantern.

'What's going on?' Molly called out.

The proceratosaurus jerked upright at the sound. It tilted its head to the side, tentacles belonging to its partially devoured food hanging from the side of its mouth. Molly squinted at the shape that was staring at her, her eyesight not as good as it once had been.

'What is that?' she asked.

The creature looked past Molly, towards the stairs behind her, up towards the shop.

Mary realised its intentions.

'Close the door!' she yelled to her mother. 'Quickly!'

But the creature sprinted across the cellar quicker than Molly could react, its little, thin legs making light work of the short distance across the room. Mary ran after it, but it was too quick. It ducked and dived, quickly escaping Mary's grasping arms. She launched herself towards the creature, attempting to dive on top of it. She missed and toppled forward, instead crashing straight into another ammonite tank, which joined the others as another broken pile of glass, water spilling and tentacles writhing on the floor.

Something was intoxicating about the sea air, Buckland always found. Something that made him feel at peace with the world. Something that relaxed and soothed the soul. He closed his eyes and breathed in that wonderful, life-giving air, then lifted a hand ready to knock at Mary Anning's front door.

Glass smashed from somewhere within the building.

'Whatever was that?' Mantell asked.

Buckland pounded on the front door.

'Mary? Mary!' he shouted.

A woman's scream sounded from inside.

Molly tripped on the last step leading out of the cellar. She had reached the top in record time; it had been years since she had moved as quickly as that. As it turned out, the only motivation she required to forget about her infirmities briefly was to have a sharp-clawed, razor-toothed monster of a creature running towards her.

She dragged herself forward on the floor, pulling herself into the main shop. The creature slowed down; its prey was clearly at a disadvantage, and there was little point in expending more energy than was required when going in for the kill. Molly turned her head and looked over her shoulder.

The proceratosaurus was right behind her. Stalking her. Ready to pounce.

Molly put her elbows into motion, pulling herself away from the steps, faster, faster, but pain and exhaustion were kicking in. Her elbows gave way underneath her. They buckled, and her face fell to the floor.

Mary ran through the open doorway from the cellar.

Seeing the situation unfolding before her, she knew she had to act fast.

Someone was pounding on the front door.

It sounded as if they were trying to get in. But she could only deal with one situation at a time, and saving her mother was probably the highest priority.

She grabbed a shovel from beside the wall that was already propped up there, ready and waiting for those occasions when Mary needed to dig for the fossils on the beach.

Molly screamed.

The proceratosaurus reared back its whole body, its jaws wide, its claws ready.

It charged directly towards Molly.

She screamed again.

The front door to the shop burst open loudly. Buckland and Mantell tumbled inside, the door giving way in front of them as they tried to force their way into the property.

Mary swung the shovel towards the creature.

It made impact with the beast's neck and kept going, slicing clean through. The momentum of the swing caused the removed head to be carried with it, finally flung through the air and straight towards their visitors. Buckland caught the head, launched in his direction, as the decapitated body of the proceratosaurus slumped to the ground.

'Mary!' Buckland cried out. 'What in the world is going on?'

Mary spun around at her visitor's voice, only seeing him there for the first time.

'Reverend Buckland!' she announced in surprise.

Mrs Anning pulled herself up from the floor, panting with exhaustion and pained from the exertion.

'Oh, Mr Buckland! What fortuitous timing!' she exclaimed.

II

"And God said, 'Let the earth bring forth the living creature after his kind, cattle, and creeping thing, and beast of the earth after his kind'. And it was so."

Genesis 1:24

SIXTEEN

'Fortuitous?' Mary cried, staggered at her mother's peculiar choice of words. 'How in the world is the Reverend Buckland's arrival at this premise moment in time fortuitous?'

'He saved me from that... that... monster,' Molly told her daughter, waving a hand vaguely towards the fallen body of the proceratosaurus.

Mary lifted Molly from the floor and pulled her into a more comfortable position in a seat.

'It was not William who saved you, Mother, but I. William merely caught the creature's head like a cricket ball tossed his way.'

Buckland looked at the head, still held in his hands, and tossed it to the side of the room as though it was nothing unusual. Mantell hovered in the doorway, as yet not introduced to the household and feeling uncomfortable about moving further within the room before making his name known. He did find himself desperately wanting to step across to the fallen creature to take a closer look, and his feet, perhaps involuntarily, started moving slowly in that direction.

'I came as soon as I could,' Buckland told Mary with a slight bow.

'And it is as well you did,' Molly replied.

'Why?' asked Mary as she bustled around to produce a warm flannel to put across her mother's forehead.

'I was, of course, intrigued and excited to view the specimen.'

Mantell found himself beside the creature. He crouched next to it and examined it, prodding it gently to ensure it was dead. He had never seen anything of the sort.

'William,' he hissed across the room.

Buckland, though, ignored him.

'What specimen?' Mary asked Buckland.

'The one in your magnificent rendering, of course.'

'I do not - '

'William!' Mantell repeated, hissing only slightly louder than before so as not to appear impolite.

The skin of the beast was scaly and leathery to the touch. Almost reptilian. Mantell lifted one of its arms and examined the claws. Three digits, long and slender, ending in pointed talons. Despite their small size, they would make light work of any prey on which the creature set its sights.

'You have a most remarkable hand, my lady,' Buckland continued, oblivious to Mantell's whispered cries in his direction.

'William!' Mantell finally cried out.

'What is it?' Buckland snapped.

'Is this creature what I believe it to be?' Mantell asked him, indicating towards the proceratosaurus.

'And what, pray, do you believe it to be?'

'A beast that should be long since extinct,' he declared.

Mary moved behind her mother's chair as though she needed to hide from whatever was to come next. If she was not there, perhaps she could refuse responsibility. Yet she knew that was not true, and whatever happened, she would have to face up to the facts. Sooner than she had hoped.

'If that is what you believe, then it cannot be,' Buckland replied, smiling at Mary and practically rolling his eyes as though his friend was distracting from a more critical conversation.

He laughed lightly, expecting Mary to join in and do likewise, but she looked at him motionless, her face ashen, drained and exhausted from keeping a secret for too long. A secret that had weighed down upon her and allowed her little rest over the past few years. A secret her mother had told her would cause much trouble to come.

She looked towards Mantell.

'You are correct, sir,' Mary said with timidity.

'Nonsense,' Buckland scoffed.

A peculiar sound came from the still-open doorway to the cellar. Apparently the only one to have heard it, Mantell turned his head to listen for it coming again. It sounded a second time: a strange mewling noise, like a creature in pain or afraid. He collected a lit lantern from beside the cellar door and stepped through, venturing away from the others.

'It was I that sent you the drawing, Mr Buckland,' Molly declared proudly from her chair. 'Not my daughter.'

'Mother! How could you - '

Mrs Anning brushed off Mary's protests with a wave of a hand.

'My daughter, bright as she is, is in over her head, Mr Buckland,' she continued. 'A knowledgeable gentleman like yourself needs to take charge of the situation. It is not something for a young woman to be getting herself involved with. I sent you the illustration as I knew that would convince you to visit with haste. You are unable to refuse such a tantalising invitation, are you not?'

'How correct you are, madam,' Buckland smiled. 'But tell me, my dear Mrs Anning: what exactly is "the situation"?'

Mantell rushed back into the shop to join them from the cellar. Out of breath, wide-eyed with excitement or fear, it was hard to tell which, he hurried across to Buckland and grabbed him by the arm.

'What in heaven's name are you doing, man?' Buckland asked as Mantell attempted to drag him across to the cellar door.

'You must see what's in here!'

Mary rushed across and stood in front of the door, blocking the two men from entering.

'I think it polite to be introduced to a gentleman before he snoops around my private areas,' Mary told Mantell, her arms folded tightly across her chest, her face resolute.

'My apologies, my dear lady. I thought my good friend would have made introductions before now.' He cast a glance towards Buckland. 'Doctor Gideon Mantell, at your service.'

Mantell gave her a slight, embarrassed bow.

'You are Dr Mantell?'

'The very one.'

'I expected someone…'

'Older?' Mantell ventured.

'Less intrusive.'

'Forgive me, madam. But I must insist that Reverend Buckland - '

Mantell tried to move around Mary and gain access to the cellar, but she continued obstructing his path.

'There is nothing of interest for you in there.'

'On the contrary, my dear. I have already seen what is down there, and I am sure Reverend Buckland will be equally fascinated. Now, if you would please step aside.'

Mary glared at Mantell.

Slowly, her conviction in keeping them away from the cellar began to slip away. They had already seen the creature she had killed in the shop with the shovel. Buckland had even held the head in his own two hands. There was no possible way of getting around the reality of the situation, no way of making everything magically disappear and return to normal. She realised that she had little choice but to let these two gentlemen in on her secret world. Perhaps they could be of some use after all. Perhaps her mother had been right, and she did need some assistance. She had kept the secret long enough and so far succeeded in keeping it safe and quiet. But things were starting to happen in that small town of Lyme Regis.

Things that Mary worried were inadvertently of her doing.

She looked from Mantell to Buckland. She had known the Reverend for several years, initially through written correspondence around the latest discoveries, occasionally sending him illustrations or actual finds for identification. He had been one of the few men of science who acknowledged her and was willing to speak with - and more importantly, listen to - a woman about such matters. She knew that she could trust him. It was difficult to introduce anyone to this hidden part of her life; if it had to be anyone, she was glad it would be William Buckland.

Sensing Mary's inner turmoil, Buckland smiled at her and shrugged slightly as if saying it was her decision to let them through.

Mary looked from one man to the other.

She sighed and moved aside.

Mary led the two men down the cellar steps, each carrying their own lantern. Tray trotted along beside them, initially hiding upstairs, wary of all of the noise going on. His curiosity got the better of him, and he went down to the shop to see what was happening. As far as he was concerned, two more people could make a fuss over him, so all was well.

'Take care,' Mary warned them as they reached the bottom of the stairs, stepping onto the cellar floor.

Their footsteps crunched through the broken glass like they were walking through fresh, crisp snow. Mary scooped Tray into her spare arm to prevent him from cutting his paws on the sharp shards scattered across the floor.

Mantell reached down and picked up an ammonite from the ground. The life ebbing from it after being out of the water for too long, its tentacles moved weakly, looking for something to grab onto that might give it hope for survival. Mantell held the lantern close to it to examine it better. The tentacles withdrew into the spiral shell, hiding from possible danger.

'What of this ammonite?' he asked Buckland. 'Is this not also impossible?'

'I am sure there is some logical explanation we have yet to hear,' Buckland replied.

His words and voice sounded firm and definitive, but Mantell could see on his face that he was already beginning to doubt whether that was true.

The group continued across the room, surveying the damage that had been done. There must have been hundreds of ammonites scattered, dying, across the ground. Some were no larger than a fingernail, others the same size as Tray. All had exquisite, delicate patterning around the spiral shells that had protected them. Yet all of them were reaching the end of their lives from being tossed out of their watery habitat by the creature that had somehow gotten into the cellar. A sound grew louder within the cellar as they crossed the room like running water, as though there was a pipe somewhere spewing forth a constant stream. Perhaps an underground spring, Mantell wondered, but it seemed a strange place for one, and the watery noise was not the gentle trickle of a spring but more a gushing sound.

Less calming and natural, more forceful and unnatural.

Mantell suddenly stopped, causing Buckland to almost collide with him.

He held his lantern high and gaped in wonder.

'And what is the logical explanation for *this*?' he whispered.

Buckland lifted his lantern, further illuminating what Mantell was looking at. His mouth, too, fell wide open, astonished at what was presented before them.

A large creature, all of eight feet in length, with a small head attached to a long neck, four flippers extending from its rotund belly, and a long tail behind it. A *plesiosaur*. It was immediately recognisable to Mantell and Buckland from the fossils they had found and the scientific papers they had poured over. And from the illustration Mary had produced and her mother had secretly sent to Buckland. The creature sat within a large tank, half filled with water. Pipes ran from it along some crudely constructed homemade apparatus up to the ceiling, where it poured back down on top of the creature through a container that gave the appearance of rain falling — a water recycling system designed and produced to ensure a steady supply of constant hydration for the plesiosaur.

'Who built this system?' Mantell asked Mary.

'I did, sir.'

Mantell cast an eye over her, unsure whether to believe that a woman such as herself could produce such a feat of homemade engineering, as crude as it may be.

'May I?' he asked, indicating towards the plesiosaur.

Mary nodded her head slightly in agreement.

No one had ever been down there before, much less been permitted to view the beast she kept there. It felt like a whole new world to her now, and she knew there was no going back now that events had been set in motion.

Mantell stepped forward to see the creature better while maintaining what he believed to be a safe distance. He cast the light from the lantern across the length of its body, up its long neck to the small head perched on top. Small eyes peered back at him, and as it opened its mouth, he saw rows of small, sharp teeth, perfect for catching and devouring fish and other marine creatures for its food. He suddenly understood the purpose of the ammonites. They were not all there to be kept as decoration or pets. They were food for the plesiosaur.

He returned the lantern to the flippers to get a better look. A chunk of the end of the front right flipper was missing. It looked to have been torn off.

Mary stood beside him.

'She was injured when I found her,' Mary told him.

'She? How do you know?'

Mary shrugged her shoulders.

'She seemed nice. It had to be a she.'

'We must leave,' Buckland suddenly declared. 'Right now.'

He turned on his heels and marched back towards the cellar steps without further explanation.

Mantell and Mary looked at each other, unsure exactly what had caused this reaction from Buckland. He wasn't unknown for his peculiarities and occasional mood swings, but to the pair, this felt like something he would be particularly fascinated by, something he would want to study, examine, and write about for days, possibly weeks. Mantell could not even imagine why he had such a strongly adverse reaction to what they had just witnessed.

SEVENTEEN

The atmosphere in the living room was frosty despite the roaring fire blazing in the fireplace.

Buckland paced back and forth in front of the flames, lost in thought. His hand rubbed his chin mercilessly as he pondered the ramifications of what he had just witnessed. Mantell had helped Mary to bring her mother up the stairs from the shop and place her into a more comfortable chair beside the fire where she now sat, wrapped in a blanket. Molly was trying her hardest to remain awake despite the late hour and the warmth of the place she was seated, never mind the company's coolness.

They had brought Mantell and Buckland's bags upstairs from the shop. Tray excitedly poked his nose inside a partially open bag and pulled out something that looked vaguely edible. He put it on the floor, sniffed it and carefully picked it up again with his teeth. He chewed and immediately spat it back out. Even a dog was particular regarding William Buckland's specific brand of *hors d'oeuvres*.

Mantell perched on the edge of another chair, watching his friend and thinking about what they had just seen. Buckland's reaction had been most peculiar and extreme, and Mantell was still unsure what to make of it. He had calmed Buckland enough to persuade him not to leave immediately, at least wait until first light and see if he still wanted to leave then. Buckland had told him in no uncertain terms that they would, indeed, be going, and his mind would not be changed on that matter.

Mary returned to the room carrying a tray of drinks for everyone: hot, steaming and hopefully soothing. They were all in need of something with a calming effect, she thought. At least, all of them except for her mother, whose eyes were so heavy they were practically closed. Mary placed the tray on a table and crouched beside her mother's chair. She put her hand gently on Molly's arm, accidentally surprising her and jerking her fully awake.

'Why don't you go up to bed?' Mary asked.

Molly sat straighter in her seat and forced her eyes wide open, trying to hide the sleepiness that had taken hold of her.

'We have guests,' she reminded her daughter.

'I can handle them.'

Molly looked at the two men: one sitting across the room, nervously tapping his foot on the floor whilst watching the other, who was doing nothing but stamp back and forth in front of the fire, causing a draft whenever he passed nearby, oblivious to anything else happening. Loathe as she was to leave her daughter alone with these two characters, Molly was exhausted. They were, after all, respectable gentlemen, so they were unlikely to cause any trouble.

She took hold of Mary's arm and allowed herself to be lifted from her seat.

'It seems I am to say goodnight, gentlemen,' Molly said to whoever might be listening.

Mantell rose to his feet and gave a small, polite bow.

'Goodnight, Mrs Anning.'

They watched and waited for any response from Buckland, but he was too far lost in his own mind to pay them notice.

'And a goodnight to you too, Reverend Buckland,' Molly snapped.

Buckland turned his head slightly and cast Molly a cursory glance as her daughter led her from the room. He quickly resumed his examination of the floor in front of him as he continued to pace the breadth of the room.

Tray returned to the bag of potential edibles, willing to risk giving it another go, having realised that it was unlikely that anyone would pay him much attention or stop him from rummaging through the contents. He stuck his head inside and sniffed his way to the back of the bag. Something in there was leaking meaty juices, which smelled delicious. He tugged it out of the bag, managing to spill the remaining contents as he did so. He bit into his find, more cautiously this time after learning his lesson from the first time. This particular snack didn't seem as bad. He wolfed down the rest and swallowed it quickly before anybody could stop him.

Returning to join them, Mary passed a drink to Mantell.

'Thank you,' he said to her, accepting the hot beverage. 'How is your mother?'

'Tired,' Mary replied. 'But that is nothing unusual. She sleeps most of the day, especially with the daylight being shorter. I am surprised she stayed up as long as she did.'

'She is a good woman, I can tell.'

'That she is,' Mary agreed with a slight, sad smile.

She took another steaming cup over to Buckland. Blind to her presence, he continued his intense stomp.

'William,' Mantell called across to his friend. Then, having received no response, again: 'William.'

Buckland finally stopped moving. He looked across at Mantell, confused as to why he should interrupt this vital part of his thinking process. Mantell nodded towards Mary, who stood nearby, offering the steaming hot drink. Buckland took the cup from her and placed it beside the fire without even taking a sip. He turned his whole body towards Mary, clasped his hands behind his back, and stood straight. He wasn't a tall man, but he cut an imposing figure when he wanted to.

'How many more of them are there?' he asked.

'Of what, sir?' Mary replied, averting her eyes and knowing exactly of what he was speaking.

'That - *thing* - you have in the cellar. Are there others?'

'Not that I am aware of.'

She looked directly at Buckland with that response, but Mantell wondered if she was looking a little too hard, a little too forcefully and trying a bit too much to appear as though she might be telling the truth.

'Good,' Buckland said, though unconvinced. 'The ones you have must be destroyed - the sea monster and the ammonites. All of it.'

Mantell leapt up from his seat in shock at Buckland's words.

The fire reflected brightly in Mary's eyes.

'I cannot destroy them!' she responded furiously.

'You can, and you must,' Buckland told her.

'They are living creatures, sir.'

'They are an abomination. Against God's will.'

'*Every* creature is part of God's will. They are all His creation.'

'If but that were so,' Buckland sighed sadly, staring into the flames in front of him.

'You cannot be serious, William,' Mantell said. 'This is the perfect opportunity for study. Flesh and blood, rather than stone and mud. I do not know how it is possible, but we cannot ignore the fact that it is real.'

'The samples you and I have collected are relics of a time long before our Creator felt it necessary to begin his creation again, wiping out all that came before with the Great Flood. These... things... should not exist. They are not of God.'

Mary glared at the Reverend and then stormed from the room.

Mantell looked at his friend and could see the conflict on his face. The same conflict was evident as he presented the lecture at which Mantell had arrived for the end. The conflict between science and religion has always been a particular struggle. Many saw them as two opposing forces: the religious claiming that science was attempting to destroy God and overturn everything written in the Bible, making a mockery of all they knew of their Creator and His Creation. They saw the scientists as heathens, Pagans, some even going so far as to denounce them as something akin to druids. On the other hand, science sought to prove the facts of the universe. More often than not, the research was immediately discredited because something they had found could potentially be read to be in opposition with the One True Word of the Bible by those who took every syllable in its most literal sense.

For geologists like William Buckland, this caused significant issues. Their time period was split between pre- and post-diluvian: before and after the Flood. More and more, Buckland and his peers were finding the remains of creatures in rock formations that could only have been created in the post-diluvian era. On its own, this perhaps did not seem like such a bad thing, but after the Flood, God had promised that he would never again wipe out life from His Creation. The fossilised creatures being discovered were long since extinct. This led scientists such as Buckland to conclude that either the Word of the Lord could not be taken literally and at face value, or God Himself had lied about never again wiping out some of His Creation.

Either of those two possibilities caused scientists much concern and hand-wringing, especially a man like William Buckland, who was both a man of God *and* a scientist. Somehow, he had to reconcile these two notions within his mind: the Truth that he believed from the Bible or the evidence that he saw with his own eyes through the investigations he had carried out as part of his scientific research.

Mantell could tell that some days the scientist within Buckland would be able to come to the fore and present his case with ease, credibility and a cool head. On other days, the reverend in him would take precedence, and his strong Christian beliefs would take over; beliefs that he had been brought up with formed the bedrock of his life and provided him with strength, hope, and faith each passing day. There were also days, or even moments, like this particular time when those two personalities could not help but collide. Buckland knew precisely what he had seen and the importance of what he had witnessed. But his belief would not allow him to acknowledge that; indeed, he seemed to want every trace of it removed.

Regardless of what happened next, Buckland would have to deal with the memories of this day for the rest of his life.

A gnawing sound drew Mantell's attention away from Buckland's introspective stance in front of the fire. He looked across the room and saw Tray chewing on a large bone he had discovered within one of Buckland's bags. Mantell could not even say what species the bone was from, but it was certainly not something a dog should be chewing on.

He walked across and picked up the dog, who tried clinging to the large snack with his teeth. It was too heavy. It soon lost its fight with gravity and clattered to the ground. Mantell kept hold of the dog, gripping him in his arms and stroking him until he settled.

At that moment, Mary returned to the room, her arms full of documents, books and other assorted papers. She dropped them on the table, spreading them out to be more easily seen.

'You think that they are not God's creation?' Mary asked Buckland. 'If they were not of God, why would He allow so many to have lived?'

As she spoke, she fanned out documents, pointing out specific ones that she thought were particularly interesting to boost her case.

'Illustrations. Notes. Diagrams,' she showed them. 'All manner of *scientific* reporting.'

The emphasis on the word "scientific" was not lost on Mantell. Mary, too, had known Buckland for quite some time, and she was well aware of the conflict he faced daily, yet she was not quite so strong in her faith as he, and more willing to accept scientific evidence over the Bible. She believed in God, but the Word could not be taken at face value; it was a book to live by and learn from rather than to explain every detail about the world around them.

'And here,' she said, pulling a stack of bound letters from the pile. 'Correspondence with a gentleman in Scotland, who has many a year looked after a creature which sounds remarkably similar to my plesiosaur.'

Buckland scoffed.

'If there were another, I would have heard of it,' he said.

'And yet you did not hear of mine, sir,' Mary retorted.

Mantell carefully placed Tray back on the ground. The dog immediately darted back to have another go at the bone. Mantell picked up a selection of documents and poured over them. Facts, figures, illustrations, detailed descriptions. It was an impressive collection of work, rivalling even his own, though he would not be willing to admit to that out loud, of course.

'This is excellent research,' Mantell told Mary.

'Thank you, sir.'

He placed the documents back on the table and looked thoughtful. He glanced across at his friend, unsure of how we would react when he spoke next, but he knew he had to either do it now or regret it for the rest of his life.

'Might I examine the creature myself?' he asked quickly, almost breathlessly, wanting to get the words out.

Mary thought about it. He had already seen the plesiosaur, so there was certainly no point in keeping it further a secret, and he did seem to be interested in the work she had presented before him. He may be of some use. Certainly more so than her supposed friend, William Buckland, who appeared to want nothing more than to destroy everything she had.

'Very well,' she eventually conceded. 'But I shall join you.'

'Of course,' Mantell agreed with a slight bow. He turned towards Buckland. 'Will you be joining us, William?'

Buckland turned to look at them briefly. A flicker of something in his eye quickly disappeared as he turned to face squarely towards the fire, stiff and proud.

'Certainly not.'

Eighteen

The plesiosaur flapped its flippers and mewled in agitation as Mantell approached with his lantern held high to examine the extraordinary creature. It pulled against the chain that held it there, nervous of the oncoming figure. The chain was not tight, but rather an extra precaution against it launching itself over the edge of the tank. The plesiosaur created waves, spilling some of the content of its tank over the edge as it thrashed around. Water sprayed over the sides, splashing Mantell.

He looked to Mary for guidance and some help calming the beast.

Mary stood on top of a small step beside the tank and reached her arm, which was not holding a lantern over the side. The plesiosaur moved towards her. It recognised her. She waited until the creature brought itself close enough, then gently placed her hand against its long neck. She stroked the wet skin in the same manner as she did with Tray when he was upset. Those gentle strokes helped to soothe the creature. The splashing slowed, and the noises it produced decreased in volume until the movement and sound gradually stopped, and the plesiosaur was at peace again.

'Incredible,' Mantell whispered.

Mary smiled at him.

'It is that, sir.'

'May I?' he asked, indicating towards the creature.

'Be slow and be gentle,' Mary advised him.

Mantell cautiously trod across the front of the tank and up the step to join Mary, who moved out of his way to give him more room. He did the same as he had seen Mary do: with his free hand, he reached across the top of the tank towards the plesiosaur's neck, fingertips straining forward to touch the creature.

The long neck twisted around, swinging the creature's head towards Mantell. Teeth bared, it snapped at him. Shocked, Mantell stepped backwards and fell from the top of the step, his fingers close to having been taken clean off. Mary couldn't help but laugh at the look of terror on the doctor's face.

'Try again,' she told him.

'Are you out of your mind, woman?' Mantell shrieked. 'That thing could have taken off my entire hand!'

'She would not hurt you; she's a gentle creature at heart.'

'By all appearances, she most certainly is not.'

'It's taken time for her to trust me,' Mary told him. 'She needs to know that you will not hurt her. Give it another go.'

Mantell stared at her for a long moment, unsure whether it was worth the risk. She was right, though, and the creature did trust her. If he could avoid being eaten, touching a living plesiosaur would be a real-life occurrence that few others would ever be able to experience for themselves. Not that he would likely be able to tell anyone about it and have them believe him. But he knew he could not leave that place without trying again.

He climbed back onto the step and reached out his arm again.

The plesiosaur hurried across to the other side of the tank, out of reach.

Mary made a sound with her mouth, much like she would use to call Tray back when he had wandered off. It seemed to attract the creature's attention as it looked at her, watching. She tilted her head towards Mantell. The plesiosaur looked across at him, then back at Mary. She tilted her head again, once, twice, clearly trying to indicate for it to move. Slowly, the creature headed towards him. It stopped halfway across the tank, still well out of reach for Mantell. He tried to make the same noise with his mouth as Mary had done. The plesiosaur looked at him inquisitively. He had caught its attention. He made the sound again, and the creature headed towards him. So close that he actually *could* touch it. His hand hovered just above the plesiosaur's skin, still wondering if there was a risk to touching it. But it had certainly calmed down now, and it did not look like it was about to snap at him again. Creatures were unpredictable, of course, so it was still a risk.

But it was a risk that he decided he was willing to take.

Mantell lowered his hand and rested his fingertips softly against the plesiosaur's neck. Then, when there was no warning sign from the beast that it was about to come after him, he flattened his fingers so that his whole palm was in contact with the creature. The skin was soft and slippery from the water, the texture of something like a marrow, perhaps, feeling as though it was fragile but at the same time firm. He ran his hand up and down gently, feeling where muscles tensed and relaxed. Pressing down slightly harder, he could make out all of the different bones that made up the length of the neck, allowing it to keep the head upright when required. The creature turned its head and looked straight at him. Making eye contact with this extraordinary, impossible creature sent a shiver down Mantell's spine, and he knew there and then that this would be a moment he would remember for the rest of his life.

'Would you like to feed her?' Mary asked.

And in that moment, the already extraordinary experience became even more so.

'Really?' he cried, barely able to contain his excitement.

'Help me collect some ammonites. They will not be fresh for much longer, I am afraid.'

Mantell patted the plesiosaur's neck and slowly withdrew his arm. He jumped down from the step and crouched down to pick up some ammonites from where they had been spilt on the floor by the rampaging proceratosaurus.

He did not notice the long, thick tentacles stretching towards him until they touched his foot and grasped him around the ankle.

They gave a tug, and Mantell found himself tumbling onto his face with a cry of surprise.

He twisted his body around to see what had grabbed him.

He found he was being pulled towards the sharp beak of the hugest ammonite he had ever seen. They usually did not eat meat, but rather small marine creatures, crustaceans, and anything they could find as they travelled under the sea. So the grasp on Mantell was unlikely to be to try to devour him, but instead, trying to find a way to survive this environment outside of the water. Nevertheless, being dragged towards this gigantic creature by some thick, rubbery tentacles was a terrifying experience for the doctor, and he could not help but let out a shriek of fear.

'Get it off!' he screamed at Mary.

'You're scaring it!' she called back.

Mantell could not imagine how *he* was the one scaring *it*; *it* was the one pulling him inch by inch towards its mouth. He tried pulling himself around to attempt to unlatch the tentacles from his leg, but the position where he had fallen prevented him from doing so. He reached out, trying to grasp anything that might help at least slow the drag, but there was nothing to grab hold of other than other scattered ammonites. He picked up any that his hand touched and launched them towards the larger creature that had hold of him, but to no effect.

'Do something!' he cried.

'What?'

'I do not care - anything!'

Mary looked around. She found a loose piece of wood on the floor and picked it up. Opening up her lantern, she placed the end of the wood in the flame and held it there until it set alight. Then, she carefully trod over to the giant ammonite and waved the flame in its vicinity. The creature scurried away from her using its free tentacles, but those holding Mantell didn't budge. They kept a tight hold, perhaps even gripping tighter, Mantell thought.

'It's not working,' Mantell told Mary, though she could see full well that was the case.

Mary looked at the flame she held and looked at the ammonite's outstretched tentacles. She had never deliberately hurt a living creature before, and she wished it was not something she would ever have to do. But at this point, it did seem to be the only possible option open to her.

'I'm sorry,' she whispered, touching the burning piece of wood against one of the tentacles that held on to Mantell.

The ammonite let out a peculiar shriek, and the scalded tentacle let go of Mantell and immediately withdrew into its host's shell. It was working. Mary did the same thing to another tentacle, and that, too, immediately retreated to safety. One final tentacle remained gripping Mantell's leg, but before Mary could reach it with her flame, the ammonite decided that enough was enough and voluntarily removed that one as well, to avoid having three burnt appendages.

Mantell, free from the ammonite's grip, leapt to his feet.

'I think we are done down here,' he announced and rushed towards the cellar steps.

Nineteen

The second large brandy seemed to be doing the trick in helping Mantell's nerves to steady after the incident in the cellar. Despite marching back up the stairs to the living room in what he believed to be a proud and brave manner, as soon as he collapsed within the chair previously occupied by Mrs Anning, he found that his hands would not stop shaking. Mary had taken it upon herself to fetch him a warm brandy, which he gulped back, barely noticing as it slid down his throat. She plucked the glass from his hand and brought him another. He sipped on this second glass more slowly and calmly than the first, and slowly, gradually, the shaking began to subside.

Exhaustion seemed to have overcome Buckland as he, too, sat slumped in another chair, eyes closed and barely moving, unaware of the short adventure that had taken place in the cellar minutes before. He would be upset to have missed out on a couple of warm brandies whenever he was to wake up, but that's just how it was.

Mantell reached forward and picked up a small bundle of the documents Mary had placed on the table. He looked through them, marvelling at the professional, scientific nature of the investigations and the superb markings that had rendered some astonishing illustrations.

'Whose work is this?' Mantell asked of the documents in front of him.

'Beg your pardon, sir?' Mary asked.

'I mean: which gentleman conducted this exemplary work?'

One of Buckland's eyes opened. Perhaps he was not asleep after all but was silently listening in on the conversation. This particular line of dialogue prompted some interest.

It received a reaction from Mary, too, as her face reddened and her jaw set firmly, lips pressed together until they were white.

'The "gentleman", sir,' she uttered through gritted teeth, 'is me.'

Mantell laughed lightly and brushed away Mary's response, sure she had misunderstood what he was asking her.

'I am sure you perhaps assisted with gathering evidence, collecting samples and so on. But what I am asking is: whose *research* is it?'

'Again, *sir*,' Mary's face continued to redden, 'it is me.'

'Who tutored you?' Mantell asked, his voice unable to contain his disbelief.

'I have corresponded with gentlemen such as the Reverend Buckland,' Mary answered, looking in Buckland's direction, who immediately snapped his eye shut again. 'But most of what I know is learned through years of experience.'

Mantell looked over the woman in front of him. This poor, young woman, in this tired little shack of a house in this tired little town by the sea. She somehow expected him to believe that she had, for the most part, taught herself enough about the sciences that he had researched for years, under the very best tutorage, to be able to produce the papers that he held in his hands at that very moment. It was a preposterous notion, yet who was he to argue? He had known the girl all of a few hours. He knew nothing of her life except what he could hypothesise from the environment in which she lived and had grown up. Stereotypes were rarely wrong in Mantell's experience, yet he supposed that there could potentially be exceptions to the rule.

'I did not mean to imply...' he began, but did not know how to finish that sentence without revealing his true feelings about the matter, so he changed tact: 'It is just that a girl - '

'Woman,' Mary snapped.

' - a *woman* of your... position... could not under normal circumstances produce such work.'

'If I may, sir, these are not *normal* circumstances. And I am no normal woman.' She stood up straighter, then, her face filled with pride rather than anger. 'I am, in fact, known throughout Europe, sir.'

'I am sure you are. Yet - '

Buckland suddenly jumped to his feet, causing Tray to yelp with fright, disturbed from his sleep in front of the fire.

'It is clear that we are neither wanted nor needed here,' he exclaimed and headed to the steps back down towards the shop.

Mantell leapt out of his chair, intent on stopping Buckland.

'You are not of a mind to leave?'

'Miss Anning has made it plain that she does not require our assistance. It was, after all, her mother who summoned us rather than Mary herself. She feels she has everything under control here, and our presence is nothing short of a nuisance.'

As Mary was distracted by Buckland's speech, Mantell picked up a small journal from the papers on the table. He discreetly tucked it inside his shirt, hidden from sight.

Sure that it was concealed, he sighed heavily.

'Very well,' he muttered. 'If that is what we must do, then so be it.'

Buckland trod heavily down the steps towards the shop, Mantell behind him and Mary bringing up the rear. She was even now in two minds about whether to stop them or to ask them to stay and help her. Her mother was probably right: things were getting out of control, with the proceratosaurus having been loose in the cellar and the boat washed up on the beach. It would likely be her fault if anyone else were hurt or killed.

But at the same time, Mary was a proud woman.

Everything she had done over the years had been a result of her own hard work. Yes, she had help here and there, but, on the whole, it had been a solitary endeavour. Mantell's words had stung. She was used to not being taken seriously in the world of science due to her gender; the old men who sat on the various committees and panels and societies refused to believe that women had anything of value to offer them, as far as science and academia were concerned. She had been told many times in not so many words that a woman should know her place and should not so much as even consider the possibility that she may produce anything important.

Mary wanted to show them, show everyone, that she could do it, that she was as capable of just as many - if not more - incredible things as those so-called gentlemen.

For now, then, she would let them go.

She had overcome much in the past and would continue to do so.

Buckland and Mantell collected their coats from inside the shop's front door and picked up their remaining bags. Mary's coat, placed on a hook for easy access by the door, caught Buckland's attention. He saw that it was caked in mud but also covered in fine dust, like that one would find in a quarry.

Mary ushered the two of them out of the front door.

'Destroy them,' Buckland told her. 'Destroy them all. Before things get completely out of hand.'

'It was a pleasure to meet you, Miss Anning,' Mantell told her with a tip of his hat.

'Likewise,' Mary snarled in response and immediately slammed the door on them.

TWENTY

The sun was already beginning to rise as the carriage started the long journey back.

Mantell was surprised at how much time had passed since they had first set foot in the Anning's shop, but, on the other hand, it also felt like that had been a lifetime ago. So much had happened in that period.

Buckland was not in as much of a rush to get back as he had been to arrive in Lyme Regis, moving the carriage forward at a far slower pace than before. That was perfectly understandable, considering the horse barely had time to recuperate, and neither of them had achieved much by way of sleep since they had arrived. Mantell wasn't even convinced that Buckland's time with his eyes closed had involved any sleep. More likely, it was nothing but a cunning way of listening to conversations without being noticed. His friend was still behaving strangely, even as he drove the carriage: he kept looking behind them as though checking up on the way from which they had come or looking to see if anyone was following them.

Mantell had had enough of his companion's peculiarities for one night. He put it from his mind, settled back in his seat and took out the journal he had stolen from Mary. He flicked through the pages distractedly, looking at them but not seeing anything on them.

'It makes no sense,' he finally declared.

Buckland snorted a grumpy laugh.

'That is one point on which we can agree.'

Mantell closed the journal and placed it on the seat beside him.

'There is something peculiar about Miss Anning's story,' he said. 'Besides the obvious, I mean.'

'How so?'

'The creature we saw chained to the wall in the cellar seemed docile. Yet the other, more wild, creature we encountered when first we arrived roamed loose.'

'That is strange,' Buckland agreed, but without conviction.

He seemed to still be too distracted by peering behind them every few feet of their journey to be paying Mantell much attention.

'I have seen no mention of the wildling in her documents,' Mantell continued. 'Yet the plesiosaur is spoken of numerous times.'

'Hmm.'

'What I am trying to say,' Mantell said as he turned to face Buckland, attempting to receive his full attention, 'is that it is as though Miss Anning did not know of the smaller beast before tonight.'

Mary, too, would not be getting any sleep that night. She had far too much clearing up to be done to risk taking a rest any time soon. The cellar was a site of total devastation, but she could leave it in that condition for the time being. The shop itself, however, required her immediate attention. There was, after all, a dismembered body and the accompanying head of the proceratosaurus to deal with. They, for one, most certainly could not stay where they were. The shop was a place the public attended, so the parts of the creature needed to be removed, and the spilt blood required cleaning from the floor before anyone spotted them.

She had her work cut out for her, and the sun was already beginning to rise.

There was one other thing she needed to do on top of the cleaning.

The beast had ruined the supply of ammonites in the cellar. They were the only food Mary could supply the plesiosaur, and, being the size it was, it was a hungry beast. Mary needed to acquire more food for the creature, and soon - before it started to make the whining noises she had heard it making whenever it was hungry. Those sounds could even be heard from outside the shop.

That was *another* risk she wasn't willing to take.

First things first, though: the proceratosaurus body parts had to go.

She found a rope and fastened it tightly around the creature's back legs. Mary pulled an axe from one of the many drawers scattered around the shop floor. She unlocked the cellar door and dragged the dead creature forward by the rope, closing the door behind them when they were through.

The carriage continued onward, yet they were still moving languidly. Even Mantell wished Buckland would increase the speed; it would be weeks before they reached home at that rate.

The constant checking behind them was starting to irritate Mantell as well, and it was more than clear that Buckland was not paying him even the slightest degree of attention, lost in his thoughts about something, though he had not said a word to Mantell of what that "something" might be.

'Are you listening to anything I'm saying?' Mantell suddenly blurted out, unable to take it any longer. He didn't want the entire journey to proceed like this, so he thought raising the issue sooner rather than later was best. 'How could you walk away from such a situation?'

'We're not walking,' Buckland told him. 'We're riding. In a carriage.'

'That is all you have to say for yourself?'

'Indeed it is not.'

Buckland looked behind them again, then steered the horse to the side of the road, slowing him to a complete stop.

'Why have we stopped?' Mantell asked.

Buckland turned in his seat to face directly behind them, peering down the street from where they had just come.

'We are not walking - or indeed riding - away from anything.'

Mary opened the door to her mother's room and peered inside. Molly was in bed, eyes closed, perfectly still and breathing peacefully. Content that she was okay, Mary went to pull the door shut again, but her mother spoke, apparently not asleep after all, but laying, unmoving in the darkness.

'You're going again, aren't you,' Molly said. 'You always check on me before you go there.'

'I was simply making sure that you are well,' Mary lied in response.

'It's as though you know you might not come back,' Molly continued, ignoring her daughter's reply, 'and you want one last look at your dear old mother.'

Molly sat up in bed and lit the lantern beside her as if she wanted to grant Mary her wish of seeing her mother again.

'Mother, please - '

'Don't go. I'm begging you, please don't.'

'I have to,' Mary replied.

'They could have helped, you know. That's why I sent for Reverend Buckland.'

'*Reverend Buckland* wanted nothing more than to destroy them.'

'Perhaps that would be best,' Molly told her with a sigh.

'I will set things right, somehow,' Mary declared.

'You're too proud for your own good.'

Mary closed the door, leaving Molly inside the bedroom, begging and crying for her daughter not to go.

She had no choice, Mary kept telling herself. This was something that she had to do.

'I don't understand,' Mantell told Buckland as he, too, twisted in his seat to look down the road.

'We can see it from here,' Buckland told him.

He pointed his finger down the street. From where they had stopped, the front of the fossil shop was visible, though they would be hidden in the shadows for anyone who might leave the shop.

'You are watching her?' Mantell asked.

'We cannot leave without making sure those abominations are destroyed.'

Mantell could not believe that Buckland was still of this position.

Those "abominations" were living proof of everything that Mantell, Buckland and their peers had been studying for years. Proof that their science was correct, and these strange, vicious creatures had once roamed the planet. On the other hand, the fact that some were still alive perhaps threw doubt on their "proof" that they had been wiped out a long time ago. But this could be more of an anomaly; some strange discrepancy in nature had caused a select few individual creatures to remain whilst the others were eradicated from the planet. Mantell could understand Buckland's discomfort at reconciling these new facts with existing hypotheses to an extent, but wasn't that what science was all about? Forming a hypothesis, finding proof that it is correct, or indeed finding evidence that it is *wrong*, and then developing new hypotheses to support these findings. That's how it worked. To wipe out evidence in the way that Buckland was suggesting was not only unscientific; the fact that it was living creatures he wanted to destroy was also barbaric.

'I cannot believe that you, a man of science, would want to slaughter those creatures,' Mantell told him.

'Did you notice Mary's coat?' Buckland asked, once again seeming to dismiss Mantell's conversation and begin on a new topic that seemed to bear no relation to what they had previously been discussing.

'What of it?' Mantell asked, feeling he had no other choice.

'It was covered in chalk dust.'

'She collects fossils. What would you expect?'

'Mary hunts the beaches and cliffs,' Buckland told him.

'Where are you going with this, William?'

Buckland turned to look directly at Mantell and smiled at him.

'There is no chalk around Lyme,' he said, as though that solved the mystery.

'So?'

'So, she has been venturing elsewhere.'

'That is allowed, I believe. I know of no reason why Miss Anning should not be allowed to visit places other than the immediate vicinity of where she lives.'

'Indeed,' Buckland told him. 'Of course, I am not for one minute saying that young Mary should remain within Lyme Regis. Though if I lived here, I am not sure I would ever venture away from it. It really is quite beautiful.'

'Focus,' Mantell told him, snapping his fingers in Buckland's face. 'If that is not what you are saying, then what is it that you *are* saying?'

'I am saying that I do not think our young friend Mary Anning is in the business of only collecting fossils.'

Buckland nodded his head towards the shop.

Mantell turned and looked.

Mary was leaving through the front door, holding a large, heavy sack.

She looked up and down the street as if checking if she was being watched. Not having noticed Buckland's carriage and the two people watching her from within it, she trod down the steps and onto the street, Tray skipping closely at her heel.

Buckland stepped down from the carriage onto the street.

'Come on,' he whispered to Mantell.

The fresh air helped as Mary stepped outside. The smell of the creature's blood as she had hacked it into smaller, more manageable pieces, combined with the stench of the dying ammonites in the cellar, had started getting to her, making her feel quite queasy. Mary usually had a strong stomach, and nothing much fazed her, but tonight had been the first time she had found it necessary to cut the limbs from a dead creature.

She had stuffed the pieces inside a sack, thinking it would make for a more straightforward disposal. But it wasn't until she tried lugging the full sack back up the cellar steps that she discovered how heavy it was. She had no choice, though; it had to be eliminated.

The scent of the sea in the outside air cleared most of the lingering smell of iron that had built up in her nostrils, though she was sure that it was a smell she would remember and most likely keep smelling over and over again even when it wasn't there.

At the bottom of the steps, she stopped and examined the front of the building.

There was a hole in the brickwork. Not huge, and not noticeable unless it was being looked for, but large enough that the proceratosaurus could have squeezed itself inside, straight down into the cellar. It must have smelled the ammonites from outside and found its way through. Some loose bricks and rubble were scattered across the ground in front of the hole, so Mary rearranged those pieces across it to try to block it. At least to ensure it was entirely unseen unless anyone moved the pieces out of place again.

Mary looked around, again making sure she wasn't being watched.

She thought she saw something moving into the shadows at the side of the street, but it didn't move again while she was watching, so it looked like she was most likely alone.

She heaved the heavy sack over her shoulder and continued her slow walk down the street.

Twenty-One

Oxford.

It was generally not considered polite to knock at someone's door so early in the morning for a seemingly arbitrary reason, but Richard Owen could wait no longer.

He had heard much of the discussion between William Buckland and Gideon Mantell during the lunch at Buckland's home, and the pair of them had sounded excited about going to examine a particular specimen. But the part Owen had missed hearing was where precisely they needed to go to see the item. He had tried to glean that information from other guests at the party, talking around the subject to avoid appearing just that bit *too* interested, but none of those in attendance seemed any the wiser than he. By the time the two men left, he still had no real idea of what the item was that they were going to examine or where it was that this examination would take place.

There was only one course of action left open to him, he decided:

Deception.

That was how he found himself cold and banging on Buckland's front door in the early hours of the morning.

It was eventually opened by a young maid, who stood in the doorway drying her hands on her apron, apparently disturbed part way through cleaning some pots.

'Can I help you, sir?' she asked.

'Apologies for the early morning interruption,' Owen said with a slight bow and a smile that offered little warmth on that frosty morning. 'I wish to speak with the Reverend Buckland, if I may.'

'The master's not here at the moment, I'm afraid, sir,' the maid replied.

As she tried to close the door, Owen pressed his hand upon it to keep it open.

'Oh, dear, that is a dilemma,' he said, shaking his head sadly and tut-tutting for extra effect.

The maid looked him up and down for a moment.

'Is there something I can help you with, sir?' she asked out of duty.

'My name is Richard Owen,' he told her. 'I was here yesterday at the Reverend's lunch. You may remember me?'

'Can't say as I do, sir, no.'

'Not to worry, not to worry. You see, the unfortunate thing is that I seem to have lost something, and the last place I remember having it was here.'

'What was it?'

'It is but a handkerchief. You will think me rather foolish, but it has sentimental value, you understand.'

'Sentimental value?'

'Yes.'

He realised then that of all things he could have chosen to gain access to Buckland's house, a handkerchief was possibly not the strongest contender for something that may have sentimental value attached to it. He felt the maid wanted him to elaborate, but he could not conjure up anything to continue that line of thought, so he let it hang.

'I have not seen anything like that myself,' the maid told him. 'If you could wait here, I can ask the others.'

She tried closing the door again, but once more, Owen prevented that from happening.

'I can see that you are very busy. If I may, perhaps I could take a quick look around myself.'

The maid looked him over again, weighing up her options. She could let him in and possibly be reprimanded for allowing a stranger into her master's home, or she could not allow him in and possibly be reprimanded for not helping one of her master's friends in his time of need.

'I believe I last saw it in the Reverend's study,' Owen told her. 'I shall only be five minutes. Ten at the most.'

The maid finally gave a stiff nod and opened the door.

Owen stepped inside, and the maid closed the door behind him.

'Five minutes,' she told him.

Owen watched until the maid was out of sight, sure that she was away carrying out her duties and not about to disturb him, then quietly closed the door to Buckland's study. He looked around at the site before him and wondered how he would ever find what he was looking for within the mountain of *stuff* that littered the room.

He had, of course, seen Mantell and Buckland discussing things at Buckland's desk, so that seemed like the best place to begin his investigations.

The large illustration the two men had been poring over was no longer there; Owen was pretty sure that he had seen Buckland roll it up and tuck it away after their discussions, so he was not expecting to find that anyway. The top of the desk was almost empty. Buckland had cleared it when placing down the illustration, so the papers that had been on top were scattered across the floor.

Owen crouched down and looked at them.

Various scientific papers, journals, correspondence... nothing particularly interesting.

It was not interesting until he realised that many of the correspondences came from one person: Mary Anning.

Owen frowned at the name.

It was not someone that he had heard of before, and why would he? Women were unimportant to his studies and career, so he had no cause to become acquainted with one at that point in his life. One may come in useful in later years, but for now, they were nothing short of a distraction and an annoyance. Yet the fact that the great William Buckland was corresponding with this Anning woman intrigued Owen. He did not think Buckland would have taken her as a lover: he already had eyes on another, a young woman also called Mary, but this one was Mary Morland, and by all accounts, he was sure that Buckland intended to take her for his wife.

Aside from Mary Morland, the only thing in Buckland's life was his work.

So that could only mean that this Mary Anning was somehow involved in that.

Owen snatched the correspondences from the floor again and looked at them more closely. They spoke of plesiosaurs, ammonites, and ichthyosaurs, all of which were already known of, so nothing particularly extraordinary there. But then he came across one letter dated just a few days previously. It was written differently from the other letters. It was excited, pleading with Buckland to go and visit, promising to show him something of great significance.

Owen smiled. This was it, he was sure.

In the top corner of the letter was the writer's address, in Lyme Regis.

That's where they had gone.

He crumpled the letter into his coat pocket and got to his feet.

About to head for the study door, he glanced back and looked at the desk. The closed drawers at the front of the furniture beckoned to him. He looked towards the closed study door and listened: no sounds of footsteps outside the room just yet. He stepped around the scattered papers and tried the drawers. They were unlocked. Buckland had an incredible mind for science, but sometimes he was too focused on that to think about simple things, such as locking desk drawers.

The topmost drawer contained more correspondence. Nothing of great interest as far as Owen could tell from rifling through it.

The second, middle, drawer was host to a bag of something that smelled particularly nasty but looked as though it was possibly intended to be edible. He closed that one quickly, gagging at the stench.

The bottom drawer, larger than the others, presented him with the real treasure.

The megalosaurus jaw.

Owen's eyes widened greedily as he saw it. He checked again that he wasn't being watched and carefully took it from the drawer. He held it up high to examine it in the light. It truly was astonishing.

The study door opened, and the maid looked in.

Owen shoved the jaw under his coat and slid the desk drawer shut with his knee.

The maid looked at him suspiciously but had not seen enough to be able to make a judgement call on whether the visitor was up to no good, so she thought it best to keep quiet for the time being.

'Did you find what you were looking for, sir?' she asked.

'Indeed I did,' Owen told her cheerily as he stepped over the papers towards the study door. 'Indeed I did.'

TWENTY-TWO

Lyme Regis.

In hindsight, a canvas bag was not the best choice of container for storing the separated body parts of the proceratosaurus. Despite putting the contents inside another bag within the canvas bag to prevent leakage, the bottom began to turn a dark shade of red as Mary walked. As that red spread across the entire underside of the bag, it started to leak, dripping splashes of crimson blood here and there, a trail of bloody crumbs for anyone to be able to follow. A few spots even landed on Tray's back as he scurried alongside Mary, making him look like an extraordinary variation of a leopard.

There was nothing she could do about it now, though, as she had arrived at the floor of a quarry.

The place was vast. They had been digging there for a couple of years now, extracting limestone, for the most part, for use in construction. They had already cut a significant chunk out of the landscape, but fortunately, until you fully came upon the site, it was impossible to see from the side of the road. The plan was also to dig lower, rather than expanding the site to swallow up any more of the surrounding countryside, forming giant cliff-like faces around the outside of the bowl-shaped extraction. Most of the work had been done through the use of explosives, the sound of which echoed for miles around, much to the annoyance of the locals.

Mary swerved the leaking bag behind her back as she approached the worker's shelter near the entrance to the site. Several men were already in there, ready to begin their day's work. Seeing Mary heading in their direction, the site's foreman, a Mr George Fletcher, emerged to greet her. A large man, who had worked hard labour all his life, had to stoop to get through the hut door, clutching a slab of bread in his thick fist. For his size and rough demeanour, Mary always found him a pleasure to deal with and very accommodating of her despite her often odd requests.

'Early this morning, Mary,' Fletcher said as he ripped a mouthful from the chunk of bread.

'Is that a problem?' Mary asked, trying to get away with providing as little information as possible.

'Could be,' Fletcher told her.

He glanced back at his crew, who watched the exchange from the hut.

Fletcher took Mary by the elbow and led her to one side so they could not be overheard.

'I can't keep letting you in here, you know,' he warned her. 'It's against the rules.'

'I thought you were in charge,' Mary said, attempting to rile up his ego.

'They're *my* rules,' he snapped, Mary's plan backfiring.

But the giant turned gentle once again as he looked down at Tray. He smiled happily at the little dog, who wagged his tail at Fletcher's attention.

'Here you go, lad,' he said, tossing a piece of bread towards the dog.

Tray snatched it out of the air as it fell towards him.

'What do you say?' Mary asked Tray.

The dog gave a small bark of appreciation and gulped down the mouthful.

'You're welcome,' Fletcher replied with a loud but short laugh.

Tray looked pleadingly at Fletcher, who was more than willing to oblige and passed the dog some more food. Fletcher crouched down and stroked Tray's back as the dog continued to eat. He looked up at Mary.

'Still searching for that something special?' he asked her.

'Always.'

Fletcher smiled and turned his attention back to Tray. He felt something wet and sticky on his hand from where he had stroked the dog. Looking at his palm, he saw something dark on it, rubbed off from the fur. He glanced towards Mary and noticed for the first time the bag that she was trying to keep concealed from him. The bottom of the container appeared to be coated in the same substance that Tray had on his back — some thick, dark liquid. In the low light of the early morning, it was hard to make out exactly, but Fletcher was sure it was red. A drip fell from the bottom of the bag and splashed upon the ground.

Mary noticed that Fletcher was staring at the bag.

She shifted position so that it was even less visible than it had been, but she knew it had been spotted. She made eye contact with the foreman as if daring him to question her. She could only hope that Fletcher wouldn't say anything. He was already risking his job by letting her on the site, so it was unlikely that he would, but Mary knew she was already risking being told she couldn't return there. She had to be more careful in the future, assuming Fletcher allowed her to continue visiting there.

Mary was the first to break eye contact, looking across to the opposite side of the quarry, where she wanted and needed to be.

Fletcher followed her gaze. Whenever she came there, she always went over to that side of the quarry and disappeared for hours. She was a nice woman, always kind to Fletcher and his men, bringing them treats whenever she was able, so Fletcher had looked the other way. But he was starting to suspect that it was more than his job was worth, particularly not knowing what she did over there.

'What are you up to, Mary Anning?' he asked, fully expecting not to be told.

'Nothing,' she replied.

'That "nothing's" going to get us both into trouble one of these days, I should wager.'

'I am sure that is not the case, sir,' Mary said with a small smile.

Fletcher sighed and rubbed his thick skull with his hand. He quickly realised that it was the hand with the red substance on it and dropped it back down to his side. But not before he had spread it onto his bald head. Mary looked away, unsure whether to laugh or be worried.

'Don't be long,' Fletcher told her.

'I won't.'

'You know where I am if you need anything.'

'Thank you.'

'I mean it,' he said, staring straight into her eyes. 'Anything at all; if you need help, let me know.'

'I will.'

He sighed again and turned away with a shake of his head, back towards the hut where his men were waiting for him.

Mary hurried across the quarry floor towards the other side.

Twenty-Three

The path to the quarry's floor was steep and narrow, slippery with loose rubble and uneven underfoot. Buckland and Mantell had followed Mary to her destination from a safe distance behind, but now there was more space between them as she seemed to have been more sure-footed on the path than those two men were; she clearly knew the best footing for navigating the route.

Trying to keep up while simultaneously attempting to remain unnoticed was tricky on such a path. On more than one occasion, the two men had to throw themselves to the ground to avoid being seen as their footsteps, scuffling in the rock, had drawn Mary's attention. Fortunately, they had been too far behind for the sound to attract more than a passing glance from Mary, but they had been close calls nevertheless.

From their high vantage point, they could see Mary walk away from the site foreman, heading across to the other side of the quarry floor.

'Quickly,' Buckland commanded. 'Otherwise, we shall lose her.'

'Where could she go?' Mantell asked, stopping briefly to rest against the physical exertion. 'It is a quarry - there is nowhere for her to become lost.'

Buckland ignored him and marched onward, leaving Mantell to hurry after him to catch up.

Finally, they made it to the quarry floor.

Mary was almost at the far wall.

Buckland set her in his sights and strode forward, his coat flapping behind him with the momentum.

As they passed beside the crew's hut, Fletcher stepped outside.

'Help you?' he called out to them.

Mantell turned to look briefly at the large man, but Buckland obliviously ploughed onwards.

'I said: can I help you?' Fletcher said again, his voice louder and firmer; not a voice that could easily be ignored.

The two men stopped, and Buckland returned to join Mantell standing before the foreman. Fletcher looked the two men up and down. Dressed in their fancy Oxford and London clothes, they certainly did not look the part for two men stumbling through a quarry in the early hours of a December morning. It would almost be comical if he hadn't been so concerned about what trouble their presence there might bring him.

'We would like to look around, if we may,' Mantell told Fletcher.

'What for?'

'We are scientists. Geologists, in fact,' Mantell explained.

'So?'

Mantell looked towards Buckland for help, but the Reverend crouched on the ground. He scooped up a handful of rock dust, raised it to his face and touched the tip of his tongue against it. He withdrew his tongue and looked thoughtful. Finally, he smiled at Fletcher.

'You have some delicious stone here,' he announced.

The foreman stared open-mouthed at the strange, balding man who had licked his rubble. Realising they were losing him, Mantell tried to reel the conversation back in again.

'We're here to see a... friend,' he said.

Fletcher's head slowly turned back in Mantell's direction, though his eyes flicked back and forth between the two men as if he thought it safest to keep an eye on the stone licker, just in case he might try anything even more extreme than that.

'Who might that be?' Fletcher asked.

'Mary Anning.'

Fletcher frowned and scratched his chin for dramatic effect.

'Anning, you say? Don't know no one by that name.'

A member of his crew named Joseph emerged from the hut, his arms laden with explosives. Fletcher turned to him.

'Know anyone by the name of Mary Anning, Joseph?'

Joseph looked from Fletcher to the two strangers speaking with him, then back to his foreman.

'Don't think so, boss,' he said, getting the hint, and went on his way.

'He doesn't know anyone by that name neither,' Fletcher told them.

'She was speaking with you but a minute ago,' Mantell snapped.

He instantly regretted it as the foreman stepped up close to him, looming above him by a full head and shoulders. He gestured his thick arms across the landscape.

'No one here but us,' he said.

The two men looked around. The quarry floor was now empty, save for Joseph carrying his explosives to wherever they might be required. There was no sign of Mary anywhere. She had, somehow, completely disappeared.

'Indeed,' Buckland said quietly.

Without another word, he marched away from Mantell and Fletcher, heading with long strides towards where they had last seen Mary, across at the opposite wall to the quarry. Fletcher chased after him, with Mantell following close behind.

'You can't go anywhere without my permission,' Fletcher yelled to Buckland.

'I am a man of God and a man of science,' Buckland retorted. 'I can do as I please.'

'Boss!' a yell sounded from behind them.

Fletcher stopped and looked back. One of his men was waving him over, needing his assistance with something that apparently couldn't wait. Fletcher looked from his crew member to the two intruders and back again. He had a responsibility to his crew that didn't extend to trespassers on his site. He'd warned them that they shouldn't be there, so if anything happened to them, it was their own fault. He had things to attend to and people he knew and respected to take care of.

He waved a dismissive hand towards the two men, who were already halfway across the quarry, and headed back to work.

Twenty-Four

Wondering what in the world he had got himself into by joining the eccentric professor in what had already been an eventful journey to the south coast of England, Mantell had to almost jog across the quarry to keep up with Buckland.

The man was driving forward at great speed, eager to discover where Mary had disappeared. As far as they could see from where they stood with Fletcher previously, there was nowhere that she could have possibly gone. There was nothing before them but the great cliffs formed while excavating the quarry.

They reached the walls and stopped.

Buckland placed his hand upon the chalky surface, and Mantell was worried for a moment that he might try and lick it, as he had done with a handful of grit before.

'Wherever did she go?' Mantell asked, more as an attempt to distract him than a question that he thought his friend would be able to answer.

'Quiet!' Buckland snapped at him.

He placed a finger to his lips and pressed his ear against the cliff.

Based on previous experience, it was hard to know if Buckland was listening for something or merely embracing the rock face.

But he suddenly jumped back from the cliff in glee.

'Did you hear that?' he asked with delight.

'What?'

Mantell had heard nothing.

'Listen,' Buckland told him.

The two men stood in silence. At first, Mantell could not hear anything. But then, after a moment, there was the clear, unmistakable sound of a dog barking, and that bark sounded like it belonged to Tray.

'Listen again,' Buckland said, pressing his ear against the rock face.

Mantell did likewise. It was cold against his face, but he forced himself to stay in place until he once again heard the sound of little Tray yapping. This second time, it was even clearer than the first.

'They're in the cliff?' Mantell asked, astonished.

'So it would seem,' Buckland replied thoughtfully.

He examined the wall in front of them, running his hands across it as though looking for a hidden lever that he could pull to spring open a secret door. But there was nothing. No door, no entrance, nothing. Buckland looked up, examining the rock face slightly above his head. He ran his hands across that surface as well, then suddenly stopped.

His fingers touched something, his fingertips pressing against a flat surface. On tip-toes, he reached further and found that the flat surface extended further back into the cliff face. It was like a ledge formed in the rock.

He heaved himself up, pulling his whole body weight onto the ledge. To look at him, one would not have thought William Buckland would have the upper body strength to be able to achieve such a thing, but he had spent years investigating and digging up fossils in even the most extreme conditions; he had grown surprisingly accustomed to physical work, and had found it necessary to remain in good physical condition to be able to perform some of the hunts and excavations himself. After all, there was no one that he trusted more than himself to perform such activities with the professionalism they required.

Buckland was finally standing at the narrow ledge, looking down at Mantell on the floor below. As Mantell watched him, Buckland glanced across to the side of where he stood. He looked surprised.

'Aha!' he exclaimed, then stepped to his right and promptly disappeared.

'What in the world?' Mantell blurted out, astonished that Buckland could have suddenly vanished from sight. He tried calling out to him: 'William! Where have you gone?'

But no response came. Mantell felt that he had no choice but to try to follow.

He rolled up his sleeves and extended his arms to where he had watched Buckland grab at the ledge. His hands found it easily enough, but the struggle was getting himself up there. Buckland had easily achieved it, but Mantell found that he perhaps wasn't quite as strong as his friend. He tried to pull himself up, in the same way Buckland had managed, several times, but always found that he didn't have the strength to lift his own body weight quite that high. He thought for a moment, analysing the situation in scientific terms. Formulate a hypothesis; test said hypothesis; analyse the results; if the results do not match the original hypothesis, a new hypothesis must be formed. His initial hypothesis was that he would be able to do what he had witnessed his stronger but slightly older friend accomplish. Testing that out, he found the hypothesis to be false, so a new theory was required.

Momentum. That was what he needed, he realised.

He stepped a few feet away from the cliff face, keeping a careful eye on where he had found the ledge, since it would be very easy to lose again, almost invisible within the rock unless you knew exactly where to look. He hoped that none of the men who worked on the site were watching him. What would they have thought of a well-respected doctor and his reverend/scientist friend and peer launching themselves at rock faces in this manner? But he could not chance looking away to check if he were being subjected to a crowd of spectators.

He ran straight towards the cliff. At the last moment, he jumped, grasping hold of the edge of the ledge and using that forward momentum to propel himself up the rock at speed. His foot slipped, not entirely resting firmly on the ledge. He came close to finding himself falling back down to the quarry floor. At the very last moment, he regained his balance. Clutching himself tightly against the cliff, he stood on the ledge. He had done it. Hypothesis proven.

Mantell inspected his surroundings. The ledge upon which he stood was narrow - little more than a few inches deep - so he remained firmly pressed against the rock face, not moving his feet until necessary.

He looked to his right, the same direction Buckland had gone when he had disappeared.

There was an opening in the cliff behind a rock face. It was barely wide enough to squeeze through, but it could accommodate a man with a little effort. Mantell moved his head forward as he looked at it. The rock covering the entrance blended seamlessly with the rest of the cliff, making the entrance disappear — a remarkable optical illusion and clearly the cause of Buckland's earlier vanishing act.

Mantell stepped carefully towards the entrance, hands flat against the wall as he trod across.

He ducked his head and stepped inside.

TWENTY-FIVE

Stepping through the opening in the cliff face, Mantell found himself in a narrow, cramped tunnel.

Though the rock walls were cold to the touch, it felt warmer in there than outside, with it not being fully exposed to the cold Winter's air. As he stepped further into the tunnel, it started to become dark. The beginning had been fine, as the daylight had continued to seep through the entrance, but the way forward grew less and less illuminated. It wasn't long before Mantell found himself in pitch darkness. He placed his hands against the sides of the tunnel to feel his way through, no longer able to see where he was going, treading with the utmost care as he worried about invisible obstacles on the floor, steep drops, or even holes that he might fall through. The tunnel gradually inclined downward, giving Mantell the impression that he was slowly walking into the very centre of the earth.

'William?' he called out into the darkness. 'Where are you?'

His voice echoed back hollowly, bouncing off the rock walls that surrounded him, refusing to travel further than a few feet in front of him. As he felt his way forward, the tunnel turned a corner. Mantell followed it around.

A soft light was ahead of him. The silhouette of a figure stood in front of the light, motionless and looking out at the soft illumination. Mantell could tell immediately that the figure was Buckland, his Oxford gowns providing an unmistakable outline. He wanted to pick up his pace to rejoin his friend, but he was still wary of where his feet might land - or if they might *not* land on anything - so he erred on the side of caution, taking it slowly and steadily as he gradually approached.

'There you are,' he panted as he finally reached Buckland's side.

'What in heaven's name - '

He couldn't finish the question as he looked out upon the sight that had frozen Buckland in place.

Natural light streamed in from above the cavern. Perhaps some other entrances, maybe just holes in the surface above, hidden from the view of the casual observer. The soft light revealed a vast underground cavern spread out before them. Bigger and more incredible than anything either of the two men had ever encountered, despite years of fossil hunting within cave systems.

Where they stood at the end of the tunnel, they were high up above the base of the cavern, staring down at all that it contained, a giant bowl carved out of the earth like a subterranean quarry. But this particular quarry did not look as though it was manufactured. Instead, it looked as though it was as old as time, lost and left as it once had been millions of years ago. Even the climate in that cavern was different: Mantell and Buckland were used to cool and damp cave systems, but it was somehow practically tropical down here. It was still damp, but that was more from the humidity than anything else. That climate had caused something incredible within the cavern.

Plant life bloomed across the floor, thriving despite the peculiar environment. Tall trees; thick, giant green ferns; even flowers - they were all there and in abundance. Pools of water were scattered here and there, some appearing shallow, like ponds, but others containing far darker water, giving the impression that they were of a considerable depth; they could even be classed as lakes, they were so vast. A river stretched from one end of the floor to the other, flowing gently until it reached the cavern wall and disappeared somewhere.

But it was not so much the plant life and the water features that had caused Buckland and Mantell's utter astonishment.

The most extraordinary creatures they had ever witnessed were within the trees, hidden in the ferns, swimming in the lakes, and drinking from the ponds. Like the one Mary Anning had in her cellar, Plesiosaurs paddled across the water's surface. Ichthyosaurs swam with them, co-existing peacefully with one another. Ammonites drifted through the ponds, tentacles flexing to help with the movement and search out possible food within the water. On the ground, *iguanodons* paraded: solid creatures with a horn on the back of their heads and four legs for walking upon - the two of which at the back were slightly longer than those at the front, making them appear stooped, swinging a thick stumpy tail behind them as they walked. Winged creatures -

pteranodons - soared through the air, fighting amongst themselves over scraps of food, then coming to rest in their own individual tree tops, where they perched silently, their beady eyes watching all that was going on around them as though on the lookout for some potential prey.

There were other creatures, too, more numerous than they first appeared as some were hidden away within the foliage, others practically camouflaged against the rock or hiding in the shadows the gentle illumination of the cavern had not yet reached.

'What is this place?' Mantell whispered in awe.

'I don't know, but I think I might know someone who does,' Buckland replied.

He pointed his finger at a spot on the floor of the cavern.

Mantell followed the finger, looking across the vista, until his eyes came to rest upon Mary. Tray beside her, she walked through the prehistoric landscape as though the sight of it was nothing to her. She knew this place, and she knew it well. The pieces were starting to fit together in Buckland's mind.

'Come on,' he told Mantell.

'Are you out of your mind? We could not possibly go down there.'

'Look at Mary,' Buckland said. 'Does she look afraid?'

'That is hardly the... That is to say... I am not... Very well. Lead on,' he conceded defeat.

Buckland turned to his side, where a natural pathway led towards the cavern floor. It was steep and looked treacherous, but there appeared to be no other way of getting down there.

This narrow path was their only option.

Tray lapped at the warm water of one of the several lakes in the cavern, drinking greedily from the pool. A scaly back emerged from the surface close by, tail flicking side to side to aid its silent swimming, heading straight towards the dog, curious as to what might be causing the ripples within the otherwise still waters. Tray noticed the fin. Ever the brave creature, he backed away slightly and gave a yap that would not even scare the most nervous of animals.

'Tray - quiet!' Mary warned.

The dog continued to growl but at a lower volume.

The scaled back continued to head in his direction.

'Come. Now,' Mary commanded.

Tray growled again, turned to his owner and joined her a few feet from the water's edge.

Mary opened the top of the bloody, dripping bag she had lugged down the rocky path to the cavern floor. Tray immediately jumped at the scent and tried to stuff his head straight into the bag to see what was available for him to eat. Mary shooed him away; nothing in there was for him.

She pulled out a large chunk of meat and tossed it into the water.

A frenzy of motion erupted around where the meat landed. The water bubbled and boiled with violence as two, three, and then four ichthyosaurs fought over the scraps Mary had thrown in there. The water stained red, the pool briefly looking like a volcanic eruption, and then all was suddenly still again, the food devoured, the creatures stealthily awaiting anything else that might be headed in their direction.

Mary continued throwing the meaty chunks of the cut-apart proceratosaurus into the pool until the red-stained bag was finally empty. The same vicious scenes played out whenever she threw some in the water. Those creatures were hungry, and anything that they did not have to find and capture themselves was always more than welcome.

Tray barked excitedly and scampered away from Mary.

She looked up from the empty bag, about to reprimand the dog and tell him to return to her side when she noticed Mantell and Buckland walking straight towards her.

At first, she was shocked at the sight of them - this had been her place for so long, hers and *only* hers. She had never seen another human in the cavern, so seeing these two gentlemen strolling in her direction was a surprise. Then, that surprise turned to anger. How dare they follow her down there? Clearly, they hadn't trusted her, and they felt it necessary to pretend to leave her home only to stop and follow her to this place, her own place, her sanctuary. How could they even think of invading her privacy like that? She should have been used to it, of course, with the men always wanting to take over anything a woman did that they felt she shouldn't be. It had been the same throughout all of her time carrying out scientific research: she would submit her investigations to some gentleman or other for publication, and he would outright refuse it for the most ridiculous reasons. Then, in the months to come, she would discover exactly her work but published under the name of the gentleman to whom she had submitted it in the first place. Word for word, not a single line changed. The only thing wrong with the research was the gender of the person who had carried it out.

Then, of course, the anger gave way to begrudging acceptance. Mantell and Buckland had seen things in her home and her study that no other but her and her mother had previously witnessed. Of course, they would be curious. Of course, they would want to know more about it, where the creatures had come from, and how she had been looking after them. They could not possibly have called themselves scientists if they had not shown at least the slightest inclination towards wanting to find out more. Yet, of the two gentlemen, it was her old friend William Buckland that she was now the most wary of; he had insisted that the creatures in her home should be destroyed, and now here he was, in their very place of origin. Mary did not know what was going to come next. Still, she hoped that the other gentleman, the doctor, Gideon Mantell, might be able to persuade the Reverend otherwise, that he might be able to speak some reason with him and stop him from doing anything that will cause this wonderful, extraordinary, beautiful place to come to an end.

'How did you find me?' Mary asked.

'It was quite by chance - ' Mantell began, trying to play the situation tactfully and with some degree of diplomacy.

'We followed you,' Buckland interrupted.

'I thought as much,' Mary replied. She looked down at Tray, who stood beside her. 'Not much use guarding me against predators now, are you?'

The dog wagged his tail happily, unaware that he was being insulted rather than praised.

Mantell looked at the sights that surrounded him. The pools, he could now see, were sparkling and contained the cleanest water he had ever seen. Living in London for most of that time, and the nearest water source being the Thames, that was hardly surprising; nevertheless, the blue tint and the shining, shimmering surface were a delight to see. The trees, ferns and other plants looked so much bigger now that he was within them, rather than looking down upon them from the cavern entrance, so high up on the cliff face. Some ferns came up to his chest, probably spreading to several feet in length.

Of course, if the foliage was larger than it had appeared from their earlier vantage point, what of the creatures they had also seen? He could not begin to imagine the immense scale of some of those.

'What is this place?' Mantell asked.

'I discovered it quite by chance. Some months ago now,' Mary told him.

'And you have kept it secret all this time?' Buckland asked, and Mary could not help but notice a chiding tone in his voice.

'What would you have me do, sir?' Mary asked. 'Let others know of it that they might destroy it?'

Buckland shrugged noncommittally at that particular option.

Mantell ran his fingers along a tree's thick, rubbery leaves close beside him. He stared up into the branches. A pteranodon stared straight back down at him. The vicious, long beak pointed in his direction in what could have easily been a malevolent grin. It shifted its feet on the branch on which it was perched, extending its wings as though it was putting on a display to show Mantell that he was no match for the winged creature. Mantell felt a shudder run through him as he realised how easily and swiftly the pteranodon could take him out. It could launch itself straight at him, and he could be dead before he even realised what had happened. Or, the creature could play with him, taking its time, prolonging his agony until the end came as a blessed relief. He tried to put it out of his mind but found himself continuously glancing up at the creature nervously as he spoke.

'It is like some sort of ancient ecosystem,' Mantell spoke his thoughts aloud, saying them as he worked through them in his mind. 'Preserved for thousands of years.'

'Millions, I should wager,' Mary corrected him.

'Impossible,' Buckland grumbled.

Mary turned to him.

'You have great trouble believing your own eyes, don't you?' Mary said. 'As a man of faith, then, *Reverend*, how can you believe that which you *don't* see?'

Mantell turned away so that Buckland could not see him smiling at Mary's thoughts, as the Reverend himself could do little but stand and stare at her, for a change at a loss for any meaningful comeback.

The doctor took the opportunity to once more look across the impossible landscape he had found himself within and marvel at the sheer beauty of it. He watched as an iguanodon chewed peacefully on some greenery beside the river, its jaw moving in much the same manner as a modern-day cow. He gazed in awe at a group of proceratosauruses, like the one Mary had so efficiently decapitated in her home, as they flocked like birds across a grassy area, occasionally turning to one another and giving what looked to be a friendly, playful nip with their teeth. He stared with fear and wonder as pteranodons circled overhead, prehistoric vultures waiting for the perfect opportunity to pick off anything that looked as though it might be edible.

And there was Mary, the poor, ordinary girl from the little town by the sea, who had someone discovered this magnificent, incredible, prehistoric utopia.

TWENTY-SIX

The quarry crew huddled around their boss, waiting for his approval. Scaffolding had been placed against the quarry wall, ready for the next part of their job. The plan had never been to extend the quarry further, instead to go deeper. But someone higher up in the food chain had insisted that the quality of the material they were extracting from the site was becoming inferior with each passing day. Therefore, extending outward was the only way to get back on track. Fletcher wasn't happy about it, and he knew he would be the one to take the brunt of the anger of those living nearby. But it was either do as he was told or find himself out of work before Christmas.

'Ready?' Joseph asked him.

Fletcher looked out across the expanse of the quarry. It appeared empty, though he hadn't seen Mary or her two visitors leave. He'd been busy getting things sorted on the site, so they might have passed him by, and he hadn't noticed. There had been plenty of previous occasions in which Mary Anning had headed off to do whatever she was doing, and Fletcher didn't see her again until she returned the next day or a couple of days later, as it sometimes was.

He couldn't hold things up any longer anyway. After setting up the scaffold, the crew had already been waiting for him to give the all-clear for half the morning. He couldn't afford to wait on the off chance that anyone else was there. Mary and her friends shouldn't have been there in the first place, and Mary herself had been warned of the dangers on multiple occasions.

'Boss?' Joseph prompted him.

Fletcher let his eyes give one last sweep of the quarry floor.

He nodded his head firmly.

'Do it,' he confirmed. 'I don't want to be here all day.'

'Let's light it up!' Joseph told his colleagues.

They headed towards the scaffolding.

A sound like thunder echoed throughout the cavern. The creatures stopped what they were doing and looked about them, wondering what was happening. Their human visitors likewise did the same. It was not a stormy day, and the thunderous noise sounded and felt like it had come from very close by.

Another violent rumble resounded loud enough to shake the whole floor.

'What's happening?' Mary cried as dust and rocks came loose and fell to the ground from the cavern's roof.

Outside, the explosives went off like clockwork. A detonator triggered the first explosion, which in turn ignited the second explosive, causing a chain reaction along the quarry wall. Great chunks of cliff face exploded, sending rocks and rubble flying into the air like waves across a stormy sea.

Creatures rushed around in terror within the cavern, chaotically trying to avoid the debris falling from above as if the sky was collapsing upon them. It was every beast for itself in an attempt to escape the devastation. Large boulders fell, raining upon some poor animals who became trapped underneath or even killed outright if they were lucky enough to avoid massive injury.

'We have to get out of here,' Mantell told them.

With a tremendous ripping sound, a crack formed in the cavern wall. As they watched, it grew in length and width until it was wide enough to be classed as a hole rather than a crack. Daylight came streaming through, basking the interior landscape with golden rays.

This did not go unnoticed by the creatures.

They turned their heads and stared at this sight as though it was a divine vision. All at once, they headed towards the opening and the promise of freedom from the cavern that continued collapsing around them.

'Go. Quickly!' Mantell cried out to Mary and Buckland.

But the creatures were quicker off the mark and stampeded towards the hole before the humans could even begin to move. If they moved now, they would likely be trampled to death by the horde of rampaging beasts, desperately trying to get out of there, knocking others out of their way as they raced to be first out into the fresh air. Tray, though, took the opportunity to join them, weaving expertly between the legs of the giant beasts, his tiny stature making it possible to be nimble and dodge around the sprinting legs of the creatures.

'Tray!' Mary called out to her dog, but her voice got lost in the cacophony of stampeding animals and walls collapsing around them.

She had no choice but to let him go and hope that he made it out safely and perhaps waited for her on the other side of the wall, ready to be picked up and coddled when she managed to get out of there.

With the way things were going, the rapidly increasing destruction of the cavern, escape from there was looking increasingly unlikely.

'What's that noise?' crew members asked themselves as a tremendous rumbling sound came from the devastation of the exploded cliff face.

The explosions had finished detonating, and most of the debris settled to the ground, so as far as they were concerned, that should have been the end. But there was a definite noise, increasing in volume, coming directly from where they had just been at work.

Everyone stared at the site of the explosions.

The rumbling became louder.

A cloud of dust grew in size.

Something - or some *things* - were heading towards them out of the dust.

A great swarm of the most extraordinary beasts.

And they were swarming straight towards the workers.

Realising they were directly in the path of the rampaging creatures, they turned and fled. The only place on the quarry floor that provided any possibility of safety was the small hut they used for shelter and rest. They headed straight for that, ran inside and shut the door behind them.

Watching through the small windows in the hut, they saw the horde barrelling straight in their direction. As the great beasts passed by, the whole structure of the hut shook, the walls vibrating with the impact of those many giant footsteps stomping across the ground. Some creatures were faster than others, some stronger and more forceful at ploughing a path.

A *hylaeosaurus* trundled past the hut. Short-legged but long from snout to tail-tip, it had no real need to sprint. Its back was covered in thick plated armour, long thick spikes offering further protection against any creature that might try its luck and attack it because it was moving more slowly than the rest of the herd.

Quicker than the hylaeosaurus, a *baryonyx* sprinted by, its long legs allowing it to cross great distances with minimal strides. It turned its large head, with a long, sharp, tooth-filled jaw, towards the hut. Seeing the crew standing inside watching it, the creature slowed down a fraction, seemingly considering whether they were worth stopping for in the middle of this rampage. But in its brief distraction from the main event that was taking place, it accidentally kicked at the hylaeosaurus. The hylaeo retaliated, ramming its spiked back into the larger creature's legs. The baryonyx roared in pain. It snapped its large jaw at the hylaeo, but its sharp teeth were no match for the armoured plates on its opponent's back. The crew hiding in the hut could only watch as these two prehistoric beasts turned an accidental bump into a full-blown combat of jaws, claws and spikes, violently coming at one another in a quest to gain the upper hand; the baryonyx with its height advantage, but the hylaeosaurus with its armour, it was a surprisingly well-matched fight. The baryonyx gripped its opponent's back in its jaw, somehow getting its teeth around one of the individual plates on its back. It gripped hard and placed a foot on the hylaeo's back, tugging with its jaw, trying to remove the piece of armour. Then, it could do some real damage.

The hylaeo twisted hard, trying to escape the baryonyx's clutches. It turned, angling itself desperately to somehow work its spikes into the baryonyx's fleshy body, vulnerable without armour similar to the hylaeo's own. It got there, successfully embedding a spike in the baryonyx's stomach as the creature was bowed down, trying to bite. The baryonyx let it go, let out another almighty roar, and swung its tail viciously against the hylaeo.

The impact sent the smaller creature flying straight into the side of the small hut.

Not designed to withstand the impact of a flying creature, the hut's walls immediately collapsed to the ground.

Now that the crew members were fully exposed to the outside world, the hylaeo wasn't of quite as much interest to the baryonyx anymore. It turned its vicious little eyes towards the now vulnerable humans and stalked towards them.

Its opponent distracted, the hylaeosaurus limped away, sensibly favouring the chance of escape over the possibility of revenge.

Within the cavern, the walls continued to fall. The roof, too, was collapsing inward. They had to get out of there very soon; otherwise, even if they survived being crushed by falling boulders, they would be trapped alive with no hope of escape.

The last few creatures fled through the hole in the cavern wall, having to leap upon fallen rocks to reach the small area of sunlight that was still accessible; the rampage, with the giant creatures bashing against the rocks as they fled from inside the cavern, had caused the new hole being used as an escape route to quickly become covered over again, with only a small space left by which they could leave.

The land-based animals had gone, so all that was left to keep Mary, Mantell and Buckland company were those creatures that lived in the waters: the plesiosaurs, ichthyosaurs and ammonites. Even the flying pterosaurs had made a break for freedom, able to swoop above the heads of those that had to walk and break out into the fresh air with relative ease.

Until the larger animals had moved out of the way, the humans could not make it out of there alive. But now, with the path to freedom diminished in size, the chance of escape decreased by the second.

'We have to go,' Mantell told them. 'Right now.'

Together, the three of them ran to the last hope of breaking free. They scrambled desperately up the rocks towards that small piece of sunlight.

A load *crack* came from directly above them.

'Look out!' Buckland yelled.

They jumped back just as a huge rock fell and landed directly in front of them, narrowly avoiding being squashed flat.

As the dust cleared, they realised that the boulder had landed right in front of the last chance of survival, completely blocking that small exit out of the cavern. The path Mantell and Buckland had used to get down there in the first place was gone, destroyed as the explosions ravaged the cavern walls.

There was no hope.

Outside, the quarry was finally, eerily, silent. The last of the creatures had disappeared, fleeing from the quarry and escaping to some new place, leaving behind nothing but footprints and dust.

The workers' hut, too, was gone.

The collapsed walls had been ripped to shreds, trampled upon, and destroyed in every conceivable way until it was unclear how it could have possibly been in the shape of a hut in the first place. Only splinters of wood remained of the outside walls. As far as the hut's contents went, there was little left of that either. A few body parts had been taken to be consumed later, but most had been devoured on the spot.

There was so little trace left of the quarry workers, save for splashes of crimson staining the quarry floor, that it was as though they had never even existed.

TWENTY-SEVEN

The rocks that blocked their escape route stubbornly refused to budge.

The three of them had managed to move aside the smaller pieces of rubble, but that was not enough to allow them to squeeze past the larger boulders that had fallen into place. They were too big and heavy for them to move even slightly.

'Do you have a lever and a fulcrum, perchance?' Buckland enquired of Mary.

She stared at him blankly.

'If you do, we can fashion a system for easily moving the rocks,' he explained.

Mary stared at him for a long moment, eyes no longer blank but gradually filling with anger and annoyance.

'Does it *look* like I have a lever and fulcrum?' she exploded.

'I was simply suggesting - '

'It was a ridiculous suggestion.'

'There is no such thing as a ridiculous suggestion.'

'That is where you are completely incorrect.'

'One cannot be "completely" incorrect. One is either correct or incorrect.'

'Then you are incorrect.'

'Quiet. Both of you,' Mantell demanded.

Buckland and Mary turned to him. The doctor had one ear pressed against the side of the wall, listening through the rock just as they had done before they knew of this place and well before they found themselves trapped.

'What is it?' Mary whispered.

'I thought I heard something.'

'What?'

Then it came again — the unmistakable sound of Tray's bark.

'Tray!' Mary exclaimed in delight, thrilled to hear the sound of her dog and knowing now that he was still alive and waiting for her outside.

If only they could get out there to join him.

'Tray, speak!' Mary commanded, wanting to hear the sound of his bark once again.

But there was no response from the dog.

'Tray: speak, boy, speak.'

Still, no sound came from the little dog.

'Tray?' Mary called out, now concerned that he might be gone, perhaps for good this time.

A splash came from behind them. The three of them span around, fearing the worst, with the only creatures left in there with them being those in the water.

But it was nothing more terrifying than the sight of Tray jumping out of the river that ran through the cavern. He shook himself on the riverbank, sprinkling water every which way as he attempted to dry his fur, then ran straight towards Mary, his tongue lolling out of the side of his mouth and his tail wagging happily at the reunion.

Mary scooped him up and wrapped him in her arms, trying to warm him after being in the cold water.

'What have you been doing?' she asked the dog as he licked her face joyfully.

Mantell wandered across to the edge of the water where Tray had reappeared. He looked downstream to where the indoor river hit the cavern's wall and then seemed to stop. But it couldn't have stopped there, as the water flowed in that direction. Without coming from, and going to, somewhere beyond those cavern walls, there was no way that the water should have been running like that; it would have been perfectly still. The water was getting out, somehow.

'I think Tray must have found a hole in the wall somewhere under the water,' Mantell called across to the rest of the group.

He stared down at the river as Mary and Buckland joined him. It certainly made sense - Tray had left with the other creatures, but he had somehow found his way back inside. The only possible explanation was that there was another undiscovered hole in the cavern wall.

'If only we had some way of checking,' Mantell muttered.

Mary stared at him, stupefied. The man was a doctor *and* a scientist, yet his inability to come up with simple solutions to simple problems beggared belief. If you wanted to know what was under some water, there was a straightforward way of finding out.

She crouched down on the bank's edge, as close to the cavern wall as possible.

Taking a deep breath, she plunged her head into the river.

The water was surprisingly warm against her skin; she had felt the temperature of it before, of course, when fishing for ammonites to feed the plesiosaur, but this was the first time she had ever needed to expose her entire face to the river. Forcing her eyes to stay open against the stinging sensation of being underwater, she looked around, thankful that the waters were clear, so visibility under there was good.

Starting to run out of oxygen, she pulled her head back out of the river and gulped in large lungs full of air.

Mantell looked at her in disbelief as she wrung the water from her long hair, her clothes sodden and filthy, her entire appearance dishevelled.

'If you wish to be treated like a lady, you should probably act like one,' the doctor told her.

Mary flicked her wet hair away from her neck, deliberately showering the nearby Mantell with water droplets.

'If you wish to stay alive, you should shut up and listen to me,' she warned him.

Buckland couldn't help but chuckle at the exchange, which earned him glares from both Mantell and Mary.

She was undoubtedly a feisty woman, but Buckland had already known that, which was one thing he liked about her. She knew her place in the world, but she refused to accept it, and time and time again, she fought against conventions and stereotypes, and the "natural order" of things, fighting with all her strength and ability (which were both considerable) to make her mark on the world. Buckland had helped out wherever he could, of course, but some things were beyond his power. His peers and other scientists and scholars already had enough ammunition against him to forever cast him out from their societies without him giving them even more to use against him. He somehow had to toe the line while also trying to boost Mary's respectability within those circles. He knew it was a battle he was unlikely to win, but one he felt necessary to continue fighting.

'Could you see anything down there?' Buckland asked Mary as he composed himself once more.

'There's a tunnel under the water,' she told them.

She pondered it momentarily, thinking of what had happened over the past few days: the boat wreck for which she was sure she was somehow responsible, the proceratosaurus turning up in her cellar. There were sure to have been other events that she had not personally witnessed. The tunnel had to be the way out for those creatures. Ichthyosaurs could have quite easily swam through the hole she had seen under the water, allowing for a reasonably straightforward escape. The proceratosaurus, too, could have fit through there, though it may have been pure chance that it had stumbled upon the opening, perhaps having fallen into the water and desperately looked around for some means of escape. She hadn't seen that particular species swimming before, but it was a possibility.

'That must be how they all escaped,' she whispered, continuing her train of thought.

'I beg your pardon?' Mantell asked, not quite hearing what Mary had said.

'Nothing,' she said louder. 'I am sure the hole is large enough to fit through.'

'That's all well and good, but how does that help our situation?'

Buckland and Mary stared at him as he once again failed to grasp the simple solution to a relatively simple problem. He looked between their staring faces, knowing that there was something he was missing, some missing link he had not quite spotted.

And then, finally, he realised what was being suggested.

'You cannot be serious,' he declared.

'Do as you please,' Mary told him.

She began stripping layers from her clothing and tossing them onto the ground at her feet. Mantell looked away, embarrassed to be looking at a woman in such a state of undress and embarrassed for Mary herself that she should be doing such a thing in front of two well-respected gentlemen. Of course, Mary was wearing multiple layers of clothing, as she always did when she went fossil hunting at that time of year, offering protection against the inclement weather and allowing for a softer landing should she tumble from the rocks. Even after removing three or four layers of clothing, Mary still wore more garments than most women Mantell would have bumped into in a typical street without even batting an eye.

He heard a loud splash and turned just in time to see Mary's feet submerging in the river's waters. Tray dived in after her, paddling along the surface of the water.

Buckland removed his jacket and threw it to the ground. He rubbed his hands together, bracing himself for the plunge at the river bank.

Mantell could not believe what he was seeing.

'William? Really?'

Buckland shrugged.

'What choice do we have? Really?'

He jumped in, diving straight under the water.

Mantell looked around. He was utterly alone, save for the few remaining creatures - who happened to live in the waters, he reminded himself, adding that to the mental list of reasons why he should not follow the others. But, then, the boulders would not shift any time soon. The underwater passage looked to be their only chance of escape. He thought of his wife, Mary-Ann, and their son, Walter. He had promised to be home by Christmas, and even though they no longer lived together, he wanted to ensure they spent Christmas as a family. He could give them that much, if nothing else. He could not perish in this godforsaken cavern with no one there beside him, his boy not seeing his father for one last time, not knowing what had happened to him and wondering whether he was ever going to return, probably thinking that he did not care any longer and had decided to disappear from their lives without any hope of reunion.

No, he could not do that to either of them.

He *had* to leave that cavern alive.

And there seemed to be only one way in which that would happen.

He sighed.

Mantell took off his jacket, folded it neatly and placed it carefully on the ground after brushing away the dust from the area where it was going to lay as best as he could. Mantell presumably did not think about how he would ever hope to retrieve it from there later, but at least the neatness of the pile he left behind was something that he could control, unlike most of the rest of the current situation in which he found himself.

He peeled off his stockings, rolled them up and placed them carefully within his shoes.

He gingerly placed the tip of a single toe in the water, testing the temperature.

It wasn't entirely unpleasant, he had to admit.

Mantell looked around one last time as though he might find another way out they had previously missed. But there was no other option.

He took a deep breath, pinched his nose shut with his fingers and jumped into the river.

TWENTY-EIGHT

The darkness of the tunnel Mantell found himself in was beyond
anything he had ever experienced before. It was thick and oppressive,
and, submerged in that water, he had never felt so claustrophobic. He
could hear motion in the water somewhere in front and could only
assume, and hope, that it was Mary and Buckland that he could hear
and not something that would devour him in the dark.

The tunnel seemed to wind on and on, nothing but narrow walls of
rock and water. He had nowhere to stop, nowhere to put his feet down
to take a short breath.

His lungs started to burn from the lack of fresh oxygen being made
available to them.

He felt like he might pass out, right there and then, and be forever
lost within those pitch-black tunnels, with no chance of survival or
rescue.

Mantell stopped moving his limbs, needing to give them a short
break.

The stillness felt peaceful. Intoxicating, somehow. He felt like he
could stay there now and would be quite content. Realising that
continuing to hold in the breath he had taken when first jumping in the
river was causing him pain and preventing him from entirely giving
himself over to the restful caress of the water, he slowly released the air
through his nose. Bubbles rose up and away from him, and he slowly
drifted downwards.

He closed his eyes, tired and ready to be led into a peaceful sleep.

Mary-Ann was there, somehow, behind his eyelids, holding hands
with Walter. He wondered briefly how they could be there; they were
supposed to be in London. But that didn't matter - they were there
now, with him. They smiled at him, beckoning him towards them,

wanting him to join them so that they could all be a happy family once more. If he could make this small effort, they could be together, and things could be back to how they once were, back when they were happy, and, really, that's all that he wanted, to be happy with his family. Everything else was a bonus. He reached out his arms towards them. The gap was closing, fingertips about to touch, a spark of joy shared between them...

And suddenly, the stillness was gone as he was jerked unceremoniously upwards by his arm. He tried to fight it, wanting to stay in that place of peace, but then he was also pulled by the other arm, and very soon, he was exploding out of the water.

The next thing he knew, he was being held in someone's arms, his head resting against their shoulder. He was coughing violently, water spilling from his mouth like he had become one with the river, and now it was flowing through him.

'He's going to be fine,' he heard a woman saying somewhere in the back of his mind.

Slowly, things became clearer.

He looked around and saw Mary and Buckland's heads bobbing beside him. Mary herself had hold of him, clutching him tightly with his head against her shoulder. Similarly, Tray was perched upon Buckland's shoulder. Their three heads and Tray making the most of a small air pocket Buckland and Mary had come across, drawing in some new air while they had the chance. As Mantell breathed it in greedily, it tasted stale, but at the same time, it was the most delicious air he had ever experienced.

'What happened?' Mantell eventually croaked.

'We almost lost you,' Buckland told him. 'You stopped moving and began to sink. You would have drowned if Mary had not noticed you in time. Between us, we hauled you up here, where we managed to find this small air compartment.'

'You saved my life?' Mantell asked Mary.

'I suppose I did, sir,' she replied.

'Then I am forever in your debt, my lady.'

'Think nothing of it.'

On top of Buckland's shoulder, Tray shook himself, spraying the excess water still clogged in his fur straight into the Reverend's face.

'This one I would have left behind,' Buckland said, indicating towards Tray.

'Then that would be the last thing you would ever do,' Mary warned, and Buckland was sure she meant it.

'How much further do we have to go?' Mantell asked weakly.

'How would I know?' Mary replied.

Tray jumped from Buckland's shoulder, splashing lightly onto the water's surface, paddling with his little legs to keep himself afloat.

'We should probably keep going,' Buckland suggested, then turned to Mantell. 'If you are feeling up to it, of course.'

'I fear we have little alternative.'

'After you, Tray,' Mary told her dog.

Tray dived under the water's surface and headed through the tunnel.

'Ready?' Buckland asked.

'No,' was Mantell's reply.

The three of them took a deep breath and prepared themselves to re-submerge.

But before they could enter the water, Tray suddenly reappeared. He practically leapt out of the water, climbing up Mary, whimpering and shaking. He looked to be afraid of something.

'What is it?' Mary asked.

Her question was shortly answered as two long, dark shapes travelled towards them from the direction in which Tray had just returned. Scaly backs, sharp teeth and long tails, two ichthyosaurs drifted silently through the water.

'Keep absolutely still,' Buckland suggested.

They all took heed of the advice and, pressing themselves as close against the tunnel walls as they could manage, remained motionless, watching the long creatures pass uneventfully by. They let out a collectively held breath in relief when they were gone from sight.

Tray shook himself again, sending water droplets back into the river.

The droplets created ripples upon the surface.

The ripples upon the surface caused small vibrations within the water further below.

The vibrations in the water let the ichthyosaurs know that something was moving nearby and that movement could equate to food.

The shapes turned and glided back towards the group, faster this time, with a greater, more pressing intention.

They were close and getting closer by the second.

'Go. Now!' Mary yelled.

No hesitation this time, the three of them launched themselves back under the water and swam as fast as they could force their bodies to manage, Tray once again leading the way. The ichthyosaurs were fast, though, with the advantage of being in their natural environment for the chase. The humans kicked their legs and moved their arms, splashing around under the water in desperation. Still, their hunters glided silently, occasionally using their fins to push them faster, closing the distance between themselves and their prey.

Everything hurt Buckland - his arms, legs, throat, and lungs. He couldn't keep this up for much longer, and he knew it. At the group's rear, he would be the first to go. He turned and looked over his shoulder. He couldn't help but let out a small scream, bubbles of precious oxygen leaking from his mouth, as he saw an ichthyosaur's jaw near his feet. He tucked himself into a ball, then stretched out again, kicking with all his might. One foot landed against the creature's jaw. It shook its head but blinked it off quickly. The kicking action had propelled Buckland forward slightly, and the ichthyosaur had been jolted back. There were a few extra seconds of safety between them. Those few seconds could be the difference between being devoured and leaving there alive.

Then a light appeared in front of them: almost celestial, as though a multitude of angels was waiting for them on the other side. However, Mantell couldn't be sure if the heavenly hosts were waiting to greet them into death or to protect them against the adversities they were currently facing.

The light grew larger as they got closer, and then, suddenly, they burst into blinding daylight, emerging from the tunnel and onto the beach.

The river continued down the beach, more of a fast-flowing stream than a river, as it emerged from the cliff face, cut through the sandy beach, and headed into the sea. Mantell, Buckland, Mary and Tray pulled themselves out of the water and launched onto dry land. The ichthyosaurs snapped their jaws at their prey, but they were out of reach from where the creatures remained in the water, and, as the waters had been theirs, so too was the land the dominion of the humans. The ichthyosaurs turned sulkily and drifted back into the cavern through the underground tunnel river.

Seeing the ichthyosaurs depart, the exhausted humans sat on the sand at first but then collapsed onto their backs, unable and unwilling to move for the foreseeable future.

TWENTY-NINE

The walk back to Mary's house was slow, cold and painful. Soaked through from being underwater, the three of them wrapped their arms around themselves, rubbing their flesh to try to warm up. But the weather was also cold, of course, making it all but impossible to increase their body temperature. Their shoes gone - either removed before entering the water or lost during the swim - made the ground harder against their feet, the cobblestones more slippery, and the whole walk an even more miserable affair.

Only Tray seemed to take it in his stride, although whenever he stopped for a moment, he began to shiver and always seemed to have excess water to shake from his fur whenever he tried to do so.

People stopped and stared as they passed by: they were used to seeing Mary Anning in some state from her fossil hunting expeditions, but to see her accompanied by two saturated, half-undressed, angry-looking gentlemen... Well, that was something altogether new, even for her. They had learned from experience that Mary was a proud woman who, on the whole, would not accept help and became quite annoyed at the suggestion that she needed some in the first place. So they felt it best to look rather than try to get involved and check that she was alright.

A foul mood had descended upon the group as they continued to walk. Buckland decided they weren't moving quickly enough and so brushed straight past Mary and Mantell, marching in front.

'You should have stopped this sooner,' he said to Mary as he passed her.

'Everything was fine until you two showed up and interfered.'

'Nonsense.'

Of course, it wasn't true that they had caused any of this to happen, but it was undoubtedly a fact that things had worsened upon their arrival. Creatures had already been escaping through the cavern by way of the river - hence the attack on the fishing boat and the animal Mary had discovered in her basement - but it was only when Mantell and Buckland had betrayed her trust and followed her to the cavern that things had got well and truly out of hand.

'What would you have me do?' Mary asked, feeling the anger swelling inside her, ready to explode free. 'Seeing as though I am incapable of doing anything for myself.'

'That is not - '

'Even my mother thinks so.'

'I am quite sure that - '

'If she did not think so, she would not have sent for you. Is that not so, Reverend Buckland?'

Buckland could not think of what to say to appease Mary, so he decided to stay quiet. They were already in enough trouble and pain as it was without adding further to their quarrel. Plus, it seemed that Mary was correct in what she was saying: her mother had slyly invited him to their home under false pretences, presumably in the hope that he would see what was happening and then help to either put a stop to it or persuade Mary of some alternative course of action. Now, things had indeed gotten out of control. The creatures Mary had discovered were loose somewhere, free to roam wherever they pleased, and while they were not directly responsible for their escaping, Buckland could not help but feel some level of guilt over what had happened.

He turned to Mantell, who shuffled behind them, his head low and staring at the ground where he was walking.

'What of you, Dr Mantell?' Buckland said. 'You are unusually quiet.'

'Once we have got ourselves warm and dry again in Miss Anning's home, I intend to depart for home. I must return to family in time for Christmas.'

Mary and Buckland stopped dead and spun around to face him.

'You cannot leave now,' Buckland declared.

'I must,' Mantell told him, still staring at the floor, unable to meet his friend's eyes.

'People are in danger,' anger flushed across Mary's face as she spoke.

'As long as we are here, *we* are also in danger.'

Mantell finally lifted his head to look directly at the other two. The words sounded selfish even as they spilt from his mouth, but he felt it was true. He needed to make sure that he got out of there in one piece and return to his family. The visions of Mary-Ann and Walter that he had experienced under the water had haunted him since then, and he realised that more than anything in the world, he wanted to see them and hold them, even if just for one more time. If they could reconcile, that would be an additional bonus, but for now, he would be content with whatever short time he might be granted in their company.

Staying there in Lyme Regis with those creatures on the loose was a surefire way of practically ensuring that would not happen.

'We are not the only ones in danger, *doctor*,' Mary reminded him. 'The whole *town* is in danger.'

'That is not my concern.'

Mantell ignored Mary's comment, but her words stung with the truth in her statement that he had also told himself.

'I think it may have just become your concern,' Buckland said enigmatically.

Mantell looked towards his friend, who nodded toward Mary's house, which they were not far from.

Outside the house was a carriage, beside which stood Mary-Ann and Walter. Mantell baulked at the sight of them. It was what he had hoped and wished for - the opportunity to spend even one more brief moment with his family - but it wasn't supposed to happen there, not in the place from which he was desperate to escape. They should not have come here, of all places, where the real danger lurked.

Walter saw his father heading towards them. He broke free from his mother's grip on his hand and ran towards him, a wrapped Christmas present clutched in his other hand. Mantell grabbed him as the boy launched himself in his direction, lifted him in the air and held him tightly against him, closing his eyes at the feeling of physical contact with his only son.

'You're wet,' Walter told him.

'I am.'

The boy looked into his face, his blue eyes large with worry.

'Your eyes are wet, too,' he said.

Mantell shifted Walter's position in his arms to free up one hand, with which he wiped away the tears that he had not realised until that point had formed and begun to spill down his cheeks.

'Better?' he asked Walter.

The boy smiled and nodded his head in agreement.

Mantell carried him back to join Mary-Ann in front of the shop,

Buckland and Mary trailing behind, giving him space for this unannounced meeting with his wife.

'What are you doing here?' he asked.

'I cannot see my husband, our son, his father?' Mary-Ann snapped at him.

This was not how he wanted the first conversation with his wife to play out, immediately getting her back up by saying the wrong thing. His question had not been meant in the way that it was taken, but he should not have been surprised that Mary-Ann was looking for alternative ways of interpreting his words negatively.

Their separation had hardly been the most pleasant of experiences. He had hardly been there for most of it, as he had returned from a dig one day to find her gone and nothing but a note to say what was happening. It was almost ironic, as it was the amount of time he spent looking for those ancient treasures that had caused the most significant rift in their relationship, with Mary-Ann accusing her husband of putting his scientific endeavours before his family and medical practice. After all, the medical practice afforded them the lifestyle in which they were accustomed to living and the house in which they lived it. Mantell's reputation in the medical world was sliding, with more and more reports of him neglecting his duties and even completely forgetting about scheduled appointments.

It wasn't so much that this was happening that upset Mary-Ann so much. It was that her husband did not seem to care, certainly not about how it was affecting her and Walter. So long as he had his fossils and his friends in the world of science, nothing else seemed to be of any importance to him.

That was untrue, as far as Mantell was concerned, even if it might sometimes seem that way. Balancing his medical, scientific and family lives was difficult, and he knew he needed to work out how to do it better. He had lessons to learn if only he were given the chance to do so.

'I merely meant that I was not expecting you,' Mantell explained.

Mary-Ann looked her husband up and down, taking in his dishevelled appearance: half-dressed, soaked through to the skin and shivering.

'Clearly not,' she said.

Walter squirmed in his father's grip as he noticed Tray peering up at him from the ground. Mantell lowered his son, and Walter crouched, stroking Tray as best he could as the dog ran around and around in circles, excited to have yet another new person to play with.

'This is not the best time,' Mantell told Mary-Ann, leading her away from the rest of the group by the elbow so that he could speak with her more privately.

'The boy wanted to give his father his Christmas present,' Mary-Ann said. 'I trust that is sufficient enough reason to visit.'

'Of course,' Mantell agreed. 'But not here. Not now.'

'Why ever not?'

'It isn't safe.'

'We are in the way, is what you mean.'

'Yes. I mean: no,' Mantell quickly corrected himself. 'You are not in the way. It's just - '

'You need not explain,' Mary-Ann said, turning away from her husband to watch their child playing happily with the small dog, oblivious to the tensions between them. 'I know your *hobby* is of more importance to you than your family.'

It wasn't just the words that stung at Mantell. It was the particular choice of inflexion in her voice that Mary-Ann had used when pronouncing the word "hobby". As if geology and palaeontology were not respectable pursuits for a gentleman but rather some dirty little secret that she felt necessary to keep from everyone else for fear of what they may think of her husband for practising such things.

Something had been bugging Mantell about their appearance at Mary's house, and he couldn't quite put his finger on what it was other than the fact that it was a complete surprise to him until he looked once again at the carriage that had brought them there.

'How did you know where I was?' he asked, speaking the doubt that had quietly plagued him.

'A gentleman brought us,' Mary-Ann told him, once again using the pronunciation of a single word to stab at her husband emotionally:

Gentleman. She sounded the word out as if it was something that he could no longer claim to be. She sounded the word out like she had found someone better than him, more worthy of her affection. She was playing the jealousy card. Mantell knew it and fought everything within him not to rise to her taunts.

Nevertheless, when he replied to her, Mantell could not help but notice a trace of a waver in his voice: anger, hurt, or betrayal. He wasn't sure which of those he felt at that moment. Perhaps a combination of all three.

'What gentleman?' he asked.

'I believe you already know him,' Mary-Ann smiled and looked towards the carriage.

As if waiting for that exact cue, the carriage door opened, and a figure stepped out, placing his hat on his head, obscuring his face for them to see until he was fully erect on the ground. Richard Owen.

'Owen?' Mantell exclaimed. 'What are you doing here?'

On hearing the name of Richard Owen being uttered, Buckland's interest was piqued. He had intended to allow Mantell and his wife time to themselves, but Owen's arrival changed things. He had, after all, been the one to introduce him to Mantell.

'Good day, gentlemen,' Owen said with a slight tip of his hat. He eyed them up, then sodden clothes still sticking to them. 'I trust you are keeping well?'

A smirk crossed his face, and it was all Mantell could do not to strike at him there and then.

'What are you doing here?' Mantell repeated.

Mary-Ann stepped in to fill them in on the story.

'Justine told me you had visited Reverend Buckland,' she said, glancing sideways at Buckland, her true feelings for him on display for all to see. 'So I headed out with Walter to give you a piece of my mind. Imagine my surprise, then, to come across Mr Owen leaving the premises having gone to Oxford in search of Reverend Buckland, only to discover that the pair of you had decided to travel here together.'

Buckland jerked his head towards Owen.

'You went to my home?' he asked accusatorially.

'I had left my hat behind at the luncheon the previous day.'

Buckland looked at him thoughtfully for a moment.

'You had no hat at the luncheon,' he told him.

'Then that is why I could not find it at your home,' Owen shrugged away the remark.

'And who, exactly, told you where we would be?' he demanded to know.

'Discreet servants are few and far between these days,' Owen told Buckland, clearly with no intention of telling him that he had ransacked his office to find the location. 'And their tongues are easily loosened with the prospect of a couple of shiny coins.'

'Indeed,' Buckland said.

He doubted every word out of Owen's mouth. The people who worked for Buckland had done so for years, and he had never questioned their discretion. He paid them handsomely enough that a couple of coins should not swerve their allegiance away from him. He was sure that Owen was lying and had discovered their location through more deceptive means than he was admitting.

'Walter?'

Mary-Ann's worried voice cut through the conversation, drawing Mantell's attention away from the other two gentlemen.

He turned to look in the same direction as his wife, towards their son, who stood in the middle of the street. Tray stood beside him, but they were no longer playing. They were staring off into the distance. Tray growled quietly, backing away a few steps, looking for somewhere safe.

'Walter,' Mary-Ann said again, more firmly.

Walter turned to look at her. His eyes were wide and afraid.

'What is it?' Mantell asked, moving to stand beside his son.

Then they heard it.

A stomping sound came from down the street.

It was growing louder and louder.

Something - or several *things* - large and heavy were heading in their direction.

THIRTY

Creatures of all shapes and sizes rounded a bend, revealing themselves to the gaping onlookers, running straight in their direction.

A great herd of prehistoric beasts swarming together like a flock of birds. Gigantic, scaly birds, sharp of tooth and claw. Still standing outside the shop, the group of humans watched the creatures from the quarry rush towards them in fascinated fear.

Mary was the first to break from the trance the spectacle had cast upon them, realising they were in great danger, standing exposed in the street like that.

'Inside the shop,' she commanded. 'Quickly.'

Everyone else was quick enough to respond to her words. They followed Mary in rushing up the steps to the shop door. Mary pushed it open and held it as she ushered everyone inside, practically shoving them through the doorway to speed things along. That was everyone: Reverend Buckland, Dr Mantell, Mrs Mantell, Walter Mantell - who had also scooped up Tray and carried him inside, Mary noticed, and of course, the newest of the new arrivals, Mr Owen. Mary slammed the door shut behind them.

Even from the apparent safety of the shop, the sound outside was so loud, the footsteps so heavy, that the shop windows rattled, threatening to break free from their surroundings and come crashing to the floor. Having let Tray go free now they were inside, Walter pressed his fists tightly against his ears, trying to block out the roar. His eyes, too, were squeezed shut against the terrifying sight. Mary-Ann crouched beside him, her arm around him, soothing her child against the unimaginable experience. The other adults gathered around the windows that looked out upon the street and watched as the creatures barrelled past, fascinated by the stampede.

As they disappeared, and the sound gradually diminished to be low enough that it was possible to hear what another person was saying, Richard Owen turned to the other three.

'What, in the name of all that is good and holy, was that?' he asked.

Mary, Mantell and Buckland shared a look between them. Not subtle in the slightest, it confirmed what Owen had already guessed: these creatures were already known to these three people and that *somehow* they had something to do with the whole affair.

Mantell ignored the question and looked at Buckland.

'Look after them,' he told his friend, indicating towards Mary-Ann and Walter. 'I shall be back shortly.'

Before Buckland could argue or even react, he had opened the shop's front door and stepped outside.

'I shall go with him,' Mary announced.

Mary-Ann shot her a look but knew that, for now at least, her place had to be by her son. Whatever it was between Mary Anning and her husband, she would have to deal with it later. If, indeed, there was anything: Mantell barely had the time for Mary-Ann and Walter as it was; she could not work out how it could be possible for him to find the opportunity in his self-imposed schedule to meet with another woman.

'Then I am going, also,' Owen told the room.

Mary sighed, but she had little choice in the matter. Richard Owen had seen the beasts as well now - as, most likely, had the majority of Lyme Regis. There was little point in trying to keep things a secret. That moment had long gone.

Mary and Owen stepped out the shop door and joined Mantell on the outside steps.

Buckland closed the door behind them and watched as they descended the steps, then turned to find Mary-Ann and Walter staring at him. Walter with an expression that looked as if it was asking what they should do next; Mary-Ann with an accusatory glare that seemed to suggest that it was his fault her husband was involved in this whole mess.

Technically - *technically* - that was true.

But even Buckland did not know the exact situation when they headed for Lyme Regis that fateful afternoon. As far as he had been aware, he was going to examine a fossil specimen. A unique, extraordinary fossil specimen, admittedly. But never in his wildest dreams would he have guessed what they would see once they arrived.

He looked back at the two faces staring at him.

'Who's hungry?' he asked.

Mary was right: the chance to keep these creatures a secret had long passed. She, Mantell and Owen followed the beasts towards the small square just along the road from the shop. Even if they had gotten further than that before being found, it would not have been difficult to track them down, with the noise they were making and the ensuing chaos and destruction they left in their wake.

In the centre of the square was a large Christmas tree, a good thirty feet tall, decorated with white streamers and a variety of ornaments, mostly made by town residents to bring a sense of community to the Christmas decor. That tree did not look like it would remain upright for much longer; needles, decorations and twigs fell from its branches as the creatures bustled past, oblivious to the damage they were causing.

Mary and company ushered onlookers, dazed and stunned by the appearance of these magnificent creatures, away from the area, trying to prevent any further scenes of carnage.

An iguanodon stumbled on the cobbled ground and tripped, falling heavily against the tree. Decorations dropped from its branches onto the creature, who seemed to take it as a personal attack. It turned on the tree, butting against it with its horned head, thwacking its thick tail against the trunk. People hiding under the tree from the creatures hurriedly moved out of the way, ducking behind other branches, skirting around as best they could to avoid the blows from the iguanodon. The more it attacked the tree, the more branches and decorations fell upon the creature, so the more it continued its attack. Going into a frenzy against its opponent, it rammed, hit, scratched, and whacked, and the people using it for shelter realised there was nowhere safe for them under there any longer. As the creature looked away from their direction for a moment, they ran as fast as they could from the tree, across the street, desperately hoping to avoid the other creature.

The iguanodon shoved hard against the tree. It was finally victorious as the whole thing tumbled, falling upon smaller creatures sheltering under the branches. They pulled themselves out from under it and scattered in different directions.

Seeing that it was now alone, the iguanodon watched where the other creatures were going and followed suit, galloping away to see what else it could discover.

Mantell watched as the square emptied of the animals, leaving nothing but destruction and silence in their wake. There was no single direction in which they were heading, as they branched out in different ways depending on how their senses led them.

Owen stood directly before Mary and Mantell, blocking their view. He clasped his hands behind his back like a headmaster ready to berate two unruly students.

'I think you have some explaining to do,' Owen told them.

THIRTY-ONE

Despite initially being annoyed at being selected for babysitting duties, in hindsight, Buckland was quite relieved to stay inside. He had stoked the fire in the living room, and the flames danced and waved merrily at him as he warmed himself in front of the fireplace, his hands burning pleasantly as the warmth spread back through his body.

The fire alone was not enough to melt the iciness of the atmosphere in the room, though.

Mrs Mantell had never been fond of Buckland. They had got along well enough, to begin with, but she held him at least partially responsible for the collapse of her family. She believed her husband ended up spending more time with Buckland than herself. Whenever Mantell came across something in one of his digs or saw a paper of interest in a scientific journal, he found it necessary to immediately set forth to Oxford to speak with the great William Buckland. Before his introduction to the scientific crowd, it was Mary-Ann whom Mantell had spoken with excitedly about whatever he had found; it was her who saw the joy in his eyes as he talked with great enthusiasm about what it might be, what it could mean, how important a find it could turn out to be.

Later, she saw none of that.

It was Buckland and the rest of that group who got to share in that part of her husband's life rather than her. She soon grew to despise those men and all they stood for and loathe Mantell's "hobby", which she had initially felt a part of.

Mrs Anning had joined them in the living room, sitting in her usual chair beside the fire. A thick blanket wrapped around her knees as protection against the cold, she watched Walter playing with Tray on the floor, her eyes sparkling with delight at seeing something joyful in

165

her home for the first time in years, despite the frosty atmosphere between the other two of her uninvited guests.

'I am sure they shall return shortly,' Buckland said to no one in particular as he watched the flickering flames.

Mary-Ann looked up at him, her eyes hard, the light from the fire not giving them a sparkle but a sharp, flint-like edge.

'For what purpose did you drag my husband to this godforsaken part of the country?' she asked. 'Did you intend to place him in danger?'

'"Godforsaken" is the correct word for it,' he muttered, receiving a similar glare from Mrs Anning at the insult to her home town.

He moved away from the fire, then, rubbing his hands together, spreading the warmth, and placed himself heavily into another oversized chair facing the flames.

'Your husband did not need "dragging",' he continued. 'Not once he saw what we were coming to research.'

'You knew of these creatures before you came here?'

'I did not.'

'How can I believe you?'

'My dear Mary-Ann. If I had known of them, I would not have come here myself, never mind "dragging" your husband along with me.'

Walter scurried across the floor to where sticks were kept beside the fireplace to help bring the fire to life. He pulled a small stick from the basket and waved it at Tray, drawing the dog's attention to what he held in his hands.

'What, then, would you have done?' Mary-Ann asked.

'I do not know,' Buckland answered quietly. 'But now they have escaped, they will be far more difficult to destroy.'

Walter threw the stick for Tray. It went further than he had intended, out of the living room door and onto the staircase that led down to the shop, click-clacking its way down the steps.

Walter headed out of the room after it.

Mantell and Mary had filled Richard Owen in on the situation in as condensed a form as possible. Owen's eyes had narrowed and widened at the appropriate points as he took it in, but it was clear that his mind was ticking over the facts, thinking, calculating. Despite the outcome as it currently stood, Owen never seemed worried or frightened. He looked as though he was taking the whole thing as an opportunity. For what exactly, they weren't sure. Indeed, Mary herself had used the creatures as an excellent opportunity to study, learn, and discover, but that was before they had escaped and were now scattered across the entirety of Lyme Regis.

'Well,' Owen said as they reached the end of their story. 'We - or, rather, you - seem to be in quite a predicament.'

'What do we do?' Mantell asked.

The question wasn't specifically aimed at Owen but more a general wondering for the whole group.

'I thought you would have all the answers, *Doctor*,' Mary retorted.

The sarcasm that ran through her voice was lost on Mantell, as he was lost in thought.

'In this instance, I am afraid I do not,' he told Mary.

They scanned the town square in front of them where the creatures had been but moments ago. It was deserted, save for a few people who stood speaking excitedly, fearfully, amongst one another about what they had just witnessed.

The creatures were gone, scattered in all directions.

Walter found the stick he had thrown at the bottom of the stairs. Tray had followed him and leapt up and down at the boy as he picked up the stick and showed it to the dog, begging for it to be thrown again so that this time, he might have a chance of retrieving it himself.

But Walter's attention was drawn away from Tray by a lit lantern beside the cellar door. The door had a key in the lock, left in all the confusion from before. The fact that the door had a lock, unlike most of the rest of the house, and the key was in there just waiting to be turned, intrigued Walter.

He found himself moving towards it.

Tray followed, practically tripping over himself as his full attention was captured by the stick that Walter still held but was not throwing.

Walter turned the key in the lock.

It clicked open.

He pushed the door open a little and peered inside. It was dark on the other side, so it was fortunate that the lantern beside the door was already lit. It was as though he was being encouraged to explore. He placed the stick carefully on the floor, which Tray immediately pounced upon, picked up the lantern, and stepped through the doorway. He pushed the door to, not closing it completely - he had enough sense to want to make sure that he couldn't get locked in - but enough to not make it immediately clear that he went through there, leaving Tray on the other side.

He found steps in front of him leading down into a dark space.

It was like an adventure story: a dark, secret room hidden away that only he had found. Perhaps treasure would be waiting for him at the bottom of the steps, he wondered.

But when he reached the bottom of the steps, it wasn't shiny coins or jewels that he discovered, but shiny sharp shards of glass scattered all over the floor, damp with spilt water.

A strange-looking creature with long tentacles and a beautifully intricate spiral shell lay there on the ground, its tentacles spasming occasionally but otherwise not moving. Walter picked it up carefully by its shell. Despite being close to death, the ammonite shrugged its tentacles back inside their protective housing, hiding away from any possible danger that Walter may pose. The shape of the shell intrigued him. He was sure he had seen something like it before, but without the tentacles.

Then it dawned on him.

He put the lantern on the floor and retrieved a small box from his pocket with his now spare hand. A square box, covered neatly in wrapping paper and with a small tag attached to it, written on with a child's hand: *To Father*. He ripped the wrapping away and opened up the box. Inside was a small, polished ammonite fossil, sitting isolated in the middle of the box. Something his mother had picked out for him to give his father for Christmas. She had called it a "wretched thing" at the time of purchase, but the look in his mother's eyes when she saw it made her look so sad yet so happy at the same time; he knew that it must be something special. But it was about a quarter of the size of this ammonite he had just found himself. And surely his father would want something he had found, not something his mother had *bought*? That would make it *even more* special.

Walter pulled the small ammonite out of the box and dropped it to the ground, replacing it with the other creature he had just retrieved from the floor. He pressed the lid back into place and stuffed the box in his pocket. He would have to try to do something about the wrapping later, but for now, there was more to explore down there in the dark cellar.

Like the sounds of water splashing from somewhere at the back of the room, for example…

Buckland drummed his fingertips against the arms of the chair where he sat, a rhythmic tapping born out of boredom and frustration. He turned and looked across at Mrs Mantell. The glare she gave him made it more than evident that she did not appreciate the sound he was making with his fingers, so he immediately stopped. He thought briefly about how he might occupy himself and then remembered something.

He twisted in his seat and pulled a small bag from his pocket.

He opened it and held it out to Mrs Mantell.

'Toasted woodlouse?' he offered.

'Certainly not,' Mary-Ann refused, squirming at the thought.

Buckland aimed the bag towards Mrs Anning. She held a hand up in polite declination of the offer. Buckland shrugged, took a small handful of the snacks in his hand and dropped them one by one into his mouth, crunching lightly against each before swallowing, Mrs Anning and Mrs Mantell watching in disgust.

Tray knocked against him, bashing his shin with the stick he was carrying, and stared up at Buckland with wide eyes, waiting for him to play. As Buckland looked down at him, the dog dropped the stick straight onto Buckland's foot. He kicked it away lightly.

'Get off, you horrible little creature.'

But the dog took the kicking of the stick to be the start of a new game and immediately fetched it back, landing it again on Buckland's toes.

Mary-Ann jumped up at the sight of the dog.

'Where's Walter?' she cried out.

The last time she had seen Tray, the dog had been playing with her son. Now, the dog was there with them, but there was no sign of Walter.

'Walter!' she called to her son, but no response came.

Buckland turned in his seat and looked towards the door to the room, leading out to the staircase, which in turn led to the shop floor, which in turn could lead down to the cellar.

He leapt from his chair and rushed from the room.

The plesiosaur looked asleep, laying still in the water, its head sticking out from the surface to enable it to breathe while it slept. Walter had thought that the ammonite he had found was amazing, but this - this living giant creature - was truly something else. Sadly, there was no way he could put *this* in a box for Christmas for his father. He watched it through the glass tank, resting on the surface of the water, the only movements the occasional involuntary flick of a flipper or slight movement of its head. It looked peaceful, relaxed and harmless.

Walter moved closer and tripped onto the small step in front of the tank. On his tiptoes, he stretched up, trying his hardest to reach the top of the tank and touch the plesiosaur. It looked so gentle; he just wanted to see what it felt like under his fingers, whether soft or scaly, like leaves or wet stones.

A firm grip on his shoulder spun him around, causing him to jump from the step to save himself from falling.

It was Buckland who had grabbed him. He stood there, brandishing a torch as though he was about to set fire to the place.

'Move away from that beast!' he yelled at the boy.

Walter looked past Buckland and saw his mother and Mrs Anning running towards them in the cellar. He sprinted over to meet his mother, running straight into her arms, away from the shouting man who was infinitely more terrifying than the creature.

Buckland's shouting had awakened the plesiosaur. It flapped its flippers, splashing water over the rim of the tank, onto the floor and across Buckland. Seeing Buckland standing there with a torch, it hissed, baring its teeth. Buckland waved the torch at the creature, warning it to leave the child alone, even though it had been asleep with no intention of harming anyone. As Buckland moved the torch between his hands, the plesiosaur moved its head, watching carefully. Buckland jabbed forward, forcing the hot flame quickly towards the creature.

It didn't like that.

The plesiosaur screeched.

It lifted its long neck from the water, swung it over the edge of the tank and thwacked Buckland hard. He dropped the torch and flew across the room, crumpling to the ground as he landed. The creature was surprisingly strong, for all its generally calm demeanour.

'Let's go,' Mrs Anning said, ushering Walter and Mary-Ann back towards the cellar steps.

Mary-Ann screamed in fright as someone blocked their path.

It took her a second to regain her composure as she realised it was her husband, Mary and Richard Owen, who she was looking at, who happened to be descending the cellar steps just as they were trying to leave.

'What's going on? We heard shouting,' Mantell asked.

'That... beast... attacked Walter,' his wife told him, waving vaguely towards the plesiosaur.

'I am sure that is not what happened,' Mary said in defence of the creature.

'I am sure you were not there to witness it,' Mrs Mantell snapped.

Mantell moved his wife to the side so that he could see into the cellar. Buckland had unsteadily got to his feet. He reached out for the torch he had dropped, which was still blazing hotly, staring straight at the creature that had knocked him to the ground.

Mantell could see precisely what was on Buckland's mind.

He rushed across the cellar and jumped between Buckland and the creature.

'Move aside, Gideon,' Buckland snarled, his eyes fixed on his quarry in the water tank.

'You are a man of science, William,' Mantell tried pleading with him. 'A man of nature. Men of nature do not destroy that which lives.'

'But this *thing* is not of nature. It is an abomination. Therefore, it must be destroyed.'

'By whose authority?'

'My own,' he growled and pushed Mantell aside.

He struck out once again with the torch at the plesiosaur.

Enraged, the creature swung its solid head around on its neck, striking Mantell and Buckland simultaneously as though they were nothing more than a pair of skittles to be knocked down. Having braced himself for the impact this second time, Buckland sprang back onto his feet much more quickly than before. He rushed to the plesiosaur, ready for another round with his opponent.

But this time, Mary was already there and waiting for him.

Buckland practically ran straight into her fist as it swung towards his face.

He crumpled to the ground on impact, out cold.

Thirty-Two

It did not take Buckland too long to come around from the punch to the face; he was soon back on his feet, but he came out of it in an even more foul mood than when Mary had struck him to the ground.

It was perhaps more to do with it being Mary - a woman - who had knocked him out cold rather than the fact that he had been struck at all that upset him so much.

The embarrassment of taking a blow from the supposedly gentler sex was all but too much for him to bear, and as he looked up at the shocked faces looking down at him as he lay on the ground, he realised that any chance of respect from within that particular group was long gone. Perhaps he had deserved it, but he could not fully comprehend how; he had, after all, been trying to defend a young boy against a beast. Indeed, he should be commended for such an act rather than hit in the face.

But as he was led upstairs, nursing an eye that he could already feel swelling, Buckland knew that he was in the minority over his opinion of the creature locked in the cellar. Some - Mantell and Mary, specifically - saw it as an opportunity for study and a unique, living creature that should be kept safe and alive by all means necessary. A one of a kind, incredible find.

Though, of course, having seen the cavern, it was clear that this was *not*, in fact, "one of a kind"; there were many more of them out there, creatures of different shapes, sizes and ferocities.

Buckland still firmly believed that their only course of action was to destroy the creature before anything else happened. It was unique, yes. But it was an anomaly. It should not have existed. *Nothing* they had seen in the cavern should have existed at that time. The Creator had wiped out entire species during the Great Flood, that much they knew, though Buckland's research suggested that others had been wiped out, even since then. This was difficult enough for him to reconcile in his mind with the words of the Bible. But for there to be more of these creatures living and breathing in these modern times... It was as though God had missed them when he wiped the others from existence. And if God had missed them, God was not infallible. He had made a mistake. And if God was not infallible and capable of making mistakes, what implications did that hold for everything Buckland and millions of other people believed?

It was all too much for him to be able to think about, and he allowed himself to be led to a large chair and practically dropped into it. He immediately closed his eyes through a combination of weariness, soreness, and simply wanting to be able to ignore everyone around him for at least a few precious moments of peace. He had too much on his mind; it was beginning to hurt even to think.

The mood in the room was once again tense and subdued.

Mrs Mantell sat in a chair with Walter on her lap, holding him tight to ensure he could not escape again. Richard Owen sat opposite her, laid back and looking the most relaxed out of the group, his fingertips pressed together in a pyramid in front of his face. His small eyes watched, surveyed, and took everything in as if he was calculating... something. Even Tray was tired and had splayed himself out in front of the fire, extending his body and laying in a position to receive the maximum warmth possible. He likely wouldn't last like that for too long before he had to get up, panting from overheating, and have to move somewhere cooler.

Mary and Mantell, meanwhile, were talking in hushed tones in the far corner of the room, not wanting to be overheard but feeling like it would appear suspicious if they left the room entirely to converse. Mary had sent her mother to bed; it was all too much for the poor woman, and she looked beyond exhausted from all the excitement the day had produced so far.

Mantell could see his wife watching them from across the room. She had a way of making him feel guilty, though he had done nothing wrong. He couldn't believe for one moment that the plesiosaur had carried out an unprovoked attack on Walter. There was clearly some misunderstanding, and from seeing Buckland's actions and emotional state down in the cellar, he was sure that if anyone had provoked the beast, it was Buckland himself.

Walter was, after all, unscathed.

Mantell had taken a solid whack to his side from the plesiosaur's head, and he was sure that he was bruised, but it was nothing to worry about. He took it more as a warning from the creature than an attempt to attack them. It was fair enough, he thought, since Buckland was swinging a flaming torch wildly in its direction, and the two of them were shouting at each other right in front of it. They must have been causing the poor thing some considerable distress. It could hardly be blamed for wanting to defend itself against any perceived threat.

Yet Mrs Mantell's eyes glared straight at him, watching his every move. She was trying to see what it was that he was saying to Mary, so Mantell subtly shifted position to try to make that task at least a little more difficult for her, turning so that he could watch his wife from over Mary's shoulder, but his face was more-or-less hidden from view. Mary's back was now facing the room, unable to see what was happening behind her, only able to see Mantell himself in front of her and the wall against which he stood.

'We must do something,' he told Mary. 'Those creatures are spread far and wide throughout the town. If we do not stop them soon, they could be anywhere, and we would have no hope.'

'I'm not doing anything until my creature is safe. Away from him,' Mary replied, casting a pointed look across at Buckland.

'There are bigger things at stake than one creature,' Mantell reminded her.

'If this creature is the only one I can save, then I will do whatever it takes.'

Mary's eyes were hard, her jaw firm, and Mantell could see that there would be no dissuading her otherwise. He nodded slightly in hesitant agreement. He understood her position and even supported it to a degree. He genuinely hoped that there was some way that they could bring an end to the current situation but still save as many of the creatures from extinction as possible. How that would happen was beyond him at that point, though, and he could see no possible way in which that particular scenario might play out.

Mrs Mantell rose to her feet and marched across the room towards them. Mantell quickly touched Mary's arm, glancing over her shoulder towards his approaching wife, indicating for her not to say anything else for the moment. Mary looked behind her, saw Mrs Mantell heading towards them, and immediately took heed of what Mantell indicated.

'We're leaving,' Mrs Mantell declared.

'I can't,' Mantell told her firmly, but immediately wished that he had said something a little less direct, something which could not be misinterpreted to mean that his priorities lay there, with Mary, rather than with his own family.

'Not you. Walter and I. We are the ones who are leaving.'

Mantell breathed a sigh of relief. The sooner they were away from there, the better. With those creatures on the loose, there was no definite way that this whole scenario would end. It would be better for them if they were back home in London, far away from all that was going on in Lyme Regis.

'Good idea. It's not safe here - '

'You still don't understand, do you?' Mary-Ann sighed, her expression filled not with anger but disappointment and great sadness.

On the other hand, Mantell's expression proved that she was correct, and he did not understand what she was saying.

'You protected that beast over our son,' she explained. 'It attacked Walter - '

Mary, trying to keep out of the conversation until then, felt the need to jump in there and defend her creature. She had looked after it long enough to know it was far from aggressive. It was the most passive animal she had ever encountered, perhaps even more so than Tray.

'I'm sure - ' she began her defence.

But Mrs Mantell held up a hand, stopping her from speaking, as she accosted Mary with a fixed glare.

'I am talking to my husband,' she said, but with an undercurrent of menace loaded within every syllable she pronounced.

Mary took the hint and backed away, leaving them to their private conversation. Mantell looked panicked at Mary's retreat, as if being left alone with his wife could have potentially disastrous consequences for him.

With Mary now far enough away for her to continue speaking, Mrs Mantell turned back to face her husband.

'It attacked Walter,' she said quietly, 'and you defended it.'

'Do you not see how remarkable this specimen is?' Mantell pleaded with her. 'How important such a discovery would be? This is above and beyond anything that I have ever dreamt of finding. It is everything I have ever wanted.'

'Everything you have ever wanted?' Mary-Ann repeated. 'What about me? What about Walter? I recall you saying those words about us at some point in what now feels like the long-distant past. How a *wife and son* is "everything you have ever wanted".'

'That is not what I am saying,' Mantell explained. 'You are twisting my words. I meant that this is everything I have ever wanted in my *scientific world*. The world of science and the world of my family are two separate and distinct entities.'

'I am aware of that, Gideon. But one of those entities is consuming the other, taking over and growing while the other is shrinking into insignificance until it is barely even visible to you.'

His wife's refusal to see the importance of what they had discovered there was beginning to frustrate Mantell. She was twisting everything that he said to use his own words against him, casting him as a man who cared nothing for his family, where the only thing that mattered was his scientific discoveries. She was unable or unwilling to accept the fact that they were both of great importance to him. They were like two sides of the same coin that made up his life: completely different worlds, but both of the same significance.

'Do you not see that I love you?' he tried again to persuade her.

'What I see,' she said through gritted teeth as she tried to fight back the tears stinging at her eyes, 'is a husband and father who cares more for his work than he does for his own family.'

'That is unfair,' he snapped.

'Is it?'

They stared at each other for a long moment. Mantell could not think what else he could say that he hadn't already said. She was firm in her conviction that he did not care, so what could he do or say that would persuade her otherwise? Certainly not much, while there were creatures on the loose outside that he needed to help contain.

Seeing that her husband had no reply, Mrs Mantell turned and marched back to where Walter sat in the chair she had vacated. She grabbed him by the hand and pulled him down from the seat.

'Come along,' she told her son. 'We are leaving.'

'I haven't given Father his Christmas present yet,' Walter replied.

'It would be wasted on him,' Mary-Ann replied, marching the boy from the room.

Darkness was already falling as Mrs Mantell and Walter stepped into their carriage. A fog was drawing in, thick blankets of white rolling across the beach from the sea towards the town. Lanterns shone somewhere within the thick fog, only their lights visible, like halos from some guardian angels sent to watch over the town on that strange night.

Mary and Mantell watched from the bottom of the outside steps that led up to the shop as the carriage rode away down the street. Mantell could just about make out young Walter waving to him through the back of the carriage. He waved back, hoping that he could be seen through the fog separating them, drawing a veil across his family and perhaps any hope he might have had for reconciliation. That seemed beyond hope now. Short of a Christmas miracle, he doubted he had much of a future left with Mary-Ann. He could only hope she would allow him to see Walter occasionally.

The carriage was out of sight now, yet Mantell still stared down the street after it, hoping it might have turned around and be heading back towards them, Mary-Ann having changed her mind about leaving.

Mary wrapped her clothes more tightly around herself, the fog adding an extra chill.

She took hold of Mantell's elbow.

'Come on,' she said, leading him back up the steps.

He continued to watch down the street as he was pulled back inside.

Always hoping.

'I'm going to need your help,' he heard Mary say as she closed the door behind them, shutting out the outside world.

Thirty-Three

The day's events had exhausted Mrs Anning, as she was fast asleep when Mary crept into her room. Even the sound of footsteps treading on the unavoidably creaky floorboards did not raise the slightest stirring from her as she lay in bed.

Mary could not help but feel bad for all she had put her mother through. The woman was unwell enough as it was, practically on the verge of collapse most days. Still, for her to have had to endure everything that had happened in the recent past... it was a wonder that she had not keeled over on the spot. But Mary knew that her mother was a strong woman, made of sterner stuff than most, and she was capable of far more than the doctors suggested she would or should be, due to her ailments.

Mary tiptoed carefully across the floor to a small wooden cabinet beside the bed.

She slowly pulled one of the hinged doors open and peered inside.

Various bottles and herbs littered the shelves. Mary scanned her eyes across them until she came across the one she required. She delicately extracted it from the cabinet, careful not to clink glass against glass, and closed the cabinet again.

The plesiosaur was very much awake, ducking and diving as much as it could within that relatively small tank. It was nowhere near the size of the environment the creature was used to living within, but it was making do. The display it was putting on seemed purely for Mantell's benefit as he stood before it, watching, the plesiosaur occasionally looking across at him as if to ensure it still had a spectator to its show. With Buckland not there, Mantell could swear that the creature seemed

178

happy, if a beast like that could exhibit such an emotion. If Buckland had seen such a spectacle, perhaps it would have gone some way to change his mind about his thoughts of simply destroying the plesiosaur; if he could see that it emoted, it *thought*, then maybe that would go some way to persuading him that it was more than some vicious ancient beast for which there was no place on this earth. Most likely, it wouldn't make any difference, but Mantell thought having a hopeful wish for a change was good.

Mary placed a hand on his shoulder, causing him to jump and drawing his attention away from the magnificent display.

She passed him the bottle from her mother's room as he turned to face her.

'What is this?' he asked as he examined the unmarked bottle.

He pulled the top off and sniffed the contents, which smelled surprisingly not terrible.

'A sleeping tonic,' Mary explained. 'It is my own concoction, purely natural ingredients sourced from the surrounding countryside.'

Mary began stalking around the cellar, searching for any relatively fresh ammonites that might have tumbled during the rampage that she *still* had not yet had the opportunity to clear up. Any that she found, she placed inside a large bowl that she held, which was already half full of water. Having decided she had sourced enough of the tentacled creatures, Mary held out the bowl before Mantell.

'Pour some in here,' she told him, indicating the bottle she had given him.

'How much?'

'I don't know,' she admitted. 'Half the bottle should do.'

'*Should*?' Mantell queried.

'I don't make a habit of tranquillising plesiosaurs, you know.'

Mantell shrugged. It was a fair point: who amongst them would have thought that the dosage of a home-brewed sleeping tonic required to knock out a prehistoric sea creature would be information of use before that day? He did as instructed and poured roughly half of the tonic into the bowl with the water and ammonites, sliding the half-empty bottle into his jacket for safekeeping.

Mary stirred the concoction with her hand, ensuring that the tonic was mixed through with the water nicely and couldn't be missed.

She climbed up on the step in front of the tank and held it over the edge, near the plesiosaur's head. The creature came towards her and sniffed cautiously at the bowl. For the briefest moment, they wondered if the game was already up, that the plesiosaur's sense of smell was strong enough to detect the tonic within the water and decide that what it was being fed was tainted. But that moment passed quickly as it threw its head into the bowl, almost causing Mary to lose her grip on it, and wolfed back the ammonites, some of them sliding down whole as though they were oysters, others having their shells crunched between the creature's teeth.

The ammonites devoured, the plesiosaur licked around the bowl with its long tongue, making sure to get the last morsels of ammonite-flavoured water from within. And, then, the bowl was empty. Ammonites and drugged water were both consumed.

Mary gave the plesiosaur a gentle stroke on the head and trod off the step.

Mantell moved closer to her and whispered conspiratorially as if the creature might understand what they were saying should he speak any louder.

'How long will it take?' he asked.

'Again, this is my first time doing such a thing.'

'But if you were to guess?'

'Not long,' Mary answered vaguely. 'Hopefully.'

Thirty-Four

Nothing made the town feel more festive than the sight and sound of groups of carol singers spreading the cheer of the season through song. Away from the town square, where the ultimate Christmas decoration - the tree - had been destroyed by rampaging beasts, there was little indication that anything was wrong on that particular evening, save for the occasional peculiar growl that would from time to time drift through the air. But the thick fog had been known to create strange sounds, carrying the noise of the waves crashing against the shore across the town, for example, and distorting those sounds so that they sounded nothing like what they had been when they were first plucked into the atmosphere.

As of yet, nothing was stopping the carollers from performing what they believed to be their good Christian duties of spreading the Word in musical form to those who would listen to them from their doorsteps.

One particular group had already visited many properties along Pound Street, finding most residents to be accommodating and generous with their gifts in exchange for the pleasant tones of the carols sung in beautiful four-part harmony. There were, of course, some who had no interest in hearing tidings of joy and peace, but for the most part, they had already known which houses to avoid not to be pelted with old fruit and vegetables for their efforts.

They were presenting a rendition of *Silent Night* to an entire family who stood in their doorway listening - the mother and father of the house, plus their three young children - enraptured by the joys of Christmas.

Jesus, Lord, at thy birth.
Jesus, Lord, at thy birth.

They finished the song and stood expecting the applause that had greeted them at the end of each of their previous carols, but the family in the doorway did nothing but stare at the singers, mouths open and eyes wide. Then they realised that they were not staring *at* them but rather at something *behind* them.

The singers slowly turned around.

They looked up.

They screamed.

Before them was a *neovenator*. As tall as two men, the creature stood on two large rear legs supporting its gigantic body and long tail. Two short forearms stuck out on either side of its body, ending with sharp claws. But the most fearsome sight was that of the head. The creature's mouth was practically as large as a child, its teeth alone the size of a full-grown man's hand. A growl formed in the belly of the beast, rising through its long neck towards its head. It opened its huge mouth, revealing rows of deadly teeth and the hollow blackness of the tunnel that was its throat. The growl became a roar as it emerged from the creature, its breath blowing in the faces of the terrified singers, foul smelling and surprisingly warm.

They broke free from their fear-filled hesitation and turned back towards the household for which they had previously been singing, just in time to see the front door slamming shut, the family hiding behind the somewhat limited protection that it could provide against such a creature.

Their only option was to run.

And so they did, scattering in different directions, each of them secretly hoping that the beast would follow those going the opposite way, that they might be able to escape.

The neovenator spun around, watching the tiny people below it, its prey trying to get away before it could gobble them down.

It swung its huge tail, catching the legs of some of the singers and sending them tumbling to the ground. They returned to their feet quickly enough, but the creature would deal with them later. It had already set its sights on one particularly delicious-looking woman who did not seem to be able to run quite as quickly as the others.

It took little more than a couple of long strides for the beast to catch up with her.

In one swift motion, it lowered its neck, opened its jaw wide and snatched at the woman.

Lifting its head back in the air, the woman was tossed to the back of its mouth. She did not stop screaming until a loud *crunch* signalled her end. The neovenator gulped her down. She was little more than an appetiser.

The creature turned back to those who were fleeing down the street.

They should be relatively easy pickings, but it would be fun to play with them for a short time beforehand.

There was nothing quite like the thrill of the hunt…

Richard Owen practically jumped out at Mantell and Mary as they emerged from the cellar.

'What are you two up to?' he demanded to know.

Mary quickly shut the door behind them as Owen tried peering past her. Without turning to see what she was doing, she fumbled with the key, locked the door, and slipped the key into her hand.

'That is no concern of yours,' Mantell told him and tried to brush past.

Owen moved, blocking them.

'Whatever is going on, I want a part of it,' Owen told them.

'Nothing is going on,' Mary told him, 'except that people are in danger, and we must help them.'

'It seems to me that this is all your doing,' Owen said, pointedly looking past Mary towards the cellar door. 'You knew of these creatures and allowed this to happen.'

Mary opened her mouth to rebuff him, but Mantell stepped in.

'What has happened has happened. We must now work to fix it.'

'How very noble of you,' Owen replied with a cold smile.

'If you would be so kind as to keep an eye on Reverend Buckland and my mother, I have things to do.'

Owen looked from Mary to Mantell and back again.

'I can see where I am not wanted,' he told them. 'Very well. As you wish.'

'Thank you,' Mary replied.

Owen bowed slightly, smiling a cold smile.

'I am sorry about what happened with your wife earlier, Dr Mantell,' Owen said, the sentiment of the words failing to make its way through to his voice. 'Perhaps you should head back and join them? I am more than capable, I am sure, of assisting Miss Anning.'

Mantell swallowed hard and took his time before replying, knowing that if he did not do so, he would more than likely say something that he immediately regretted.

'I believe that giving my wife some space is the best thing I could do for the moment.'

Owen smirked.

'You know best, doctor.'

With no indication that Owen had any intention of moving in the near future, Mary spoke up.

'Perhaps you would not mind checking on my mother now, Mr Owen? I am sure that if she awakens, she will be in a state of some confusion.'

'As you wish, my lady.'

He looked at them both again, knowing that they were scheming about *something*, but it seemed unlikely that he would get anything out of them at that point. Feigning indifference would have to be the way forward for the time being.

He bowed slightly once more, turned and headed for the stairs.

Mary and Mantell watched him until he disappeared, then listened for his footsteps treading towards Mrs Anning's bedroom.

Quite sure that he was, for now, gone, they set about preparing what was required.

The suspicions of Richard Owen were pushed to one side for the time being, though they were sure that they had done nothing to quash them but rather to delay the inevitable further interrogation.

Mary and Mantell exited the shop.

Between them, they carried, pushed and pulled a large wooden cart with wheels attached to it. On top of the cart was something of not inconsiderable size, draped in a tarpaulin to hide it from view. The tarpaulin expanded and contracted slowly, rhythmically, as though whatever was underneath it was breathing in the relaxed manner of something fast asleep.

It wasn't easy to get down the stone steps of the shop, and more than once, it seemed that their load would slip from the cart. Getting it on there in the first place had been more than enough effort, and neither felt they had the strength or energy to do it again. Fortunately, slowly and steadily, they reached the ground level without incident.

They stopped to catch their breath and check that everything was in place to make the bumpy ride along the street's cobbles as frustration-free as possible.

A group of figures emerged through the fog before them, heading in their direction.

Mary and Mantell shifted position so they were as hidden as possible in the shadows of the buildings at the side of the street.

Then they realised the figures heading towards them were paying them no attention.

They were running.

People dressed in clothes that looked like they had recently been engaged in some festive activity. Like carol singing, perhaps.

They glanced behind themselves as they ran, running from *something* further behind them in the fog.

Mary and Mantell could easily guess what that something might be.

They looked at each other.

'We need to hurry,' Mary said.

The Cobb at Lyme Regis is a large, artificial harbour made from stone and in the shape of a horseshoe, the ends of the shoe jutting up into the sea, with the curve at the edge of the water. The structure's shape provides a haven for boats, protecting against wind and waves, and a place to dock when the boat isn't required. Steep steps lead up to the top of the tall walls, along which you can walk as if you are walking straight out into the sea itself.

It was here that Mary led Mantell as they pulled their heavy cart. They went to the opposite side of the Cobb, to the side of the wall away from where the boats were moored, away from most of the traffic from the sea. A more private, less travelled spot where they were less likely to be noticed by anyone else. They looked to see if anyone was around who might witness what they were about to do. They appeared to be alone, though the fog was thick enough that it was unlikely that they could be seen regardless of the tall brick wall between them and any spectators. From where they stood on the beach beside the water, the street they had travelled along was no longer visible; it was as though a thick white veil had been pulled down, hiding the real world from this, what was to Mantell the most surreal of missions.

They untied the tarpaulin from over their load, revealing the plesiosaur, still asleep from the tonic they had administered, and manoeuvred the cart as close as possible to where the sea met the sand. Careful not to awaken the creature just yet, Mary clipped a thick metal clasp around its neck, attached to a length of chain. The clasp was loose enough not to cause discomfort but tight enough that it could not slip its head through and get free. She held on to the other end of the chain herself.

They were ready.

'Tip it gently,' Mary instructed.

She and Mantell carefully lifted the end of the cart they had been pulling, tipping it at an angle towards the sea. The plesiosaur slowly began to slide off of the cart towards the water. First, the tip of its tail went in, then its back flippers, and then its whole body was in there. At the point where the cold water hit the bottom of its neck, the plesiosaur was stirred from its slumber.

It lifted its head slowly, still groggy from its sleep, but when it discovered that it was no longer where it had been when it had fallen asleep, it began to panic. Flapping its flippers wildly, swishing its tail, swinging its long neck side to side, Mantell had to grab onto the chain to assist Mary before it was pulled from her hands. They tugged it towards them, Mary trying to angle the creature's head so that it could see her and, perhaps, be comforted by the sight.

It worked. As the plesiosaur noticed a familiar face, it calmed somewhat, not so much thrashing but still flapping its flippers agitatedly. Mary stepped towards it and stroked the side of its face and down its long neck, shushing it until it was more relaxed. Slowly, it settled down. After the initial shock of a change of scenery, it looked around properly and saw the vast expanse of the sea stretching out before it. It flapped around again as if testing if its flippers would still work within this larger body of water.

'Everything will be fine,' Mary whispered to it. 'Everything will be fine.'

It was a mantra that she repeated over and over for her own benefit as much for - if not more than - the creature's.

She carefully stepped to the side of the beach, against the Cobb wall, and climbed up the narrow steps. Still holding on to the chain connected to the plesiosaur, she watched it as she walked, keeping eye contact so the creature would know she had not forgotten about it. She walked along the top of the wall, gently pulling the plesiosaur with her as she ventured further into the sea. Towards the end of the wall, she laid down on the stone, reached over the side, and attached her end of the chain to a thick metal ring embedded in the stonework.

'I'll be back for you,' she called down to the creature in the sea below.

It whined up at her as if understanding that she was about to leave it behind.

'I promise.'

She brushed a tear from her eye as she walked back along the top of the wall towards the shore, feeling surprisingly emotional at leaving the creature behind after caring for it for so long. She turned to look back at it. Its long neck was still sticking out of the water, staring at her.

'Keep out of sight,' she whispered into the fog, beginning to separate the two. 'Please.'

Mary turned away again, determined not to show any signs of emotional weakness to Dr Mantell. They had work to do, and she wanted to ensure she was a part of it.

Thirty-Five

The building was filled with shouting and arguing as Mantell and Mary returned to the shop. On the whole, the voices belonged to Owen and Buckland. But Mrs Anning joined in occasionally to let her opinion be known. From the shop level of the property, the words being said were muffled and incomprehensible, making the meaning behind the argument unclear.

Heads turned, and silence descended as Mantell and Mary made their presence known within the living room. The three who had been huddled together in heated discussion separated as if nothing had happened and drifted to their individual corners of the room.

'Mother?' Mary asked in an accusatory tone.

'We were beginning to worry,' Mrs Anning replied.

'I'm sure you were.'

Buckland approached Mary, his head low, his expression and demeanour contrite, his whole posture practically bowing before her.

He clasped Mary's two hands in his own.

'I owe you an apology,' he began.

'Indeed?'

'My behaviour was inexcusable, and I am sorry.'

'That is good of you to say,' Mary replied, though the words took her a moment to spill from her mouth.

This was the last thing she had expected to hear from William Buckland after all that had gone before and the argument raging upon their return to the shop.

Buckland was a showman, though, an expert at putting on a display and persuading others of his views and opinions. But right there and then, he did seem genuine in his apology, which was good enough for Mary for the time being.

'I have concluded that the best course of action would be to return the creatures to the cavern from whence they came and seal them in.' He lifted his head, meeting Mary's eyes, fixing her with a stare that showed he was firm in his resolve when he ended his speech with a single word: 'Permanently.'

Permanently sealing any entrances to the cavern would mean, of course, that Mary could no longer get in there. She could no longer examine, study, and walk amongst those creatures she had discovered, which had provided her with so much joy, enthusiasm, and wonder over the past months. She would no longer have the opportunity to watch them as they lived together, as no one had seen them do for thousands, perhaps millions of years, depending upon which version of the scientific research available could be believed. Her whole reason for being would be taken away from her, and she would once more return to being nothing but the strange, lonely woman who wanders the beach day and night, searching for her peculiar objects in the rocks. Not that any of those who judged her knew anything about her secret "research project" within the cavern, but just knowing that it existed made her feel somewhat superior to their opinions. Once it was all gone, their opinions would return to being correct.

She *would* be the strange, lonely beach lady who had become a common sight on their walks along the beach. Someone to watch and talk and laugh about behind her back as they continued about their days.

Yet, she knew that Buckland was right. They could not risk the creatures escaping again. Enough people had been hurt or even died, which was partially on her. At least Buckland had changed his mind about destroying them all and would be happy enough to see them contained, presumably to die off naturally as and when the Creator decided.

Mary sighed and nodded her head slightly in agreement.

'That sounds like a reasonable compromise,' she said.

'Containing them is not enough,' Mrs Anning piped up. 'They are sure to find another means of escape, and then this whole mess begins again.'

'Madam,' Buckland said calmly, holding his hands up to cut off Mrs Anning's words. 'Madam, please. I implore you to trust me on this. I shall ensure that further escape is not possible.'

A look passed between Buckland and Mrs Anning, caught only perhaps by Mantell. Buckland had lifted his eyebrows at Molly and stared at her as if trying to communicate something by thought alone. She had looked confused for a moment; then, her face softened as if the silent message had been received.

'Very well, Reverend Buckland,' Mrs Anning said. 'If you believe it will be safe, then I shall put my trust in you. You are, after all, a man of your word.'

Buckland smiled slightly and bowed humbly.

Mantell wondered what the look had meant, what the secret message was that had passed between the two of them that so quickly changed Mrs Anning's mind about Buckland's decision not to destroy the creatures. But they had spent long enough arguing. The beasts were still out there, terrorising the town. They needed to come up with a plan, and they needed to do it quickly.

'How will we go about it?' Mantell asked, keen to set things in motion.

'What drove the creatures out from the cavern in the first place?' Buckland asked him.

Mantell knew that he was being tested. It was the same strategy that Buckland used with his students, asking them a question to which he knew the exact answer for which he was looking, but most likely a solution that no one but Buckland himself would ever come up with. That was how Buckland's mind worked - differently from everyone else's - and that was what made him so brilliant but also so difficult.

'The fresh air? The daylight?' Mantell tried.

Buckland shook his head.

'Wrong.'

'Fear,' Mary said.

Buckland clapped his hands in delight, that old sparkle returning to his eyes for the first time in a while.

'Exactly!' he exclaimed. 'The explosions terrified the beasts, causing them to run for their lives.'

He looked at the faces staring back at him as if he had given them all the answers they needed to solve the riddles he presented. The faces stared back at him, waiting for him to unravel the layers of mystery.

'How does that help the current situation?' Mantell asked.

Buckland rummaged through the papers scattered around the room, searching until he finally found what he was looking for: a map of Lyme Regis. He laid it on the floor, spread it out, and crouched beside it, leaving the others no choice but to follow suit.

'Carefully rigged explosions, in the right locations, at the right times,' he said, jabbing a finger at various locations on the map, 'could be used to force the beasts back to the cavern. What drove them out could drive them back.'

'It sounds risky,' Mary said.

'There are a few too many *coulds* in that plan for my liking,' Mantell agreed.

Buckland shrugged and pulled himself back up to his feet.

'I would be most pleased to hear of any alternative course of action.'

He stood, arms folded, looking almost smugly at those assembled around him.

Mantell and Mary looked at each other.

'I have no other thoughts,' Mantell admitted.

'Nor I,' Mary agreed.

Mrs Anning shrugged, also unable to think of a better course of action.

'Mr Owen?' Buckland asked, looking behind him, as Owen was not standing before him like the others.

But the rest of the room was empty. Owen was not there.

'Where has he gone?' Buckland wondered aloud.

'He must have left when we were speaking together,' Mantell said.

'Perhaps he was in need of some relief,' Buckland suggested.

'Reverend Buckland!' Mrs Anning exclaimed. 'There are ladies present.'

'Oh?' Buckland retorted sarcastically, with a cheeky wink in Mary's direction.

'I am not so sure that… that… is what he is doing,' Mantell said.

He frowned in the direction of the staircase. He had been too engrossed by what Buckland was saying to have noticed anyone coming or going. It was certainly possible that Richard Owen had snuck away from them during their conversation. Though, to what purpose was anybody's guess.

'Never mind that now,' Buckland said. 'We must continue with our preparations.'

'What would you have us do?' Mary asked.

'I shall seal the tunnel through which we escaped, then reopen the blocked hole in the cavern wall from which most creatures fled. It shall be rigged with explosives to collapse again once all of the beasts are contained. You two should set explosives strategically throughout the town, drawing the creatures in my direction.'

'That is too much for you to do alone,' Mary told him.

'I am quite sure that, for the right price, I shall be able to enlist help from somewhere.'

'Very well.'

'How shall we light the fuses of the explosives? We cannot be carrying lanterns or torches with us.'

Buckland smiled. He reached inside one of his bags and pulled out several of his lighter devices. He handed them to each member of the party.

'These should do the trick,' he told them. 'We shall meet back here once we have everything we require.'

THIRTY-SIX

The fog had come in quickly, covering the docks with thick white blankets. Visibility was reduced so much that it was hard for the fishermen to see much further than the end of their arms. They were glad to have safely returned to shore before the fog landed; there would have been little chance of returning anytime soon if they had still been at sea.

They had the more arduous task of unloading their boat ahead of them now. It was hard work, lugging hundreds, sometimes thousands, of fish from the boat's deck into containers on land, and it was the last thing any of them felt like doing after a long day at sea. But it was a necessary - in fact, vital - part of their job, packaging everything up while it was still fresh so that it could be sold and they could get paid.

Rumours were already spreading of creatures being spotted in the town. Those who had worked on the sea for all of their life knew better than to pay attention to tales of monsters; they had heard enough rumours and been warned against far too many legendary dangers to pay them much heed, even though most of them had been part of at least one experience on the waters for which they could not come up with any rational explanation. But monsters? No. There were never monsters.

Yet Lyme Regis wasn't a town known for its superstitious locals or for spreading dangerous gossip such as the tales they had heard since arriving. So, despite putting little stock in what they had heard, the men still felt a little anxious as they set about their work, especially with the fog wrapping around them so tightly that they would struggle to see if anything was coming at them from the other side.

As they worked, a peculiar sound found its way through the blanket of fog. It was as though something large and heavy was plodding through the darkness, making strange snuffling noises which sounded like it was sniffing at the air.

The fishermen stopped, listening for the sound and trying to peer through the fog to see what might be making it. They were used to the occasional dog or having to fend off many a fat gull from their wares, but this sounded like neither of those things.

It snuffled again. Then the plodding came after, quicker this time, as though whatever made those sounds was moving more quickly.

Then they saw it.

Its head broke through the fog first, followed by its long, spiked, armoured body: a hylaeosaurus.

Despite the fearsome points on its back, the creature presented an almost comical sight: supporting its long, thick body with four stumpy little legs caused it to waddle, its whole body rocking from side to side as it walked. The fishermen watched it with some amusement as it sniffed the air and moved towards an open container half filled with fish.

It carefully backed up slightly, then, with great effort, lifted itself onto its hind legs, placing its front legs on the edge of the container. The whole container fell. It crashed down, burst open and spilt the fish inside to the ground. The creature set to work, immediately devouring one fish after another.

The thought of losing their day's work made the situation somewhat less amusing for the fishermen.

'It'll eat through the whole catch!' one of them - John - cried out.

He grabbed a pole from the ground and picked up one end of a large net with his other hand. He indicated silently for one of his crewmates, Peter, to pick up the other end. Together, they slowly advanced towards the creature, still eating the fish and oblivious to anything happening around it. It barely seemed aware that anyone was there with it at all.

John jabbed the end of the pole at the creature, hard enough to let it know he meant business but hopefully not hard enough to rile the beast and cause it to attack. The hylaeo turned its head and looked at them. Deciding they were not enough of a threat to warrant leaving its delicious feast, it simply moved its body around so that it was out of reach but could keep an eye on them. It picked up another fish and gulped it back.

Peter looked to John for guidance. John held up three fingers and slowly stepped towards the creature, holding the net high. He put down a finger: two left. The hylaeo watched them warily but carried on eating. Another finger down: one. They were practically on either side of the beast now.

John put the final finger down, his hand in a fist. Peter got the hint.

They dropped their respective sides of the net, and it tumbled down upon the hylaeosaurus.

The creature went wild. It struggled hard against the net containing it, swinging its tail and launching its whole body any way it could, trying to get free. Wherever it went, the net followed, and it was soon knocking things over and bashing into the fishermen as it tried to get out of there. The net snagged against a rock. It tore, creating a large opening in the mesh.

The hylaeosaurus broke out.

It turned its full attention towards the fishermen.

They backed away, hoping the fog would envelop them, keeping them out of sight of the crazed creature.

It let out a deep, guttural growl.

'Grab one of those - quickly!' John yelled to Peter, indicating a wooden crate on the dock nearby.

It was a heavy crate, the wood thick and robust, allowing it to be thrown around with relative ease by anyone with enough strength without destroying it. Peter picked it up as if it were nothing and carried it to John.

'Throw it over the top,' John instructed. 'We've got to contain the beast.'

Peter looked at his skipper as if he had lost his mind.

'I'm not going anywhere near that thing!' he said.

'If you don't, you also won't be going anywhere near my boat in future,' John warned him.

Peter looked from John to the creature, weighing up the choice between approaching a strange creature he had never seen before in his life and the prospect of losing his job and no doubt being made a laughing stock, never able to show his face again in his home town for fear of humiliation.

Being attacked by a mysterious creature seemed like the less traumatic of the two options.

Peter stepped slowly around to the outside of the group, circling to the side of the hylaeosaurus, careful not to draw its attention.

He stumbled slightly, his boot striking loudly against a cobble.

He froze.

The creature turned its head to face him.

Apparently, either not seeing him or deciding his was of less interest than the remaining crew members it had been watching, the hylaeo turned back to the rest of the group, hissing and growling at them, taking occasional small steps forward. Peter, too, stepped forward, stalking his own prey.

At one step behind the creature, the crate held above it, he looked to John for final guidance.

John nodded his head and mouthed the instruction: *now*.

Peter dropped the crate over the top of the creature.

It immediately went wild, striking against the sides in a fury, whirling around underneath the wood-like spinning top, trying to find a weakness within the wooden crate. Splinters fractured away from the boards that made up the crate, and it looked like even that strong structure might not be able to withstand the impact of the beast within.

'It's not going to hold,' John admitted. 'We're going to have to take alternative action, boys.'

John unsheathed his long knife and strode towards the crate as it rocked from the impacts within. The other crew members stepped back, not wanting to be in the creature's path should it make a bolt for freedom.

John crouched in front of the crate and placed one hand on its side, ready to raise it. The other hand held the knife, his fingers wrapping around the handle, ensuring the best possible grip. He raised the blade and took a breath, preparing himself.

A hand grabbed the wrist of his knife hand.

John jerked around, ready to have strong words with whichever one of his men thought they knew better than him, stopping him from doing what he knew needed to be done.

To his surprise, it was not a face that he knew but the long, thin face of a gentleman with small beady eyes that bore into him.

'It is more valuable alive than dead,' Richard Owen told the fisherman. 'Help me, and I shall make it worth your while.'

Thirty-Seven

The stench on the quarry floor was almost unbearable. It was like visiting a butcher for some fresh meat only to find that everything had gone sour a few days prior, but it had all been left out to rot and decay. Flies buzzed around the few pieces that remained of the quarry workers, dancing around the pools of blood and patches of *stuff* that had been left behind, stuff even the creatures had not wanted to devour. A few of the beasts themselves remained in the form of half-eaten carcasses. Those unlucky few that had somehow got on the wrong side of the larger, stronger creatures, or been easy targets for those who were hungry and making the most of their newfound freedom.

Mary and Mantell trod carefully through the remnants of this scene of carnage, trying not to step in anything so revolting that they would have to discard their footwear.

Darkness was drawing in, the short winter afternoon coming to a close, and evening on its way. The hour and the fog would make their task even more challenging, but leaving it until the morning was not an option; enough damage had already been done. They needed to try and fix things, as far as they could do so, that very evening.

They stepped over entrails, skirted around crimson puddles, and brushed large black flies away from their faces, reaching where the workers' hut had once stood.

The hut's walls were well and truly destroyed; if they had not known that it had once stood there, there would have been no way of identifying it as such now. The wood was cracked, splintered, torn, smashed, trampled upon, and ripped apart.

They picked through the pieces, lifting the larger wall fragments and casting them aside to reach what had once been the hut floor.

Several containers, still remarkably intact, sat waiting underneath the rubble. They were locked, but Mantell made light work of the locks by smashing down upon them with a discarded shovel he found lying nearby. He pulled the first container's lock from its latch and pried open the lid. He looked at Mary and smiled.

'Found them,' he announced.

Inside were enough explosives to level half a town.

Mary opened the lid of the second container. It was similarly stocked. It appeared they had enough explosives to go around, with plenty to spare.

They scooped the explosives from the containers, filling up large sacks they had brought for such a purpose.

The public house looked deserted from the outside; no one was coming or going, and there was no sign of movement or even illumination from within. Buckland had visited Lyme Regis on multiple occasions in the past and - though he had not been known to frequent such an establishment, being, after all, a man of the church - he had never known a time when there was not at least one soul within the building baring his soul to the bottom of a jug of ale, the landlord and his bar acting as the confessional to the drunkard.

Buckland tried the front door, shut now though it was usually left ajar, presumably to allow the smell within to escape or to ensure that no one walked into it, causing themselves an injury on the way out after having a few too many.

The door wouldn't budge. It rattled in its frame as Buckland pushed and tugged at it, but something inside stopped it from opening as if it had been barricaded or barred from within.

He raised his fist and bashed hard on the thick wooden door. It vibrated with each strike, the heavy sound sure to have been heard by anyone inside.

The massive, round face of the establishment's landlord - Henry Asquith, Esq., as the plaque above the doorway read - appeared at the window to the side of the entrance. His face was generally a crimson colour, his nose bulbous and a similar flush to his cheeks, through years of not infrequent sampling of his own wares. But today, as the face peered out at Buckland through the window, he looked positively ashen, with very little of the redness he usually sported, replaced instead by a pallid white. He glared at Buckland, eyes wide, with what looked like fear rather than annoyance.

'Quiet out there!' he hissed through the closed window.

'Might I come in?' Buckland enquired.

'We're shut.'

'Whatever for?'

The face momentarily turned away from the window, and Buckland heard whispering coming from close by. Asquith seemed to be conferring with others within the premises over Buckland's simple question.

'Personal matters,' the head told him when it reappeared. 'What happened to your eye?'

Buckland lifted a hand to his eye and prodded the large blue bruise that had sprung up from where Mary had hit him in the face. He cringed more at the memory of the blow than the sensitivity of the touch.

'I was attacked,' he said.

'Oh?'

'It was a big man,' Buckland elaborated. 'Two big men, in fact.'

'Is that so.'

'You wouldn't be hiding in there, would you?' Buckland teased, keen to draw the conversation away from his encounter with the clenched fist of a lady. 'From monsters, perhaps?'

Asquith again turned away and whispered with whoever was in the building with him.

'There's no monsters in here,' he said on his return. 'Them's all on your side of the walls.'

'Indeed,' Buckland agreed. 'But I ask again: might I come in?'

'What for?' Asquith asked.

'I need to enlist the help of a strong, capable man.'

'What for?' he asked again.

'To help capture the beasts, naturally.'

Laughter sounded from within. Asquith's guests could quite clearly hear what was being said. Buckland imagined them all standing just beside the window, ears pressed close to the walls, trying to listen to every word. Even the head in the window bobbed up and down as it chuckled.

'I don't think you'll find what you're looking for here,' the landlord told Buckland.

Buckland positioned himself to be seen over Asquith's shoulder through the window, addressing the others within the public house directly.

'Whoever helps will be paid handsomely,' he told them.

Sounds of scuffling came from within. The head in the window turned and looked to its side, displeased about something. It kept moving back and forth as if it was being pulled but unwilling to move, then suddenly, it was jerked forward and disappeared entirely.

The large head of Henry Asquith was replaced by the equally large but differently built face of Jessie.

'How much?' he asked as he nudged his way in place.

THIRTY-EIGHT

The shop door burst open, and Richard Owen marched inside, closely followed by three fishermen, between them carrying the heavy crate containing the hylaeosaurus. The creature was not happy about being moved around and kept lurching from side to side, shifting the balance of the crate and making it incredibly difficult to carry. There had been more than one close call on the way back to the shop with the beast, as the crate was jerked out of their hands, landing on the ground. Despite a few bumps and splintered edges, it had survived the impact.

'Bring it in. Quickly,' Owen demanded as they struggled to carry it up the steps and through the front door.

Owen closed the door behind them, and the crate was unceremoniously dumped in the middle of the floor.

The fishermen stretched their backs and unclenched their fingers from where they had remained in a gripping position for far too long. It would have been an impossible task for anyone not so used to a hard day's physical labour as they were.

'You can't leave it there,' Owen told them. 'Pick it back up.'

He left the groans and curses of the fishermen behind him as he went across to the cellar door. He tried the handle and found that it was still unlocked. Owen picked up a lantern from close by and lit it.

'Bring more light with you when you come down,' he told his "volunteers" and descended the steps into the cellar.

A short time later, Mantell and Mary returned to the shop, laden with bags full of explosives. Buckland, too, arrived back with Jessie at his side, appearing at the front door just as the others were going in, as though he had been standing outside waiting for them.

Mantell looked Jessie up and down, taking in the full size of the gigantic man.

'And who might you be?' Mantell asked him.

'Who might *you* be?' Jessie responded. He gave a curt nod towards Mary and tipped his hat. 'Mary.'

'Jessie,' Mary returned the greeting.

'Jessie,' Buckland said in response to Mantell's question.

'Jessie, is it?' Mantell replied sarcastically.

Buckland clapped the tall man on the back.

'Jessie here is my secret weapon,' he said with a smile. 'With a fine specimen like this beside me, we'll have the job done in no time.'

'So, he... knows?' Mantell asked secretively.

'Hardly a soul round these here parts that don't know about the creatures by now, sir,' Jessie told him.

'I suppose not.'

'Perhaps we should get inside?' Mary suggested.

She pushed open the door to the shop and allowed everyone in, closing it again gently once they were all within.

'Who's there?' a shrill voice cried in the darkness.

A flicker of light emerged from the bottom of the steps, illuminating the pale, wrinkled face of Mrs Anning, a spectre haunting the building to ward off any intruders. She held her stick in front of her, aiming it like she might have a chance to use it against anyone who might think about attacking.

'It is just us, Mother,' Mary told her.

Mrs Anning visibly shrank with relief at the sound of her daughter's voice. She lowered the stick and used it to guide herself across the shop floor.

Tray, hiding behind the older woman for safety, yapped excitedly at Mary's voice. He rushed past Mrs Anning, darting across the room to Mary, who crouched down and scooped him up from the floor, letting him lick at her neck and face in unadulterated joy at her return.

'This is Jessie,' Mantell told Mrs Anning as her eyes fell upon said person.

'I know who Jessie is,' she snapped at Mantell, then nodded politely at the new arrival. 'Jessie.'

'Mrs Anning,' he returned the greeting.

'Whatever were you doing at the bottom of the stairs?' Mary asked.

'I thought I heard someone in the shop. Loud banging about - it sounded like someone was breaking in.'

Mary glanced around the shop floor, which was empty except for those they expected to be there.

'There's no one here, Mother,' Mary told her. 'Just us.'

'One moment,' Buckland said.

He trod across to the cellar door and pushed against it with a single finger. It was open.

'If there is someone here, they're down there.'

'Stay here,' Mary told her mother. Then, knowing she was unlikely to cooperate, she added a pleading: 'Please.'

Mrs Anning harrumphed but agreed to stay where she was.

Buckland held the cellar door open for the others to go through. Somehow, he arranged it so Jessie would be the first through. If anyone was down there looking for trouble, Jessie was best placed to be the first responder; one look at him and whoever it was would likely have a change of heart.

There was definitely someone down there. Multiple people, in fact. Murmuring voices echoed indistinctly within the cellar, forming the shape of spoken words without providing enough detail to be identified. They trod slowly and carefully down the cellar steps, not yet ready to let their presence be known until they could assess the situation more thoroughly rather than walking straight into potential danger.

They could see four men down there, surrounding a large wooden crate that seemed to occasionally judder and jolt with movement as if it had a life of its own.

Despite their cautiousness, a face turned to look at them as they descended the steps, and the eyes of Richard Owen bored into them.

'There you are,' he said with a half-smile. 'I had wondered when you would return.'

Seeing a familiar, if unwelcome, character in the cellar, they sped up their descent and soon joined Owen and the three fishermen.

'What's in the crate, Mr Owen?' Mantell asked.

Owen gave him that peculiar half-smile again, darting his eyes toward the doctor.

'I think you already know.'

With his foot, he gave the crate a sharp tap, and the creature inside once again sprang to life, thwacking itself fearlessly against the wooden sides.

'Why do you have it?' Buckland asked him. 'You know that we mean to return them all to whence they came.'

'Indeed,' Owen seemed to agree. 'Yet, should I not be entitled to retain one such beast for my own studies?'

'Most certainly not!' Buckland exploded.

Owen turned to look at Mary as he continued to address Buckland.

'Others seem to have bestowed such a privilege upon themselves.'

Mary's entire face tightened, her cheeks practically glowing with rage. Owen had spied on them, after all. He had known what she and Mantell had done, taking the plesiosaur to safety at the Cobb. And because of his deceit, that had now been a waste of time, and she would likely lose the opportunity to keep the creature in secret.

'I do not know of what you speak,' Buckland said, looking from Owen to Mary.

Mary could not meet his eyes but instead continued to glower at Owen.

'See for yourself,' Owen told him, pointing towards the rear of the cellar where the plesiosaur had previously been held.

'I do not need to see. I just need to hear Mary say it is untrue, and I shall be satisfied with her word.'

All eyes turned to Mary, though her gaze remained fixed on Owen. She could feel the anger continue to build up inside of her. She had to be careful, or else she would likely do to Owen what she had already done to Buckland - or, quite possibly, even worse. With those other three men standing alongside Owen, she might have fared the worst in the situation should it escalate.

'What Mr Owen says is true,' Mary said quietly but with pride. She had done what she believed to be correct, and though it may cause her trouble, she knew that, given the opportunity, she would do the same thing again.

Buckland looked at her sadly.

'Oh, Mary,' he said with quiet disappointment.

'It was my idea,' Mantell announced.

He could see the looks on Mary and Buckland's faces: Mary's indignance about what she had done and Buckland's annoyance and disappointment. He knew that the two had been friends for longer than he and Buckland, and he did not wish to see that friendship eroded and lost over this. It seemed only fair that he should be the one to take the brunt of responsibility for the actions with which he had assisted.

But Mary's anger turned swiftly and unexpectedly towards him.

'I do not need rescuing, Dr Mantell,' she hissed.

'I only meant - '

'I am not some poor, meek, helpless woman who needs a gentleman to swoop in and gallantly save the day.'

'That is not - '

'What do you hope to achieve? You are a married man, sir, and I can give you nothing in return for such an act.'

Mantell's cheeks flushed at the notion that he should be doing such a thing to win Mary's hand. Despite their difficulties, he was still very much in love with his wife, and the thought of taking another was the furthest from his mind.

'If you would let me finish!' he snapped at Mary. But then he realised that he no longer knew what else to say. He trailed off to silence for a moment. 'I only meant to help,' he finally said quietly.

'How very noble of you,' Owen sneered.

'You helped her with this?' Buckland asked him.

'I did indeed.'

Buckland looked at him, and momentarily, Mantell saw the old Buckland again. There was that mischievous twinkle in his eye, and a small smile threatened to appear at the corners of his mouth.

'I would have never thought you had it in you,' Buckland said.

'Then, sir, perhaps you do not know me so well as you thought.'

'Indeed.'

Owen clapped his hands together sharply once to draw the attention back to himself.

'This is all very touching,' he said, 'but I have work to do.'

He turned to the fishermen who had accompanied him to the cellar.

'Keep them here,' he instructed. 'No one is to leave.'

He spun around and strode across to the cellar steps as astonished cries followed behind him. Jessie was the first to reach him. He grabbed Owen's shoulder and whirled him around, arm raised and ready to strike. But the three fishermen between them were just about enough to stop the attack, holding the large man back and allowing Owen to create some distance between them.

'What are you going to do?' Mary asked.

'I have one specimen,' he told her, 'but there are plenty more out there to be "saved". Imagine having a whole menagerie of the creatures. A zoo, perhaps, or some touring exhibit, showing a whole host of creatures all discovered by me.'

'You'll be killed,' Mantell told him.

'Oh, I doubt that,' Owen replied. He smirked at the three fishermen.

'Getting someone else to do the dirty work for you doesn't cost much around these parts.'

He spun back around to the steps and strode away.

Thirty-Nine

'You have to let us out,' Buckland tried pleading with the fishermen. 'People's lives are in danger.'

'Can't do that, I'm afraid, sir,' John told him. 'I made a gentlemen's agreement with that other chap. Paying us more than a month's wages for this, he is.'

'Does a "gentlemen's agreement" stand when the person you made it with is no gentleman?' Mantell asked bitterly.

Jessie stepped towards them again. His gigantic stature was imposing, and they each took an involuntary step backwards. But they knew he was just the one man, large though he was, and between them, the three of them would surely be able to control him. They didn't especially care to test that theory out, but it gave them some degree of confidence that they could do what had been asked of them.

'What if we gave you *two* months' wages each?' Buckland asked. 'I am quite sure we could put together that kind of money between us.'

'*What?!*' Mantell exclaimed in surprise.

Buckland gave him a look, and Mantell took the hint to be quiet.

The fishermen looked at each other. The offer provided them with some degree of temptation to fight against. John spoke up on their behalf:

'Sorry, sir, but a deal's a deal.'

The other two fishermen looked disappointed; clearly, that wasn't the way their minds saw that scenario playing out. But it was what it was, and their skipper was correct in what he was saying. They couldn't very well be going back on their word, even if it was double the money they would be getting once all this was done and dusted.

'Why are you doing this, John?' Mary asked. 'I've known you all my life, and I've never seen you do something like this.'

'I'm sorry, Mary, I really am. But you don't know half of what I've done in my life.'

'Are you doing this just for the money?'

'Times are hard. You know that. Catches lately haven't been what they should be. Like something's out there gobbling up all the fish before we can get to them.'

Mary glanced across at Mantell at this statement. Chances were that John was correct in what he was saying, even if he had only meant it as a throwaway comment. Mantell picked up on that, too, and the look he returned to Mary was filled with understanding and compassion for both her and those affected by what was happening.

'You need to let us go,' Mary demanded. 'Think of all the people in the town - people you know, some people you even love - your wife and family. Think of the danger they're in because you got greedy and wanted more money.'

John flashed angry eyes at Mary.

'It's not greed, Miss Anning. It's survival,' he told her.

'Survival, indeed,' Buckland joined in. 'Survival is exactly why you should allow us out of here, so that others, too, might survive this night. The creatures could already be further away than we would like, but if we are kept here much longer, it will be too late. They will be gone with no hope of recapture. Please. If there is an ounce of decency within you, you must allow us to leave.'

John's face softened slightly, and although he and his crew did not move out of the way, something about their posture made it look as though Buckland may have been beginning to get through to them.

Much to Richard Owen's annoyance, he was finding the creatures surprisingly tricky to track down. He would hear their sounds echoing in the darkness from time to time, but whenever he was sure of where they had come from, and reached that spot, he heard the same noise from somewhere further away. The darkness, fog, and cramped, narrow streets all conspired against him.

But he would not give up hope. He already had the hylaeosaurus, which was proof that he could achieve whatever he wanted. He was sure he would have at least three or four more additions to his collection before the night's end.

If only he could find the stupid things…

And there it was:

As he turned a corner into yet another cobbled street, lined with houses that all looked the same, tiny and decrepit, and nothing like his own home back in wonderful, modern, thriving London, a creature was finally before him — standing right in the middle of the street and looking straight at him. A neovenator. It was only small, perhaps a baby, Owen deduced, its legs running shorter than his own. They were thin and spindly at that; the creature was probably fast, but Owen was sure it could not do him much damage. Its teeth were likely sharp, so he would have to avoid those as far as possible. Otherwise, it was easy pickings. He had intended for other men to do the work for him, but those he had already enlisted were otherwise occupied, and the streets he had walked through were all but deserted. As usual, he would have to carry out the task himself.

Owen pulled out a length of rope from inside his coat and approached the creature slowly.

It tilted its head, watching him with interest rather than suspicion or fear.

Stupid animal.

'That's it,' Owen whispered. 'Hold still.'

He was close to it, then. So close that he could reach out and *almost* touch it.

Just a few more steps, and it would be within his grasp.

The neovenator moved its head to the side and peered up, past Owen's shoulders, his head, up somewhere in the air behind him.

Owen felt something warm on the back of his neck.

Whatever it was, it smelled terrible.

Like the worst possible case of halitosis he had ever encountered.

A shiver ran through him as he realised what it could be.

He slowly turned his head to look over his shoulder.

Huge nostrils flared in front of his face.

The full-grown neovenator exhaled heavily.

Owen practically gagged at the smell.

The younger of the species jumped forward a few paces, closing the gap between them.

Owen dropped the rope to the ground.

He ran.

Jessie stretched himself to his full height, towering above the fishermen by a whole head. Enough was enough, he had decided. They were getting out of there now, one way or another.

He moved towards the fishermen swiftly, his face set and determined. At that point, to him, they looked like nothing more than skittles he would happily bowl straight through to get past.

'I'm warning you, Jessie,' John said, the words brave but his voice choking a little on them as they emerged from his suddenly dry throat.

Jessie advanced, and the fishermen backed away until they were all crowded at the bottom of the cellar steps. Huddled together, there was little room to manoeuvre and even less space for Jessie to get past them. He would have to go through them if he wanted to get out of there. Whether or not that was a good thing was yet to be determined.

Left behind in the middle of the room, Buckland gave Mantell a silent nudge to get his attention.

When he was sure that Mantell was looking, he cast his eyes to the crate on the floor in front of them. Mantell's own eyes widened as he realised what Buckland was suggesting. He shook his head slightly: *no!* But Buckland only nodded: *yes*, the twinkle in his eye returning at the thought of the mischief he was about to cause. Mary tapped Mantell's arm, and as he turned to look at her, she, too, nodded in agreement with Buckland's idea. Mantell gave her an expression of disbelief, but Mary shrugged. It was their only chance, and it was right there in front of them. The fishermen were still distracted by Jessie looming large right in front of them, threatening them with violence either there and then or once they were finally out of the cellar. His bulk blocked their view of the rest of the room, affording them no knowledge of what was happening behind him.

Buckland crouched on the ground and examined the crate.

The opening was on top, so they would have to be quick to make it work.

Buckland pulled on the catch, trying to loosen it. It wouldn't budge. He tugged on Mantell's sleeve, inviting him to join him on the ground. They pulled at the crate between them, attempting to free the lid. It released with a crack that was louder than they had anticipated.

'What's going on back there?' John called out.

He moved so that he could see past Jessie, peering out from behind the large body in front of him.

Buckland and Mantell were frozen with their hands on the crate lid.

'What are you doing?' John cried.

And then everything happened far too quickly for anyone to do anything about:

210

The cellar door opened, and Mrs Anning called down the steps:

'Mary? Are you alright down there?'

The fishermen turned and looked up towards the source of the voice, surprised by it.

Taking advantage of their surprise, Jessie pushed them aside and bounded up the steps for freedom.

'Don't come down here, Mother!' Mary called.

Mantell and Buckland gave the crate lid a final great tug, springing it loose. As soon as the lid was off, the hylaeosaurus within the crate poked its long head out of the box, sniffed the air and clambered out, knocking the crate on its side as it escaped. Still held in Mary's arms, Tray yapped at the creature, which turned its head towards him and snarled, but then it saw the fishermen at the bottom of the stairs and decided it was they to whom it would turn its attention.

It waddled at speed straight towards them, thrashing its spiked tail from side to side and advancing at them as they tried to flee up the steps and out of the cellar.

'Go!' Buckland cried to Mary and Mantell, who were watching everything unfold alongside him. 'Now!'

Mantell grabbed the bag of explosives, and the three of them ran to the steps just in time to see the fishermen launch themselves out of the door and into the shop, the hylaeo following closely at their tails. They sprinted out of the front door, the creature skidding and sliding to catch up.

Buckland ran to the door and slammed it shut behind them.

Mary put Tray down and attended to her mother, who had collapsed in a nervous state against the shop wall.

'What now?' Mantell asked.

'Now,' replied Buckland, 'we finally go about our business.'

FORTY

'I have never ridden before,' Mantell complained.

They had left the shop, and Buckland had led them to the stable where they had left Buckland's horse all that time ago when they first arrived in Lyme Regis. It had been less than twenty-four hours, incredibly; so much had occurred since then that it felt as though they had already been there for a week or so. Mantell realised then that they had not had the opportunity to eat since they had first arrived. He dared not mention it to Buckland, though, in case he was offered anything of an unsavoury nature that the reverend seemed to believe was edible. It was likely to get to a point soon, though, where even those mice on toast would seem an attractive option. He hoped he could hold on long enough without food that they might not tempt him.

'Although I am hopeful that most of the creatures will have stuck together, unnerved by their new surroundings, they are still likely too far apart to be able to do this by foot,' Buckland explained, patting and stroking his horse's back. 'She is fast, as you know, and the only chance we have of containing them.'

Mantell looked at the large horse in front of him, its head standing tall and proud above his own. Buckland had already saddled her, and she was ready to go. They were waiting for him.

'How do I...?' Mantell began as he angled his foot towards the stirrups, trying to figure out how to mount the creature.

Mary rolled her eyes, and Buckland tried to contain a chuckle as Mantell got one foot through the stirrup and attempted to hoist himself up, only managing to kick the poor horse and land himself the wrong way around and only halfway up the creature's back.

'Why don't you - ' Mary began to suggest.

'I can do it,' Mantell snapped.

He tried again, only managing to demonstrate that, in actual fact, he *couldn't* do it, as his foot slipped from the stirrup and he found himself falling back onto the ground.

'We're wasting time,' Mary said.

She pushed Mantell gently aside and grabbed hold of the edges of the saddle.

'I think it should be me,' Mantell protested. 'You are, after all - '

Mary cut him off.

'If I hear you say one more thing about me being a lady and how I shouldn't be doing this, that or the other, you'll feel the full force of exactly what a lady is capable of, Dr Mantell,' she threatened.

Buckland subconsciously lifted a hand to his eye and prodded at the tender flesh, Mary's threat very much real in his memory.

Mantell stepped back, raising his hands in surrender.

With a grunt, Mary heaved herself up and into the saddle, expertly manoeuvring herself in place on the first attempt.

'You are clearly more practised than I,' Mantell said with a slight bow of admiration.

Mary shrugged.

'First time I've done that, as it happens.'

Buckland did not even attempt to suppress the chuckle that time, drawing Mantell's ire.

'It will be more than just you and I that this one shows up before she is through, I am sure of it,' Buckland said, slapping his friend good-naturedly on the back. He lifted Tray from the floor and passed him up to Mary, who tucked him securely within her coat.

Mary held out her hand for Mantell. He hesitantly took hold of it and used her as support as he lifted his first foot. Buckland heaved him upwards as Mary pulled, and Mantell soon found himself sitting on the back of the horse. Buckland flung the bag of explosives across the horses' back. They had already split the load to ensure that Buckland and Jessie had enough for what they were required to do, and then Mary and Mantell should have sufficient for their specific task.

'Hold on,' Buckland advised Mantell.

'To what?' he asked, looking for anything he could cling to.

Buckland shot his eyes meaningfully towards Mary.

Mantell's face flushed.

'I do beg your pardon, Miss Anning,' he said and gingerly wrapped his arms gently around Mary's waist.

'You're going to have to hold tighter than that,' Mary told him.

'Are you quite sure?'

'If you do not wish to fall off, then, yes, I am quite sure.'

Mantell shuffled forward slightly so he was closer to Mary's back, gripping her a little tighter.

'I shan't break,' Mary promised.

'Of that, I am sure.'

Mantell and Mary looked down at Buckland and Jessie, ready to set off. The time had come. If this did not work, there was no backup plan. The creatures would be too far gone for any hope of returning them to the cavern. At that point, they would have to be individually tracked down and destroyed. But there was no knowing what damage they could cause between now and their ultimate capture. It had to be done now, and it had to be done quickly.

'Good luck to you,' Mantell said.

'And to you,' Buckland replied. He slapped the horse's rear end. 'Godspeed!'

The horse galloped out of the stable, and Mantell's grip on Mary immediately tightened, his fear of hurting her, or what people might think of his gripping a lady in such a way, replaced with fears for his own safety.

Forty-One

The hardest part was not knowing where even to begin. They knew there was little real chance of succeeding in rounding up all of the creatures, so they would have to settle on making it as many as possible. But where to start? They also knew they could not waste time thinking about it, so they allowed Buckland's horse to carry them onward. At that point, a random path seemed to be as helpful as attempting to plot a route.

They discovered their first pack of creatures quite quickly, as it happened, by the harbour.

Several species were feasting on crates of freshly caught fish, discarded by whomever it was who had brought them to shore, and left for any scavengers to find and take for their own. Larger beasts pushed aside the smaller and weaker, while the more cunning amongst them ducked between the taller one's legs, grabbed what they wanted and darted away with it before they could be stopped or rammed out of the way.

Mary urged the horse to a halt a safe distance from the group, keeping it, and themselves, hidden within the shadows as far as possible. The last thing they needed was for the creatures to notice their mode of transportation and decide that it would be more delicious than the fish they were consuming. Actually, that was the *second* last thing they needed: the absolute last thing they needed was to be noticed and *themselves* taken to look like a tasty meal.

Mary helped lower Mantell off the horse, then slid off herself, leaving Tray behind to sit on top until they returned. Mantell pulled an explosive from the bag. They nodded a signal of readiness to one another and crept through the darkness of the fog-drenched night towards near where the creatures were feasting.

Mantell carefully set up the explosive inside a crate that the creatures had already emptied of its contents. In all the time he had spent in quarries digging for fossils, he had picked up a few things from the men who worked there. There had been occasions when he had call to use them himself to extract a particularly obstinate specimen. However, he had to use them sparingly and carefully, lest the fossil he was trying to extract should itself be destroyed in the extraction process.

'Ready?' he whispered to Mary.

She nodded in agreement.

'As soon as this goes off, we need to be ready to continue to chase them forward, edging them towards the quarry,' Mantell told her.

'I am aware of the plan,' Mary scolded him.

'I know. I did not mean... I was merely...'

'Hurry along, would you?'

'Go back to the horse and be ready.'

Mary did as told, climbing back on the horse and safely tucking Tray away.

Mantell lit the fuse for the explosive.

He ran.

His movement drew the attention of some of the creatures. They lifted their heads from the fish and watched him. Some of them even began to move towards him.

Mary yanked Mantell back onto the horse, and they watched, waiting for the explosive to detonate.

More creatures became interested in the pair, plus their ride.

'Come on, come on, come on,' Mantell whispered.

'Have you done it right?' Mary asked.

'Of course I have done it right,' he snapped.

'Only, nothing is happening.'

'I can see that.'

'Why don't you - '

An almighty *boom* cut off Mary's words. The crate exploded with a great flash of fire, taking out other crates nearby and sending wood and pieces of fish flying into the air. The creatures screeched in fear and ran from the explosion, heading away from the harbour. Despite previously fighting together over the fish, they seemed to find comfort in numbers and travelled as a group away from the site.

The plan was working.

The creatures were moving as they needed them to.

There was just the simple task remaining of rounding them all up and ensuring they all travelled in the right direction.

The next hour or two continued similarly. They had to approach the situation like a shepherd might try to round up his sheep, although this flock of creatures had considerably sharper teeth and claws than any sheep they had seen before.

Mary and Mantell darted around the town on Buckland's horse, setting explosives here and there, where they found groups of creatures, forcing them onward, then occasionally having to gallop to the side streets for the smaller beasts, using the horse to draw them into position, much as a sheepdog might do.

They were soon directing a large flock of the creatures, and Mantell had become so adept at sorting the explosives that he found he no longer had even to dismount the horse to set them off. He would set them up as they rode to their target, light the fuse whilst on horseback and drop it into place at the right time. Not having to dismount made it far easier for them to keep the creatures together, not allowing them to stray away from the main group for too long. There were a few stragglers they lost here and there, but they decided that it would be easier to try and "tidy up" those last few later; so long as the majority made it back into the cavern, Mary could live with that.

Having reached a point where they had not encountered more of the creatures for several minutes, Mary and Mantell decided they must have collected the vast majority.

'Let's get going,' Mantell suggested. 'The roads we took to the quarry before were narrow, so we should have little trouble keeping them under control.'

'I hope so.'

As they headed to the outskirts of the town, Mantell continued watching for anything they might have missed.

A figure darted between two houses, running as fast as it could.

A moment later, a small creature followed after it.

Close behind that, a much larger beast brought up the rear.

The figure appeared again, dashing across the street, trying to find sanctuary. Slightly closer this time, Mantell immediately recognised him.

Richard Owen.

They had a plan to stick with, and Owen had caused them nothing but trouble. Mantell could quite easily ignore what he had seen, putting it down to a shadow, a trick of the light, a deer, perhaps. But he knew what he had seen and could not bring himself to turn his back on someone in trouble. He was, after all, a medical doctor by trade, and the ethical code of such a position meant that he had to help those in need, regardless of personal opinions about them.

He sighed.

'Stop a moment,' he told Mary.

'Whatever for?'

'I need to sort out a situation.'

He pulled some explosives from the bag as Mary halted the horse.

'The creatures will get away,' Mary told him.

'You continue,' he said, jumping down with now practised ease. 'I shall deal with this and catch you up.'

A large creature roared somewhere close by.

'At least,' Mantell continued, 'I hope to catch you up.'

'Be careful,' Mary told him, and he could tell from her eyes that she meant it.

'Make haste. Don't let them get away.'

Mary set the horse in motion.

'I shall see you at the quarry,' she called back to him as she rode away.

'I do hope so,' Mantell whispered to himself as he watched her disappear into the fog.

He stood there for a moment, alone in the street, with explosives in his hands, but he had no clue what his plan would entail.

FORTY-TWO

The collapsed rocks blocking the exit through which the creatures had previously escaped the cavern were huge and heavy. Even Jessie was struggling with the weight of some of them, and it quickly became apparent to Buckland that there was no way that just the two of them could shift it all out of the way to re-create the opening. Even fifty men working together would be unlikely to be able to perform such a feat.

Buckland stood back, examining the area, his hand stroking his chin. He looked around to see what was available to him. Any tools he could form from the natural landscape to fashion some type of tool that might help them move the rocks and apply the rules of physics to the situation.

'It's obvious, isn't it,' Jessie said, standing beside him and imitating Buckland's posture as though it might make him, somehow, more intelligent. His words should have been a question but came out more as a statement of fact, which riled Buckland, though he did not know why.

'Would you be quiet? Please. I'm thinking.'

'I know that, but, like I say: it's obvious.'

'*What* is obvious?' Buckland snapped.

'How to shift the rocks.'

'My good man, if it was so obvious, I am quite sure that I would have thought of it by now.'

Jessie shrugged.

'Maybe I'm just smarter than you,' he sniffed, matter of fact, not a trace of boasting or pride in his voice.

Buckland chuckled.

'Yes. I am sure you are a very smart man,' he replied, his voice dripping with condescension.

Buckland stared at the rocks in silence, pondering their next move.

Jessie allowed him a moment but then piped up again.

'We just blow 'em up, don't we,' he said.

'We can't just - ' Buckland began.

Then his eyes widened and sparkled with realisation. He moved his hand away from his chin and held a finger in the air as if he could feel the idea forming in the atmosphere.

'That's it!' he cried. 'I have it! We must use some of the explosives we already have to blast our way through those rocks and create a new opening.'

'That's exactly what I - ' Jessie began complaining.

'No time to lose!' Buckland cut him off. 'To work!'

When he agreed to join his friend William Buckland on a trip to the coast, Mantell expected a gentle, relaxed journey, followed by some time examining fossils and reading through their associated papers. That had promised to be the most exciting thing to have happened to him throughout the previous year: an actual, near-complete, full-size plesiosaur fossil! He had never thought that one would be discovered in his lifetime, never mind the opportunity to be one of the first to examine it. Alongside studying the fossil, he thought a pleasant stroll in the fresh sea air would do him good, breathing in the fresh atmosphere away from the increasingly industrialised London. The slower pace of life and the gentle nature of the locals had been something to look forward to. Although it was, in essence, a scientific expedition on which he had set out with Buckland, he also thought it a good - and rare - opportunity to afford himself a small break.

Had he been given a chance to sit down and think about where else that "break" might take him and what side roads he might end up taking along the way, never in a million years would he have thought that he would be treading cautiously through the foggy streets of Lyme Regis on the trail of a prehistoric creature that should by all accounts no longer exist, in the hopes of rescuing a gentleman he had the misfortune of meeting at one of Buckland's luncheons.

Yet, that was precisely where he somehow found himself.

He trod quickly but as quietly as possible in the direction he had seen Owen going. Stomping footsteps sounded from somewhere up in front of him, clearly belonging to the larger of the creatures rather than Owen himself. He wondered again why he was doing this; he could easily have stayed on the horse with Mary and gone with her to the quarry.

But his sense of moral duty prevailed, and he still had no plan. He had two explosives with him, and there were two creatures. His ultimate end goal was still to get them to the quarry so that they might live out their remaining days peacefully, but how he would be able to get them all the way there with so little to work with, he was as yet unsure.

He turned a corner onto Clappentail Lane, very much aware that he was now on the outskirts of the town. If he lost the creatures now, there would be no hope of tracking them down again.

But, as luck would have it, he saw them up ahead.

They were standing at the roadside, staring at the top of a tall tree.

The large neovonator bashed against the trunk, shaking the bare branches and sending loose, dead twigs tumbling to the ground. The younger of the two dashed excitedly around the tree, jumping into the air and snapping its jaw towards the higher branches as if it thought it could leap high enough to reach.

Mantell followed the tree trunk from the ground upwards with his eyes. A figure was nestled amongst the branches, clinging on for dear life, mere feet away from the giant jaws of the taller creature. Every time the tree was shaken, he held that bit tighter, swaying with the force of the impact. From where he stood, the person's features were vague, softened and blurred by the fog between Mantell and the tree, but Mantell could not for a moment imagine that it was anyone other than Richard Owen.

He stepped to the opposite side of the street to the tree and, crouched low to the ground, trod forward, trying to avoid being seen but making his visibility of the situation a little clearer. The creatures had their backs towards him, as yet unaware of his presence.

Owen, though, spotted him almost immediately from his high vantage point.

'You there!' he cried out. 'Do something!'

Mantell made an exaggerated show of putting his fingers to his lips and pleading for Owen's silence.

'For the love of God, help me, would you!'

Be quiet! Mantell screamed inside his head. As yet, the creatures must have thought that Owen was shouting for the sake of it, but it was only a matter of time before he did something stupid that drew attention towards Mantell instead.

And Mantell did not have to wait too long for that time to happen.

'Can you hear me?' Owen screamed.

He pulled a branch from the tree and flung it towards Mantell over the heads of the creatures. It landed with a thwack no more than three feet from where Mantell crouched.

The larger neovonator paid it no interest, but the younger followed its path and trotted after it like a dog fetching a stick for its master.

It ducked its head and sniffed at the stick. Discovering that it was nothing edible, it turned and was about to head back to the tree when it suddenly stopped. It lifted its head and sniffed the air. Mantell backed away, trying to duck further into invisibility. But his scent had been noticed. The neovonator stepped forward; its head cocked as it peered into the gloom. Mantell backed into the wall of a building.

There was nowhere left for him to go.

The neovonator passed through the fog blanket and saw his prey properly for the first time.

Mantell could have sworn that he saw the creature grin a little.

It turned to look over its shoulder and made a sound within its throat, calling to the larger of the two.

The full-grown creature looked towards the younger and seemed to say something back. They called to each other as though having a full, though brief conversation, as Mantell edged his way along the wall he had found himself against. The larger knocked against the tree again, harder this time, rattling it right through to the roots. Somehow, Owen managed to cling on as the creature strode away from him towards the infant, taking little more than a couple of long strides to reach its side.

It lowered its head and moved closer to Mantell until he could feel the warmth of its breath on his face.

There was no way that he could run to escape them. It was too late for that; they would be upon him within seconds.

He realised that he had no choice.

There was no chance that he would be able to get them safely to the quarry.

There was little chance that he, himself, would be getting out of there alive unless he did this one thing.

He slowly pulled out an explosive, keeping two eyes on the creatures before him, expecting them to pounce at any second.

He closed his eyes and lit the fuse.

The sudden emergence of flame startled the creatures, and they took an involuntary step back.

Perhaps… Mantell wondered.

He held the lit fuse in front of him at arm's length.

The creatures kept their distance.

He moved along the wall, then away from it, stepping around so he was back in the middle of the street. The creatures followed him, but they were still wary of the flame.

Mantell smiled. He was doing it. He had a method of escape.

But then it dawned on him: he was holding a lit explosive.

He couldn't keep hold of that forever, or even more than a few seconds, before it went off.

He panicked and threw the explosive over the top of the creatures, as far away from him as possible.

The neovonators watched it sail through the air. It landed on the ground behind them.

No one moved for a long, tense moment.

Then the ground exploded. A mighty *boom* rang out as flames erupted, and stone and dirt were flung into the sky, showering down upon them.

Mantell was already running as the creatures roared.

They ran away from the explosion.

He was unsure whether they were running for safety or chasing after Mantell.

The one thing he was sure of was that there were two angry creatures gaining ground on him quickly. The larger of the beasts had its head close to the ground, its jaw wide open, displaying a dazzling array of long, sharp teeth, as if it was ready to scoop Mantell up within it as it reached him, without so much as stopping.

Mantell saw the jaw loom larger, the black hole of the creature's throat ready to welcome him inside.

As he ran, he prepared his final explosive. He had hoped that it would not come to this, that he might be able to save both himself and the creatures. But it was clear that there was no longer any path that would save them all.

He lit the fuse and held tight to the explosive for as long as possible.

He felt a bump against the back of his legs.

He almost fell forward but managed to save himself just in time.

He risked a look over his shoulder.

The neovonator was right there; the beast's mouth had brushed against him, almost sending him to the ground.

It was time.

He twisted around and flung the explosive forward, launching it into the creature's mouth.

It gulped in surprise and stopped in its tracks.

The younger of the two skidded to a halt and cocked its head inquisitively at its elder.

Mantell backed away, hoping above all else that the fuse had remained lit.

He ducked down a little, trying to shield himself from the aftermath of his actions.

And then the creature exploded — a violent, sticky, grotesque explosion. Slabs of the creature's flesh, shards of bone and dollops of internal organs were flung viciously away from where the creature had stood less than a second beforehand. Mantell cowered as the ungodly showers fell upon and around him, and he wondered, strangely, how Buckland would have reacted to it raining blood as though they were back in Egypt at the time of the plagues.

As the squelchy pitter-patter of falling debris subsided, Mantell opened his eyes. He wiped some gloop off his face and stood up straight. There was an almighty mess in the street. The younger creature was still alive, but it paid him no attention: it was working away at the splattered remains of the elder creature, gnawing happily at whatever seemed to be edible. Nature, red in tooth and claw, it seemed.

Mantell stepped past the feasting creature, receiving no more than a cursory glance in his direction as he tip-toed by. He stood at the bottom of the tree where Owen was still hiding.

'Come down from there,' he called up.

'Is it safe?' Owen asked.

'As far as possible,' Mantell replied.

Owen hesitated, unsure whether to believe him, but, seeing that Mantell had yet to be devoured, decided that it could not be especially *un*safe out there at present.

He laboriously clambered back down the tree, awkwardly pushing aside twigs and reaching nervously out with his feet for branches to stand upon. He practically fell the last few feet, landing heavily on his backside on the ground below.

Mantell held out a hand to help him, which Owen begrudgingly took.

'What are you doing here?' Owen asked as he brushed the dirt and twigs from his clothes.

'You're very welcome,' Mantell replied with annoyance and sarcasm.

'Yes, yes, thank you, of course,' Owen threw up a vague acknowledgement of his gratitude. 'But how did you get out of the cellar?'

'We escaped,' he said simply.

'And the creature I had captured?'

Mantell shrugged.

'That escaped, too.'

'That is a pity,' Owen said.

He turned to look over his shoulder at the fallen feasting neovonator and, more particularly, the puddle that had once been the larger of the two.

'A great pity,' he muttered thoughtfully.

Forty-Three

The process wasn't going as quickly or smoothly as Buckland had hoped. They had managed to successfully re-open the entrance to the cavern, using the explosives as Jessie had suggested, but now, rigging the remaining explosives to all detonate at the same time, causing the entrance to collapse in on itself one more time was proving to be less straightforward. He had tasked Jessie with clearing as much rubble from the entrance as possible to ensure there was a clear path for the creatures to return to the place they had known as their home for who knew how many years. Buckland had placed the responsibility for wiring up the explosives on himself. He knew exactly how they needed to be laid out and exactly what the outcome of the blast should be. If anything went wrong, then the blame would fall solely on him. But if it went right, as he expected, he would have the satisfaction of a job well done.

When taking on the task, though, he had not yet thought through exactly how he would carry out such a job. The cavern entrance was high, and the rocks around it were loose and treacherous. He needed to run the explosives around the top rim of the entrance, which meant clambering up there at great risk to life and limb.

It was this precarious position in which he found himself when a great rumbling vibrated across the quarry floor. Loose rubble fell from close by, and the whole ground shook.

'What is that?' Jessie asked, looking up from his clearance task.

'That,' replied Buckland, 'is the sound of our time running out.'

The two men stood and watched the direction from which the sound was coming.

It was getting louder, nearer, with each passing second.

No longer just a distant rumbling, but now the unmistakable sound of feet running - hundreds of them, stomping, sprinting; some large, some small, but a great mass of feet between them.

And then they were visible: a horde of creatures entering the quarry and heading straight in their direction.

But they were not yet ready: the creatures could get back into the cavern, but nothing stopped them from returning, meaning that all of their work had been for nought.

Mary brought up the rear of the pack, riding atop Buckland's horse. She skirted around the creatures and galloped to where Buckland and Jessie were working. Tray yapped a greeting from within Mary's coat as he poked his small head out to look around.

Buckland looked at Mary, concerned that only one person was riding the horse.

'Where is Gideon?'

'He will join us shortly. He stopped to help... someone,' Mary replied, unsure of the response she would have received should she have let Buckland know that it was Richard Owen that Mantell was busy assisting.

Buckland smiled slightly.

'Always the doctor,' he said with a hint of sadness, despite the smile.

'Are you ready?' Mary asked.

'Not quite,' Buckland admitted.

He looked out upon the sea of creatures that now ambled aimlessly within the quarry. Any sense of purpose or direction had gone now that they were not being forced ever forward by explosions being set off behind them. Unrest was growing within the group, and they started turning on each other, jostling for space. Some were beginning to wander back towards where Mary had brought them into the quarry, looking to leave.

'You need to send them this way,' Buckland told her. 'Now.'

Mary's eyes widened in alarm. Buckland was half-crouched on top of the very place through which the creatures needed to go, his balance only maintained by clinging on as tightly as he could. One large creature knocking against the side of the rock could send him tumbling down amongst them, an easy target to be trampled or devoured.

'You'll be killed!' Mary objected.

'There's no time for arguments. They will leave again if we don't force them forward immediately.'

Mary looked at the creatures and could see that Buckland was right. To delay much longer would mean disaster.

She nodded her head slightly in agreement.

'Very well,' she said. 'But work quickly. Get it done and get away from there as soon as possible.'

'You have my word.'

Mary looked at him for a long moment, this strange, clever and ultimately brave man. His eye was still swollen and bruised from where she had hit him, and she wished now that she could take that back, but all she could do was forgive him for what had gone before. His actions now made up for past events.

She nodded again, unsure what else to say or do, then pulled the reigns on the horse, sending it into a gallop, away from the entrance and around the side of the creature swarm.

Buckland watched her go, then turned his attention back to Jessie.

'Let's get this done,' he said. 'And quickly.'

At the rear of the crowd of creatures, Mary saw that a single explosive would not have the required impact. They were spread too far apart, and one detonation would cause the group to drift in a specific direction rather than drive them forward to where they needed to be. She would have to set the explosives out across the quarry floor and detonate each in sequence for any chance of success.

She looked in the bag.

There were three explosives left.

Placed correctly, that should be sufficient.

She stopped the horse and started linking the three devices with a fuse, ensuring they might all detonate in a chain reaction. Satisfied that everything was as it should be, she moved the horse forward and dropped the first explosives towards the horde's rear, ensuring it was positioned to drive them forward straight away.

Next came the tricky bit:

She would need to navigate the creatures to place the other devices, drawing a line of detonations leading directly to where she needed them to be.

She decided that galloping into the midst of the beasts would be unwise: seeing another creature - in this instance, a horse - moving at speed among them might make them think that they were being attacked, and so turn on the horse, and in turn Mary also.

Instead, she trod the horse forward slowly and cautiously, trailing the length of the fuse behind them as they went.

Buckland's horse wasn't happy about it, she could tell. For every two steps it took forward, it took one back, unsure about the swinging tails and sharp teeth and claws surrounding it. Mary stroked the horse's neck gently and whispered soothing words to it, trying to keep it as calm as possible, hoping she would not be thrown from its back in fear or agitation.

Halfway into the group, she carefully dropped the second explosive to the ground. This one should ensure that the beasts veered towards the right whilst still stampeding forward, moving in the general direction that was required of them.

She continued the slow, steady approach until she reached the point where the final explosive should be laid, directly across from the cavern opening, a final push for the creatures to go to their final (*not resting place, which sounded like they were being sent to their death*) destination.

Mary saw Buckland and Jessie still hard at work preparing the way. She did not wish to disturb them, as she knew there was little time left for them to complete the job. Instead, she left them to it and slowly turned around to the edge of the group, picking up speed once she was on the outside, hoping that none of the creatures were watching her and ready to strike.

She made it.

It was time to light the fuse and set things in motion.

She could only hope and pray that Buckland and Jessie got out of there in time. Once the fuse was lit, their safety - their *lives* - was out of her hands.

She lowered herself off the horse, taking Tray with her and setting him beside her on the ground.

Mary crouched beside the tail end of the fuse and pulled out the little device Buckland had given her. She flicked the switch. A spark formed, which became a flame. She looked across the quarry, towards where Buckland and Jessie were working, but the creatures were blocking her view of the progress being made. She had no choice.

She held the flame to the fuse until it lit, got back to her feet, grabbed Tray from the ground, and backed away. Mary held Tray close as she watched the flame travel the length of the fuse, edging closer and closer towards the first explosive.

It reached its first destination, and for the briefest moment, nothing happened. Mary thought that everything had gone wrong and there was no longer any possibility of the plan succeeding. It was all her fault, and now there was no way of stopping the creatures. But that moment lasted longer in Mary's mind than in reality, and she was soon thrown backwards by the force of the explosion. The sound echoed wildly throughout the quarry, rattling in her ears, and rock flew into the sky, launched from the ground into the heavens, only to inevitably fall back down again in a shower of stones.

It had worked.

The first explosive had detonated successfully, and the creatures, terrified by the sight of the flames and flying stones and the incredible noise of the explosion, roared and squealed and ultimately did as they were supposed to: they headed forward, away from the rear of the quarry, and towards the cavern entrance. A couple of them were too close to where the explosive had been and did not survive the blast. Mary saw their fallen bodies as the dust settled and couldn't help but feel terrible about that. But it was inevitable that a few would be lost; she just hoped there would not be too many more.

The detonation of the first explosive lit the fuse linking it to the second, and the flame on that, too, travelled forward, seeking something else to feast upon.

It reached the explosive and set that one off as planned.

Once again, the explosives were doing the expected job as the creatures fled this new blast, veering to the right-hand side of the quarry. Mary climbed back onto Buckland's horse and slowly trod across the ground, heading towards the final explosive that would send the creatures straight back into the cavern. Then, it was down to Buckland and Jessie to trigger their explosives and trap the beasts back inside, sealing the entrance from any possible escape.

The flame travelled the length of the fuse towards the final explosive.

It reached its destination.

And...

Nothing happened.

Mary stared at the device, expecting it to detonate at any second. Practically *willing* it to go off.

But, still, nothing.

The creatures, previously huddled together in safety over the ongoing onslaught that seemed to be going on against them, began drifting apart.

'No, no, no, no, no,' Mary whispered to herself as she watched the group start to break apart.

If they got too far apart now, too far away from where they needed to be, there was no chance of getting them back together. All of the explosives had been used. There was no other way. Mary wondered about charging at them, just her, Tray and Buckland's horse. Perhaps she could scare them enough to drive them forward. But, in comparison, she was not a fearsome sight, and she was pretty sure she would be thrown from the horse before she could make it into the group.

'The fuse may have come loose,' a voice said behind her, startling her from her reverie.

She spun around and looked down to see Mantell and Owen standing behind her, Owen a couple of feet back and refusing to look at her, both men sweaty, exhausted and dishevelled.

'You made it!' Mary cried with delight. She turned her attention to Owen. 'And you're here, too,' she said bitterly.

Mantell nodded towards the creatures, particularly a small faction splitting off from the others.

'They're starting to get away,' he told Mary as if she was not already aware of that. 'See if you can round them back together, and I'll deal with the explosive.'

'You could be trampled.'

Mantell shrugged slightly.

'I see no other option.'

'What should I do?' Owen asked, though it was clear from his face that his offer of assistance was not something he particularly wanted to give.

'Stay out of the way,' Mary snapped at him.

Owen held up his hands as if to acknowledge that he knew he wasn't welcome.

'Be careful,' Mary told Mantell and trotted to the creatures.

They must have been more afraid than they looked, as the sight of the advancing horse made them back away slightly, rejoining the main group, but not without making sure that Mary knew they weren't happy, baring their teeth and hissing at her as they retreated.

In the meantime, Mantell worked his way between the creatures. They had initially paid no attention to anything else, but now that nothing much was happening, they were actively looking for things to do. Things to eat. He ducked down low, trying to avoid their line of sight as much as possible, but the height differences between each creature made that near impossible. He opted to try and avoid the largest-looking ones in the hope that he might be able to outrun, or perhaps even incapacitate, smaller animals, should they cause any trouble.

He reached the explosive without consequence and knelt beside it on the ground. He was correct in his original assumption: the fuse had indeed come loose. Hardly surprising, he thought, with all of the creatures stomping around. They were lucky that it hadn't been wholly crushed underfoot. Mantell set to work, trying to reattach the fuse. It wasn't quite as clear-cut as he had initially thought, and there was a little damage to the side. It was still fixable, but it would take him a little longer than he had anticipated.

A baryonyx spotted him. Alone and vulnerable, and something altogether different from the other creatures that roamed nearby. It tilted its large head, taking him in with its small eyes, set into a skull that seemed like a million miles from the end of its enormous jaw.

It stepped forward on its huge hind legs, its shorter forearms hanging limply in front; they would be useful for tearing the human meat apart once incapacitated.

Mantell, engrossed in his work, failed to notice the approaching creature.

It took another step forward.

And another.

Closing the gap between itself and its food.

Mary had been watching Mantell intently, waiting for the very moment that he completed his task. The giant creature advancing upon him drew her attention. She watched it carefully. There: it was *definitely* heading towards him.

A wall of creatures separated her, mounted still on Buckland's horse, and Mantell, hard at work on the quarry floor. She didn't think she could get through them in time to reach him.

'Get out of there!' Mary yelled across to him instead, hoping that would not be enough to draw the attention to the horde of creatures upon herself.

But her shout was lost in the quarry's noise, the growling, roaring, grunting, scuffling, and stomping that continued unabated. She had not drawn the attention of the creatures, but she had also failed to draw Mantell's.

Tray seemed to understand like dogs sometimes do. That strange second nature that allowed them to work things out or sense them in ways that humans could never comprehend. He pulled himself loose from the covers of Mary's clothing, and before she could react, he had leapt from the back of the horse onto the ground.

'Tray!' Mary shouted, but to no avail.

The little dog wove between the legs of the creatures, ducking, dodging and swerving to avoid being stepped on by the oblivious beasts. He reached the spot where Mantell was working, skidded to a halt and turned around to face the baryonyx.

Tray barked at the beast.

The baryonyx stared down at him. A look that seemed to be wondering if this tiny little creature, which didn't look like anything of a threat, could in any way be a danger to itself, a beast with its long legs, scaled back and huge jaw lined with sharp teeth. This tiny creature that dared to stand before it and effectively *shout* in its direction as though warning it away. Tray growled, and the sound was practically lost between where he stood protecting Mantell and the baryonyx glaring down at him.

Mantell looked up for the first time. He noticed Tray first and wondered what the dog was doing there alone. Then his eyes drifted past the dog and up the legs of the baryonyx, and he swiftly understood that Tray was protecting him from this gigantic creature that had materialised before him without him even realising. *Too wrapped up in your own work to notice what's going on around you*, his wife had always told him. Here was proof of that and that not heeding your wife's words could land you in danger.

Mantell jerked forward and grabbed Tray from the ground, pulling him against his body for shelter. The baryonyx roared and stepped forward. Mantell closed his eyes tightly and cowered.

But then he felt his arms suddenly empty.

He opened his eyes.

A pteranodon was flapping away with Tray gripped in its claws.

The baryonyx roared again, this time at the flying creature. It snapped at the air with its great jaws, but the pteranodon was out of reach.

They were too far away for Mantell to be able to do anything about it.

He had completed the work on the fuse, so that had to be his priority.

Mantell lit the fuse with one eye watching the pteranodon swooping across the quarry. He ran in the direction of the flying creature, rushing after them in a perhaps ridiculous hope that he might be able to save Tray.

The explosive went off.

Another great roar sounded across the quarry as fire and rock sprang up from the ground. The creatures were once again thrown into a panic but forced forward.

Shocked by the sudden noise, the pteranodon dropped Tray in a panic.

Mantell leapt forward. He caught the dog but continued to tumble forward, rolling and toppling onto the ground. He curled into a ball as the horde of creatures flocked across and around him, desperately trying to flee the blast.

Buckland watched as the great swarm galloped towards him. The explosives were nearly ready, but they weren't *quite* as prepared as he had hoped. But now they had no choice. If he and Jessie stayed where they were, they would be crushed to death, either by the creatures or the rocks that would be falling when the explosives were detonated.

'Go. Now,' he told Jessie.

The large man didn't need to be told twice.

He darted to the side of the quarry. Buckland half-skidded, half-leapt down from his place above the cavern entrance.

The creatures marched onward, following the path set for them.

It was working.

They were heading directly for the cavern.

Buckland saw Mary was again bringing up the rear, using his horse to help round up the stragglers so that they were all continuing to advance.

'Light the fuse,' he told Jessie.

'It's too soon,' came the reply.

'Do it - now! We can't chance them escaping again.'

Jessie huffily lit the end of the fuse on their side of the cavern. It sparked to life, the flame trailing along the fuse towards the first explosive.

'I would stand back if I were you,' Buckland suggested.

Both men moved as far from the scene of future destruction as they could.

The creatures entered the cavern, rows at a time, squeezing and squashing their way in. They may have recognised the scent of the place; maybe it seemed like a natural refuge from the madness outside. Whatever it was, they made no qualms about venturing back into that space.

Buckland watched the flame continue to move.

'Come on, come on, come on,' he muttered to himself.

The last of the creatures were inside.

The flame reached the explosive.

Nothing happened.

'Come on,' Buckland repeated his mantra.

The first explosive went off. Rocks fell across the cavern entrance; smaller stone fragments whizzed into the sky, launching towards those watching.

A moment later, a second explosive ignited.

Then, a third.

And a fourth.

Several layers of rock completely covered the entrance. Nothing would be getting through there any time soon. A cloud of dust hung in the air as smaller rocks and stones continued to tumble, skittering down the fallen rock face.

Buckland turned to speak with Jessie.

Mary looked over her shoulder to where the shape of Gideon Mantell lay, curled up, on the ground in the middle of the quarry. He wasn't moving.

Tray stood beside Mantell's still form, nudging at him with his nose and whining quietly. Mantell was covered in dust from the stampede that had gone on around him, his clothes torn and filthy. Mary crouched beside him and hoped above all hopes that he had survived, especially after he had kept Tray safe and unharmed during the ordeal.

The dog forced his nose through the crack between Mantell's arm and his face and licked at him, cleaning his cheek of the dirt that caked it and perhaps hoping to use the healing power of his tongue to revive him.

Mary stroked Tray and tried to pull him to her so they could comfort one another, but the dog did not want to know. He pulled back and immediately resumed licking at Mantell's face.

An arm moved weakly and gently bashed away the dog.

Mary couldn't help but let out a gasp of surprise.

Mantell was alive!

She gently reached out and eased Mantell onto his back so she could see him better. Even more excited now, Tray furiously lapped at the newly exposed parts of Mantell's face. Mantell shooed him away. He finally opened his eyes.

'I never should have saved you,' he croaked hoarsely at the dog.

Mary smiled.

She held out her hand and helped Mantell to sit up. Buckland and Jessie joined them, then, and Richard Owen scowled from where he had kept himself out of the way during the incident, just as he had been told.

'I'm glad you're okay,' Buckland said.

'As am I,' Mantell replied.

He grabbed Buckland's arm for support, lifting himself upright to stand with them and not be looked down upon.

'You should go now. Be with your families,' Buckland told Mantell and Mary. He turned his attention to Owen. 'And you go back to wherever it was you crawled out from. Jessie and I will finish off here.'

'Thank you, William,' Mantell said as he shook Buckland's hand in genuine gratitude. 'We have some tidying up to do before I can return to London. A few lone creatures to round up, though I fear they will have to be... dealt with... separately.'

The sadness about that admission was apparent to Mary, and she felt it, too. She tenderly rubbed Mantell's arm in sympathy.

'I shall help you with that,' she told the doctor.

He smiled slightly, glad for the company on such a barbaric mission.

'Mary,' Buckland said with a slight bow.

'Reverend Buckland,' she replied, mimicking his movements.

Mary and Mantell walked side by side, away from the cavern and the creatures contained within. Owen followed a few steps back, realising that his presence was neither needed nor wanted.

Mantell turned to look over his shoulder at the sight of all that had gone before. The place had held so much mystery and wonder when he first saw it, having followed Mary there with Buckland. The discovery of a whole ecosystem, hidden for millennia in a cavern on the south coast of England. A truly incredible thing. But perhaps it was never meant to have been discovered. The creatures had been living there without disturbance for year after year, and the moment humans invaded their space (excluding Mary, of course, who had been able to dwell among them for some time prior), things went horribly, horribly wrong. Now, the creatures were back in there, and Mantell hoped they would stay that way for as long as they could survive. No one else must ever discover the place. On his return to London, he would see to it that the quarry be sealed off and the area where the cavern was located be made a protected site that no one could dig, excavate, or detonate upon the property. He would somehow find the funds to purchase the land himself if it came to it.

He looked across the cavern wall and only then noticed the extra explosives.

They were attached along the length of the wall. More of them than had been used to seal the cavern entrance. The explosion would be enough to -

Buckland gave Jessie a nod, where he stood on the other side of the cavern wall to Buckland. Jessie nodded in acknowledgement, and the two men ignited their individual ends of the fuse that linked all of the explosives together.

'No - wait!' Mantell cried, rushing back towards the wall.

But too late.

The first explosives detonated, causing the second to go off, then the third, then the fourth:

BOOM-BOOM-BOOM-BOOM-BOOM-BOOM-BOOM!

So many detonations in such a short time, Mantell felt as though the inside of his head was rattling at the noise. The whole cavern wall came crashing down, collapsing into a gigantic pile of rubble and dust. There was little hope for the creatures inside; they would surely have been crushed under the weight of the falling rocks.

Mary rushed at Buckland, her fist raised and ready to strike.

'What have you done?' she yelled.

Mantell grabbed her just in time to prevent her from giving Buckland a matching pair of bruised eyes.

'What needed doing,' Buckland replied.

'You tricked us,' Mantell said.

'This was the only sensible solution.'

Mary struggled in Mantell's grasp, trying to get at Buckland. Mantell thought momentarily about letting her go, allowing her to give Buckland everything he deserved. But once again, his morals prevented him from doing what he would have liked to have been done.

'You're safe,' Buckland continued. 'Your family is safe. The town is safe. We did the right thing.'

'*You* did it,' Mary hissed. '*You.*'

Mantell felt Mary go limp in his hands, her anger seeping from her as exhaustion took over. He let her go.

'Go home,' Buckland said. 'It's over.'

And then human nature took over from his morals, and before he realised what he was doing, Mantell swung his fist towards his old friend, knocking him to the ground.

It was the first time he had ever hit anyone. In the immediate moment afterwards, he wondered why he had never done it before. The feeling of power, that raw moment of violence, was intoxicating. But then the pain set into his knuckles, bruised from the impact with Buckland's cheekbone. He rubbed them as he looked down at Buckland sitting pitifully on the ground in the dirt, his hand pressed gently against the second eye to be bruised in as many days.

They stood, Mary and Mantell, looking at the rubble and dust slowly descending, a cloud easing to the ground and gradually clearing.

'Come on, Tray,' Mary said, scooping her dog into her arms.

Mantell gave Buckland one last look, then turned and joined Mary in finally leaving that place.

Jessie held out a large hand for Buckland and jerked him onto his feet. Buckland shrugged away from his grip, his pride hurting almost as much as his face. He brushed down his clothes, shedding the layer of dust that clung to them, and made his way to his horse.

'Can I join you?' Jessie called after him.

Buckland ignored the request, climbed onto his horse's back and trotted away.

Jessie watched him go and gave him a dismissive wave of the hand, along with a choice string of words he was glad his mother wasn't around to hear him using.

He looked back towards the destruction site and was surprised to see Richard Owen still there. He thought Owen would have skulked away before the others, wanting to avoid any possible consequences for his actions. But instead, he was standing, staring at the rubble that had been created mere moments before. Jessie stepped up behind the other man and gripped his shoulder.

Owen jumped at the touch.

He spun around and saw Jessie there, his face changing from alarm to suspicious delight in a fraction of a second.

'How would you like to earn yourself a few pounds?' Owen asked.

'What do you need?' the large man replied without hesitation.

Owen smiled as he slipped something from his pocket: a bottle containing some particularly potent sleeping tonic he may have acquired somewhere along the way.

He and Jessie stepped towards the rubble, where Owen had spotted movement within the debris — an almost imperceptible motion underneath the rocks and dust. Something moving.

Something still alive.

III

"...it would not be wonderful to meet a Megalosaurus, forty feet long or so, waddling like an elephantine lizard up Holborn Hill."

Bleak House, Charles Dickens

FORTY-FOUR

Lyme Regis.

Mary had slept fitfully following her return home after the events at the quarry. Her dreams and thoughts had been troubled by all that had happened. She had thought and believed that they would save the creatures - her creatures - in the cavern, allowing them to go about their existence safely and securely, albeit without her. But the one person in the world who she thought would understand, who she thought would respect the sheer volume of scientific analysis that could have come from the situation, who she thought was her *friend*, had betrayed her. His fear of the implications of what he had seen had overwhelmed him and caused him to act rashly, working against everything for which a man of science should stand.

Buckland could try to rationalise it as much as he wanted, but he had murdered those creatures. There were no two ways about it. *Thou shalt not kill* was surely applicable to *all* living creatures, not just those made in His image. Especially when they were such extraordinary, unique creatures. He had killed them and tried to justify it.

And Mary herself had been an unwilling accomplice.

She and Gideon Mantell had spent several further hours hunting out stragglers from the horde but had been unsuccessful in finding any. That came as a relief to both of them, as neither had looked forward to doing what they knew had to be done to protect the town's residents. The creatures were no doubt out there, somewhere, but hopefully, they would find a quiet place to live out their remaining days and not be of bother to anyone.

After the fruitless hunt, they had all gone their separate ways, and

Mary had brought Tray home.

She had gone straight to her bed and laid there for what felt like hours, tossing and turning, thinking and wondering, vaguely aware at times that her mother had crept in to check on her, worried that she might be unwell. She had a fragmented recollection of telling her mother the whole story of all that had happened, in fits and starts throughout the day, perhaps no more than a line or two here, a paragraph of information there. She thought she eventually made it to the tale's end, though she couldn't be entirely sure. She may have even told her something wholly untrue or inaccurate, considering how out of it she had been; recollections of the day made her feel as though she had been suffering from delirium, so goodness only knows what had spilt forth from her mouth by way of storytelling and, perhaps, confession.

Mary awoke fully at some point in the late afternoon.

It was Christmas Eve.

But the festive spirit was not something she felt particularly full of at that time, and she was pretty sure that the feeling would not be returning at any point soon. After all, work was to be done, starting with clearing up the debris scattered across the cellar floor.

Mary dragged herself down the two flights of stairs.

She grabbed a large broom propped against the cellar wall and began to sweep up the mess. She felt she was doing little more than just moving the shards of glass around, rather than clearing anything up, but being busy was helping to take her mind off other things. Things she would rather not be thinking about just now, though it was hard to push those thoughts out of her head, considering the scale and importance of it all.

Mary saw something move underneath a cabinet.

She cleared the broken glass from in front of the furniture and crouched on the ground to look. It was an ammonite, somehow still alive, weakly moving its tentacles as if they were enough to keep danger at bay. Mary reached under and took hold of it. The creature was too far gone to even attempt to withdraw into its shell, instead allowing its rubbery limbs to hang limply in the air as Mary carried it across the cellar to a large glass jar, half filled with seawater and holding several other ammonites she had already discovered during the cleaning process. She dropped the latest find in the water with a plop and stared at the contents momentarily, thinking.

That would do for now, she decided.

She placed a lid on the top of the jar and sealed it tightly.

It was the first time Mary could remember when she did not want to go outside. She had practically lived her life outdoors, but the thought of venturing into that big, strange world again made her feel uneasy. Especially now that she could not return to her special, secret place. But she had things to do out there, and she thought doing those things might make her feel better. She pulled on her coat and collected her hat. Just before leaving the house, she thought she had better check on her mother.

Mary pushed open Mrs Anning's bedroom door a fraction, meaning only to peer inside to check that she was asleep. But her mother was propped up in bed, watching the door as though she had been expecting a visit from her daughter. Mary quickly shut the door again, hoping she had not been noticed. Of course, she loved her mother; she was just not in the mood for conversation or another refrain of *I told you so.*

But it was too late; Mrs Anning's position in her room made it impossible to go unnoticed.

'Where are you going?' she asked as Mary tried to disappear.

'Just to get some air,' Mary replied.

She stood outside of the partially closed door, reading the atmosphere. She wanted to go, suddenly so badly, but she felt that her mother needed to see her. To know that she was okay after what Mary had put her through during the day. That she could be trusted to leave the house on her own, perhaps.

Mary pushed the door open and stepped inside. Her mother looked tired, perched at the end of the bed, propping herself up on her thin arms.

'What's wrong?' Mary asked.

Mrs Anning sighed.

'I can't sleep, is all.'

Mary walked over to the medicine cabinet, opened the hinged wooden doors and peered inside. There was a space where the glass bottle of sleeping tonic should have been. She hesitated, her hand outstretched automatically to reach for it, wondering where it was. She had taken it, of course, but what had she done with it after that? She had given it to Gideon Mantell, she remembered. But what then? She did not recall having received it back. Through all the misadventures, he must have forgotten to return it to her, that's all. She would have to make up some more when she had the opportunity.

She closed the cabinet again.

Mary touched her mother's forehead and gently pushed her downwards into the bed.

'Lay down and try to sleep,' she whispered. 'You're exhausted.'

'Where are you going?' Mrs Anning repeated as she slid down onto her back.

'I'll be back soon,' Mary replied.

She slipped out of the bedroom door, pulling it shut behind her. Before she could close it fully, a voice called out from inside.

'None of this is your fault, you know,' her mother said.

Mary hesitated, unable or unwilling to reply, then closed the door.

FORTY-FIVE

London.

Upon returning to his home in London, Gideon Mantell, too, felt disheartened, disillusioned and overwhelmed, physically and emotionally. He found himself in his study, standing and looking at everything surrounding him: books, journals, samples, artefacts... All of it now somehow rendered meaningless. He had seen the *real thing*, and they had been snatched away from him. How could a fragment of bone discovered at the back of a cave in the middle of nowhere continue to hold that much importance for him now, having seen the creatures in the flesh, living and breathing? Having been chased by them and having even touched one. After all that he had seen and experienced, how could he go back to digging through dirt for hours on end and try to get excited about the smallest fragment of bone, tooth, or imprint that had been left in the ground for so long? There were - there *had been* - living specimens. His so-called friend William Buckland had, in effect, betrayed science through his actions. Mantell wondered if he should have words with the Dean of Oxford University or the chairman of the Royal Society and get Buckland removed from his positions within the respective institutions. The man did not deserve to hold such status after what he had done. But Mantell knew he would be laughed out of the building should he try to present his case. If he was serious about doing such a thing, he would have to invent some reason for Buckland to be removed rather than telling the truth, and wouldn't that then make him almost as guilty as Buckland himself? Almost.

The sea air had also done him good; despite the genuine threats against his life during his time on the coast, he realised how much more easily he could breathe during his visit to Lyme Regis. Arriving back in his home city, his throat had felt constricted, his lungs half their size. He was unsure whether it was the smog, the fires of industrialisation, the unending crowds and busyness of the place, or something more psychological than physical. But Lyme Regis had quite literally been a breath of fresh air.

Mantell looked at the surface of his desk, littered with documents.

A thundering rage ran through him suddenly.

He swept his arms across the entire length of the desk, yelling at the top of his lungs as he flung everything to the floor.

His desk now bare, he stood still again, panting as the adrenaline surged through his system until gradually the anger subsided, and he felt nothing but remorse.

He knelt on the ground and began collecting those items he had just scattered, placing them into neat piles ready to put back on the desk.

A bell rang, indicating that someone was at the front door.

He glanced up briefly at the jangling interruption but continued his business. Justine would see to whoever it was so they would not bother him.

The bell rang again.

Mantell paused completely, listening to the sounds of the house for any indication that Justine might be rushing through the building to do her job. But the house returned nothing but silence.

'Justine!' he called and listened again.

Nothing. No movement, no shouts of apology heading his way from a young maid who had been lost in her own world, oblivious to the duties she was expected to be carrying out.

The bell rang a third time.

Mantell shot to his feet. The anger had returned. He was in the sort of mood that meant he quickly got annoyed. The slightest thing was likely to set him off, and one thing he could not abide was people neglecting their duties and responsibilities. He realised this was ironic, considering that was exactly what his wife had accused him of in the past, concerning his general practitioner duties taking second place to his more scientific endeavours.

He stormed out of his office and into the large entrance hall.

He looked around to be sure that Justine wasn't lurking somewhere nearby before yelling her name as loudly as possible straight up the stairs.

Still nothing. Where was that girl? She never seemed to be around when he needed her, but she always got under his feet when he was busy doing other things. It was probably high time that he had words with her. He was in just the kind of mood for such a conversation.

He strode angrily towards the front door and jerked it open.

His wife and son were standing on the doorstep, Mary-Ann with an impatient look on her face. In his surprise at them being there and seeing his wife's expression, Mantell could think of nothing better to say than:

'I don't know what Justine is playing at.'

Mary-Ann brushed past him with a sigh, stepping inside, with Walter following her.

'It's Christmas Eve, Gideon,' Mary-Ann told her husband.

'And?'

He continued to cling to the door he had opened, unsure whether his wife and son would be staying or leaving again immediately.

'And she is home with her family,' Mrs Mantell explained, stripping the gloves from her hands. 'Which brings me on to why we are here.'

Mantell's brain still seemed unable to function correctly, and he could do little but stare at his wife. She had a habit lately of dropping by without notice, and Mantell was expected to accommodate her at the drop of a hat. She was the one who had wanted to live apart from him. She was the one who had a problem with everything that he was doing. Yet she seemed to be there every five minutes. Bringing the boy as well - whom Mantell loved dearly, of course - meant further disruption to his schedule. He could not be expected to work with a child running around the house just as Walter was doing at that moment, galloping up and down the hallway as though he were the horse which had pulled the carriage within which they had just ridden.

'Walter never had a chance to give you his Christmas present,' Mrs Mantell said, realising that her husband was in some peculiar state of mind and was unlikely to continue the conversation without prompting.

Mantell stared across at his boy, who began to gallop straight back towards his father. Walter grabbed him around the waist, squeezing him in a tight hug. Mantell could only stand there and allow it to happen, his hand still holding the door.

'Are you closing the door?' his wife asked. 'Or do you need Justine to do that for you too?'

Mantell closed the door, shutting out the cold and a wind beginning to whistle its way inside his house.

FORTY-SIX

No one was around when Mary reached the Cobb, much as she had hoped. Those who had witnessed what had happened the previous night were likely too afraid to leave their homes, still trying to process what they had seen and experienced, and those who were oblivious to the events that had occurred were probably settled down with their families for a pleasant Christmas Eve night in front of the fire. She envied them, in a way. Part of her wanted a proper family, not just her and her mother forced together by circumstances, her brother having left years ago to pursue his own dreams halfway across the world. On the other hand, she valued her freedom, such as it was, and the ability to go out and stroll the shore searching for her treasures as and when she felt like it. The responsibility of a husband and children to deal with would change that significantly, and she wasn't sure how she would cope with being unable to get up and walk for hours without a care.

Care: that was one thing she knew that she could do. Not for people, necessarily; they, more often than not, rubbed her up the wrong way. But for creatures: for Tray, the wildlife surrounding her, for…

She leant over the side of the wall of the Cobb and dropped an ammonite into the sea below.

She waited anxiously.

Ripples formed as something moved through the water towards where the ammonite had landed.

Mary smiled.

The surface of the water broke as the head of her plesiosaur pushed through and appeared to her. It looked straight up at Mary, and she was sure she saw it smile as it recognised her. She stretched out as far as she could, and the plesiosaur reached up its long neck until Mary's fingertips made contact with its head, and she was able to stroke it in a fashion.

She took another ammonite from her jar and tossed it down to the creature, who expertly caught the food straight in its mouth and gulped it down. They weren't the freshest creatures to feed the plesiosaur, having been out of the water for some time as she had other things to deal with, so those that weren't already dead were close to that point. But they were the best that she had.

Mary had been so afraid that something might have happened to the plesiosaur in the time that she had been gone: that it might have somehow broken the chain she had attached to it, that someone might have spotted it and either taken it away or killed it; that it might simply have died from lack of food. But the creature seemed in good spirits. Mary had given it enough length of chain to move around relatively freely, so it should have been able to find food from somewhere while stuck there. She smiled again as she thought about the possibility of taking it back home with her but then wondered if that was such a good idea after all, considering what had happened before. And now, seeing it enjoying more freedom than it had in her cellar, she felt it would be almost barbaric to take it back to that makeshift aquarium she had put together in her home.

As her thoughts drifted, more ripples appeared nearby on the water's surface.

A scaled back broke through the surface of the waves, a long leathery tail swishing silently behind it.

An ichthyosaur.

Mary jumped to her feet before remembering that she was in a precarious position on top of a high stone wall above the sea. She felt unbalanced in the rush, her feet worryingly close to the edge of the wall and her body struggling to remain fully upright. She put her arms out and concentrated on her posture, finally steadying herself.

The snout of the ichthyosaur appeared through the waves.

Of course, there would be an ichthyosaur in the sea - perhaps more than one. She had forgotten about the wreck of the fishing boat, and any of the water-dwelling creatures that had escaped the cavern were more likely to have found their way out to sea through the river, like the ichthyosaurs that had chased them, than on to the streets to be rounded up. How could they have been so stupid to forget about such things? But she could do nothing about it except hope that they ventured further out into the sea and found food for themselves without attacking other shipping boats. The fact that this one was there, in the Cobb, was troubling.

And it was heading straight towards her plesiosaur.

Mary picked an ammonite from her jar, pulled her arm back and flung it into the water as far away from them as possible.

The plesiosaur looked at her quizzically, most likely wondering why she would make it move for its food after having been hand-fed the last few tasty morsels. The ichthyosaur swerved immediately upon the ammonite's impact on the water. It turned its whole body, darting towards where the ammonite landed. Diving under the water, it snatched at the food, devouring it quickly. But the ammonites Mary had to hand were small and unlikely to satisfy such creatures' appetite. It turned around, heading back towards Mary and her plesiosaur.

Behind it, a second ichthyosaur surfaced from the water, slyly stalking its way through the waves towards them.

Mary threw a handful of ammonites towards them.

The ichthyosaurs darted towards the food as it plopped into the water, sprinkling the surface like heavy rain. The water boiled around them as they wrestled and fought and shoved and bit, trying to be the first to reach the ammonites. The tips of their thick tails swung back and forth, sticking out of the water as they dove and struggled together.

Mary looked in the jar she held. There was only one ammonite left. She felt terrible for feeding them to the ichthyosaurs rather than her friend, the plesiosaur, but she felt like she had little choice; she had to appease the fearsome creatures' hunger to get rid of them.

She pulled the final ammonite out of the jar and launched it towards them.

The ichthyosaurs practically leapt out of the sea, trying to be the first to reach the ammonite. One snatched it from the air, gripping it firmly between its teeth. The other turned on the creature who had the ammonite, snapping at it with its sharp teeth. It received a hiss of retaliation and a solid whack with a tail against its body.

The plesiosaur slowly sank its neck back down and tucked its head under the water as though it might somehow be able to escape the violence that was playing out.

But the motion of the water around the moving plesiosaur drew the ichthyosaur's attention. There could be food there, and it was likely to be far larger than the less-than-filling ammonites provided to them. Their disagreement temporarily forgotten about, the two ichthyosaurs glided in single file towards where the plesiosaur had disappeared, a V-shaped ripple formed in the surface of the water as they pushed through it.

'Oh, no, please no,' Mary whispered a plea, helpless to do anything to prevent whatever might be about to happen.

But then the ichthyosaur at the back disappeared. The ripples stopped, and there was no sign of it being there.

Mary stared out at the water, wondering if the darkness of the late evening was playing tricks on her eyes or if she had just seen what she thought she had seen. And, if she *had* just seen what she thought she had seen, where had the ichthyosaur gone?

The sea's surface broke open with an eruption of water, and the head and long neck of the plesiosaur emerged from the depths. It held the ichthyosaur in its strong jaw, its captive struggling against the plesiosaur, trying to break free of the sharp teeth that held it, thrashing its tail wildly and trying to latch on to something - anything - with its claws and teeth. But the plesiosaur had hold of it in a position that stopped its attempts at attack from being effective. The plesiosaur turned, twisting its long neck. Then, in one swift motion, it swung its neck back around, opening its jaw and releasing the ichthyosaur at just the right time to send the flailing creature flying into the stone wall of the Cobb. It made contact against the brickwork with a sickening thud, squealing briefly upon impact before sliding down the wall and into the water, its back broken, towards its death.

The other ichthyosaur turned on the plesiosaur. It swam straight towards the larger creature as fast as possible, but the plesiosaur was quick. It ducked out of the way of the teeth heading towards it and viciously swung its neck at the ichthyosaur, striking it hard. The ichthyosaur stopped in its tracks, dazed by the blow. It lost its momentum and consciousness just long enough for the plesiosaur to launch its large body on top of the ichthyosaur. The plesiosaur forced the ichthyosaur under the water below it with a gigantic splash.

Mary watched, eyes wide and open-mouthed.

A red cloud appeared in the water, bubbling up to the surface.

And then, finally, it was still.

FORTY-SEVEN

Leaving their son happily playing with a ball on the living room floor, Mantell returned to his study. Mrs Mantell followed close behind and froze at the sight before her as she entered the room. She was used to it being something of a mess - the one place that Mantell refused to let Justine clean or tidy, in case she broke anything or shuffled his papers around so that he was no longer to find anything within his "organisational system". But this time, stuff was scattered over the floor as if thrown down in a rage. On the other hand, she had never seen his desk so tidy, as it was now empty.

'Whatever is going on?' she asked.

Mantell gazed at the evidence of his sudden outburst, somewhat ashamed at what had happened.

'I'm having a clear out,' he told her, unable to think of anything else he could say that would allow him to escape the situation unscathed by embarrassment.

Mrs Mantell raised her eyebrows at him.

'You're done with all of this - ' she waved an arm vaguely around the room at all his papers and artefacts ' - foolishness?'

'It's not fool - ' Mantell began to snap.

But then he cut himself off. The look he was getting from his wife was one reason for abruptly halting himself mid-word, but the other was an internal admission. An admission that, after all that he had seen, now was the time to put his geological days behind him. He had already argued with himself about what he could hope to do, see or achieve after all that he had witnessed. He was frequently told (by one person in particular) that he was spreading himself too thinly and not giving as much attention and care as he used to towards his work as a general practitioner: the work that paid his wage. Fossil hunting had started as a hobby, something that interested him and was a helpful distraction from the pressures of being a doctor. But, he had to admit, it had taken over more and more of his time, to the detriment of the service he provided to his patients. It may be time to hang up the shovel and brush once and for all.

'Yes,' Mantell sighed. 'I'm going to concentrate purely on my general practitioner duties from now on.'

'Oh?' his wife replied, proclaiming more disbelief than he would have thought possible in a single syllable.

'And, of course, my duties as a husband and father.'

'Of course,' Mrs Mantell repeated.

The water's redness slowly spread through the waves until it finally dissipated, dissolving in the sea without a trace, as though it had never been there in the first place.

Mary lay on the wall of the Cobb so that she could watch the waters below more carefully.

Since her plesiosaur had taken the second ichthyosaur under the water and the explosion of blood had appeared under the surface, there had been no further signs of movement. She had no idea which creature that blood belonged to. She didn't know if her plesiosaur had killed the ichthyosaur that had attacked it or if the ichthyosaur itself had managed to get the upper hand during the dive under the water. Perhaps they had killed each other as they fought below the waves. Maybe they had become entangled in the chain Mary had attached to the plesiosaur. She had told herself that it was to keep the creature safe, but she knew that really it was to make sure she could get it back for herself later. She might have killed the poor thing through her selfishness.

Yet Mary continued to search for even the slightest hint that her plesiosaur had survived. She found herself willing the ichthyosaur to be dead, and it made her feel a little guilty, wishing that upon a wild creature who was only doing as its instinct dictated. Still, she could not help herself hoping for the plesiosaur to be the one that was alive. After all, she had looked after it all by herself for several months, nursed it back to health following the injury it had received to its flipper (quite possibly also caused by an ichthyosaur, she wouldn't be surprised), and kept it fed and watered to the best of her ability.

The waters remained still. Dark and lifeless, other than the continual cycle of waves.

Mary suddenly felt the chill of the late evening air and realised she could not stay out there much longer, laying on her stomach on the cold rock wall, in case she were to become unwell from the cold. She slowly and carefully got to her feet, still watching the sea.

Begrudgingly, she walked along the wall back towards the shore.

A splash came from somewhere in the water beside her.

She turned excitedly. Could it be…?

A gull squawked as it flapped its wings, lifting itself from the waves, empty-beaked after diving for a fish which must have escaped its grasp.

Mary began to turn away, once more saddened at broken expectations, when she noticed a shape emerging from the water.

Something large and smooth.

Something long.

It was her plesiosaur.

It looked at her and barked its own form of a greeting, then thrust itself out of the waves and dived back under the water, the chain rattling behind it as it disappeared underneath the surface.

Mary smiled, laughed, and clapped her hands joyfully at the wonderful sight.

Mantell collected the papers and books he had thrust upon the floor, forming them into separate, tidy piles to try to neaten the place. His wife picked up a book that was near her feet. She flicked through the pages, briefly scanning the content. Early on, there had been a time when they shared Mantell's passion for the subject, when he would come to her with a new find, and joy and excitement spread across his face like a child with a new toy. He would talk to her about it, explaining exactly what it was, where he had found it and what made it of any importance. Then he had found others with a similar interest - other *men*; those who were in a position to make his finds more than just something that he shared enthusiastically with his wife. Men who could make him feel distinguished and that what he was doing benefited the scientific community. And little by little, he had stopped sharing the discoveries with her. He would rush into his study as soon as he arrived home, scouring through his papers and books to see if whatever he had dug up had previously been identified. If not, he would immediately send word to all he knew in that community -

more often than not the Reverend Buckland - that they might write back with praise and adoration over such a remarkable discovery. Mrs Mantell wasn't resentful that he was making a mark in the scientific world. Good for him, after all. She was upset that she had been shut out of what he considered a significant part of his life. He no longer wanted to share that with her, and that withdrawal had come at a cost to both his personal and professional life. It was she, after all, who received word whenever her husband missed an appointment with a patient or when Mrs so-and-so from such-and-such a place had taken a turn for the worse after the doctor had failed to attend to her ailments in good time.

Yet, Mrs Mantell also knew how much this stuff meant to her husband, and she couldn't help but feel that perhaps she had been a little unfair. Maybe they could find some balance; he could work fewer hours as a general practitioner and get some help with his duties, which would afford him more time to spend on his geological research projects.

She handed the book to her husband, keeping hold of one end of it as he moved to take it from her.

'Whatever I say, I don't want to be the reason for you giving up your passion,' she told him.

Mantell plucked the book from her hand, placed it on the desk and took both of her hands in his own.

'My dear,' he said, looking her straight in the eyes with utmost sincerity. 'You and Walter *are* my passion.'

Mrs Mantell couldn't help but be moved by her husband's words. As brief and, admittedly, sickly sweet as they may have been, she could see in his face that he meant every word. Before she could help herself, before she allowed herself the chance to think about what she was doing, she pulled her husband against her and kissed him. It was like the first time they had ever kissed: gentle and unsure to begin, but moving into the easy familiarity of the situation until it was as though they had never missed a step in their relationship.

Mrs Mantell became aware that they were being watched.

She reluctantly pulled away from her husband and turned. Walter stood in the doorway to the office, smiling at the sight of his parents sharing an embrace. She straightened out her clothes, flustered to have been caught, as though they were doing something they shouldn't be.

'Let's not rush things,' she told her husband. 'It shall take time to heal.'

'Of course.'

Mrs Mantell coughed to clear her throat. She straightened her posture and turned back towards the study door, head held high in her usual manner. Mantell grabbed her hand before she could leave and turned her back around to face him.

'I'm glad you came,' he told her.

Her face softened again, and she allowed herself a smile.

'As am I,' she replied and truly meant it.

FORTY-EIGHT

Having left her plesiosaur, Mary realised she was not ready to return home. She was out of the house now and felt like she wanted to stay that way rather than return to her small, dark home only to go straight to bed yet unable to sleep. Tray was there waiting for her, of course, but he was likely dozing in the corner of the room, unaware she wasn't there with him.

She walked by the Rock Point Inn, where the path beside the sea met with Broad Street. Sounds of laughter and conversation drifted outside despite the windows being closed against the cold. Mary didn't so much want social interaction but rather to be lost within a crowd. She was sure she would regret it as soon as she set foot within the building, but she pulled the heavy wooden door open and stepped inside.

The smell of the place hit her first: alcohol, sweat and dirt. It was simultaneously off-putting and welcoming. Heads turned as she ventured towards the bar. Other than her, there were only a couple of other women amongst the hordes of men within the property, and the men were certainly making the most of those they could find. It was very infrequent that Mary went to the public house, so her appearance surprised the locals within. But they were so used to Mary being something of a strange creature that they thought little of it and quickly returned to their conversations, songs, rhymes and drinks.

The landlord of the establishment, William Fletcher - or Bill to those who knew him, which was the majority of Lyme Regis and indeed the surrounding areas - looked Mary over with a curious eye.

'Now then, Mary,' he said with a slight smile, his cheeks flushed and speech slightly slurred as evidence that he had been consuming almost as much of his wares as he had been serving that night. 'What are you doing here tonight? This is no place for a lady.'

'Good evening, Bill,' Mary replied. 'I appreciate your concern, but as you know, I am no lady.'

She smiled, and Bill guffawed loudly.

'What'll it be?' he asked.

'Your finest ale, please.'

'There's nothing fine about the ale here,' he retorted as he wiped a glass with his soiled apron.

'Then I'll take whatever it is you're serving these layabouts,' Mary told him, gesturing towards the loud, drunken crowd that littered the room.

'Right you are.'

Mary looked around as Bill poured her drink. Half the town's men were in there, enjoying a few drinks before Christmas Day, when those who were married would have no choice but to hunker down and enjoy some "quality time" with the wife and children. Those without families tended to visit friends who did; in those situations, the alcohol may have flowed more freely in the interest of "hospitality". But on the whole, Christmas Eve was one last hurrah before the business of family duties took over.

Bill passed Mary her drink. She gave him her money and pushed her way through the crowds to a small table in the corner, left unoccupied due to only having one seat available. She sat nursing the drink for a while before taking a sip and wincing at the taste. A few more sips in, and she became used to the flavour and enjoyed it a little more. Her hands were finally beginning to stop shaking from the emotional mountains and valleys she had traversed at the Cobb previously, and the alcohol was helping to warm her from the inside out.

A roaring cheer from the bar drew Mary out of her reverie. She looked up and saw Jessie surrounded at the bar by a group of men clamouring for his attention. Bill stood behind the bar, arms folded across his chest, looking decidedly unimpressed.

'Money first,' Mary heard Bill tell Jessie as she tuned in to their conversation. 'We'll see about the drinks once I see the money.'

Jessie grinned and pulled a bag from inside his coat. He dropped it down on top of the bar, and the unmistakable sound of coins bashing together emanated from within. Bill opened the top and peered inside. He looked at Jessie in surprise, then suspicion.

'You been out robbing some rich folk, Jessie?'

Jessie looked shocked at the accusation, though it wasn't the first time that such a thing had been thought of him.

'This money's hard-earned and legitimate, I'll have you know,' he protested.

'What do you know about hard work?'

'Got it from a gentleman from London, I did.'

Mary's attention perked up at this news. There had been two "gentlemen from London" around town in the past few days, both of whom had been in direct contact with Jessie. It would have been an extraordinary coincidence for there to have been *other* gentlemen from London making conversation with Jessie.

'Come to think of it, what do you know about gentlemen, either?' Bill taunted.

Jessie playfully swung an arm across the bar, half-heartedly trying to hit Bill, who, despite his drunken state, easily dodged out of the way.

'Asked me to transport something for him, he did, and paid me handsomely for my services.'

Mary jumped out of her seat in the corner of the room and pushed her way through the crowd so that she might be able to stand beside Jessie. She received some opposition from the men closest to him, most likely afraid that they might miss out on the drink already promised them by the recently wealthy Jessie, but in the interests of not wanting to appear to be fighting with a woman, they let her through without too much protest.

'Which gentleman was it?' Mary demanded, grasping at Jessie's arm.

Jessie turned and saw her for the first time. He looked sheepish, trying to avoid her gaze, looking anywhere but at her face.

'Hello, Mary. Didn't see you there,' Jessie said.

'Which gentleman was it?' she repeated more forcefully, stressing each syllable to ensure Jessie fully understood her question's importance.

Jessie shrugged out of her grasp and turned to face the bar once again, avoiding looking at her completely.

'Sworn to secrecy I am, Mary,' he told her with an air of importance that rubbed Mary the wrong way.

'You have to tell me.'

'I don't have to do anything of the sort.'

'Then tell me of the item you had to deliver.'

'What of it?'

'Was it… large?'

He glanced at her briefly, neither confirming nor denying what she was asking through words, but the look on his face said it all.

'Please,' Mary pleaded. 'I must know. Was it large?'

Jessie gulped down the drink Bill had just placed in front of him and slammed the empty glass back down on the bar in front of him.

'Maybe,' he said.

'What was it, Jessie? What were you asked to transport?'

'I can't break my word to my employer, Miss Anning.'

"Miss Anning". As long as they had known each other, Jessie had never called her "Miss Anning". It had always been "Mary". Now here he was, with a bit of money in his purse - all of which he was ready to spend immediately within a public house - and speaking of his "employer", she was suddenly known to him as "Miss Anning". It seemed unlikely that he would offer up the information she required. She was sure that she already knew the answers to her questions, but she wanted them confirmed. She needed to know for sure. If he would not answer her questions, perhaps there was another way of discovering the truth for herself.

Mary realised that she would have to appeal to Jessie's true nature in the same way that the "gentleman from London" had appealed to him in the first place.

'If you drive me to the gentleman in London, I'll get you double whatever he paid you when we get there,' she told him.

Mary could see immediately that her proposal was being thought through very carefully. Jessie stared down at the refreshed drink before him, concentrating hard as though he might find the answer to his dilemma within the alcoholic beverage placed before him. Mary could practically hear the thoughts ticking through his head as he processed the idea, probably trying to calculate precisely how much double the money would equate to in terms of drinks, how many days he might be able to sleep straight through if he consumed that much money's worth of alcohol in one go.

He picked up his drink and raised it to his lips.

He tipped his head back and poured the liquid straight down his throat.

Jessie sighed with satisfaction and wiped his mouth with his hand.

'When do you want to leave?' he asked.

Forty-Nine

The picture-perfect Christmas Day morning: the family sitting together in front of a roaring fire as snow fell outside, the windows edged in white as it gradually built up until it obscured their view of the world outside. But inside and together, they didn't mind feeling like they were the only people in the world. Gideon Mantell sat in a large, comfortable chair while Mary-Ann knelt on the floor with their son, both watching Walter open his presents. Their faces mirrored Walter's delight with each gift he unwrapped. Mantell couldn't have imagined this Christmas morning would turn out this way. The previous couple of Christmasses or so, he had been itching to get back to his study to continue the analysis of something or other, resenting every moment that spending time with his family took him away from his work.

This year was different.

This year, he was - dare he even think it? - happy.

They had awoken in their separate rooms, and Mrs Mantell had made breakfast for them. After they had eaten, Walter was too excited to wait any longer before opening his gifts, so they had come through to the living room to do so. All this - a good couple of hours or so - without a single disparaging, disagreeing, spiteful word shared between them.

It had been a good day so far.

Mrs Mantell looked up at her husband and smiled at him as if she had read his thoughts; she probably had, Mantell thought, based on previous experiences where that had been the only possible explanation for her knowing exactly what he had been thinking or feeling at the time. Today, though, she would have only received good, kind words from his mind.

'I almost forgot!' he cried out and jumped to his feet.

Walter and Mrs Mantell looked at each other, confused about what was happening, as their father and husband rushed from the room.

'Mama?' Walter asked.

His mother shrugged her shoulders, as clueless as he was at his father's sudden disappearance.

Almost as quickly as he left, Mantell returned, clutching a small box wrapped and tied with an extravagant bow. The bow itself was far larger than the box, dwarfing it in comparison to the point that it looked almost ridiculous. But as he handed the small parcel to his wife, Mrs Mantell knew that it was the thought that counted, and her husband had clearly thought about it, regardless of what the outcome might have looked like.

'Merry Christmas,' he said, kissing her softly on the cheek.

Mrs Mantell slowly and carefully undid the bow and removed the ribbon from around the box. The wrapped container itself was barely more than an inch square. She wondered what it could be as she pulled off the wrapping, revealing the box inside. She tossed the paper to the ground and gave the box her full attention, straightening up before doing anything else. She slowly lifted the lid on the box and gasped in surprise.

Laying inside was a necklace. But it was no ordinary necklace: it was a piece of white glass, smoothed from being tossed around in the sea for years, attached to a small but perfectly formed ammonite. Dark grey, the bumps and ridges of each shell segment were perfectly preserved, and the detail that remained despite having been hidden in the water for countless unending years was incredible. The sea glass and fossil were, in turn, attached to a silver chain, turning the whole piece into a one-of-a-kind piece of jewellery.

'It's beautiful,' Mrs Mantell said, genuinely delighted by the gift.

Her husband took the necklace from her and moved behind her. She stood and pulled her hair away from her neck so he might put it on her. A shiver ran through her body as his fingertips lightly scraped the skin on the sides of her neck, where he smoothed out the chain and clipped it together. She lifted the ammonite to look at it more closely.

'Do you recognise it?' Mantell asked.

She frowned, trying to remember. She had seen so many hundreds and thousands of ammonites over the years, but this was one that she was supposed to remember for some reason. Yet to her, they all looked more or less the same; some fared better in the water than others (like this one), but generally, she found that there was little to tell one apart from another.

She looked at her husband, concerned that she was forgetting something important.

Rather than a look of annoyance on his face, he smiled.

'It is the first ammonite we found together, before… everything else happened,' he explained. 'Do you remember?'

Of course, she remembered. Gideon had been speaking for months about these incredible *things* people were finding on the beaches and in quarries; relics and remains from years ago - perhaps many years in the past. Remains of creatures that had once been but no longer existed. Evidence of a time long since past. In some places, one could stroll along the shore and find samples of these long-extinct creatures lying in the sand, waiting to be discovered by any old layman with a keen eye and a little patience. One such place had, of course, been Lyme Regis and the nearby beach of Charmouth. He had nagged her for weeks that they might head to the coast. It would be good for her to spend some time in the invigorating sea air, Mantell had told her. He had always had a way of twisting the idea of something that he wanted to do to make it sound as though it would also benefit her, that she might more readily agree.

Agree she did, and they ventured down to the south coast for a weekend.

Her husband had been right: the sea air had done them both wonders. Walking beside those crashing waves on one side and the tall cliffs on the other was refreshing and intoxicating. They had walked for two hours without finding anything, and Mrs Mantell could see that her husband was beginning to get impatient and annoyed. *Just laying there, they said*, he whined, *just laying on the shingle waiting to be picked up.*

And then, finally, his eyes widened, and he plunged his hand into the sand by his feet. His hand clasped firmly shut, he rushed to the sea's edge and washed off the sand surrounding whatever he was so excited about. He ran back to his wife, smiling ear to ear with pure, unadulterated joy.

'Hold out your hand,' he had told her.

She did as asked.

Mantell paused for a moment, allowing the tension to build.

'Well?' Mrs Mantell prompted him.

He finally placed it in the middle of her palm: a small, perfectly formed ammonite fossil. The very same that she was wearing around her neck now. She had to admit at the time that it was the most incredible thing to find such an item on a stroll along the beach, especially knowing what it had once been and for how long it had been waiting to be discovered.

That one ammonite had led to many more, and those many more led to everything else that had followed. Good and bad.

'Of course, I remember,' Mrs Mantell told her husband as she ran her fingers over the gift that now hung around her neck. 'You were so excited. Like a child.'

'I was?' Mantell asked, almost in protest at the choice of words.

'It was a long time ago.'

The words hung there with a kind of sadness. It *was* a long time ago, that was true. Even before Walter had been born. A lot had happened since then. A lot of good things and a lot of bad things. Until that day, the bad stuff had outweighed the good, but Mantell hoped he might be given a chance to address the balance, tipping it in favour of the good.

Mantell put his arms around his wife and pulled her into an embrace.

'We can only look forward to the future,' he whispered in her ear. 'Things will be different. I promise.'

Mantell felt a tug at his sleeve and reluctantly pulled away from his wife, who, he noticed, had tears shimmering delicately in her eyes. She brushed them away, hoping he might not have seen, but it was too late. The tugging was young Walter, trying to get his father's attention.

'Father, father!' he pouted as the attention did not come quickly enough.

Mantell crouched in front of his son.

'And what can I do for you, young man?' he asked.

Walter pulled a box from behind his back and handed it to his father. It was battered and bruised and a little torn in the corners. It must have been the same gift that Walter had taken with him all the way to Lyme Regis, only for plans to go awry, and he never had the opportunity to hand it over.

'What is this?' Mantell asked.

'A present,' Walter told him.

'For me?'

Walter nodded his head with an emphatic *yes*.

'Well, thank you,' Mantell said.

He kissed Walter on the forehead and took the gift from him. Poised to open it and discover what was inside, a loud knock came at the house's front door.

Husband and wife looked at each other as if each expected an indication from the other that they knew who it might be.

'Who could that be?' Mrs Mantell asked, dissipating any thought Mantell had that she might know. 'It's Christmas morning!'

Mantell placed the gift from Walter on the floor, still unopened, and stiffly got to his feet.

FIFTY

Things had been going too well; Mantell should have known to expect some disruption to the special time they were finally sharing as a family. But for someone to come knocking on his front door on Christmas Day, it had better be nothing short of a medical emergency, or so help him, someone was going to pay for breaking the spell of that enchanted morning.

He pulled the door open, ready to give whoever was standing there a piece of his mind.

He stopped short, however, before he could launch into a tirade.

'Miss Anning?' he gasped in surprise.

Mary stood on his doorstep, her head and shoulders covered with a fine dusting of snow, Tray clutched tightly under her arm to protect him from the cold. The dog yapped excitedly upon seeing Mantell, wriggling to get free so that he might greet the doctor with a licked face. Mercifully, Mary clung to him.

'I beg your pardon for disturbing you, Dr Mantell,' Mary said.

'That's quite alright; I am just surprised to see you. Whatever are you doing here?'

She slid a hand underneath her coat and pulled out a crumpled sheet of paper. She handed it to Mantell.

'I thought you might want to see this,' Mary told him.

'Something has come up,' Mantell announced to his wife. 'I have to go out for a short while.'

Mrs Mantell spun around in her seat before the fire and glared at him.

'Whatever could be more important than spending Christmas Day with your family?' she demanded to know.

Walter looked up from his new toys, his eyes shimmering with sadness at the thought that his father might not want to be there with them after the fun and enjoyment they had shared over the past few hours.

Mary stepped forward, revealing herself in the doorway.

'Oh,' Mrs Mantell said. 'I see.'

'No, you don't,' her husband told her.

'Is that what these little trips have been all about? And now you bring her *here*, to *our home*?'

'Begging your pardon, Mrs Mantell - ' Mary began trying to explain.

'Don't you even talk to me,' Mrs Mantell snapped.

'It is not what you think,' Mantell told her, 'but I don't have time to explain. You have to trust me.'

'What is that?'

She had spotted the paper Mantell held in his hands, given to him on the doorstep by Mary.

'It is why I must go out,' Mantell told her.

His wife held out her hand, waiting for him to pass the paper to her for her examination. Mantell did as instructed and took a safe step back.

Mrs Mantell moved her glare from her husband's face to look at the paper he had placed in her hand.

It was an advertisement for a lecture. A lecture to be presented later that very day by Richard Owen, declaring in enormous letters that he would announce the most extraordinary discovery ever known to man, woman or child. It was gaudily decorated with an illustration of a fantastical beast, composed, it seemed, entirely of fangs and claws. It looked more like an advert for a travelling show than a scientific lecture, Mantell thought, but it was sure to have drawn attention.

'These are posted all over the city,' Mary said but sank back again upon receiving a look from Mrs Mantell.

She turned her gaze back to her husband.

'You are leaving us on Christmas Day to attend a lecture?' she asked with terrifying calm.

'I must,' Mantell told her. 'I do not know what Owen has planned, but - '

Mrs Mantell got up, dropped the paper into her seat, and calmly wandered out of the room, brushing past Mary and her husband and heading straight towards Mantell's study.

Mantell followed her through, where she began putting the books and papers back on the shelves that lined the room's walls.

'What are you doing?' Mantell asked.

'I never should have forced your hand,' his wife replied. 'It's clear your priorities lie in your books and studies.'

'That is not... I *have* to go to this lecture, Mary-Ann,' he protested. 'I must stop him before he puts many people in danger.'

'You're going to the lecture to *stop* the lecture?' Mrs Mantell scoffed.

'That is exactly the case.'

She laughed humourlessly.

'Are you that petty and jealous,' she asked, 'that you would try to stop someone else's lecture because they got one up on you?'

'Certainly not! I have told you I am going because - '

'Walter!' Mrs Mantell cried out, cutting her husband off. 'Say goodbye to your father. We're leaving.'

They stared at each other as they waited for a response from their son, both angry at the other for entirely different reasons. Perhaps last night and this morning had been a mistake all along. He couldn't let it go as promised, and she consistently failed to allow him to express his side of the argument, reaching conclusions without allowing him to explain the situation. Perhaps it was best that they left, after all. The lecture would begin soon, and Mantell knew that he had to be there, ready, somehow, to help when things inevitably went awry.

They heard footsteps running towards the study, and Walter appeared in the doorway, excitedly holding out the advertisement for the lecture.

'What is this, Father?' he asked.

Mantell crouched in front of his son.

'It is the reason I have to leave for a little while. A man is giving a talk about a big, scary monster, and your father needs to go to hear what he has to say.'

Walter's eyes widened, a huge smile stretching across his face.

He whirled around to look at his mother.

'Can we go too, Mother?' he asked. 'Pleeeeease?'

Terrified at the thought of putting his son in danger, Mantell emphatically shook his head - *no* - at his wife, clearly expressing his wish that she should deny Walter's request.

Mrs Mantell smiled.

'Of course, we can,' she said sweetly. 'We can all go together.'

Walter wrapped his arms around his mother's legs, an appreciative embrace. Higher up, where he couldn't see, his parents once again shared a look that was none too friendly.

FIFTY-ONE

The lecture was scheduled to take place at three o'clock in the afternoon in a town hall in Holborn, at the intersection of Gray's Inn Road and Theobald's Road. The building itself was not exceptionally spacious, and by the time Mantell arrived with his wife, his son and Mary, the place was already close to being full. Coming in through the main entrance to the hall, they were led straight into the back of the meeting area, rows of seats in front of them, leading down to the front where Richard Owen would give his talk. They edged into the few remaining seats where they could all sit together as the crowd chattered excitedly amongst themselves, eager to see whatever Owen had to show them. Mantell was surprised by such a high turnout on Christmas Day, but by then, the dinner would have been digested, and it seemed to be a reasonable alternative to falling asleep in a chair in front of the fire. The poster had promised excitement, and that's clearly what the crowd was looking for.

That was, the crowd other than his small group.

Mrs Mantell looked bored and annoyed even before the lecture had begun.

Young Walter sat perched on the edge of his seat, eager for the show to begin. Mantell had not realised until then that the boy had brought the gift, which he *still* had not had the opportunity to open. He promised himself that he would give it, and Walter, his full attention once this was all over and be sure to make a show of making it a special moment for the boy.

Mary and Mantell himself looked anxiously around the room. Crowded, with barely any space to move, never mind to run, flee or hide. It was as though they had brought themselves into a trap from which they knew there was likely no chance of escape.

At the front of the room, a small stage was set up, empty, not even a lectern behind which Owen could stand to deliver his talk. By Mary's feet, Tray stood up, turned around and slumped back down on the floor, immediately falling asleep once again, having found himself a more comfortable position in which to lie.

The hall door was pulled shut, blocking the sound of the wind and the chill from outside.

A hush fell upon the room, the chatter gradually subsiding as the room noticed Richard Owen himself striding onto the stage from where he had been waiting in the wings. Mantell and Mary looked at each other. It was time; whatever was going to happen would happen soon.

Owen waited for silence, scanning the room with his small, dark eyes, allowing time for all attention to fall upon him.

'Good afternoon, ladies and gentlemen,' he finally addressed the room. 'And a "Merry Christmas" to you all.'

The more responsive members of the audience replied with their own murmured Christmas greeting, while others remained passive. Mantell sat on the edge of his seat, his chin resting on his fingertips, pointed upwards like a church spire, almost willing Owen to get on with it and be done with whatever madness was to follow.

'I'm glad so many of you could make it today of all days,' Owen continued. 'A day for celebrating miracles, is it not? And what I have to show you today, I can assure you, is nothing short of a miracle in itself. A miracle of nature.'

The door to the hall opened, letting a blast of cold air back in.

Mary pulled her coat higher up her neck to block the breeze and turned to look over her shoulder at whoever the newcomer might be. She was surprised to see that it was none other than the Reverend Buckland. He still sported two black eyes from the various altercations he had been a part of, though the swelling had decreased somewhat. He must have been placing ice over the bruises to ease his suffering. Buckland caught Mary's eye as she watched him. He gave her a brief but polite nod, then skirted around people to place himself in a single seat in the middle of a row at the very back of the room.

'William Buckland is here,' Mary whispered to Mantell.

Mantell whipped his head around at the news.

'Where?' he asked.

Mary nodded her head in Buckland's direction. Mantell followed her gaze and saw him sitting there. Buckland had noticed Mantell but was making a point of not looking in his direction, avoiding eye contact with him at all costs.

'Whatever is he doing here?' Mantell asked.

'Most like the same as us,' Mary replied.

Shushed by a member of the audience sitting in front of them, Mantell and Mary turned their attention back to the stage.

'For those of you who know anything about the scientific studies of geology and palaeontology, you will know that much of our work is based on little more than conjecture: analysis of existing scientific data and trying to form an opinion on something new through nothing short of guesswork, based on pre-existing notions and ideas.'

Owen clasped his hands together, rubbing them one over the other as though he was washing them thoroughly. He looked around his assembled audience, smiling at them and increasing the tension as everyone waited for some big reveal.

'Today,' he finally continued, 'that guesswork ends. Today, we deal in nothing less than cold, hard facts.'

He paused again, using all the tricks in the showman's manual.

'Before continuing, I would ask those of you of a nervous disposition to leave now. This is not something for the faint of heart. I know we have at least one doctor in the room,' he said as he looked specifically towards Mantell, 'but I am sure they would prefer not to work on Christmas afternoon, given the choice.'

Nobody moved. The whole audience wanted to stay to see whatever it was that Owen could be about to show them.

Owen smirked. He had them in the palm of his hands.

He turned to his right and nodded towards the stage wing.

At his nodded command, three assistants wheeled an enormous cage onto the stage. It must have been nearly thirty feet long and eight or nine feet high. The thing was huge. A large cloth was draped over the top of the cage, hiding whatever was contained within from the audience's view. Mantell could feel the collective tension of the room building as people edged forward in their seats as if that might allow them to see what was in there sooner than anyone else.

Mantell turned to look over his shoulder at Buckland in the back of the room. Buckland maintained his stance by deliberately not looking in Mantell's direction, but Mantell could see that Buckland was concerned. His posture had stiffened, and his eyes widened with worry.

'Ladies and gentlemen. Boys and girls. I give you: *Megalosaurus!*'

Richard Owen stared straight ahead at William Buckland. He had spotted him, too, as he had entered the room and was glad the Reverend was there to witness his unveiling. Owen smiled at Buckland and took hold of an edge of the cloth covering. He whipped the covering away with a great, practised flourish, revealing the cage and its inhabitant underneath.

The audience gasped.

Some even screamed at the sight that was before them.

Inside the cage was an enormous beast, practically filling that gigantic cage. The megalosaurus stood on two large back legs, swishing its long tail behind it, rattling against the cage bars as it looked around with its small, inset eyes, opening its mouth to reveal its rows of sharp, pointed teeth. It was a fearsome sight to behold.

'My God, Owen,' Buckland whispered to himself. 'What have you done?'

FIFTY-TWO

Based on the scientific evidence they had at hand, the megalosaurus looked nothing like Buckland had expected. He had described it and illustrated it in his papers as more of a crocodilian species, practically waddling on four thick legs, supporting a large, slightly humped body. The face was more-or-less the only thing that fit with his expectations: a long, fearsome jaw and two eyes on either side of its head. That part was relatively easy to surmise since he had a reasonable specimen of a fragment of the creature's jaw, enabling him to estimate the size based on actual physical resources. The majority of the rest of it had to be worked out based on pre-conceived notions of expected size based on the small pieces of evidence they had to hand.

It was so different, in fact, that Buckland could not be sure that it even *was* a megalosaurus at all. After all, how could Richard Owen know that this creature and his megalosaurus were one and the same?

Buckland realised that he was focusing on entirely the wrong thing.

It didn't matter *what* it was: what mattered was that Owen had brought it there, a survivor from what had happened in Lyme Regis, and now it stood at the front of a room filled with people.

From the stage, Owen tried to continue with his lecture, but there was too much excited, anxious chatter around for him to be adequately heard. He decided instead to take a step back and, with a smile, allow his audience time to soak in the vision he had brought before them.

Within the cage, the creature scanned the ranks of people before it as though it was trying to pick one out that it thought might be the most delicious, should it be allowed to partake of this buffet. It stopped moving and tilted its head. It sniffed, gulping in air through flared nostrils. Something out there had got its full attention. It lifted its head and sniffed more, homing in on the scent. There it was: it caught the precise location.

It tilted its head down slowly, keeping track of that delicious aroma.

It stared directly at Walter.

And licked its lips.

Mary noticed the creature's gaze falling in their direction and looked across to where it was staring. There, on Walter's lap, was the gift for his father. She frowned at it, wondering if that could be what the creature could smell. She would rather that than the megalosaurus deciding that Walter himself looked like the tastiest of morsels.

She reached across Mantell and snatched the wrapped package from the boy.

'What do you think you're doing?' Mantell demanded as she ripped the packaging from the box.

'That's not yours - it's for my father!' Walter wailed at the sight of his wrapping being pulled apart.

Mary ignored them both and opened the now exposed box.

A pungent aroma wafted straight out at them. Mary gagged at the scent as it hit her full in the face, and Mantell had to turn away, his fingers under his nose to suppress the urge to vomit.

Mary gingerly pulled out the contents of the box between two fingers.

It was once an ammonite, now entirely dead and beginning to rot away like discarded old fish.

The megalosaurus' sense of smell must have been strong enough to have been able to detect the dead creature, even from the front of the room. Mary looked across at the megalosaurus. It looked straight back at her. It licked its lips again.

Mary thought that perhaps she saw the flicker of a smile cross its face, but she was pretty sure that could not have been possible.

The megalosaurus took a step back, as much as it could, within that cramped cage.

Then it threw itself, full force, at the bars in front of it.

The audience screamed as the sound of the beast hitting metal resounded throughout the room. Some leapt from their seats and fled down the aisles. Others remained, waiting to see what would come next.

'There's no need to panic,' Owen tried to reassure them as he backed away from the cage towards the stage wings. 'It's perfectly safe.'

The megalosaurus hit itself against the cage bars once more, twice, three times. The bars were denting somewhat, but it was making little progress in getting free. It turned ninety degrees to face one of the other walls of the cage, reared itself back, and slammed into this new metal victim. This wall reacted differently to the first: it rattled, vibrating back hard at the impact rather than remaining firm and still. Even the creature could tell that this was a more likely suspect in its quest to be free: the door to the cage.

It barged against the door again. It rattled more this time. Something was beginning to give way.

More of the audience were on their feet by now; many were trying to get out of there, but others were trying to look around those in front so that they might have a better view of this incredible sight.

'Please, remain calm,' Owen told them, his voice shaking with terror, and promptly ran into the wings.

The megalosaurus reared back once more.

It hit the cage door with the greatest force that it could muster.

The lock snapped clean off and was thrown across the stage to the other side of the room. The door swung wide open.

The audience screamed more loudly.

The megalosaurus ducked its head and stepped out of the cage.

Those who had been enjoying the show joined those who had already made a sensible move towards the exit. The crowd ran from their seats, rushing to get out of there, trampling over those in their way, pushing past in a desperate sprint for escape.

The megalosaurus leapt from the small stage straight into the audience. Its sights were set on Mary and, more specifically, the ammonite that she held. It ignored the people around it, pushing through them like they weren't even there, focusing entirely on where it wanted to be.

Mary didn't know what to do. She had no hope of getting through the crowds making their escape - not without drawing the megalosaurus' attention towards them, but she also could not stay there and allow the creature to come to her, putting herself and her friends in great danger. She felt a tap on her shoulder and looked around.

'Pass it to me,' Buckland said from behind her.

Mary frowned, confused.

'The ammonite,' Buckland explained. 'Pass it to me. Now.'

Dazed by indecision, Mary did as instructed. Buckland held the ammonite aloft, and immediately the megalosaurus' attention snapped from Mary to him. He pushed through the crowd towards the exit and into the cold late afternoon air. The megalosaurus let out a roar and stomped towards him.

Mary found herself able to think more clearly now that she did not have an eight-foot-tall beast staring at her. She looked towards the front of the hall, where Owen had been. He hadn't yet emerged from where he had hidden himself in the wings. *Perhaps…* Mary wondered. She scooped up Tray from where he sat on the floor at her feet and ushered Mantell and his family out of their seats.

'We have to leave,' Mary told them. 'Now.'

The Mantells started to head in the same direction as everyone else - the same direction that led them to be in the beast's path.

'No,' Mary hissed at them. 'This way.'

She indicated towards the opposite direction, where there were far fewer people.

They trod along the row of seats to reach an aisle at the far side, then were more quickly able to dash towards the front of the room.

'Quickly,' Mary said.

She led them to the side of the stage where Owen had disappeared.

There it was, precisely what she had hoped to find: another exit.

FIFTY-THREE

They rushed out of the side door of the building into the outside world. Snow was still falling, and a thick layer coated the ground. The darkness of a winter evening was starting to descend, and it looked like it could have been the perfect Christmas. However, Mary could not recall a gigantic fearsome creature visiting the baby Jesus in the manger as part of the Nativity story. From the side of the town hall, they could hear the screams of those fleeing the scene around the front of the building. There was no other way around from where they had emerged. It was a dead-end street. They had to head in the same direction as the others.

They trod through the thick snow as quickly as it would allow, Mantell leading his son by the hand, Mary carrying Tray in case he got lost under the white blanket, and Mrs Mantell left to fend for herself at the rear of the group.

Finally, the group emerged from the side street onto the main road, joining the crowd of audience members running for their lives. It was pandemonium; people were screaming, running, and shouting in a chaotic mass, doing whatever they could to escape from there as quickly as possible with little or no regard for the others around them.

'Which way should we go?' Mary asked.

As she spoke, a carriage pulled along the road before them. It slowed to a crawl as it approached, never entirely stopping. William Buckland was at the reins of the horse. He spotted them in the crowd.

'Get in,' he called out. 'Quickly!'

Mantell pulled the carriage door open and held it for Mary, Mrs Mantell and Walter to get inside, hoisting Walter into his seat, practically throwing them aboard as the carriage continued its forward momentum. Finally, he took up the position next to Buckland in the front.

'I never thought I would be so glad to see you,' Mantell told Buckland as they moved away.

'I have a certain undeniable charm,' Buckland joked with a smile.

Mantell looked over his shoulder at the street behind them, all those people they were leaving behind to whatever fate might befall them. A solitary figure broke from the group and ran down the middle of the road towards the carriage, yelling at them:

'Wait! Wait!'

Mantell realised that it was Richard Owen, the cause of all the madness.

'I think Owen requires transportation,' Mantell said.

'He can get his own carriage,' Buckland replied grumpily.

Mantell looked at him, staring until Buckland could feel the gaze.

'Alright, alright,' he said. 'But I'm not stopping.'

Buckland slowed the carriage, giving Owen a chance to catch up.

'Tell him to run,' Buckland instructed.

'Hurry!' Mantell cried to Owen as he stumbled through the snow-laden road.

'I'm trying!' Owen yelled back.

He tripped and fell, hands plunging deep into the cold white covering the ground.

'I have to help him,' Mantell said, as though he was convincing himself perhaps more than Buckland.

'Don't - ' Buckland began, but too late:

Mantell jumped down from the carriage and ran back towards the fallen Owen, in the high-kneed manner that has to be used when attempting to sprint through snow. He grabbed hold of the frozen man and pulled him back onto his feet.

'I didn't think you'd stop,' Owen told him.

'We almost didn't.'

'Then I am thankful to you all.'

A louder scream emerged from the road behind them.

'Don't thank me just yet,' Mantell said.

The megalosaurus burst out of the front of the town hall, smashing itself through the doorway and out onto the street. The few people who remained close by ran as the creature emerged, treading easily through the snow with its large feet and long legs. It roared violently, a great sound that temporarily drowned out the fearful screams.

'We have to move,' Mantell said.

The two men plodded back through the snow, stepping within the imprints Mantell had made on his way to rescue Owen to try to speed their return to the carriage.

The megalosaurus lifted its head and sniffed at the air. Snow flurried into its large nostrils, and the ground trembled with the vibration of its sneeze. It sniffed again, turning to detect the aroma driving its break for freedom. It spotted it, wafting through the air.

It looked directly at the carriage.

It stepped onto the road.

And ran straight towards it.

Mantell realised they were directly in the path of the creature.

'*Run!*' he screamed at Owen.

'*Run!*' they heard cries coming from the carriage in front: Mary had her head out of the window on one side of the carriage and Mrs Mantell on the other, both encouraging them onward with terrified shouts.

Mantell looked behind.

The creature was advancing quickly. Their tiny legs were no match for the gigantic strides the beast made, covering ten times the distance they could in the same amount of time.

From somewhere deep within, Mantell found the extra energy to give himself a boost. He sprinted forward, his head sticking out far ahead from the rest of his body as he tried to propel himself forward. He reached the carriage and grabbed the door, yanking it open.

'Hurry!' he yelled to Owen, who trailed behind him a short way.

'I'm trying!'

Mantell stepped onto the edge of the moving carriage and held out his hand towards Owen, who in turn reached out towards Mantell. Their fingertips touched, then their whole fingers and finally Mantell could grasp Owen's entire hand. He jerked him forward, pulling with all his might while trying to balance on the carriage. He pulled Owen onto the platform's edge and practically threw him inside.

'Go!' Mantell instructed Buckland. 'Now - quickly!'

Buckland flicked at the reins, and the carriage picked up speed. Mantell lost his footing with the sudden lurch forward. He quickly grabbed the carriage roof to steady himself.

With Owen in place, there was no more room inside. Mantell closed the door and edged along the outside towards the front. He clambered onto the edge of the seat beside Buckland, standing up but using his hands to stop himself from falling into that unsteady position.

'Whatever are you doing?' Buckland asked as Mantell pushed behind his back.

'Trying to get back to my seat,' Mantell replied.

He slid down beside Buckland and breathed a sigh of relief.

'We're not out of the woods yet, my friend,' Buckland told him.

Mantell looked behind them at the chasing megalosaurus. The speed increase had helped, and the creature was lagging behind them now. Not very far behind, and it was liable to catch up very quickly should they encounter any issues on the road, but far enough that they were in relative safety for the moment.

'It's as though the megalosaurus is coming straight for us, as though it has directly targeted us,' Mantell said after getting his breath back enough to speak.

'That is no megalosaurus,' Buckland said.

'I'm sorry?'

'Look at it,' Buckland continued, but Mantell didn't have to look at it again to remember its exact appearance clearly. 'It is nothing like my scientific research and investigations suggest it would be. This is no megalosaurus.'

'Could your scientific research and investigations perhaps be... wrong?' Mantell asked cautiously.

Buckland's head snapped in Mantell's direction.

'Wrong, sir?' he exclaimed.

'I only meant to say...'

'I have used the complete volumes of research available to assemble my paper on megalosaurus, and it is not... *that*... which is behind us. Owen has misinformed his audience as to the true nature of the beast.'

'I am quite sure that you have done the most thorough research possible,' Mantell tried appeasing him. 'But you cannot deny that theories change—research changes. Opinions change. The theories about the Diluvian era, for example.'

'Now you are questioning the Great Flood?' Buckland practically shrieked. 'You are questioning the words as written in the Good Book?'

'You said yourself - '

'I no longer wish to speak of this.'

'Very well.'

Mantell slumped back down in his seat. He peered behind them. The creature was still close by, still chasing and still following.

'Nevertheless, my point still stands: the megalo... - I mean, the *creature* - does appear to be following after us.'

'What rules the heart, Dr Mantell?' Buckland asked enigmatically.

Buckland fished around in the seat beside him and pulled out the ammonite Walter had planned to gift to his father. He handed it to Mantell. He took it from Buckland and looked at it, keeping it away from his nose as far as he could, giving the pungent aroma emanating from it.

He turned it over in his hands, contemplating Buckland's question.

It finally dawned on him.

'The stomach,' he answered.

'Precisely.'

'We must be rid of it, else the creature will continue following us.'

Mantell moved to fling the ammonite from the carriage, but Buckland gripped his arm before he could do so.

'On the contrary! That ammonite is perhaps our only chance of drawing the creature away from others.'

'You are not seriously suggesting - ' Mantell began.

But he did not get the opportunity to finish his thought.

FIFTY-FOUR

The horse slipped in the snow, sliding on the slick cobblestones of the London road. Jerking the carriage as it moved, it tried to regain its footing, but there was no hope once that first leg had gone. Its other legs also gave way as they tried to accommodate for the imbalance, and the poor creature came crashing to the ground.

'Hang on!' Buckland cried.

He frantically worked to try to detach the fallen horse from the carriage, but the carriage followed the horse, teetering precariously on its left-hand side, close to toppling over. He managed to get them loose, but by then, the carriage had taken a life of its own, following its own trajectory as the horse that had served Buckland so diligently over the years lay on the frozen ground, hurt and broken and unable to get back to its feet.

Buckland leaned heavily to the right, the opposite direction to which the carriage was trying to go, to try to force it upright again.

But the carriage was too far over, leaning at too sharp an angle to be able to fight against the inevitability of gravity. Mantell clung desperately to the door on his side, inching closer and closer to the ground by the second. The vehicle's surface was slick with the wet snow, and his hands began to freeze. It was nearly impossible to get a comfortable and useful grip on it.

The left side front wheel of the carriage crunched into a solid block of snow.

The whole carriage jerked forward with the impact.

The motion was too much for Mantell. His hands slipped, losing their grasp, and he was flung from his seat. He tumbled to the ground, rolling on the snow-covered cobbles, and crashed heavily against a lamppost.

The carriage finally gave up its fight and turned fully horizontal. Its momentum continued, though, and it slid straight across the white floor.

Straight towards Mantell.

He watched as the vehicle headed in his direction, powerless to do anything to stop it.

He could hear screams, though he wasn't entirely sure whether they were his own or if they came from his friends and family (and Richard Owen) who remained within the carriage. Buckland was half-standing, his feet on the inside of the door where Mantell had previously been sitting, as if he was sledging his way towards him.

Buckland crouched and then leapt, clearing the carriage door and landing in the snow. He tumbled lightly, then jumped back onto his feet with the grace of an ageing, slightly overweight gymnast.

The carriage continued its slide.

Mantell lifted his hands to his face, trying to prevent injury to his head. *This is it*, he thought to himself, *this is how I'm going to die: not in the jaws of a snarling, vicious beast, but hit by a runaway carriage*. At least the former would have made for a more exciting tale for his wife to tell; the reality of the situation was far more mundane.

The carriage crashed straight into him, viciously pinning him against the lamppost by which he rested.

He cried out as the most unimaginable pain wracked through his whole body, and he realised just before he blacked out from the shock that there was nothing mundane about this situation whatsoever.

The carriage finally halted, using Mantell and the lamppost as a barrier. Tray was the first to poke his head out of the fallen carriage. He scrambled out of the vehicle and plopped into the snow. Seeing Mantell crushed against the lamppost, he hurried over to him and licked his face, whining when no reaction came from the crumpled figure.

Buckland climbed on top of the carriage and opened the only accessible back door, which was now more of a ceiling to its inhabitants.

'Is anyone hurt?' he called down.

'I don't believe so,' Mary replied.

'No,' Mrs Mantell responded.

'Walter?' Buckland asked.

'No,' the boy said.

'Good.'

'I have cut my arm,' Owen whined. 'If anybody cares to know.'

'Not particularly,' Buckland muttered.

He thrust his arms inside the carriage and pulled Walter out with Mary's help lifting him from inside. He slid the boy down the side of the fallen vehicle, then continued to do the same with the others.

Mrs Mantell rushed over to her husband crying, the tears freezing to her cheeks even as they fell from her eyes.

'Don't be dead,' she whispered. 'Please, don't be dead.'

She rubbed his cheeks, gently at first, then harder, eventually slapping him across the face; anything to get a reaction.

'Do as I ask you for once, won't you?' she half-snapped between sobs.

'Help me,' Buckland instructed Owen as he began trying to pull the carriage off of Mantell.

A roar sounded somewhere close by.

The megalosaurus was catching up with them.

'Quickly!' Buckland hissed.

Mary joined the rescue party. Between them, they shifted the weight of the carriage, freeing Mantell from where he was trapped.

'Gideon,' Mrs Mantell said, kissing her husband's cool forehead. 'Gideon.'

Another roar came. It was getting closer.

Mantell's eyelids flickered open. He saw his wife in front of him and smiled weakly.

'Am I dead?' he asked.

'No, but we all will be soon if we don't move you.'

A third roar. So close this time that snow fell from the branches of trees with the vibration from the noise.

'You have to get out of here,' Mantell told her.

'We're not leaving you.'

'You have to. Think of the boy.' He turned to address Buckland, wincing at the pain of merely shifting his weight. 'Look after them for me, William.'

'Gideon...' Buckland began.

'Go. Now.'

Mantell raised his right arm. In it, he still held the ammonite. He looked at Buckland, and they shared an understanding. Buckland nodded slightly, sadly, in agreement.

'Come on,' Buckland said, ushering the others away from Mantell.

'I can't - ' Mrs Mantell said.

'We have no choice,' Buckland interrupted.

'Please leave. Keep them safe,' Mantell said.

The group shuffled away, Mantell's wife and son looking back at him, both crying now, fearing the worst.

Hopeful that they were out of imminent danger, Mantell lifted his arm as high as possible.

'I have what you want!' he shouted. 'Come and get it!'

The megalosaurus came bounding into view and suddenly looked much larger than Mantell remembered now as he was lying there, on the floor, alone and injured. The creature stared straight at Mantell and trod slowly forward.

Before she could stop him, Tray leapt out of Mary's arms and darted through the snow. It stopped between the megalosaurus and the broken carriage and faced the gigantic creature. Tray yapped, the small dog capable of little more than squeaking annoyingly rather than terrifyingly at the beast it was trying to stand up against. The megalosaurus tilted its head, eyeing up this strange little creature that would dare to stand up to it.

The megalosaurus crouched slightly and let out the full force of its roar.

Tray couldn't help but yelp in fear and run away.

The megalosaurus turned its attention back to where Mantell was.

Or, rather, where Mantell *had* been.

Tray had provided the perfect distraction. Whilst the megalosaurus was captivated, its attention entirely on the little dog, Buckland had snuck behind the carriage and pulled Mantell out from the wreckage. He dragged his friend through the snow and back to where the rest of the group waited for them. Between them, they helped Mantell onto his feet. He was too injured to walk alone, so he placed his arms around Buckland and Mary's shoulders for support.

The megalosaurus spotted them and let out another annoyed roar.

It dashed forward, slipping in the snow as the surface was starting to freeze over with the lowering temperatures.

FIFTY-FIVE

The streets narrowed, and tall buildings loomed over them as they hurried around one corner after another, trying to escape the megalosaurus that continued to stalk them close at their heels. They turned yet another bend, hopelessly lost within the maze of streets that was London, only to discover the worst possible scenario:

They had reached a dead end. In front of them was a wall, and on the other side of the wall was the Thames, flowing fast and cold, far below. There was no way out.

They rushed back the way they had come, as fast as they could whilst assisting a young boy and his father who could do little more than hobble rather than move at any great speed.

But at that very moment, the megalosaurus turned the corner and stepped into the narrow, closed-off alleyway in which they found themselves.

They slowly backed away, and then they were pressed firmly against the brick wall that marked the end of where they could go. Trapped.

The megalosaurus stalked forward, matching their steps, taking its time.

'Father?' Walter cried, looking up at Mantell with terrified, tear-filled eyes.

Mantell crouched in front of him, slowly and painfully, until he was eye to eye with his boy.

'Whatever happens, you know I love you, don't you?' Mantell asked.

Walter nodded his head in agreement.

Mantell reached out and took hold of his wife's hand.

'And I love your mother, too.'

Mantell felt her grip his hand more tightly. Vibrations passing down her arm and into his hand made him realise that she, too, was crying, but she was trying hard to keep it inside for the sake of their son.

'If we can't be together here,' Mantell continued, 'then we shall be together someplace else. Someplace so much, much better. Isn't that right, William?'

He turned to look at his friend but discovered that Buckland was no longer standing with them. He was striding away from the group, straight towards the megalosaurus.

'William, wait!' he cried out.

Buckland held out a hand to him, indicating for him to be quiet and patient.

Buckland pulled a paper bag from his pocket as he approached the creature. He opened it and pulled something from it.

'It isn't much,' Buckland told the creature, 'but perhaps you would prefer to consume a toasted mouse rather than us?'

He flung the small snack towards the megalosaurus. It bounced off the giant creature's nose and landed on the ground at its feet, burying itself slightly within the layer of snow. The megalosaurus leant its head to the ground and sniffed at the food Buckland had provided. Buckland looked over his shoulder and smiled at the group; his plan seemed to be working. But, rather than consuming the mouse, the megalosaurus instead grimaced at the smell and put a large foot forward, stomping it down into the ground.

'Ah. Another critic,' Buckland complained.

The creature growled, the sound emanating from low down in its throat. It kept its head down, level with Buckland, as it continued to move forward, its jaw threateningly wide open. Buckland backed away quickly, rejoining the group against the wall.

That was when Mantell remembered.

'What rules the heart?' he asked himself, pulling the rotting ammonite from his coat pocket.

The megalosaurus stopped at the smell of the very item it had been chasing since the town hall. It sniffed the air and licked its lips hungrily.

'This is what you want, isn't it?' Mantell said to the creature.

He motioned to the rest of the group with his eyes to move out of the way, then held the ammonite aloft.

'Here it is,' he said. 'Come and get it.'

The megalosaurus reared back on its hind legs and charged straight towards Mantell and the ammonite.

Mantell swung his arm around, screaming with the pain that flooded through his body at such a motion, and flung the ammonite straight over the brick wall behind them. The megalosaurus, so intent on reaching its food, was going too fast to be able to stop itself. It smashed straight through the wall. Before it even knew what was happening, the ground had disappeared underneath it, and there was nothing but empty space leading straight down to the fast-flowing waters of the river fifty feet below. It writhed around as it fell, thrashing its limbs, whipping its tail around, even snatching at the air with its jaw, trying to get a hold of anything that would stop its descent.

But there was nothing there to stop it.

With a great splash, the creature landed, plunging underneath the freezing surface of the river, consumed by the cold waters.

Above, the group reconvened around the hole in the wall and watched for any sign of motion. But there was none. The creature was gone, hopefully sunk to the bottom, frozen and drowned, never to be seen again.

FIFTY-SIX

London.
One week later.

William Buckland looked around the people assembled within the cramped, smoke-filled room, lounging in their leather-clad chairs and smoking their pipes as they listened to him speak. Most of the gentlemen there with him had been members of the Geological Society since its inception in 1807, and it showed: their faces as ragged and worn as the rocks they studied. Most members no longer practised the sciences, and there was little chance of more than a few getting back up on their feet if they crouched down to extract a fossil from the ground. They were there primarily for the esteemed honour of being a part of the society and the rules they were thereby allowed to enforce upon any new members. It was as though they believed respect automatically came with age and experience rather than with any demonstration of the characteristics they expected from those younger than them who might wish to follow in their footsteps.

Nevertheless, on that particular day, Buckland found that he could hold their interest despite - he had to admit - the dryness of some of the research he presented. The illustrated papers he had distributed beforehand were undoubtedly helping, as was the jaw fossil he had finally extracted back from Richard Owen after the disastrous turn of events on Christmas Day.

He still struggled to make much sense of those events, particularly Owen's use of the name "megalosaurus", which Buckland himself had suggested for his remarkable jaw fossil discovery, based on the estimated size of the beast to which it had belonged. The creature in

London looked nothing like that with which he had illustrated his work. *His* megalosaurus somehow looked more fearsome even than the creature that had stalked them through the snow-covered streets. Owen had tried to convince him that he was wrong with his estimations of the creature's natural design and that the London beast was indeed a megalosaurus. He had looked through Buckland's research, the jaw fossil himself, and somehow found a way to make the research and data match that beast from which they had fled.

But Buckland himself could not in all consciousness present his megalosaurus in that light. He had to stick with his research and his own scientific understanding. Seeing was not always believing, and he could not twist the facts of the matter in a way that he could not bring himself to conclude from his research.

Buckland had placed the megalosaurus jaw in the middle of the table so that it might be examined - carefully and from a distance - by the other patrons of the society as he presented his paper. Sharp teeth were always a good way of getting and keeping attention, igniting imaginations and enthusiasm that had perhaps wavered somewhat over the years after listening to one paper after another about nothing but comparisons of the layers of sedimentary or igneous rocks that outlined the magnificent coast of England.

He reached across the table and carefully picked up the fossil, holding it gently and pointing it to the appropriate places as he read his paper aloud.

'The exterior surface of the jaw presents several distinct and rugose cavities for the passage of the exterior branches of the inferior maxillary blood vessels and nerves,' he explained, though he could see that his audience had little interest in the scientific minutiae of his discovery; they wanted to know what size animal the megalosaurus could take down and how quickly it would be able to devour it.

'This character agrees,' he continued, 'not with the crocodiles, but with the other members of the saurian family.'

He had at first believed that the jaw had belonged to an enormous crocodile of some description, but further analysis had revealed that it was not a part of that family at all. Further discoveries of leg bone fossils belonging to the same specimen proved that it could not have been completely crocodilian in nature but closer to those other long-lost creatures which Richard Owen himself had labelled as "dinosaurs", a term which Buckland was not yet ready to embrace fully. It was practically the only genuinely original contribution that

Owen had brought to the table, rather than piggybacking off other people's ideas and discoveries. And for someone so relatively young to have a term used widely throughout scientific circles... Perhaps, Buckland wondered, he was becoming like one of those prehistoric creatures that sat and half-listened to his paper in that very room. Maybe he should be more open-minded and willing to listen to the up-and-coming scientists of the next generation, regardless of what they may have done to endanger the lives of him and his friends.

'Learned gentlemen,' Buckland said as he returned the fossilised jaw to the centre of the table. 'I give you "megalosaurus".'

The room erupted with thunderous applause and banging of hands on the table. It was a far more enthusiastic response than he had expected from the group, but then it was a far more interesting topic than usual, even if he did say so himself.

'Thank you, thank you,' Buckland accepted the praise as he stood waiting for the noise to quieten so that they could continue the meeting and get out of there at a reasonable time for a change.

Finally, the applause subsided, and Buckland could address the room.

'Before we close, was there any further business of which we must partake?' he asked, looking around the room and hoping that the answer would be a resounding "no".

The society members glanced at one another, looking for whoever might be about to make the meeting drag on for that bit longer before they could retire for brandy in the social room.

A solitary hand raised at the back of the room.

'Ah, Dr Mantell,' Buckland said.

All eyes turned to the owner of the hand. Hidden behind most of the society members, Gideon Mantell slowly got to his feet. He clutched the top of a thick cane in his left hand, and his right hand held on to the back of the seat in front of him for support. Even rising from a chair was hard for him since the carriage accident. A "serious back injury", the doctors had told him, confirming his assumption - which had not been a challenging diagnosis to make, considering that his spine felt as though it was twisted in knots most of the time. He could no longer walk unassisted, using a chair with wheels to go around for any distance.

He started slowly working his way to the front of the room, clutching chairs for support as he moved, looking as though he were forty years older than his actual age. The stack of papers he held supported between his arm and his body did nothing to help matters, but he believed they were important enough to bring with him.

'Please, Gideon, feel free to address us from your seat,' Buckland told him. 'There is no reason why you should stand on ceremony.'

Mantell rejected Buckland's words with a wave of his hand, which he immediately regretted as he left the full support of his body to his cane alone. He took a moment to steady himself once again, then proceeded to the head of the table where he could look at every one of the society members. As Mantell arrived at the front of the table, Buckland stepped aside and sat in a chair behind him.

'I would like to read from a prepared statement, if I may,' Mantell requested.

Buckland nodded in agreement and waved to encourage his friend to continue. Mantell set the bundle of documents on the table before him and pulled a sheet of paper from his coat pocket. He unfolded it and cleared his throat.

'Gentlemen,' he addressed the room, looking at every member of the society as he spoke, lest any of them should take offence for not being included. 'Learned colleague of the Geological Society. It is with some sadness that I announce today my retirement from the Society.'

Murmurings rose throughout the room, sounds of disbelief, perhaps even anger that someone should choose to do such a thing: they should be the ones to have the privilege of expelling someone from their Society; it shouldn't be something that was done of an individual's own accord.

Buckland rose slightly from his seat.

'Gentlemen, please,' he said to quieten the room again so that Mantell might continue reading his statement. As silence fell, Buckland returned to his seat.

Mantell nodded his gratitude towards his friend and continued:

'It has been an honour and a privilege to be amongst such esteemed gentlemen as yourselves, but I must now give my full attention to other things.'

He looked upon the sea of faces belonging to the old men who stared towards him and took a deep breath before continuing.

'However. If I may, I would like to nominate a new member to the society to take my place.'

He slid the pile of papers on the table to be closer to Buckland.

'If you wouldn't mind distributing these amongst the esteemed members of the Society, please, Professor Buckland,' he requested.

Buckland did as instructed, dishing out the papers to the members who took them with little enthusiasm, flicking vaguely through the pages, stopping at the occasional illustration which helped to pique their interest a little. It was too late in the evening to go through more scientific research in detail. Still, the illustrations alone appeared to have been produced in a highly technical, proficient manner, and if the written research was presented equally adequately, then whichever gentleman it was who had produced the papers most likely warranted inclusion within the Society. Of course, it was customary for a nomination to be at the Society on the day they were put forward, that they might be interrogated about their work before the Society voting in their favour or, indeed, against. However, no such new face was present in the room then.

Mantell allowed the gentlemen to scan through the documents and give the research at least a glance before continuing his statement.

'You will see on the papers in front of you some extraordinary specimens, scientific gatherings and factual evidence, which I have personally verified alongside Professor Buckland. I believe that the person who has produced these scientific discoveries should take my place within the society, as they have made - and no doubt will continue to make - incredible advancements and contributions to our science.'

He paused to gauge the room's reaction to his request.

Perhaps the eldest of the members, Charles Booth, slowly pushed himself to his feet. Mantell could not help but notice that he required the same degree of effort and assistance in rising as Mantell himself did following his injury.

Booth cleared his throat, hacking at some phlegm that was sat there as a result of puffing at his pipe for the past who knew how many hours since the meeting had begun.

'If what you are saying is true,' the old man croaked, 'and I have no reason to doubt this is the case - indeed, looking at these papers, it does appear to be so - I am quite sure that this person of which you speak will be a valuable addition to our Society.'

Mantell nodded his gratitude.

'Thank you, sir.'

'But why have I never heard of this...' he looked down at the papers before him and flicked through the pages until he came upon the name he was looking for. '..."Mr Anning" before?'

Mantell glanced across at Buckland. He had known that this would be the sticking point of the meeting. Not the science - the science was sound and the research solid - but the fact that it was not *Mr* Anning he was proposing as a member. Buckland smiled his encouragement.

'It is not *Mr* Anning, sir,' Mantell announced. 'It is Miss Mary Anning of Lyme Regis.'

The reaction was exactly as Mantell had feared but expected. Shouts of uproar filled the room, cries of outrage that the mere prospect of admitting a *woman* into the Society had been suggested that evening. Women were not, and could not, be taken seriously as scientists.

It was just as well that Mantell had already resigned from his position within the Society before his nomination. Otherwise, it would have been stripped away from him following his request.

Epilogue

Somewhere in Scotland.

Two carriages made their way past mountains, through valleys, across great plains of natural beauty, winding along the roads, sometimes bumpy and treacherous, other times peaceful and tranquil. But, always, the scenery made the journey nothing short of spectacular. The first signs of Spring were beginning to show themselves in the blossoming trees and flowers starting to emerge from their winter shelter.

The foremost of the two carriages was considerably larger than the other, crafted to carry a large load in the back. The heavy backend made it more challenging to manoeuvre, and any sharp bends had to be taken with the utmost care. But Jessie was skilled at the reins of a horse and managed to steer the carriage without, as yet, causing any real problems.

The second carriage, being smaller, presented a far smoother ride. Driven by one Reverend William Buckland and ably pulled by his new horse (who had yet to pick up any awkward habits of stopping beside quarries without notice like its predecessor had done), Gideon Mantell, his wife and son, and Mary Anning enjoyed a more comfortable journey. Which was just as well, as the journey from London to Scotland had already taken them several days. It was just what the doctor had ordered. Still, Mantell found that he was enjoying the company of his family and friends and the lack of responsibility for having to do anything during his period of absence. His back still pained him very much, and he struggled more with walking each day, so he was grateful for the extra padding on the carriage that had been provided for his benefit. He sat beside his wife, Mary-Ann, opposite Mary Anning and Walter. Tray was perched between the two, enjoying many days of extra attention from the boy. The dog was already gaining weight from the additional treats he received and scraps fed to him by Walter. Mary herself was enjoying the countryside. It was her first time seeing mountains, and she found them breathtaking. At the same time, though, she missed home: the silence in those parts was hard to sleep with, without the background noise of crashing waves and whistling winds that made their way through her bedroom window at night, surrounding her as she drifted to sleep. She also missed her mother. Despite having to look after her more or less around the clock these days, she was still her family, and she resented nothing. Mrs Anning had been taken in for a few days by another family they were friends with, so at least she would have some company during Mary's trip, and it was almost like a small holiday for her as well.

Mary turned her attention from outside the window and noticed Mantell was looking at her.

'I cannot say enough how sorry I am,' he said.

'You already have,' Mary replied with a smile. 'Many a time.'

'I know, but I had hoped that the Society would look at your work and think of that first and foremost when considering your nomination.'

'It is of no matter. The gentlemen of the Society are little more than -' she turned to speak with Buckland as he sat outside the main carriage. 'What is that term you have heard about your discoveries?'

'Dinosaurs,' Buckland replied gruffly, still unable to find peace with using that word.

'Indeed. The Society members are nothing but dinosaurs,' Mary continued. 'Living in the past. They are unable or unwilling to see what contribution the opposite sex may be able to make to their precious studies.'

'That does indeed appear to be the case,' Mantell said sadly. 'I just thought...'

Mary placed a hand gently on top of his and smiled again.

'You are not like them,' she told him. 'To you, a discovery is a discovery. It does not matter who made it.'

Mantell looked away momentarily, then looked back at Mary as if trying to decide whether to say what was on his mind.

'I have to confess,' he began slowly, 'when I first met you, I did not -
'

'That is in the past,' Mary said firmly. 'Whatever you may or may not have thought back then, it does not matter.'

'Thank you,' Mantell said. 'Some day, Mary. Some day, you will get the recognition you deserve.'

Mary looked away, back at the scenery outside the carriage, where a vast body of water stretched before them, the waters blue-green in the golden sunlight.

'Maybe,' she replied simply.

The carriage slowed and eventually stopped alongside the larger carriage, which had already parked right on the shore, the rear of the vehicle facing towards the edge of the water.

'We're here,' Buckland announced.

They stood together in front of the loch, the vast stretch of water spilling out before them, reflecting the golden orange of the slowly setting sun. Perched on the water's edge was a small castle, or at least the remains of what had once been a castle, still standing guard after two hundred years and watching over the shores on which it stood.

It was perfect in its tranquillity.

After all they had been through together, it felt like they finally had a moment of peace and togetherness that they could share.

'Are we ready?' Jessie asked, breaking the spell the loch had cast upon them.

'Very well,' Buckland said. 'Let's get this done.'

Jessie and Buckland headed to the back of the larger carriage and pulled down the door at the rear, hinged at the bottom so that it would lay flat once opened, spreading out like a ramp leading to the ground.

Inside was Mary's plesiosaur, seated within a smaller, more mobile version of the water showering system she had built within her cellar, keeping it comfortably moist throughout the journey. It hadn't been easy to build and install, and getting the creature into it when it was ready had presented its own challenges. But it had brought the plesiosaur there alive and well, so the effort had been worth it in the end.

Buckland and Jessie took hold of two thick ropes attached to either side of the showering apparatus. They gave it a hard tug, and the container slid towards them. Continuing to pull, they moved it closer and closer until it was on the ramp so that they could slide it more easily downward and onto the grassy bank.

'Stand back,' Jessie said.

He unclasped a pair of latches on the side of the container, and the front-most face came open, swinging like a door. Gallons of water tumbled out, watering the grass before it and cascading straight into the loch. The plesiosaur looked around: at the vast loch in front of it, the surrounding hills, trees, greenery, and blue sky with small white clouds scattered here and there. It looked at the now missing front edge of its container and the apparent freedom that represented. It raised a flipper, stretched it forward and plopped it down further in front. It did the same thing with its other front flipper. Then its back ones moved, and the creature slowly made small movements forward.

Mary moved closer so that it might be able to see her.

The plesiosaur immediately recognised her and made a slight noise that sounded like excitement. Mary held out her hands, indicating that it should continue to move closer to her, out of the container.

'Come on,' she said. 'You can do it.'

It edged closer and finally plopped down in the grass, which was in itself a brand new sensation against the plesiosaur's body, having lived within water all its life and never had the opportunity to experience the feel of soft, tickly grass against it. It reached the water's edge, standing alongside Mary and looking across the great blue lagoon.

Mary stroked its long neck and petted it tenderly. She would miss the creature immensely, but she knew that it was the right thing to do. She had kept it as best she could in the cellar, letting it recuperate from its injuries and then within the sea beside the Cobb. But all the time, it was chained, like it was her prisoner, waiting for the time when it would be granted its freedom. All the while that it was chained to the Cobb, Mary was terrified that it would be found and killed, thought to be like the other vicious creatures that had rampaged through her home town. Those who had experienced the terrifying onslaught of the prehistoric beasts still told tales about that day, but those who had seen nothing found it difficult to believe: how could there have been monsters loose in their town only for them to miss it? They put it down to some mass hysteria or some wild conspiracy amongst the townsfolk to make them look stupid for not having seen anything. Virtually everyone had heard - and felt - a great deal of what could have been explosions throughout that day and night. Perhaps that was what it had been - the vibrations and noises caused by a multitude of explosions could easily have been mistaken for a roaming horde of giant beasts.

Obviously, they were mistaken.

Even those who claimed to have seen them with their own eyes, every tooth, claw, and tail.

Somehow, the blame had never made its way back to Mary, and for that, she was immensely grateful. She had always felt like an outsider within the town, so she feared that if they found the right excuse, the other locals would not hesitate to force her out of the community.

But this was where it was going to end, she believed.

On the shores of this great Loch, a place that may have been a million miles from home.

The plesiosaur bowed its head towards the water and lapped it delicately with its tongue.

It looked up at Mary. She smiled and rubbed its neck again.

'That's it,' she said. 'This is your new home now.'

She reached down and scooped up a large handful of water, then sprinkled it across the creature's back, rubbing it into its body so it would know it was safe.

'Go on now,' she said and gave it a slight push forward.

The plesiosaur grunted and reached out a flipper, dipping it tentatively into the loch. The water was cold, but no more than the sea in Lyme Regis in December. It lifted another flipper and flopped it forward, so both front paddles were now submerged. It shifted its weight so that the front of its body was covered and finally slid forward into the waters, only its long neck protruding from the surface, its head looking towards Mary.

'Goodbye,' she said softly, realising her vision was clouding with tears.

Buckland approached and put his arm around her shoulder.

Then the Mantells took up position alongside the pair, Mantell in his wheelchair, watching the plesiosaur from the shore. Mantell reached out and took hold of his wife's hand in his. She gave it a gentle squeeze and smiled down at him.

The plesiosaur watched them for a moment, then turned around, its back to them, ducked its head and dived under the surface.

The ripples spread out in large circles and slowly, one by one, disappeared, just as the creature had done, until it was once again perfectly still.

Suddenly, there was a burst of water from the middle of the loch.

The plesiosaur's head shot out of the surface, its long neck extending out of the water. It turned and looked at its spectators, flicking its head as if in a greeting. Mary smiled and couldn't help but let out a half-sob, half-laugh. She wiped the tears from her eyes as the plesiosaur once more dived back underwater.

They watched the loch for a long, quiet moment, each of them hoping that the creature would reappear and that they might see it for one more final time. But the moment dragged on, the sun slowly setting, and darkness was beginning to descend. It was over, and time to leave.

They silently turned around as a unit, no words needing to be said and headed back towards the carriages, ready to begin the long journey home.

Walter, clutching Tray close to him to share their warmth and for a sense of comfort, turned to look back over his shoulder at the loch where the fantastic beast had last been seen.

He cried out in surprise:

'Look!'

The group spun around to face the loch, none needing more than a single word from a young boy as an excuse to remain there.

The plesiosaur's head was sticking out from the surface some distance from the shore, practically a silhouette against the darkening waters.

'Come on,' Mrs Mantell told him, taking his spare hand, 'we had better be moving.'

'No, wait!' Mantell said with astonishment.

Beside the plesiosaur, more ripples formed in the water.

The surface broke.

Another head emerged, attached to a long neck.

A second plesiosaur.

Mary's plesiosaur called out to them, and as they watched, the two creatures swam side by side, leaping and diving, leaping and diving in a show that could have only been orchestrated for them. They couldn't help but laugh at the sight.

The plesiosaur had company.

Perhaps even a mate.

Mary found herself wiping yet another tear away. She hadn't cried so much for a while, certainly not tears of happiness.

'Incredible,' Buckland whispered as both creatures leapt from the water and then dived back under the surface, gone.

'You think that's incredible?' Mary asked. 'Come back to Lyme as soon as you're able. You too, Gideon. And bring your families. I've found something that I think you might find particularly interesting.'

'Oh?' Mantell asked, intrigued.

'Tell me more,' Buckland prompted.

'You'll have to come to see it,' Mary told them. 'Make a holiday of it.'

They continued talking amongst themselves, trying to coax more information out of the enigmatic Mary Anning as they climbed back aboard their respective carriages, settled into place and set off for home.

"Thus the great drama of universal life is perpetually sustained; and though the individual actors undergo continual change, the same parts are ever filled by another and another generation; renewing the face of the earth, and the bosom of the deep, with endless successions of life and happiness."

Geology and Mineralogy Considered with Reference to Natural Theology, William Buckland

Author's Note

These are facts about what happened to the real-life versions of the main characters of this story:

Richard Owen continued to publish scientific papers and perform his own research, though he was later discredited on several papers due to apparent plagiarism. However, he established London's Natural History Museum and was instrumental in creating the dinosaur sculptures in Crystal Palace Park. And, of course, he gave us the term "dinosaur". He died on 18th December 1892.

William Buckland continued in his attempts to reconcile his views on theology and geology throughout the remainder of his life. He never fully succeeded and spent his final years in a mental asylum in Clapham. His endeavour to eat a member of every species of the animal kingdom was never quite fulfilled, though he made significant progress. He passed away on 14th August 1856.

Gideon Mantell never recovered from his spinal injury (which, in real life, was presumably *not* caused by trying to escape a rampaging dinosaur). Taking opium to control the pain, he died of an accidental overdose on the 10th November 1852. As a final act of retribution against his former rival, Richard Owen placed a preserved section of Mantell's spine in the Royal College of Surgeons, where it remained until 1969.

Mary Anning, being a woman from the lower classes of society, was often snubbed by societies and their members, who refused to take her seriously. On more than one occasion, a paper of hers was published but in the name of another gentleman. More than 170 years after her death on 9th March 1847, she began to receive the widespread recognition she deserved for her contributions to science and geology. Her legacy is now finally intact, and her importance in history is becoming more widely known and acknowledged. Some of her giant ichthyosaur and plesiosaur discoveries are still displayed in the Natural History Museum. In 2022, a statue of Mary was finally erected in her home town of Lyme Regis.

There are mild spoilers for the book below, so do not read it unless you have finished it. You have been warned!

Writing a fictional account about dinosaurs based in Georgian times was tricky, particularly in one respect: the dinosaurs themselves.

At that point in relatively recent history, most of the dinosaur names we know now had not been specifically assigned, and indeed many of the creatures featured in this book had yet to be discovered and/or formally identified.

For the sake of readability and to make it easier to explain which given creature is doing what at a particular time, I have generally used the modern names we know and love within the text. This helped with my own sanity. With regard to the descriptions of the individual creatures, I have taken a degree of artistic license (if *Jurassic Park* can do it, why can't I?) and at times used the more modern depiction, and other times I have used what the characters in the story would have believed them to look like, based on scientific reasonings of the time. For example, William Buckland realises that his original depiction of the Megalosaurus is entirely incorrect, based on what he witnesses with his own eyes, yet he at that point has no scientific reasoning for depicting the creature in its "correct" form; here, I have used the more modern "version" of the Megalosaurus. The ichthyosaurs are far more terrifying in the form they took within research papers and illustrations of the time, looking more like crocodiles than the more friendly-looking dolphin shape we now believe them to have been.

It's all for dramatic effect.

"Snake stones" are ammonites. I decided to stick with calling them snake stones at times, simply because I like the name.

Printed in Great Britain
by Amazon

37855881R10175